The

WORST

BEST

MAN

By Mia Sosa

The Worst Best Man

LOVE ON CUE
Acting on Impulse
Pretending He's Mine
Crashing into Her

THE SUITS UNDONE
Unbuttoning the CEO
One Night with the CEO
Getting Dirty with the CEO

The WORST BEST MAN

A Novel

MIA SOSA

AVON

An Imprint of HarperCollinsPublishers

THE WORST BEST MAN. Copyright © 2020 by Mia Sosa. All rights reserved. Printed in the United States of America. No part of this book may be used or reproduced in any manner whatsoever without written permission except in the case of brief quotations embodied in critical articles and reviews. For information, address HarperCollins Publishers, 195 Broadway, New York, NY 10007.

HarperCollins books may be purchased for educational, business, or sales promotional use. For information, please email the Special Markets Department at SPsales@harpercollins.com.

FIRST EDITION

Designed by Diahann Sturge

Library of Congress Cataloging-in-Publication Data has been applied for.

ISBN 978-0-06-290987-9

20 21 22 23 24 LSC 10 9 8 7 6 5 4 3 2 1

It took a village to raise us; this story is for the village elders:
Mãe, Ivany, and Reni.

The Stockton Hotel
Washington, DC
Three Years Ago

MAX

$\mathcal{M}$y phone's text tone chirps like a robin—which fails to prepare me for the clusterfuck on the screen.

Andrew: Everything you said last night made sense, M. Thanks to you, I can see the truth now. I can't marry Lina. Need you to break the news. Don't worry, she'll handle it with class. Going to disappear for a few days while I get my head straight. Tell Mom and Dad I'll call them soon.

I'm too young and hungover for this shit.

Using the few brain cells that survived the effects of yesterday's bar crawl, I try to synthesize the limited information in my possession. One, my older brother, Andrew, the quintessential people pleaser and a man who does everything according to plan, is due to get married this morning. Two, he's not in our hotel suite, which means he fled the premises after I crashed last night. And three, he never jokes about anything; the stick permanently lodged up his ass prevents him from experiencing fun. No matter how I move them, the pieces of this puzzle refuse to fit together.

Could this be a case of Andrew's dormant (and terrible) sense of humor suddenly waking up? God, I sure hope so.

I fight my way out of the bedsheet twisted around my torso, sit up, and type a quick reply.

Me: This isn't funny. Call me. Right now.

He doesn't respond, so I ring his cell. When the call goes straight to voicemail, I accept that Andrew doesn't want to be reached and wish him a speedy trip straight to hell.

Don't worry? She'll handle it with class? My brother's a bonehead if he thinks Lina won't flip out when she discovers he isn't showing up today. Easily imagining the bride's devastated reaction, I focus on the two sentences in Andrew's text that make me especially queasy: *Everything you said last night made sense, M. Thanks to you, I can see the truth now.* Problem is, I can't remember much about the prior evening—an entire bottle of Patrón tends to affect a person's short-term memory—let alone recall what bullshit I may have said to my brother during his final hours of bachelorhood. If I had to guess, though, I probably claimed that remaining single was preferable to getting married and acted as if I'd thoroughly beaten him in the game of life.

I'm twenty-five. He's my brother. This is what we do.

Christ. I flop back onto the mattress and contemplate my

next move. Someone needs to clue in the bride. My mother's *not* an option. She's tactless. At my parents' twentieth-anniversary celebration, she told my grandmother Nola—and a roomful of their guests—that her only hesitation in marrying my father had been a concern that he was a mama's boy, an affliction my mother attributed to the extended period Grandma Nola had let him drink from her tit. Direct quote. My father, for his part, would throw on his investigative reporter hat and engage in an invasive truth-finding mission, all in service to discovering why my brother had bailed on his fiancée. Dad's heavy-handed behavior will only aggravate the situation. I know this firsthand— it's one of the reasons my parents divorced a year ago. Since my big mouth is partly responsible for triggering this unfortunate chain of events, I'm the obvious choice. But damn, I don't want to be.

Massaging my throbbing temples, I drag myself out of bed and limp my way to the bathroom. Minutes later, as I'm brushing my teeth and ignoring my scruffy, red-eyed reflection in the mirror, the phone chirps again. *Andrew.* I spit out a capful of mouthwash, dart back into the bedroom, and swipe my phone off the nightstand—only to be disappointed by my father's message.

Dad: Get your asses down here. Your brother's going to be late
for his own wedding if he's not here in five.

Everything inside me freezes: atoms, blood flow, the whole shebang. I might even be clinically dead. Because on top of everything else, I overslept, effectively destroying my chance to divert the guests before they arrive and adding another layer to this shit cake of a day.

The blare of the hotel's digital alarm clock yanks me out of my stupor and pummels my skull. I slam a hand down on the *off* button and squint at the tiny snooze icon mocking me in the corner of the display. You know what? I'm never drinking again. No, wait. That's an empty promise if ever there was one. Special occasions. Yes, that'll work. Going forward, I'll only drink on special occasions. Does informing a bride that her groom won't be showing up for the wedding qualify as one such occasion? Probably not. Do I want it to? Absofuckinlutely.

LINA

*P*ity. That's what I see in Max's whiskey-brown eyes. In his dejected stance. In the way he's struggling to conceal a pout.

I motion him inside the dressing suite. "What's going on?"

My tone of voice is exactly as it should be: calm and even. In truth, I regularly monitor my daily emotional output the way some people track their daily caloric intake, and since my mother and I just shared a few teary-eyed minutes together, I'm either fresh out of feelings or close to exceeding today's quota.

After striding to the center of the room, Max turns around slowly, one of his hands fussing with the collar of his button-down. That's the biggest sign that something's amiss: He isn't wearing the light gray suit Andrew selected for his attendants.

I prod him with a different question. "Is Andrew okay?"

It can't be that bad if Max is here. I don't know him well—he lives in New York and hasn't been around for most of the pre-wedding festivities. Still, he's Andrew's only sibling, and if something awful has happened, he'd be with his older brother, right? Well, given that Max was Andrew's third choice for best man (after choices one and two politely declined), perhaps that isn't a safe assumption.

Max scrunches his brows, the resulting lines in his forehead reminding me of ripples in water. "No, no, Andrew's fine. It's nothing like that."

I press a hand to my belly and let out a shaky breath. "All right, good. Then what's going on?"

He swallows. Hard. "He's not coming. To the wedding. Says he can't go through with it."

For several seconds, I just blink and process. Blink, blink, blink, and process. *God.* All the planning. The people. The family that traveled from near and far to be here. I envision the fallout and cringe. My mother and aunts will be livid on my behalf. Before this day is over, they'll organize a search party so they can find Andrew and kick him in the balls with the agility and precision of the Rockettes. And considering their entrepreneurial spirit, I wouldn't be surprised if they sold tickets to the show and titled it *The Nutcracker.*

Max clears his throat. The staccato sound disrupts my stream of consciousness, and the significance of the situation truly hits me.

I'm not getting married today.

My throat constricts and my chest tightens. *Oh, no, no, no. Hold it together, Lina. You're a pro at this.* I wrestle with my tears and body slam them back into their ducts.

Max inches forward. "What can I do? Do you need a hug? A shoulder to cry on?"

"I don't know what I need," I say hoarsely, unable to pull off the unruffled demeanor I'd hoped to convey.

His sad eyes meet mine and he opens his arms. I step into his embrace, desperate to connect with someone so I'll feel less . . . adrift. He holds me with a light touch, and somehow I know he's restraining himself, as though he wants to keep me afloat rather than pull me under. Through the fog, I notice Max is damp, fresh from a shower possibly, and I'm struck by the absence of any detectible fragrance on his skin. I wonder briefly if my scent will cling to him when he leaves, then wonder just as briefly whether my brain's short-circuiting.

"Are you okay?" he asks in a whisper-soft tone.

I don't move as I consider his question. Maybe remaining still will help me assess the damage. By all rights, I should be hurt, angry, ready to rail against the injustice of what Andrew's done to me. But I'm none of those things. Not yet. The truth is, I'm numb—and more than a little confused.

Andrew's supposed to be "the one." For two years, we've shared interesting conversations, satisfying sex, and stability. Most important, he's never pushed my buttons—not even once—and I can't imagine a better choice for a lifelong partner than someone who doesn't trigger my worst impulses. Until this morning, Andrew and I seemed to be on the same page about the mutual benefits of this union. Today he's apparently in a different book altogether—and I have no idea why.

Max fills the silence, babbling for us both: "I don't know what's going on with him. One minute he was fine. And then we talked last night. We went barhopping, you know? Somewhere between the shots of Patrón, I said some foolish things. It went sideways from there. I'm sorry. So damn sorry."

The anguish in his voice snags my attention, gives me a hook to sink my psyche into. He's apologizing for something rather than consoling me, which doesn't make sense. I slip out of his arms and back away. "What do you mean you said some foolish things?"

He drops his chin and stares at the floor. "Honestly, I don't remember all that much. I was drunk."

I skirt around him so I'm not blinded by the sunlight streaming in from the arched bay window—the better to see this fuckery. Oh, the cloudless sky chafes, too; wasting perfect wedding-day weather should be a petty crime punishable by at least a few days' jail time. "How'd he tell you? Did you speak to him face-to-face?"

"He sent a text," Max says softly, the floor still the object of his undivided attention.

"Let me see it," I demand.

His head shoots up at the command. For a few seconds, we do nothing but stare at each other. He flares his nostrils. I . . . don't. His gaze darts to my lips, which part of their own volition— until I realize what I'm doing and snap my mouth shut.

My body temperature rises, and I'm tempted to tug at the lace on my arms and chest. I feel itchy all over, as if millions of fire ants are marching across my skin to the tune of Beyoncé's "Formation." I mentally push away the discomfort and hold out my hand. "I need to see what he wrote." When he doesn't budge, I add, "Please."

Max blows out a long breath, then reaches into the back pocket of his jeans, pulls out his phone, and taps on the screen. "Here."

With my lips pursed in concentration, I read the jumble of

sentences confirming that I, Lina Santos, a twenty-five-year-old up-and-coming wedding planner to DC professionals, am officially a jilted bride. *Wow. Okay. Just. Yeah.* I couldn't be more off-brand if I tried.

Still studying Andrew's text, I narrow my eyes on the sentence that annoys me the most: *Thanks to you, I can see the truth now.*

Oh, really? And what truth did you help my fiancé see, Max? Hmm? God, I can just imagine those two talking crap about me in some grimy pub. Makes me want to scream.

I shove the phone back into his hand. "So to sum up: You and Andrew got shit-faced last night, chatted about something you claim not to remember, based on that conversation he's decided not to marry me, and he doesn't have the decency to tell me any of this himself."

Max is slow to agree, but eventually he nods. "That's the sense I get, yes."

"He's a dick," I say flatly.

"I won't argue with that," Max replies, the beginnings of a smile daring to appear at the corners of his trash-talking mouth.

"And you're an asshole."

His face sours, but I refuse to give a rat's ass about his feelings. Whatever nonsense he spouted off last night convinced my fiancé to tank our wedding. I'd been *so close* to marrying the right man for me, and a single drunken conversation derailed everything.

I straighten and grab my own phone off the dressing table, sending out an SOS to my mother, aunts, and cousins:

Me: Eu preciso de vocês agora.

Telling them I need them now will get their attention; doing so in Portuguese will get them here within seconds. In the meantime, I scowl at the worst best man I could have ever asked for. "Max, do me a favor, will you?"

He takes a step in my direction, his eyes pleading for forgiveness. "Anything."

"Get. The fuck. Out."

Chapter One

Present Day

LINA

The limousine door opens, and the wedding guests let out a collective gasp.

Because the bride's wearing green—chartreuse, to be precise.

Bliss Donahue gracefully exits the car and fluffs the tiered taffeta skirt swallowing the bottom half of her frame, oblivious to the slack-jawed expressions of the people witnessing her arrival at the Northern Virginia inn she's chosen for the affair.

Like a veteran member of the Royal Family, Bliss stands in front of her imagined subjects and waves a single hand in the air, her face upturned to catch the sunlight just so. After a thirty-second pause for maximum dramatic effect, she takes several dainty steps along the cobblestoned path, the back of her ruffled dress fluttering in the April breeze. A few of the older female guests cluck their tongues and tut at the sight of her jaw-dropping gown. Others visibly cringe.

Discreet as always, I stand a few feet away, ready to troubleshoot any mishap threatening to ruin Bliss's day. Although I warned Bliss the dress might overshadow the finer details of the otherwise elegant event, she was adamant that the unusual color accentuated her best features. In my view, the dress highlights her questionable fashion sense, but as the wedding planner, my job is to bring the couple's vision to life, no matter how wonky that vision may be. To be clear, I'm not averse to voicing my concerns if the situation calls for it, but in the end, this isn't my day, and if Bliss wants to walk down the aisle in a dress that looks as if it was cobbled together with Post-its to satisfy a *Project Runway* unconventional-materials challenge, I can't stop her.

That's not to say I don't appreciate the unexpected. I've had great experiences with forward-thinking bridal attire (a wedding in which a lesbian couple both wore three-piece cream pantsuits is a personal favorite), and I'll gladly support outside-the-box plans whenever possible—largely because I'd prefer the box didn't exist. Sometimes, though, a ruffled chartreuse dress is just . . . tacky.

Now that Bliss has made her way inside the inn without incident, I pull out my phone and scan the ceremony checklist. I'm two lines down the list when Jaslene, my assistant and closest friend, appears at my back.

"Lina, we have a problem," she says.

The news shoots through my veins like adrenaline. *Of course we do. And that's why I'm here.* Armed with a renewed sense of purpose, I whip around and draw Jaslene away from the entrance to the wedding venue. "What is it?"

Jaslene's face bears a relaxed expression. *Good.* There's mischief in her dark brown eyes, however. *Not good.*

"Oh, no, no, no," I tell her. "Your eyes are twinkling. If it's funny to you, it'll be terrifying to me."

Grinning like a Cheshire cat, she grabs my arm and pulls me toward the stairs. "Come. It's the groom. You need to see this for yourself."

I follow her upstairs to the groom's dressing suite and knock three times. Shielding my eyes, I open the door a crack. "If you're not decent, you have fifteen seconds to cover up your important parts. I leave it to you to decide which parts need covering. One, two, three, four, five—"

"We're decent. It's okay," Ian, the groom, calls out.

The strangled edge to his voice warns me that things are most definitely not okay, a conclusion confirmed by my own eyes when I sweep into the room and drop my hand. I blink. I gulp. Then I blurt out an obvious but clumsy question: "Where the hell are your eyebrows?"

Pointing in the direction of his three attendants, Ian groans. "Ask these assholes. They're the ones who thought it would be hilarious to shave them off the night before my wedding."

All but one of the assholes study the floor. Needing a target, I lock eyes with the lone male who isn't avoiding my gaze.

Slumped in an oversize armchair, with his dirty-blond hair in disarray, the groomsman burps and shrugs his shoulders. "We were drunk. What can I say?" He turns his bloodshot eyes toward the groom. "Sorry, man."

I stride across the room and bend to the caveman's eye level, my hands clenched into fists as a preventive measure. "Sorry? That's all you've got? There's a bride out there who's been dreaming about this day for months. She wants it to be perfect. She wants to remember it for years to come. Now she'll remember it as the day she married a man with the skin of a newborn hamster above his eyes. And 'sorry' is all you have to say?"

Jaslene clutches a stretch of fabric on the back of my dress and pulls me upright. "Lina, this isn't helping the situation."

I bite the inside of my cheek as I compose my face into its usual cool-calm-and-collected expression. "You're right. Okay. I'll be back in a sec."

Internally cursing the brotherhood of asinine groomsmen worldwide, I leave the room, dash down the stairs, and race to my car. Once inside my rusty-but-mostly-trusty Volvo, I rummage in the back seat until my hands land on the emergency kit. I pop it open, rooting around to confirm my makeup supplies are inside.

I return as quickly as my legs and sensible pumps allow, once again not daring to look at any of the wedding guests mingling in the foyer. When I reenter the room, I spy a woman who apparently joined the entourage while I was gone. I don't bother to ask who she is or why she's here. Chitchat won't fix the groom's brows, so I have no time for it.

After laying out the contents of my makeup kit on the dressing table, I drag a chair to the full-length mirror and pat the seat bottom. "Sit," I tell Ian.

He regards me with a wary expression. "What are you going to do?"

"Do? I'm going to fix the mess your groomsmen created, of course."

"Will it work?" he asks.

Probably not, but part of my job is to project confidence in challenging situations. I raise a small vial in the air. "This is fiber fill. It's meant to enhance eyebrows, not create them out of whole cloth, but I'm hoping it'll do the trick. Won't be pretty. Still, you'll have something up there when you say 'I do.'"

Resembling a pack of hyenas with their tongues hanging out, the groomsmen huddle together and guffaw at Ian's predicament. With friends like these, who needs jackasses? When I direct my death stare at them, they straighten and study the floor again.

Ian peers at the vial more closely, then gapes at me. "My hair's brown. That's blond."

"Yes, well, grooms whose buddies shave off their eyebrows the night before their wedding don't get to choose from an array of hair color options. It's either this stuff or a Sharpie. I can cover the blond with brow powder closer to your natural hair color afterward. We don't have much time, though. What'll it be?"

He swipes a hand down his face. "All right. Let's do this. But don't make me look like Mr. Spock, okay?"

"Got it." With a shake of my head, and a prayer to the wedding gods, I get to work, holding in my laughter as best I can. *He should be so lucky.*

Needless to say, my job's ridiculously messy—and I love it.

———

Standing in a corner of the outdoor tent, I watch the guests mingle and dance, secure in the knowledge that I've averted another crisis. Yes, the groom appears to be sporting carpet scraps above his eyes. And okay, the flower girl *did* blurt out, "Hey, he looks like one of those Angry Birds." Nevertheless, my clients are happy, and in the end that's what matters. Considering I was literally working with nothing, I'm calling this Browtox procedure a win.

Now I can enjoy my favorite part of the reception: the phase after the couple honors their chosen traditions and there's nothing left for me to do except watch for last-minute glitches. This is when I finally relax a bit. Not *too* much, though. Many a wedding has been destroyed by the effects of an open bar. My skin still crawls when I remember the groom who removed his new partner's underwear instead of her garter. *Gah.*

"Nice save back there," someone to my left says.

I turn my head and survey the person, instantly recognizing her. "Thanks. You were upstairs in the dressing suite, right?"

"That's right," the woman answers.

"Related to the groom?"

Nodding, she presses her lips together, then lets out a resigned breath. "Ian's my first cousin."

"He's a nice guy," I say.

The woman raises an exquisitely arched brow and snorts. "A nice guy who loses his appeal whenever he's around his douchebag friends."

As if on cue, one of the groomsmen bares his overbite and begins to gyrate his hips as he passes us. Another one drops to the ground and inches his body along the parquet dance floor like a worm. Yet another does the Robot.

I watch them impassively even though her assessment is spot-on. "I can neither confirm nor deny."

"No need to say anything, really. They douche for themselves." She pivots to face me and extends a manicured hand. The move causes the ends of her razor-sharp blond hair, simply but expertly styled in a chin-length bob, to sweep across her cheeks. "Rebecca Cartwright."

"Lina Santos."

As we shake hands, I marvel at Rebecca's sleek hair, something

I've never possessed. Even now, my naturally curly hair is fighting against the millions of bobby pins holding my bun in place.
I love the versatility of my own locks, so I'm not envious in the
least, but I *am* fascinated by the symmetry of this woman's appearance. I don't doubt that if I split her in half and brought
both sides of her body together, they'd match perfectly.

"I was impressed with what you did up there," Rebecca says.
She leans in a fraction and gives me a conspiratorial smile. "That's
got to be something you don't see every day, right? A groom with
shaved eyebrows?"

I can't help smiling as I speak. "Believe me, dealing with
wacky stuff like that is a perk of the job."

Rebecca edges closer. "The wedding dress, though. There's a
story there, I'm sure."

"This time, I plead the Fifth."

Her blue eyes dance, then she nods sharply, as though she's
made a decision. "Discreet, too. Do you ever lose your cool?"

Rebecca's studying my face with such laser focus that I
wouldn't be surprised if the red dot from a sniper's automatic
weapon were trained on my forehead. But she isn't being creepy,
exactly—just intense—so I ignore the weird vibe and concentrate on her question. Lose my cool? Rarely. Still, the moment
when I wanted to throttle that groomsman immediately comes
to mind. "Sometimes I slip, unfortunately, but most times I'm
the one to hold things together, because if I lose it, my clients
will lose it, too."

"How long have you been planning weddings?" she asks.

Ah, is that where this conversation is headed? She's looking for
her own wedding planner, maybe? I chance a glance at her hands.

"I'm not engaged," she says, flashing her ringless fingers. "Just curious."

The tips of my ears warm. "Sorry, it's an occupational hazard. I've been in the business a little over four years. Dotting the I Do's, that's me."

"Clever," she says, nodding and smiling. "Do you enjoy it?"

I stare at her, taken aback by the question. No one's bothered to ask me that before. But I know what I tell prospective clients, and the pitch comes to me easily. "I enjoy the challenge of helping a couple settle on a meaningful wedding theme. Relish the opportunity to organize a couple's special day down to the tiniest detail. If something goes wrong, and something *always* goes wrong, I take pride in coming up with a workable solution and keeping everyone happy. Challenging venues, scheduling snafus, catering flubs—that stuff's a rush rather than a burden."

Rebecca tilts her head and studies me, a crease appearing between her brows. "There must be a downside, though. Or something that frustrates you to no end. No vocation, not even one you're passionate about, is without its challenges."

I would never tell Rebecca this, but planning weddings is my second shot. A valiant effort to reinvent myself after my first career as a paralegal failed spectacularly. I'm the daughter of Brazilian immigrants, both from humble origins. And after my father left us, I was raised by a single parent who worked tirelessly to ensure a better future for my brother and me. I owe it to my mother and tias to rise above my shortcomings and succeed in my chosen profession. After all, their hard-earned savings helped get my business off the ground. Now there's no more room for error. And that knowledge weighs on me. So heavily that I fear I'll botch this chance as badly as the first. That's the downside: The pressure to succeed can be stifling at times. But I'm not sharing my personal baggage with a stranger. *Never let them see you weak* is my mantra, and it's served me well for years.

I mentally tick through the minor complaints I'm comfortable sharing with Rebecca and settle on an innocuous one. "Indecisive clients occasionally test my patience, but all in all, it's a great gig."

Rebecca points her chin in the direction of the dance floor. "You've done a wonderful job here, I must say. Other than the fact that the bride looks like a celery stalk, this truly is a lovely wedding."

"Tsk, tsk," I say with a shake of my head. "That's no way to talk about someone celebrating her special day. Bliss is lovely in every way that matters."

A flush spreads across Rebecca's cheeks. "You're right. She is." Then she shrugs. "But as of today, she's family, which means we're going to talk about her behind her back whenever the situation calls for it. That's just our thing."

Honestly, I can relate. Over the years, my cousins and I have developed a set of hand signals and eye cues to talk shit about our relatives or unsuspecting dates. Because we often use them during family get-togethers, music is usually playing in the background. At this point, my mother and aunts believe our inside communication system is an updated version of the Chicken Dance.

"So let me ask you this," Rebecca continues. "Have you ever thought about expanding your business? Taking on a partner, perhaps?"

Nope, nope, nope. Despite the many challenges of being self-employed, my business is growing at a decent pace, and I don't want anything to muck up the careful equilibrium I'm maintaining. I'd only alter the status quo for an opportunity that would take my company to the next level, and I'm hard-pressed to imagine any individual fitting that description. Knowing this, I deflect her question. "Well, tell me a little about you, Rebecca. Have you ever planned a wedding?"

Rebecca draws back, her mouth falling open as she considers me. "Never had the pleasure. Looks fun, though."

Oh, now I see. I get this reaction at least once during every wedding. People get bowled over by the product—the breathtaking floral arrangements, the perfectly timed music, the stunning place settings, the heady scent of romance in the air—and convince themselves that they, too, can do what I do. "It *is* fun. But it also takes top-notch organizational skills and an exhausting attention to detail to pull off an event like this one. Thankfully, my assistant and I have a good system going. I'm hoping she'll eventually agree to work with me full-time." With perfect timing as usual, Jaslene glides across the dance floor, making a beeline for the DJ booth, the clipboard she stole from me tucked under her arm. And I know why: "Baby Got Back" is definitely on the couple's do-not-play list. "But listen, if you're interested in pursuing wedding planning as a career, an online course is a great place to start."

Rebecca presses her lips together, plainly holding back a smile. "To be frank, you're upending the plans I've already set in motion, but I think we were meant to meet today."

What's this woman's deal? She's not making any sense. "I don't understand."

She sighs and shakes her head, as if she's frustrated with herself. "Sorry. I'm being cryptic, and you're probably looking for the nearest exit. Basically, I have a proposition for you, but I don't think this is the time or place to discuss it." After removing an item from her clutch, she presents it to me. "Here's my number. I can explain over lunch in the next few days if you'd like."

Rebecca then slips away, disappearing into the circle of guests at the other end of the dance floor. I look down at the embossed business card on textured card stock as luxe as any wedding invitation I've ever seen. Along with her direct line in the 202 area code, it reads:

Rebecca Cartwright

◇◇◇◇

CHIEF EXECUTIVE OFFICER
THE CARTWRIGHT HOTEL GROUP
A Forbes-Rated Hotel

That moment when you realize you've just made an ass of yourself? Yeah. That.

Chapter Two

MAX

*F*rom the seat of her throne—granted, it's only a humongous desk-and-chair combo strategically placed above the average person's eye level—my mother swings her gaze between Andrew and me. "To my surprise, the Cartwright Hotel Group is shaking things up. Rebecca Cartwright, the original owner's granddaughter, has just been promoted and is at the helm now. She's trying to cater to a different clientele. Wants to focus on expanding its upscale restaurant, booking more weddings, and becoming *the* place in the District for weekend spa retreats. She has lots of ideas and would like our expertise on how to promote them. Immediately. I need my best people on this, and you two, *together*, will bring the right combination of charm and know-how to this collaboration."

I'm the charm. Andrew's the know-how. Or so everyone thinks.

Fact is, my mother's a bona fide hustler who can talk her way out of anything. This time, though, her explanation is pure unadulterated non–genetically modified crap. I wish she would just come out and say it: She doesn't trust me to handle an important client account on my own.

I can't say that I'm surprised. Unfortunately, this is familiar territory, a by-product of another truism I've come to accept: When my brother and I compete—and frankly, we don't know how to do anything else—he always comes out ahead. Through no actual fucking effort on his part. What's worse, even when we're not knowingly competing, Andrew excels. My ex-girlfriend Emily certainly thought so. After spending a day in my older brother's presence, she decided she was settling for mediocrity by being with me. She came to meet my mother. She left with a new dating manifesto. That was a fun Thanksgiving.

Andrew taps his pen on the legal pad resting in his lap. "We've worked with Rebecca before. Sounds great."

I want to mimic his chipper demeanor, but that would be childish. Also, I'm trying to be a professional here; I gave Mom my word that I would.

A year ago, our mother brought us on as employees of her firm, Atlas Communications, a one-stop shop for marketing, publicity, and branding services located in Alexandria, Virginia. She did so only after we'd mastered the basics elsewhere—me in New York and Andrew in DC and Atlanta. Before then, she'd had no time for entry-level marketing and publicity associates, not even if they were her children. When she approached us about joining the firm, she made the offer on two conditions: First, we had to agree to come as a package deal, on the theory that we'd bring out the best in each other and one day take over the business together. Second, we had to promise that once we stepped through the company's doors, we would forget that she'd given birth to us.

I get why she's worried about perceived favoritism, and if I screw up at work, I fully agree that I deserve to suffer the consequences just like anyone else. But no amount of pretending can change the immutable fact that she's our mother. Plus, the way she treats us here isn't all that different from the way she treated us as kids. Case in point: She thought nothing of summoning us to the office on a Sunday for a non-emergency. I'm annoyed for this reason alone, and her insistence that my brother and I once again work as a pair stretches my patience beyond its normally abundant limits. "We're not a set, you know," I've told her. "Or conjoined twins. We can conceivably function on our own if you let us."

Because here's the thing: Andrew's not as perfect as he pretends to be. Most of our great ideas originate with me. I'm not boasting, just stating facts. And if our mother ever untethered me from the robot claiming to be my brother, she'd realize it, too. If the past is any guide, though, that epiphany won't be happening anytime soon. In her eyes, older necessarily means wiser, and regardless of what I do, Andrew will always have me beat on that score by two years.

"Don't make that face, Max," she says as she stares at me over the rims of her hawkish red-framed eyeglasses. "The client has a special task in mind that requires two people to work on separate projects, so I'm sending you both. There's no need to take any more meaning from my decision than that. I'm catering to the client's wishes and nothing more."

Well, this is excellent news. My mind's already whirring,

brainstorming ways I can convince the client that what she wants is me—as her account manager. If I can step out of Andrew's shadow and impress Rebecca, taking the lead on the Cartwright account would be the next logical step. And if that happens, maybe my mother will finally recognize the value I bring to the firm in my own right.

"If you're both free," my mother continues, "she'd love to meet with you next week to explain her plans. And given the volume of work her company sends our way, I suspect I don't need to stress that you *should* make yourselves available at her convenience."

Andrew nods like an obedient puppy. "Of course. We'll make it happen. Right, Max?"

My mother surveys my face, her eyes narrowing to slits as though she's expecting me to be difficult. Whyever would she think that?

I adopt an agreeable tone. "Of course."

She rises from her chair and brings her hands together in a loud clap, essentially dismissing us. "Well, gentlemen, I really appreciate that you came in over the weekend. The client is eager to move forward on this as quickly as possible, so I didn't want to waste any time."

I'm tempted to note that she could have briefed us over email, but I just don't have the energy to be the troublemaker today. Instead, I simply salute her on the way out of the office. "See you tomorrow."

I'm almost at the elevators when Andrew jogs up behind me. "Hey, M. Hang on a minute."

I slow my steps. "What's up?"

When he reaches me, he plants his legs wide and pushes up the sleeves of his beige cashmere sweater. I'm in a fucking hoodie. I'm also itching to point out the pilling on the left side of his sweater, likely caused by his favorite designer messenger bag rubbing against it, but that's the kind of minor shit that would fuck with his day and I'm trying not to be a jerk.

Andrew cocks his head as he studies me. Then he says, "Listen, I know the client might want us to work on different projects, but we'll still brainstorm together, right? I think that'll be a good thing for whatever final product we present."

Ideally, we'd do the exact opposite of what he's suggesting. I *want* to work on my own and show the client that, between Andrew and me, I'm the better bet. How else am I going to set myself apart from him?

We eye each other in silence as he waits for my answer, until the *ding* of the arriving elevator breaks the awkward spell. Before I step on, I say, "I figure that'll depend on what the client wants, and we'll know that soon enough. You coming?"

He takes a step back. "No, I'm going to answer a few emails before I go." Smiling smugly, he taps a finger against his temple. "Might as well get some work done since I'm already here." Unable to help himself, he adds, "That's not your first instinct, though, is it? Being industrious."

I ignore the jab. *Be the better man, Max.* "I'm going to shoot some hoops. Sure you don't want to join me?"

His reaction is priceless. He shudders and scrunches his face like a pug's.

Yeah, I didn't think so, but hey, it was decent of me to ask.

"I'll pass," he says on a chuckle—make that a chortle. Andrew's definitely the kind of guy who chortles.

"Fine. See you in"—I look down at my wristwatch—"less than twenty-four hours, then."

Giving me a half-assed wave, he says, "Yeah. Sure." When the elevator doors slide shut, he's still standing in the same spot.

I wish Andrew and I were closer, but we don't have the same interests, and we've never been friends. It would be great if we interacted on some level other than a competitive one, but the more my parents shoved us together, the more we tried to pull ourselves apart. Okay, that last bit's mostly my fault. I'm mature enough to own the blame.

Who knows? Maybe this project will give Andrew and me the separation we need to connect in other ways. Or maybe we'll kill each other. Admittedly, it could go either way.

Chapter Three

LINA

*B*liss and Ian are somewhere over the Atlantic, heading to their honeymoon destination, so I'm officially off the clock for the rest of the weekend. Today's to-do list is short: restock the fridge, live in my sweats, and binge on Netflix. But first . . . pão com manteiga and cafezinho.

By unanimous consent, Brazilians must consume two items—and *only* two items—for breakfast each day: buttered bread and coffee. If a person deviates from this menu, they're probably staging a coup. Or they're first-generation Brazilian Americans like me, in which case, bring on the bacon-and-egg sandwich. This morning, though, I woke up craving a traditional Brazilian breakfast, and my favorite place to get one is Rio de Wheaton, the grocery store my mother and aunts operate out of a strip mall just off Georgia Avenue in Wheaton, Maryland. Side note: For years, I've begged them to change the name. For just as many years, they've ignored me.

It doesn't take me long to get to the store from my apartment in College Park. The bell affixed to the door jingles when I enter, and everyone inside stops in mid-motion to inspect the newest arrival. Passing a display of Havaianas flip-flops wedged between the cassava flour and masking tape, I breathe in the sweet and buttery aroma of freshly baked bread permeating the air. A third of the store's space is dedicated to a tiny café—literally consisting of three round tables and not enough chairs—where the sisters serve cafezinho brasileiro, or the equivalent of Starbucks on steroids, and pão, in this case, a warm, flaky roll served fresh throughout the day.

"Bom dia," I call out. "Como vai?"

"Filha, um minuto," my mother says with a smile before she returns her attention to the customer at the register. As she hands the man his change, she winks at him. "Obrigada."

Hang on. Is my mother flirting? That's a first, and I'd *love* to see more of it. I don't think she's dated anyone after divorcing my father over ten years ago. The flush on her cheeks is promising, though, and the way she's leaning forward, her head cocked to the side, suggests she's into this guy. Hallelujah! As far as I'm concerned, my mother deserves all the booty calls her heart desires to make up for my father's lack of affection during their marriage.

Lugging a twenty-four-pack of Guaraná Brazilia in her hands, Viviane, my mother's oldest sister and our family's matriarch, marches my way and gives me a hurried kiss on each cheek. Tia Viviane operates in two modes: "busy" and "on overdrive." Her body already moving in the direction of her next destination, she looks at me over her shoulder. "Tudo bem?"

"Everything's fine," I tell her. For a few seconds, I'm rooted to the spot in the center aisle as people shuffle past me without any real sense of direction. They don't appear to be interested in buying anything; they're just . . . here. Jaslene says Puerto Rican storeowners have bodega cats. Well, Brazilian storeowners tend to attract bodega people. Such as the guy from the neighborhood who's enamored with my younger cousin Natalia. He's currently pretending to watch futebol on the TV suspended from the corner of the café's ceiling, while the object of his unrequited love, who is *very* engaged to be married, is wiping down the salgadinhos display. Coincidence? I think not.

"Oi mulher!" Natalia says as she drapes the dish towel over her shoulder. "Scrounging for free food again?"

"Respect your elders, brat."

At warp speed, she grabs the dish towel, flicks it at my chest, and leans in, lowering her voice so only I can hear what she says next. "You have a white ring around your mouth. What is it? Pastry residue? Pre-come?"

I jump back and quickly wipe at my face before I realize she's doubled over in glee. "Har-har. Hilarious as always."

"Why was my observation even plausible, prima?" she asks through her laughter. "I mean, what the hell have you been doing in your spare time?"

Nothing. Absolutely nothing. The truth is, if there were a white ring around my mouth, there'd be no chance it came from a blowjob, considering I haven't been with anyone for well over a year. And since my livelihood depends on working most weekends from March through September, I don't have time to meet potential partners in any case. These days, my orgasms are self-induced, battery-powered, and delivered in under five minutes—if I'm really feeling sassy, I'll stretch it to ten. So, yeah, no way it's pre-come. Remnants of a powdered doughnut, though? Entirely possible. "Whatever, Natalia. My love life, or lack of it, isn't open for discussion—or dissection." I snap my fingers at her. "Now get me coffee and bread and make it quick."

"*Pfft*. Get it yourself. It's break time, and I need to call Paolo." She removes her apron and hands it over, giving me her ever-present smirk. "You're welcome to take my place for a bit. If you want to make yourself useful, that is." A loud pop of her glossy lips punctuates her point, and then she waves goodbye as she saunters toward the door.

"Don't forget we have an appointment on Wednesday," I call after her.

"It's my dress fitting. Of course I'll be there," she shouts back before she slips outside.

I throw the apron over my head, tie it around my waist, and wait for it in . . . three, two, one . . .

"Wash your hands," my mother warns.

Every. Time. As if I don't know better. But do I snap back at her? Of course not. I value my life as much as the next person. "Will do, Mãe." I look around the store for my other aunt's short, springy curls. "Where's Tia Izabel?"

My mother's other older sister is the quietest of the bunch—and the least interested in running the store.

"She went to run a few errands," my mother says.

Mãe's still busy at the register, so I sneak a kiss on her cheek, then stride to the back. After my hands are properly washed and sanitized, I return to the counter and use tongs to swipe a bread roll; I pop a piece into my mouth and sigh in contentment. *Definitely worth the drive.*

My mother finally breaks free of her register duties and slips a hand around my waist. "How was the wedding? This was the one with the green dress, right?"

She takes great joy in living vicariously through the people who hire me, and she has an excellent memory, too.

"It went well," I tell her after I finish chewing the bread. "The dress was as interesting as you thought it would be. Oh, and the groom's friends shaved off his eyebrows the night before."

My mother looks up at me, her dark eyes growing wide as saucers. "Wow. I didn't see that one coming. But you handled it?"

I give her a do-you-even-know-who-I-am look, my face screwed up playfully. "Of course I handled it."

She nods, pulling me closer to her side. "I'm proud of you, filha."

"Thanks, Mãe." Her words make me stand a little taller. That's all I've ever wanted—to make Mãe and my tias proud. When each of their marriages imploded, the sisters banded together to raise their children, taking turns cooking, babysitting, and driving to and from school and extracurriculars. They spent their remaining time cleaning other people's homes, until they saved enough to open this store. Because of them, I'm a college graduate; my older brother, Rey, is a physician's assistant; and Natalia's in heavy demand as a self-employed makeup artist. Bringing up the rear and no less impressive is Tia Izabel's daughter, Solange, who's completing graduate school and preparing to change the world.

"Think you'll get any more work out of this one?" my mother asks.

"More work? Maybe. It all depends on timing. If someone's engaged and hasn't booked a planner, they'll probably call to feel me out."

And then there's Rebecca Cartwright. She mentioned a proposition, and I'm curious to know what it is. I make a mental note to call her first thing Monday morning and set a time for us to meet. At the very least, I can add her to my growing list of contacts in the area. Even a loose connection with the CEO of a hotel as highly regarded as the Cartwright could be useful someday.

An actual paying customer with goods in her hands shuffles to the counter. My mother wanders off to help her, allowing me to return to my love affair with the bread in my hand. I'm happily chomping on said bread when in walks Marcelo, a family friend and the owner of Something Fabulous, the boutique dress shop where I rent space for my business.

"Olá, pessoal," he says grandly, his voice booming over the crowd's cheers on the TV screen. "Tudo bem?"

"Tudo," Tia Viviane says, half of her body hidden behind the reach-in beverage cooler she's stocking. "E você?"

He gestures with one hand to indicate he's so-so, then he saunters over to Tia Viviane and drops a kiss on her forehead. They've been friends for ages, having met decades ago through the extensive social network that helps Brazilian immigrants in Maryland acclimate to life in America. That same network found all three sisters their husbands, none of whom stuck around after the marriages ended.

As for Marcelo and Viviane, I suspect their friendship comes with benefits, but I've never been bold enough to confirm my suspicions. Tia Viviane's lethal when a pair of Havaianas are within reach.

Marcelo sees me and his eyes dim, causing me to question the truth of his next words. "Carolina, I was hoping I'd see you here. I have news."

My chewing slows as I place the rest of my bread on a napkin and brush the crumbs off the front of my T-shirt. "What's up, Marcelo?"

He casually rests his forearms on the counter. "The real estate company gave notice Friday afternoon that they're increasing the rent for the next leasing period. By seven percent." Sighing, he steps back and motions as though he's wiping his hands of the situation. "And as far as I'm concerned, that's it. I can't keep up anymore. Not with everyone buying wedding dresses online. Or renting them. So I'm going to join my daughter in Florida and find a little shop there to sell my inventory for a few more years. Eventually, I'll retire and spend all day fishing. It's time." Marcelo reaches over and covers my hand. "I know this affects you, too. And if I could afford it, I'd stay, but I was struggling already, and this will make it worse."

I force my words past the massive lump of disappointment clogging my throat. "When does the lease end again?" I already know the answer, but hearing the expiration date out loud will force me to confront the reality of my situation rather than bury it.

"Sixty days," he says on a sigh.

Well, that's real enough for me, and it's no small thing. An office in the District is essential to my business. Most of my clients are busy professionals who appreciate the convenience of meeting in a central location where they can also go to other shops and restaurants as part of their evening plans. A home base just off Connecticut Avenue communicates stability, a certain gravitas that doesn't need to be explained. Any charlatan can whip up some business cards at a local copy shop and call themselves a wedding planner; a registered business address assures a couple their coordinator won't pack up her portable office and run off with their money.

I don't require a lot, really—an office and a cubicle are enough—which is why my arrangement with Marcelo met my needs perfectly. Because I didn't take up much square footage, he could afford not to charge me market price for it. I know from my own abandoned efforts to find office space a few years ago that leasing even a closet in the District will make it almost impossible for me to pay the rent on my own apartment. And even if I can find an affordable alternative, it'll probably be a step down from my current location, so the optics of the transition won't do me any favors, either.

Dammit. I can't screw up. Not again.

Marcelo's decision has knocked me off-kilter, and I don't know what to do to right myself. Tears threaten to fall, but a glance between Viviane and my mother, the former of whom is wearing a stern expression, dries my eyes instantly. *Right.* Having learned my own harsh lessons when I was a wide-eyed innocent, I now know the rules well: We must never let our emotions get the better of us; doing so is either a sign of weakness, one that diminishes our well-earned respect, or a mark of combativeness, which will cause people to say we're irrational. And as women—women of color, more specifically—we simply can't afford to be perceived in those terms.

Too bad I'm a softie. Apt to cry or sob the moment anyone manages to draw the slightest bit of emotion out of me. When I was younger, my brother and cousins teased me about it mercilessly. Bebê chorão, they'd chant. *Crybaby.* It didn't bother me much then; how much harm could come from that pesky trait, really? As an adult, however, I discovered the answer was *plenty*—certainly more than I could handle. So I developed a persona over the years, to manage my feelings. I'm no-nonsense. A badass. Made of Teflon and impervious to minor insult or offense. I'll never again be that woman who made a blubbering fool of herself over a guy. Never again be that person who crumbled in a professional setting and lost the respect of her peers. Strength is a state of mind, and I'm willing it into existence, dammit.

I straighten and give Marcelo a tight smile. "None of this is your fault, Marcelo. You couldn't have predicted a rent hike this ugly. I'm sure I'll be able to find something else. So don't worry about me. Everything will be fine."

He studies my face—undoubtedly detecting my bullshit but not calling me on it—his mouth pressed into a deep frown. "You're sure, *querida*?"

The endearment tries to slip through my defenses, but I mentally build a barricade against showing any emotion. "*Certa*."

Everyone around me—Marcelo, Tia Viviane, my mother, even the guy pretending to watch soccer who's eavesdropping on the conversation—visibly relaxes, the tension of the moment cut by my assurances that all will end well. And it must. End well, that is. Because I have no other choice—my career and livelihood are at stake.

Sighing on the inside at the detour in my day, I make a last-minute addition to my to-do list: *eat my feelings*. My gaze lands on the half-eaten roll of bread. No, that just won't do; it's way too basic. I need fat, and carbs, and tons of sugar. Where's a goddamn powdered doughnut when you need one?

Chapter Four

LINA

Note to self: A dozen glazed doughnut holes can work wonders on your disposition.

After an evening of bingeing on TV and sweets, I greet the new week with optimism and a plan, one that includes an early-morning meeting with Rebecca Cartwright. Now more than ever, I need to cultivate my contacts and keep my eyes peeled for new business opportunities, so when I contacted her last night and she offered to see me first thing this morning, I jumped at the chance.

According to the quick research I did during the Metro ride here, the Cartwright is one of three boutique hotels owned by the Cartwright Group. The flagship location is in the District; the other two properties are in Northern Virginia. In another life, this building housed a bank, and remnants of its austere beginnings, such as the large white columns that flank its breathtaking entrance, complement the simple yet eclectic interior design. Thanks to a massive skylight in the center of the circular lobby, the marble floors gleam, and the sun's rays highlight every detail, from the abstract art adorning the textured walls to the steel lines of the contemporary furniture. It all comes together to give the hotel an upscale yet unpretentious vibe.

The sound of Rebecca's heels enters the space before she does. As she approaches, her tinny voice floats through the room. "Lina, thanks so much for coming to see me on such short notice."

I rise from the sleek yellow leather couch and extend my hand. Her grip is firm but not overpowering. We make eye contact for the customary few seconds and pump our clasped hands three times; I bet we both attended business-etiquette workshops in high school.

"It's good to see you again, Rebecca."

"Let's sit for a minute," she says, gesturing to a small table by a window, the hustle and bustle on New Hampshire Avenue audible just beyond the pane as we settle in. "So here's the deal. We're rebranding in several areas, one of them being wedding services. I've been searching for a wedding planner to direct this new vision for our hotels, serve as its public face, and plan weddings, of course. You impressed me on Saturday. So much so that I'd like you to put yourself in the running for the position, assuming the thought of directing wedding services for a Forbes five-star-rated hotel with an award-winning restaurant appeals to you."

I'm stunned, but I manage to drum up a decent question. "You're not looking for someone to direct general event planning, right?"

She smiles and nods. "Right. I'm looking for someone to focus on weddings and build our brand in that specific area."

"Okay, got it." I wipe my palms on my skirt and puff out a

short breath. "Another question, then. I currently work with an assistant. She would need to be a part of any venture I consider. Is that possible?"

This time, Rebecca's nod is even more vigorous. "If we offer and you accept a position as director of wedding services, you'd be authorized to hire your own select staff. If that means hiring your current assistant, I'd have no problem with that. I'd authorize 50K for a full-time assistant."

"And my salary?"

"Double that," she says. "For work at all three hotels, of course."

Inside, I'm flailing like Kermit the Frog. *One hundred thousand dollars. Holy shit.* Is this really happening? I want to squee, but I contain my excitement as I process the possibilities. If I land this job, my lease problem wouldn't even matter anymore. I'd be moving into larger, cozier digs at the Cartwright—and doubling my income, too. This is the break I never imagined I'd get, and my mother and tías would be ecstatic. But I can't get ahead of myself just yet. I'll need to keep looking for alternative office space in case this doesn't work out. Still, am I going to try to get this gig? Shit yeah. "You'd like me to interview for the position? Today?"

Until now, Rebecca's navigated this interaction confidently, but in this moment she seems less assured, her hands flitting around as though she's nervous. I can see that my question, although an obvious one, isn't easy to answer.

"I'll be honest," she says. "I knew the moment I met you I'd have a hard time choosing between you and my top prospect to date."

Oh. Bummer. There's someone else—presumably, an equally impressive and highly qualified someone else—who's already a standout in her eyes. Well, I guess I'll just need to work doubly hard to prove I'm the better candidate.

"So this is where my marketing folks factor into the equation," Rebecca says. She glances at her wristwatch and stands. "Let's move to one of our conference rooms. We can talk more there."

I jump up from my seat, a bundle of energy waiting to be unleashed, then force myself to simmer down. "Sure. After you."

Rebecca strides down the hall, her upper body twisted around so she can face me. "It just so happens that my talented marketing people are visiting today. I figure we can all get together in the conference room, and I can further explain my proposition and get them up to speed in one meeting. They'd be heavily involved in helping you present your ideas, and I think you'll get along with them splendidly. Sound okay to you?"

"Sounds great."

Rebecca leads me into a meeting room and motions to a seat at the head of a glass conference table. "Make yourself comfortable. Do you need anything before we begin? Coffee? Water?"

If there's one thing I do well, it's going an entire day without drinking a single ounce of fluid. Dehydration is a real possibility at any given moment. And when I'm nervous—as I am now—thoughts of spilling liquids on myself, or worse, thoughts of spilling them on someone else, only add to my agita. So no, I don't want anything to drink. Pasting on a measured smile in the hopes of projecting confidence, I settle into the chair and smooth my hands over the front of my pencil skirt. "I'm fine, thank you."

Rebecca, who's been leaning against the threshold, straightens. "Great. I'll grab the guys so we can get started. Back in a sec."

Now that I'm alone, I take in my surroundings, scanning the

space for a focal point to latch on to during the meeting, should I need to calm my nerves. It's a trick I've used since college, when I realized that my mother's old advice about picturing everyone in their underwear wouldn't work for me. Back then, I'd get caught up in guessing which brands my classmates and professors were using, which styles they'd favor, and so on. There's nothing worse than imagining your econ professor in a plaid tie and leopard-print thong. Nothing.

My gaze is immediately drawn to a bronze sculpture of a phoenix resting on the only credenza in the room. That'll do. And I imagine I *will* need it. Rebecca can't fool me with her business casual attire and friendly demeanor. Every step of this process is part of my interview, and the marketing people she nonchalantly referred to as "the guys" will either help or hurt my chances of landing this once-in-a-lifetime opportunity. So I need to make a good first impression. If I demonstrate my expertise and convince them of my competence, maybe they'll go the extra mile for me. And since I'm essentially competing for the position, every advantage, no matter how small, matters.

A minute later, Rebecca's laugh carries down the hall as though it's a trumpet heralding her arrival. I rise, straighten my jacket, and stretch my lips. When the door opens and "the guys" walk in, all the fresh air in the room rushes out, displaced by a sudden influx of toxic atmosphere that makes breathing a struggle. I could use a strong slap on my ass to shock me into gulping in much-needed oxygen, but I'm not a newborn, and these men couldn't care less whether I'm okay.

And I'm not. Okay, I mean.

Because there, in all his gorgeous and villainous glory, stands my former fiancé—or as I've renamed him since the breakup,

Asshole Majora. And if that's not bad enough, the worst best man ever—his brother, Asshole Minora—is standing by his side.

Fuck my life into next week.

What are they doing here? Together? Last I heard, Andrew had relocated to Atlanta and joined the marketing team of a global law firm. His brother lives and works in New York, or so I thought. Well, not today apparently. Today, they're starring in my nightmare. And if their bulging eyes are any guide, they weren't expecting this almost-a-family reunion, either. Andrew even looks a little green around the gills. So it's no surprise, then, that they don't do or say anything, presumably waiting for me to set the tone of this ill-fated encounter.

Rebecca regards me with a cheerful smile as she addresses them. "Gentlemen, meet Carolina Santos. Says we can call her Lina for short." To me, she says, "This is Andrew and Max. They're brothers and colleagues."

Merda. This is *not* how I imagined this day would go. Not even close. I wanted to show Rebecca her instincts about me were right. Instead, she'll discover in the next few seconds that one of two wedding planners she's interviewing for an amazing position was jilted by the very marketing agent she thinks so highly of. How am I supposed to convince her that Andrew and I can work together to build the hotel's wedding brand? I'm not even sure we can.

And if Rebecca's weighing the pros and cons of two comparably impressive candidates, would discovering that one of them comes with a lengthy vacation's worth of baggage push her to go with the other one instead? Why would she sign up for this drama if she discovered it before she'd invested any appreciable time in that prospect?

There's more to this than just the uneasiness of working with a former fiancé, too. I make my living creating the illusion of happily-ever-afters. Admitting I didn't succeed in finding my own kills the mood. What I do inevitably gets filtered through this lens even though it has no bearing on my skills as a planner. Sure, it's not my fault, and no, it's not a scarlet letter by any means, but if people are honest with themselves, they would readily concede that knowing I'm a jilted bride makes them feel sorry for me—especially given the nature of my business.

Honestly, I wish I could let a river of tears run down my face, but I absolutely *refuse* to let anyone in this room regard me as a weakling who doesn't deserve their respect. I need a way to neutralize the situation so I can function at the level Rebecca expects from me. I simply can't let this reunion play out in her presence.

The idea isn't even fully formed in my brain when I clasp Andrew's hand and give him a firm, desperate handshake. "It's great to meet you, Andrew. Rebecca says you're talented, so I'm excited about the possibility of our working together."

His mouth opens, closes, and opens again, while I implore him with my eyes to go along with this harebrained plan to pretend we're strangers. "It's . . . uh . . . great to meet you, too."

Yeah, stiff as always, even when he's flustered. He looks good, though. His hair's grown out at the sides and top, and his fair skin glows with vitality. The navy suit he's wearing flatters his broad shoulders and trim waist as if his body regularly serves as the mold for menswear mannequins. All that's fine and dandy, but here's what I understand now: Andrew's like a perfect résumé—there's either a ton of embellishing going on or a bunch of unflattering stuff never made it onto the page.

Max, for his part, appears to have experienced late-onset puberty between twenty-five and today o'clock—because he did *not* look this handsome the last time I saw him. Or maybe I wasn't in the right mind-set to notice all those years ago. Well, in any case, time has been ridiculously kind to Andrew's younger brother. From his dark, effortlessly tousled hair to the sharp cut of his jaw, the individual parts combine to make an impressive whole. Shorter than his brother by a couple of inches, Max still manages to dominate the room. He couldn't blend into the background if he tried. Also, he's cute in the eyes and thick in the thighs—a deadly combination that's wasted on him.

Max clears his throat and glides forward to join the introductions. "Lina, it's a pleasure."

I ignore his outstretched hand. There's a moment of unease as we stand there staring at each other, until he gestures toward the conference table, an ear-to-ear grin masking his manipulative tendencies.

"Shall we?" he asks. "I'm looking forward to hearing a little more about you."

It's not lost on me that Max has settled into his role like an Academy Award–winning actor while his older brother's flopping around like a stuffed animal being dragged by a toddler. There's a lesson in there somewhere, but I'm too anxious to absorb it.

"Sounds great," I say.

After blowing out a slow and what I hope is an imperceptible breath, I scramble back to my chair.

Andrew finally recovers and joins us at the table. His face is flushed and there's a sheen of perspiration above his brows. Good. He deserves to be uncomfortable. We talked only once

after the non-wedding, when he'd mustered the courage to explain that he was looking for *more*. More affection, more conversation, more sex, more *everything*. He'd been so calm and proper
as he rattled off his new-to-me wishes, a laundry list of items
that probably reflected Max's wants, not his. Today, though, his
unflappable demeanor is nowhere to be found, and knowing I
put him in this panicked state sparks joy in me.

"So . . . uh . . . Ms. . . . uh . . . Santos, tell us about your business," Andrew says as he wipes his forehead with a handkerchief.

Max covers his disappointment in his brother's performance
by swiping a hand down his face, but I catch the way his eyes
roll to the back of his head before he clears his expression of any
emotion.

My chest expands as I take a deep, calming breath. Okay,
they're not blowing my cover; that's encouraging. So I guess
we're doing this, then. And sure, I'm fully aware this could be
a big mistake. Huge. Like Julia Roberts in *Pretty Woman* you-
work-on-commission-don't-you huge. But there's no going back
now, is there?

Chapter Five

MAX

As subtly as I can manage, I watch Andrew's reaction to this monumental turn of events. He's sitting up straighter than usual, appearing cool and unbothered, but one of his knees is bouncing at an alarming rate. Oh man, if I had to guess, he's seconds away from peeing his pants.

This farce is going to blow up in our faces. Guaranteed. But what other choice do I have than to run with it? Lina plainly didn't want to acknowledge that she knows us, and now that we've followed her lead, extracting ourselves from this charade would strain our developing relationship with Rebecca.

I study our co-conspirator as she describes her business. Her appearance hasn't changed much since I last saw her—when she told me to get the fuck out of her wedding suite. Same almond-shaped eyes, same pouty mouth, same regal air about her. The hair's shorter, though, a cloud of curls resting on her shoulders, but otherwise she looks exactly like the woman who displayed little emotion when I told her that Andrew would be a no-show for the ceremony. Okay, maybe her brown skin tone's warmer, but she's not duping me; that sun-kissed complexion is camouflaging an icy interior. *Do not go anywhere near that woman, Max. She's a rattlesnake—coiled up tight and ready to strike at her innocent prey at any moment. Shit, you still bear the fang marks.*

"I plan six to eight weddings at various stages in any given month," she says. "So my work requires lots of juggling. But I enjoy the challenge, and seeing the result always gives me immense satisfaction . . ."

It's a script. I'm sure of it. I can see the effort she's making to recall what she's supposed to say. Every few seconds, her eyes dart to one side as though she's looking at something in her peripheral vision. I follow her gaze to the statue of a phoenix across the room. Maybe she's engaging in a visualization exercise to calm her nerves? Or maybe the bird's just interesting. Who the hell knows? In any case, there's no denying she's good. *Really* good. But she needs to loosen up. If it weren't so obviously rehearsed, her pitch would improve tenfold.

When Lina's done, Rebecca nods politely, and then our client swings her gaze back to Andrew and me. "You guys already know that I want to shake things up here. I'm taking the reins, and my grandfather's fully on board with the changes I've proposed. But there's one problem. I know absolutely *nothing* about weddings. Which means I need to hire someone who does." She turns to Lina. "I heard everything you just said, but I'm a visual person. I want to *see* what that new vision would look like, and how the person I hire will incorporate everything the Cartwright has to offer in one compelling package. How would you make use of our award-winning restaurant? How would you transform the ballrooms? What do you bring to the table that no one else does? How would you *sell* what you do so that a couple looking to hire you decides it's a no-brainer? Show me what the revamped website would look like. Brochures. A display at a wedding expo, and so on."

Damn, if Rebecca's willing to put this much effort into the search, how much does Lina stand to make if Rebecca ultimately hires her? Jesus, I don't want to know. I might be tempted to switch careers.

"Essentially a mock-up of what it would be like to have me as your hotel's wedding coordinator," Lina says.

Rebecca points at Lina with both hands. "Yes. Exactly."

"How long would I have?" Lina asks. Her brows are furrowed, the first sign so far that she's wary of what Rebecca's proposing.

"Around five weeks. I'd like to get the position locked down before the next board meeting."

Lina's pinched expression softens. "That's doable." She points at my brother and me. "And these gentlemen are going to help me package it?"

"One of them, yes."

That captures my attention like no other statement does. "Only one of us?" I ask Rebecca.

Rebecca gives us all a sheepish grin. "Well, here's the thing: Before I met Lina this weekend, I'd made inquiries about potentially hiring someone else. I was at home mulling it over when my boyfriend started watching *Hell's Kitchen* and that's when the light bulb went off. A weeks-long interview with a demo component. Hmm, I thought. Why not do something like that with Lina and the other candidate?" She looks at Lina. "I won't share his name for privacy reasons. Anyway, I got excited, emailed the agency, and here we are. So I'd like to go through this process with both candidates and choose based on my general impressions, your references—send me those, by the way—and your ability to sell me on your vision. I'm guessing it would make the most sense for us to split the group into two teams and plan for the presentations to be made around the middle of May. How does that sound?"

Andrew audibly gulps, causing everyone's gazes to land on him.

"Sorry," he says, swallowing. "I think I'm a little parched. That works for me."

"Same," Lina says succinctly.

"Me, too," I chime in.

"And I'll leave it to you all to decide how to split the teams." She looks down at her phone. "Maybe you guys can chat a bit while I make a quick call?" To Andrew and me, she says, "But don't leave when you're done here, okay? I need to speak with you about the restaurant and our spa services. Oh, and website analytics."

We nod and Rebecca dashes out of the room.

The wheels in my brain are turning so quickly they might pop off. This situation couldn't be more perfect. My goal is to convince Rebecca that I'm the better person to manage the hotel's account, and she's devised a hiring process that necessarily puts Andrew and me on different sides. How can I *not* shine under these circumstances?

Lina relaxes into her seat, her expression unreadable. "Let's get a few things straight before we hash out the details. First, this is an unpleasant development, but I'm committed to making the best of the situation. Second, if I had a choice, I wouldn't work with either of you, but I don't have a choice, so Max, we'll"—

she makes air quotes—"work together for the duration of this project. Third, I don't intend on taking your advice, Max, so don't bother offering it. Rebecca doesn't need to know the extent of our collaboration, and I'm more than willing to take full responsibility for the pitch. Your safest bet is to simply stay out of my way and let me do the heavy lifting. Are we clear?"

Well, damn. How can I not shine under these circumstances? The pessimistic voice in my head makes a rare appearance and whispers, *That's how.*

Andrew clears his throat and leans forward. "Hang on. This is getting out of hand. Maybe we should take a step back and consider coming clean to Rebecca. We can explain that—"

Lina and I shake our heads, and he clamps his mouth shut.

"How would you go about doing that, Andrew?" Lina asks. "Are we going to tell her that we got flustered and decided to pretend not to know each other?"

"It's the truth, isn't it?" he asks.

"The truth makes us look like fools," I point out.

"We *are* fools," Lina adds. "Look, I don't know what I was thinking in the moment. I panicked. And I'm not proud of myself. But telling Rebecca that we *do* know each other is going to open a can of worms that isn't going to endear her to any of us. And I really, really want a shot at this job, okay?"

I catch the slight tremor in her voice, and a part of me warms to her cause. Despite the absurdity of the situation, she's trying to maintain control over it, and I find that admirable.

Lina taps her lips with two fingers, the wrinkling between her brows suggesting she's deciding how much to share with us. Then, after sighing in resignation, she speaks. "I don't expect either of you to care, but this opportunity would solve a huge problem for me, not to mention it's the type of position that will take my career to the next level. If my and Andrew's prior relationship had any true bearing on whether Rebecca should hire me, I'd be the first to say we need to confess what we did. It shouldn't matter, though, not in a fair world. So let's just do what we need to do and hope everyone gets what they want. It's five weeks, not a lifetime." She stares at Andrew, unapologetic determination apparent in her unflinching gaze. "You owe me this."

He does owe her this—and so do I.

My brother puffs out his cheeks as he rubs the back of his neck and contemplates Lina's scheme. "You'll work with Max?" he asks her.

"Ostensibly," she says with a shrug.

Andrew looks between us, until his lips curve into a smug grin. "That's fine, then. I'll work with the other planner. We'll coordinate our schedules so that we don't run into each other to the extent that we're here." He puckers his mouth as he considers her. "Seems odd, don't you think? I'll be helping your competition."

"I'm not too worried about that," she says, her face a blank, uninterested canvas.

Man, this woman's something else. A minute ago, she admitted she was in a panic; now she's driving this conversation, and Andrew and I are just along for the ride. I wish I could say I'm partly responsible for her confidence, but she's already announced that she intends to ignore anything I tell her. How did this day go off the rails so quickly?

Lina pulls out her phone. "What's your number, Max? I'll give you a call so we can discuss the bare minimum we need to do together."

On autopilot, I recite my number and repeat it for her.

"I'll call you soon," she says, and then she strides out of the conference room without a backward glance, her hips swiveling to match the brisk pace of her steps.

After shaking out my arms and massaging a kink in my neck, I turn back to my brother. I'm itching to wipe the self-satisfied expression off his face, but there's nothing I can say that would accomplish that objective.

"So it looks like we'll be competing on behalf of our wedding planners," he says.

"I guess so. I think it's safe to say I'm working at a disadvantage." Andrew snorts.

I've never heard him make a sound like that. It startles me. Kind of reminds me of the first time I heard my mother fart. "What's funny?"

"Nothing." He raises an imaginary glass to simulate a toast. "May the best man win."

"May the best wedding planner win, you mean."

"Yeah," he says with a wink. "That, too."

Someone's acting cockier than he was just yesterday. That's fine. Because this is what we do best: try to one-up each other. I just need to come out on top. And once I remind Lina that co-operating with me will help her hit Andrew where it'll hurt him the most, she'll reconsider her stance toward me.

Damn, what a day. I bet most brothers would be having a different kind of debriefing right now, one that focused on the bizarre coincidence of seeing your former fiancée under these cir-cumstances. But that isn't and has never been us. The one time Andrew opened up to me, he ended up bailing on his wedding. It's probably better for everyone if we limit our conversations to work topics.

"What do we tell Mom?" I ask.

Andrew grimaces. "Only what she needs to know. The basics of the assignment. If we're committed to treating Lina as though she's just another wedding planner, then there really is no point in disclosing details that'll put Mom under unnecessary stress."

Andrew's not fooling me. He doesn't want to remind our mother of the *one* time he disappointed her. For weeks after his wedding was canceled, my mother tried to convince Andrew he was making the biggest mistake of his life. No woman he's dated since Lina has met my mother's approval, and unfortunately, Andrew's the type of man who needs it.

"Okay, we won't tell her," I say.

He sags against his seat. "Good. So what's your plan where Lina's concerned?"

I wave a finger back and forth in front of my face. "*Uh-uh-uh.* There will be no sharing of information, or brainstorming, or joint strategy sessions. I'll work on Lina's pitch, and you'll work with your person on his. Otherwise it wouldn't be fair."

Andrew's gaze bounces around the room as he considers the change in our usual state of play. "Fine. Good luck, then."

Remembering the way Lina skewered us in less than thirty seconds, I think it's safe to say I'm going to need it.

Chapter Six

LINA

"This is a disaster," Natalia whines as she inspects herself in the mirror. "I look like I'm starring in a Disney on Ice production. Or competing in the World Figure Skating Championships."

We're tucked away in one of the dressing areas of Marcelo's shop. He's up front speaking with a woman second-guessing her veil selection. Yesterday, whenever I wasn't meeting clients or working on proposals, I was thinking about Andrew and Max's untimely reappearance in my life. Focusing on Natalia's wardrobe crisis—which, because it involves Natalia, requires nothing less than an "all brain cells on deck" mentality—is a welcome distraction.

Jaslene, who's kneeling at Natalia's feet, shakes out the bottom of my cousin's dress and looks up at her. "Not true. You look like a princess."

Natalia pins Jaslene with a dubious stare. "Yes. A Disney princess. Wearing ice skates and doing figure eights. Besides, you're just saying it looks nice because I'm paying you both to help plan this wedding."

"No, Grumpy Bear," Jaslene counters. "I'm saying you look nice because it's true."

"Anyway," Natalia says, a hand on her hip, "even if it's true, this dress is going to give me nightmares. I can already picture one." She drops her voice to a stage whisper. "I'm walking down the aisle and both Tim Gunn and Christian Siriano pop out from behind potted plants and tell me my gown needs editing."

Now *that's* a fair point. Because, *whoo boy,* there's a lot going on here: tulle, lace, taffeta, and a scalloped bodice with intricate crystal appliqué. So. Many. Crystals. I'm tempted to sing *Frozen's* "Let It Go" at the top of my lungs, but I don't think Natalia would appreciate it. "May I make a suggestion?"

"If it's a good one, yes," Natalia says.

I ignore her sarcasm; it's a survival mechanism where my cousin's concerned. "What about a jumpsuit? It's simple yet elegant. You'd be comfortable, too. And if you want a showstopping element, you can choose a design with a train." I lean forward to make my final point. "Best of all, you could add *P-O-C-K-E-T-S.*"

"Don't spell shit out this early in the morning, Lina. I can't deal."

I purse my lips at her. It's eleven o'clock. "Pockets, bitch. Pockets."

"Ooh, ooh," Jaslene says, waving her hand. "I need that on a dress. With. Pockets."

Natalia rolls her eyes and spins to face the mirror. Letting out a long-suffering sigh, she cocks her head to the side and studies her reflection. "Marcelo will be crushed, and I'd hate to hurt his feelings. He's offering this to me for free. Just a slight alteration here and there and we'd be done."

I stand and rest my chin on her shoulder. "This is your and Paolo's wedding, not Marcelo's. Do you love it?"

"No," Natalia admits, returning my gaze through the mirror. "I actually dislike it very much."

"And is that how you want to remember your wedding day?" I ask.

She shakes her head. "No, you're right. And a jumpsuit would look badass. Totally in keeping with my personality. Plus, this might be the only time when a jumpsuit would be easier than a wedding dress to manage during a bathroom break." She widens her eyes, and I see the first glimmer of excitement in them. "I'd be able to dance at the reception with no problem. Oh, I could use the Rainha da Bateria outfits at Carnaval as inspiration."

"Let's not get carried away," I tell her. "You cannot have your ass out at the wedding."

Thanks to the Dominican stylist who presses it each week, Jaslene's shoulder-length hair swings through the air as she claps excitedly. "Purple assless chaps and a humongous headpiece would be *perfect*. You'd be channeling Prince *and* Carnaval."

"Yes," Natalia says, pumping her fists. She looks at me. "See? Jaslene gets it. That way, I could pay homage to my dual citizenship."

"No," I say. "I'm pretty sure that would violate the wedding venue's health code."

Natalia scoffs at me. "Whatever. My ass would get an *A* grade from any health inspector."

Lord. If any bride needs to be reined in, it's this one. Left to her own devices, she'd hire an entire samba school to precede her down the aisle—drummers, dancers, floats, and all. Now that I think about it, I wouldn't put it past her to plan something like that as a surprise. I need to keep her on task. "Take a look online in the next day or two and see if anything catches your eye. I can make some inquiries at other bridal shops around town. There's a reason you're five weeks away from your wedding and you haven't committed to a dress. It's time to think outside the box."

She nods thoughtfully. "Okay, you've persuaded me. I'll look first thing when I get home tonight." As Jaslene and I gather the accessories Natalia tried on, my cousin deals with the delicate task of removing the dress.

"Need help in there?" I ask.

"I think I got it," she says through the louvered double door. "The zipper stitched in underneath the row of buttons is genius. I'd stab someone with a stiletto if I had to wrestle with these tiny buttons the morning of my wedding."

Jaslene and I shake our heads, knowing Natalia's only slightly exaggerating.

"Natalia, you can't use your wedding as an excuse for everything," I say. "Everyone knows you'd stab someone with a stiletto simply for existing."

"*Exactly,*" she says from the changing room. "That's why I've always hated the term *bridezilla*. For one thing, it's sexist. Women under immense pressure who speak up for what they want? *Monsters.* But also, it erases part of my identity. My true friends know I'm like this all the time."

Even though Natalia can't see her, Jaslene hides her mouth and whispers to me, "It's true."

"So, your mom told my mom that you're interviewing for a major position," Natalia says. "What's that about? And why didn't you tell me?"

To be honest, I didn't tell Natalia because she's going to flip and I don't want her to try to dissuade me. Not until it's too late to be dissuaded, at least. I'm not sure what she'd do if she ever saw Andrew or Max again, but I suspect at some point the cops would be called.

"You still there?" Natalia asks.

"Yeah, I'm here. So the position could be a stellar opportunity. I'd be the wedding coordinator for the Cartwright Hotel Group."

"Holy shit, Lina," she says, opening the door and sticking her head out. "That's fantastic. Congratulations."

"I don't have the job yet," I say as I stack several shoeboxes on an accent table. "The interview process is involved."

She pulls an arm through the sleeve of her top and pauses. "How hard could it be, though?"

I make the mistake of letting her question go unanswered a few seconds too long.

She glances at Jaslene's face, then scans me from head to toe. "What aren't you telling me, prima? There's a catch, isn't there?"

When she retreats inside the dressing room, I exhale and silently thank the Lord for the breather. It'll be easier to disclose this if she's not staring me down. My explanation comes out in a rush, Andrew's and Max's names dropped into the narrative like tiny breadcrumbs I'm hoping she doesn't pick up. And when I'm done, the silence that follows surprises me. I look at Jaslene, who shakes out her hand as though I'm in trouble.

Before I can prod Natalia for a reaction, she bursts out of the dressing room like an Old West gunslinger making her presence known in the local saloon. "Tell me you're going to make their lives a living hell."

If the way people emoted were reflected on a scale of one to ten, most days, I'd be a three—four, tops. Jaslene's a solid seven with level ten potential when she's tipsy, an altered state that's a thing to behold if you're lucky enough to catch her in it. Natalia's a ten—seven days a week, twenty-four hours a day. And the easiest way to defuse my cousin's outbursts is to speak in soft tones. It's like calming a skittish horse. Just call me the Natalia Whisperer. "I hadn't planned on exacting any retribution, no. I told Andrew he needs to steer clear of me, and even though Max and I are supposed to work together, I intend to handle the pitch myself. I mean, isn't that what I already do for my own business?"

Natalia reaches behind her to grab the dress, which is now safely back in its garment bag, and hands it to me. "The universe is giving you the chance to right a few wrongs. Why on earth won't you take it?"

Because I'm above such pettiness, that's why. Or, more accurately, because I'm not well-versed in the art of pettiness and would never be able to do the discipline the justice it deserves. Plus, harping on old news suggests it has power over me, and it doesn't. I don't like Andrew and Max. I don't want to work with them, either. But that doesn't give me license to torture them. "Ladies, don't think I haven't imagined ways of luring Andrew into my very own Red Room of Unpleasant Pain, but when all is said and done, I'm a professional facing a threat to her business. Either I get this job or find an alternative location. And I only have five weeks. That *must* be my priority. Anything else is a distraction I don't need."

"Speaking as someone who stands to benefit from your mature take on the situation," Jaslene says, "I *should* support this plan, but now I'm wondering if you need closure."

I draw back and tilt my head. "Closure? With Andrew?"

Jaslene shakes her head. "No, you got that already. You need closure with Max."

"And I think those resale designer shoes you insist on wearing even though they're a size too small are cutting off the supply of oxygen to your brain."

She playfully purses her lips at me. "Cute. Anyway, all I'm saying is, Max isn't just some person you need to collaborate with. You have *history*. Unresolved feelings. Closure will help you address them. I suspect you're going to need it if you want to work with him successfully."

Jaslene's so wrong about this, it's cringeworthy. How could I possibly benefit from talking to Max about a day I'd prefer to forget? "Do you even know me at all, Jaslene? I'm not interested in rehashing what Max did and how it affected me."

Jaslene grabs one of my hands and shakes it. "Silly goose, when I mentioned closure, I didn't necessarily mean that you and Max needed to have some big cathartic talk about what happened." She blows a raspberry. "I'm shocked to admit this, but I actually think Natalia's on to something. Maybe the universe *is* giving you the chance to right some wrongs." When I simply stare at her in silence, she adds, "Listen, there are different ways of getting closure, and one of those ways might be to make someone miserable for the sake of satisfying your petty soul." She shrugs. "Just a thought."

"Noted and dismissed," I grumble. "I have a job to land and a business to run. Playing games is a luxury I can't afford."

Natalia rolls her eyes and neck as though she's doing her best impression of a bobblehead. "I'm disappointed in you, Lina. Especially given what you do for a living. Haven't you ever heard of multitasking? You can impress this Rebecca person *and* make the Brothers Karafuckoff suffer."

I shake my head. "Dostoevsky, Natalia? Seriously?"

She pretends to brush off her shoulders. "What can I say? My dragging skills are multifaceted." Her eyes are kind when she takes my hands. "Listen, if you need to stay within your comfort zone, that's okay, too. Your way of reacting to a situation is just as valid as mine."

"Just not as fun, right?" I ask with a smile.

She winks. "You said it, not me." With a finger over her mouth, she gestures for us to leave the dressing area quietly. "I don't want to tell Marcelo about the dress just yet. Not with an audience. He's coming over to my mom's tonight, so I'll tell him then. Please cover for me."

Jaslene and I link arms to create a human wall for Natalia, then we all tiptoe past the showroom and skulk out the door. We loiter outside, a few feet away from the shop's entrance, beyond Marcelo's line of sight.

As Natalia and Jaslene chat about the wedding timeline, I stare off into the distance, mentally urging myself to tell Natalia the full story. Before I can change my mind, I turn to her. "There's one other thing I didn't tell you."

She raises a brow. "There's *more*?"

"Yeah. So when I first saw Andrew and Max in the conference room at the Cartwright, I panicked and pretended not to know them. Rebecca has no clue Andrew broke our engagement, and there's no going back, not if I want a shot at the job."

"Shut. Up." Natalia flails. "This is mind-blowing. You, Ms. Plan Everything Within an Inch of Its Life, orchestrated a sham of epic proportions and now you'll be forced to see it through to its unpredictable end?" She makes a big show of looking around. "Where's the popcorn and the Twizzlers? I can already picture this playing out on a big screen."

"That's what I said," Jaslene adds. "Well, the part about the popcorn. I'd even plant my ass in a movie theater to see it. And you both know I don't put on a bra and real clothes for just any ol' film."

"Look, I'm not proud of what I did," I say, interrupting their musings, "but yeah, I'm going to see it through to the end. Maybe after Rebecca makes her decision, I'll find a way to tell her. By then, I hope she'll think it's more important to have me as her wedding coordinator than to concern herself with my past relationships."

Natalia worries her bottom lip as she studies me. "Hope may spring eternal, prima, but deception will bite you in the ass. You sure you know what you're doing?"

"Hell, no," I tell her. "I have absolutely no clue what I'm doing, but I'm not going to let that stop me. Andrew has every reason to keep up the ruse, and his brother's just along for the ride. I know exactly how to handle someone like Max."

Jaslene clears her throat and gives me scary googly eyes.

"Allergies again?" I ask her. "Ugh. My car was covered in pollen this morning."

"Not exactly," she says, coughing into her hand.

"Anyway, if I play my cards right," I continue, "Max won't figure into the process at all. He's so clueless, I'll be signing my employment papers before he realizes he was a nonfactor."

Natalia tips her head up and sighs.

"What?"

She looks at a spot over my shoulder, her eyes narrowing into a death glare.

My breakfast somersaults in my belly, and a tingling sensation runs up my spine. "He's standing right behind me, isn't he?"

"He is," Max says, a tinge of humor in his voice.

Shit. Maybe my life *should* be a movie.

Chapter Seven

MAX

Every opponent, no matter how worthy or skilled, has a weak spot. I can already guess Lina's. She wants to control everything. When she doesn't, her brain flounders, leaving her off-balance, agitated, and flustered enough to do absurd shit—like pretend not to know her ex-fiancé and his brother during an impromptu business meeting. By showing up here unannounced, I'm taking advantage of this vulnerability. Shameful, I know, but necessary nonetheless.

She spins to face me, her face contorted into an awkward wince. A slight wobble interrupts the fluidity of the move. *Heh.* My plan's working.

I give her my best charming-as-hell smile. "Lina, it's good to see you again."

She treats me to a drop-dead-and-die grimace. "I wish I could say likewise, but I'd be lying if I did. What are you doing here, Mr. Hartley?"

If Lina thinks I'm going to get riled up when she snaps at me, she's flat-out wrong. I'm an easygoing guy. It would take some monumental bullshit to set me off, and her snippiness doesn't even come close to reaching that level. "It's a public sidewalk, Ms. Santos. Would you believe I happened to be passing by just when you bad-mouthed me?"

A woman jumps in between us, looking up at me with venom in her eyes. "Don't answer her question with a question, creep." She takes off an earring, then another, whips out a hair tie, and pulls her long, curly honey-brown hair into a ponytail. She's getting ready for something, and given the way she's cracking her knuckles, I don't think it's a tea party.

"What do you want?" the irate woman asks.

I vaguely remember her. If memory serves, she rushed past me in the hall after Lina kicked me out of the bridal suite on her wedding day. Apparently, I'm on this woman's shit list, too. I put up my hands. "Whoa, whoa, whoa. What's all the hostility for? You're not supposed to shoot the messenger, remember?"

"Messenger?" The woman sneers. "That's rich. The person who convinced my cousin's fiancé to cancel the wedding is an accomplice, not a messenger."

My gaze darts to Lina's face. Her mouth trembles, but I don't even blink before she clears her face of any expression. Is that how *she* feels? Or am I just a douche by association? I wish she'd give me a peek inside her brain. It's where all the action happens, and it must be fascinating in there.

"Look—" I point at the woman. "What's your name again?"

"Natalia," she says through gritted teeth. She jabs a thumb in the other woman's direction. "And this is Jaslene."

Jaslene shakes her head at me gravely. "Hey, Max."

Huh. Jaslene doesn't seem to hate me. Shocker. Maybe she's a potential ally.

I turn back to the hostile one. "Look, Natalia, from what I overheard I gather you're up to speed. Which means you also know Lina and I can't avoid working together. I'm trying to make the best of an uneasy situation. So, do you mind if I talk to your cousin for a minute?"

She crosses her arms over her chest and shifts to the left. "Be my guest."

"Alone, please?"

Natalia and Jaslene take several steps back but remain within arm's reach.

"I stopped by to invite you to lunch today," I say to Lina. "I think we should talk. Maybe clear the air and figure out a way forward? What do you say?"

Tilting her head, she widens her eyes and blinks like an owl on speed. "Clear the air? Why would we need to do that? We're strangers, remember?"

Oh, we're playing this game, are we? Fun. "Well, we're strangers as long as I cooperate, remember? Rebecca's just a phone call away."

She straightens and glowers at me. "*You. Wouldn't.*"

Dammit. She's got me there. I shake my head. "No, I wouldn't. But you know how in a movie when a group of teenagers does a bad thing, there's always that one kid who cracks under pressure and confesses everything? That's Andrew. If you and I don't get our act together, he's going to get scared and sing like a canary."

She takes a small breath, her face pensive as she studies me. "We can clear the air right here."

"Or we can clear the air over a nice lunch. Like adults."

She leans over and rests her hands on her thighs, as if she's addressing a small child. "Are you sure that wouldn't put too much pressure on you to perform?"

Jesus. By the time Lina's through with me, I won't just be a shell of myself; no, I'll be a mutated version that wears V-neck cashmere sweaters, relaxes in Adirondack chairs, and chortles when someone tells a joke.

"Nice," Jaslene says.

Some ally she is.

Why am I subjecting myself to this abuse? I didn't sign up for this. Okay, so maybe a tiny part of me is enjoying this snarky side of her, but that's not the point here. If I don't reassert myself, Andrew's going to easily steer his planner to victory—and I can't let that happen. Plus, I'm tired of being punished for someone else's bad behavior. Andrew's especially. Frowning, I squish my eyebrows together and pretend to be confused. "I think I might have missed the moment when I left you at the altar." Then I rest a hand on my hip and tap my chin. "Oh, wait a minute. That was my *brother*. Sorry. I get us confused sometimes. You do too, apparently."

Lina squints. Natalia growls. Jaslene gasps.

Oh fuck. That came out way harsher than I intended. Now I'm stranded on Gone-Too-Far Island, and these women are my only chance for a rescue. Before I can apologize, Jaslene pulls Lina away. They face each other, and Jaslene rests her hands on Lina's shoulders, as though she's coaching her through a personal crisis.

"Petty is as petty does," Jaslene tells Lina, her voice urgent. "You can do this."

Lina looks from Jaslene to Natalia, and the latter nods as

though she's the Godfather, silently putting a hit out on some-one. What an odd trio.

Lina inhales, her chest rising high and proud, then she breathes out slowly. "Okay, Max. Where would you like to go?"

That's it? She's not going to flay me for that ill-advised out-burst? I feel as though the Queen has granted me a reprieve. Well, I'm taking that reprieve and running with it. I still have five weeks to smooth over any bad feelings. "Your choice. What-ever you want."

"How about the Grill from Ipanema?"

"In Adams Morgan? That's right around where I live. Perfect."

She nods. "Okay, I'll meet you there in thirty minutes."

I point at my illegally parked car. I'll probably get a ticket if I'm not gone in the next minute. "I can give you a ride if you'd like."

"Nah," she says. "I need to run an errand first. I'll meet you there." She turns in the direction of her bodyguards while Jaslene pulls Natalia away by her shirtsleeve.

I take a few steps and freeze when I hear Lina call out my name. "Yeah?"

"I'm looking forward to it," she says. "And I really appreciate the gesture." Then she tucks a lock of hair behind her ear and smiles at me shyly.

Lina's luminous as it is, but that smile transforms her face, as though she's suddenly glowing from the inside. It's not just breathtaking, it's breath snatching. I inhale deeply—because I want my fucking air back. "Uh, yeah, I'm glad we're doing this. See you soon."

She nods and turns away.

I stand in a daze of my own making, cautiously optimistic

about the quick progress we've made. Makes me realize I've been thinking about this all wrong. Interacting with Lina isn't a battle. It's more like making a great cocktail—a science I'll be perfecting over time. Take a person who thinks they're in control (Lina), add in someone bent on throwing them off-balance (me), and stir vigorously. It's effervescence in a glass, an explosion of flavors on the tongue, and it leads to tiny breakthroughs like the one we just experienced. With a few more tweaks, we'll be so good together someone will want to bottle our chemistry.

Platonic chemistry, of course.

Just, you know, chemistry between two people interacting on a professional level and working toward a common goal.

Dammit. I can't unthink it. Now I'm the one flustered enough to do absurd shit—like wonder what would have happened if I'd met Lina before my brother did.

Lina and I have just ordered our meals—an appetizer, entrée, and dessert for her (says she prefers to choose her dessert and work backward from there), and an entrée for me.

So far, so good.

I sneak a glance at her face as she sips her drink, a cloudy concoction with lime and mint in it. She's been disturbingly serene since we sat down, and I'm recalibrating how to engage with her now that she's no longer throwing daggers with her eyes. "Let me start by congratulating you on a fantastic opportunity. You must have really dazzled Rebecca. She's putting a lot into this search process."

Lina settles an elbow on the table and stabs the ice in her

glass with a swizzle stick. "I was wondering about that. Whether what she's doing is atypical for a client trying to rebrand."

Now, *this* is a step in the right direction. Lina's engaging with me as though I'm just another colleague. As though she wants to give us a fresh start. And I intend to capitalize on her mellower demeanor. "It's the first I've heard of anything like this. But I'm not surprised. Rebecca strikes me as the type of person who's perfectly happy following her own approach. The good news is, what she's asking for in terms of a pitch is very much in my wheelhouse, so I can help, especially when it comes to using social media to your advantage."

Lina nods thoughtfully. "Well, let's say I was interested in relying on your expertise. How would you propose we go about preparing the pitch?"

"Simple. I'd take Rebecca out of the equation for the moment and make you the client. What I typically do is research the client's work and how people respond to it. So in your case, I'd get a feel for what it's like to plan weddings." There's a split second of unease when I say this—on my part, not hers—mostly because the phrase reminds me that she planned her own wedding but never experienced the grand finale. Also, I'm the asshat who blithely mentioned it earlier. I shake off the thought and forge ahead. "So, in essence, I'm looking for what you bring to the table and how it compares to the rest of the market. Then I'd check your references. Get a handle on what people think of you. Next, we'd talk about how you want to position yourself in the field. Brainstorm a bit about what that would look like. Then we'd put everything together to compose your pitch."

"So you'll—"

Our server arrives with Lina's appetizer. "Bolinhos de bacalhau?"

"Sim," Lina says as she rubs her hands in anticipation. "Ob-rigada."

He places the dish in the center, and Lina pulls it closer to her side of the table.

"You sure you don't want to try it?" she asks.

I beg off. "Never been a fan of salted cod, so I don't want it to be my introduction to Brazilian food."

"Makes sense." She picks up one of the egg-shaped fritters and bites into it. Closing her eyes, she groans. "Oh, that's good. *So. Good.* And not greasy at all." She pops another one in her mouth and hums.

I don't dare look at her. Not when she's coaxing her appetizer past first base. It's fucking obscene. Unable to help myself, I peek at her with one eye. *Shit.* The visual's worse. I grab my water glass and guzzle, then mentally smack myself. *What is your problem, Max? Let the woman eat in peace.* Maybe I should give her a little privacy—or make a joke to break this embarrassingly one-sided tension. "If you'd like me to leave you alone with your cod balls, just let me know."

She jerks to attention and her eyes snap open. I truly believe she forgot I was here, and it takes everything in me not to laugh at her stricken expression.

I point at her nearly empty plate. "Satisfying, I take it?"

"Immensely." She dabs at the corners of her mouth with a napkin. "Getting back to the pitch. You said you'd like to get a sense of what I do on a day-to-day basis. So, what, you want to shadow me?"

I'm grateful she's keeping us on task; for a minute, I forgot why we're here. "Shadowing is a good way to put it. I want to see you in your regular environment. But I also want to record you, if that's okay. Some of that footage could find its way into a video package. Or help us make stylistic choices."

"You'd tell me when you're recording?"

"Of course."

"And since I'm the client in this scenario, you're going to listen to my wishes, right?"

Yes, she's right about that, but only partially. This isn't exactly a what-she-says-goes situation. It can't be, because I have another client—my actual client—to please. "I'm going to listen, sure. Bear in mind, though, that I work for Rebecca, and I need to keep her interests and the interests of the Cartwright Hotel Group in mind."

She nods. "That's understandable. Thanks for being up front about that."

If I'm not mistaken, we're experiencing another breakthrough; she seems receptive to working with me. Which confirms what I'd hoped: This lunch is exactly what we needed.

Two servers sweep in with our entrées, placing them on the table with a flourish that makes me feel underdressed. At Lina's suggestion, I'm trying moqueca de peixe, a Brazilian fish stew. Lina's having . . . the remaining items on the restaurant's menu, apparently. The servers tag-team the process of setting bowls in front of her. Chicken. White rice. Black beans. A side that looks like cornmeal. A bowl of tomatoes and onions swimming in some kind of vinaigrette. And a plate of greens.

I bend down and lift the tablecloth, scanning the floor.

"What's the matter?" she asks. "Did you drop something?"

"No, I'm looking for the other people who are going to help you eat your meal."

Her mouth twitches.

Aha. Lina's thawing before my eyes.

She lifts her fork in front of her mouth as though I need instruction on how to use basic utensils. "Eat, Max. It's the wisest thing you can do right now."

I give her a sheepish grin. "Okay, okay. Can I ask a question first?"

She sets her fork down. "Sure."

"What's the stuff that looks like cornmeal?"

Her face lights up and she gives me a radiant smile. "That's farofa. It's toasted cassava flour, a staple of any Brazilian meal. A little bit of oil, onion, and garlic add flavor. My mother's version blesses us with bacon."

She enjoys sharing this part of herself, and I wish she'd never stop talking. I scramble for more questions to keep her engaged. "And are those collard greens?"

"Brazilian-style, yes. We call it couve à mineira. Instead of slow-cooking the collards, we slice them thinly and stir-fry them in garlic and olive oil. Want to try?"

I lean in, drawn to the savory smells wafting over the table. She lifts a forkful of greens and transfers it to the side of my plate. I'm on it in seconds. "Oh, damn, that's delicious. The texture's interesting, too."

She smiles at me, but then her face falls, as though she's just remembered who I am and why she shouldn't be chummy with me. With a sigh, she digs into her own dish. A few seconds later, she straightens in her seat and snaps her fingers. "Oh, shoot. I forgot to tell you to try adding peppers to your stew." She crinkles her nose. "Actually, never mind. It'll probably be too spicy for you."

My head snaps back. *Excuse me? Too spicy?* I laugh at the insinuation that I can't handle the heat. "I'm a big fan of cayenne sauce. Eat it all the time. And since I want to experience this meal the way it was meant to be enjoyed, hit me with it."

She grins at me and waves our server over. "O senhor poderia trazer o molho de pimenta malagueta?"

Our server's eyes grow wide. "Sério? Tem certeza?"

Lina nods. "Sim."

He flashes a smile her way.

"Certeza means 'certain,' right?" I ask after he leaves. "I'm picking up a few words here and there. Probably helps that I took Spanish in high school and it sounds like Portuguese."

"Yeah, he wanted to be sure about the peppers."

"Gotcha." I wipe the lower half of my face. "The stew's excellent, by the way. Thanks for asking."

The corners of her mouth lift, but it isn't a smile. She's distracted. Probably still pissed at me for the snide remark I made outside the dress shop.

Because we need to get past this, I muster the courage to address the T. rex in the room. "Lina, I want to reiterate how sorry I am for the role I played in your breakup with Andrew."

She raises her chin and fixes her face into a blank expression; it's a move so effortless, I bet she's done it a million times. "There's no need to apologize, Max. I'm over it."

I'm not convinced. If Lina were "over it," would she have greeted me the way she did earlier? Would she retreat every time we take a step forward? I don't think so. She may not be showing any overt signs of resentment, but the resentment's there just the same. "Look, I can understand why you'd be frosty with me. But in my defense, Andrew truly wasn't ready to get married to anyone back then. Whatever I told him would have forced him to face that fact. So in a sense, I guess you could say I did you a favor."

I laugh in the hopes that she'll join me. It'd be great if one day we could look back on this episode with amusement, knowing she dodged a miserable-ever-after.

"Max, I think you should stop while you're—"

"And if you two were meant to be, you would have eventually found your way back to him, right? Besides, I'm sure there's no shortage of people who'd love to take his place."

A muscle ticks in her jaw. She picks up her cocktail and drains it. After she sets the glass down, she wipes her mouth with the back of her hand. "Right. Exactly."

The server returns with the pepper sauce, and I ladle it onto the stew.

"Thanks," I tell him. "Been looking forward to this."

Without a word, he backs away slowly.

"That's not enough to get the true experience," Lina tells me. "Make sure to get a generous helping. Oh, and you *must* try a few of the whole peppers."

I take her advice and scoop more of the sauce onto my plate, licking my lips in anticipation.

She watches me under the veil of her lashes as I eat another spoonful.

"Oh, you're right," I say. "The sauce gives it extra *oomph*." My tongue sizzles from the heat, but it isn't overwhelming.

Lina looks at me expectantly. "You good?"

"I'm great," I say, then toss one of the small red peppers in my mouth. This time, I can feel the heat working its way to the back of my throat and down my esophagus. *Whoa*. That pepper's got bite. "What kind of pepper is this again?"

"Malagueta," she says. "It's about twice as hot as a cayenne pepper, but nowhere near a ghost pepper."

"Hmm." I wipe my brow as I pop another in my mouth and chew. *Damn, is it getting warm in here?* I look around. People are laughing and enjoying their meals, but they're appearing in my mind's eye like hazy mirages, as though they'd disappear if I were to reach out and touch them. Someone's stretching my tongue, too. It feels way too big for my mouth. I fan myself with the cloth napkin as my eyes water. *What the hell did I just eat?* "Are you thure thisn't a gauche peppa?"

Lina shakes her head as if to clear it. "What did you say? I can't understand you."

"A gauche peppa. Theems a little throng."

Lina snorts. "A ghost pepper? Seems a little strong?" She tilts her head. "Max, is your tongue okay?"

I wave off her concern. "No, no, I'm thwine."

Leaning over and resting my hands on my thighs, I push away from the table. The sound of my chair scraping across the floor draws a few curious stares. *Jesus.* Maybe I'm a shape-shifting dragon and this is my first transformation. My throat certainly feels like it's capable of producing enough fire to scorch this restaurant. Trying to cool my mouth, I pucker my lips and inhale and exhale. *Swoo-hoo, swoo-hoo, swoo-hoo.* Okay, the burning sensation's dissipating, thank God. My tongue still feels like it's wrapped in sausage casing, but I'll survive.

"Would you like me to ask the waiter for milk?" she asks.

There's an airiness to her voice, as though my discomfort has eased her own. I lift my head and study my tormentor. Judging by Lina's poorly concealed grin, I'm assuming this is exactly how she wanted this to play out. Well, isn't that something—there's a prankster beneath that crusty exterior. And that changes everything. Forget being amused by her snippiness. Fuck mixing the perfect cocktail. I want nothing short of her surrender. Retreat, regroup, reengage—that's what I need to do here. "I'll be fine, no thanks to you."

"Me?" she says, a hand flying to her chest. "*You* wanted the peppers."

"Based on your calculated encouragement, yes. I didn't think the peppers would strip my taste buds." I shake my head. "Never expected that from you."

She dabs at her mouth with a cloth napkin. "Consider me a chameleon, Max. I regress to blend into my surroundings, present company included."

With any luck, she'll blend into a ghost and disappear. "This is fascinating, really. I never imagined you'd enjoy playing games. Rounds out your winning personality quite nicely."

She shoots sparks at me with her eyes. "You know *nothing* about my personality."

"Today's been a crash course on what makes you tick, so I know plenty. I also know you wanted to marry my brother at one point. I can figure out your Myers-Briggs personality type based on that info alone. ISTJ. Insensitive. Stubborn—"

"What's the matter, Max? Is coming up with an insightful comeback beyond your skill set?"

My nostrils flare all on their own; they're affronted by her condescension. I drum my fingers on the table and lean back in the chair. "I. S. T. J. Insensitive. Stubborn. Twisted. And—"

Her eyes narrow to slits. "Don't you dare say it, Max. Call me a jerk and I'll force-feed you that entire bowl of peppers."

"I'd never call you a jerk."

That seems to placate her. The aura of steam billowing around her head vanishes.

I lean forward, throwing my elbow on the table as if I'm issuing a challenge. "Besides, that's a noun. No, the million-dollar word is . . . *juvenile.*"

Lina stills, a vein in her forehead popping out like a tiny alien. Then she growls at me. *Literally* growls. And it's the most perfect sound I've ever heard in my life.

Eliciting that response from her is so fucking satisfying—and for some unfathomable reason, I want to do it again and again.

Chapter Eight

LINA

Oh God. Did I just growl? In a restaurant?

I plop my elbows on the table, throw a hand against my forehead, and peek at the diners around us. No one seems to have noticed. Except Max, of course. Max, who, despite having looked like asshole warmed over only minutes ago, now appears relaxed and unruffled as he watches me in silence.

Everything about him bothers me: his complete lack of self-awareness (genuine), his sarcasm (rudimentary), his boyish smile (insincere), his stupidly chiseled jaw that he pretends to stroke absently (totally affected), his thick so-dark-it's-almost-black hair that I wish with all my heart were dyed so I could picture him sitting in a salon with foil strips clinging to the strands (natural, unfortunately), and so on and so on. *Grrr.*

We don't mix well, that's for sure. He pushes buttons I wish I didn't have. But I'm stuck with him. For at least the next five weeks—and maybe more. Now he thinks I'm as immature as he is. Even worse, he's probably questioning my fitness for the job at the Cartwright.

Take a deep breath, Lina. You can fix this. I scour my brain for something—anything—to explain my explosive reaction to Max's needling. It doesn't take long to settle on a cause. Stress. That *must* be the reason I'm out of sorts. I channel the goddess of tranquility—who bears a striking resemblance to an actor in a Summer's Eve commercial—and say, "Max, we need to rid ourselves of this negative energy. It isn't healthy for either of us. Let's rewind the last few minutes, okay?"

He lets out a deep breath, proving he isn't as unruffled as he looks. "You're absolutely right. Sorry about that."

I lean forward and lower my voice to a whisper. "The thing is, I'm under an immense amount of pressure, and I think it's finally getting to me. If it were just one thing, I think I'd be okay. But in the last few days, I've run into one pothole after another. The bridal shop where I run my business is shutting down. The opportunity with the Cartwright, as much as I'm excited about it, brings its own set of worries. And I didn't anticipate seeing Andrew again—not in that conference room. I'm not myself. At all."

Well, I *am* being myself, but that's not the version of me I want to present to the world—or to the man who's already seen me at a low point in my life.

"That's fair," he says, frowning. "To be honest, I'm not myself, either." He gestures at the space between us. "None of that was necessary, so let's put it behind us. As for what to do about your stress, is there an activity that could help relieve it?" His eyes grow wide. "Like a physical activity, I mean." He shakes his head. "A *sport* or something. Ax throwing. Yoga." Grimacing, he gives me a half shrug. "I don't know."

I wrinkle my nose at him. "My stress relievers usually take less active forms. Watching TV, shopping, eating sweets, silencing all electronics and reading undisturbed."

He sits back in his chair and chews on his bottom lip as he considers me. Seconds later, he says, "I take a capoeira class here in the District during the week. Tonight, in fact. It's an awesome way to let off steam."

I blink at him, unable to process what he's told me. "You what?"

"Capoeira," he says. "It's a Brazilian martial arts—"

I roll my eyes. "I know what capoeira is, Max. I'm just surprised you're taking it as a class."

He raises a brow. "Why's that?"

"Because we've been eating Brazilian food for the last thirty minutes and you didn't once mention that you're familiar with any aspect of Brazilian culture."

It's also intriguing. Suggests Max has layers underneath his shiny yet annoying topcoat.

He shrugs. "Oh. Well, now you know. Think you'd like to join me?"

"What? Tonight?" I scrunch my face. "No, I couldn't."

He nods as though he's not surprised by my refusal. "I just figured you might appreciate doing something like that. Music and dancing mixed with martial arts. Yeah, it's probably too physical anyway. You said yourself you prefer less active forms of stress relief."

Our server sweeps in with my dessert, a giant brigadeiro. Max stares at the monstrosity. Yes, it's a massive ball of chocolate with sprinkles. Isn't that the definition of a stress reliever? And if Max thinks I won't enjoy the shit out of this, he's so wrong. I can eat chocolate and take a capoeira class. The two aren't mutually exclusive. "When and where's the class? I might stop by. Just out of curiosity."

"The class?" He scratches his head. "Let me text you the info when I get back to the office. I can give you the details on what to wear, point out landmarks in the area. I'll send you the link to sign up."

"Oh, okay." I dip my spoon into the thick bomb of chocolate on my plate. "Want to try?"

He waves his refusal. "No, I can't. My tongue's out of commission."

My gaze dips to his mouth. It's a nice mouth. Not that it matters.

"It's out of commission for eating things," he adds. His eyes bug out. "For eating *foods*."

"Yeah, I get it, Max."

The clarification's superfluous, of course. The state of Max's tongue has nothing to do with me. Still, when someone puts an image in your head that you'd prefer not to see, your brain grafts it onto your retina. *Oh my God, why are images of his face between my legs flashing through my brain? Make it stop. Make it stop!*

Max motions for the check and hands our server his credit card without seeing the total. "Listen, if I'm going to have any chance of making tonight's class, I'll need to get back to the office soon. Is it okay if I slip out after I pay the bill? Want me to order a Lyft or something?"

Shaking my head, I wave off his offer with my spoon. "No, I'm fine." I point at the brigadeiro. "Going to enjoy this for a bit."

The server returns with the receipts and Max signs the restaurant copy.

"Generous tip included, or do you need me to take care of it?" I ask.

"Generous tip included. Always."

I nod. At least he has that going for him. "Thanks for lunch."

"No problem," he says as he stands. "Maybe I'll see you tonight?"

"Maybe," I say.

He gives me a knowing grin. "Okay, so probably not."

"*Maybe* means maybe, Max." I say goodbye with a wave of the fingers of my free hand. "Tchau."

"Bye, Lina."

I watch him weave his way around the tables and stroll out the door. Now I feel compelled to go to the class just to prove his prediction wrong. And I bet he planned it that way.

Next time I'll give him a ghost pepper.

"Can I just state for the record that I think this is a terrible idea?" Jaslene says as we climb the stairs to Capoeira Afro-Brasilia Studio.

No, I'm not dragging Jaslene to the class just for emotional backup. She needs a stress reliever, too. Completing her college studies at night is proving more challenging than she expected, and as an older-than-average student who's been out of school for several years, she's struggling with the demands of her new schedule. As for me, with the week I've had, I'm warming to the idea of learning how to disguise my physical aggression as intricate dancing. Jaslene, not so much. "Listen, I just want to show Max that I'm not as predictable as he thinks. One class. That's it. Plus, you need a little loosening up. And it's capoeira. How could you not be excited about that?"

She rolls her eyes and tips her head from side to side as we reach the landing. "Okay, fine. But when I ask you to come to pole dancing class, saying no will *not* be an option."

"Deal," I say as we walk through the door.

I know I'm in the right place as soon as I enter the large studio. It's a mixed crowd of people—many of whom are speaking in English but with a distinctive accent that in my mind immediately pegs them as native Brazilians—and the energy they're generating is positively electric. Max doesn't appear to be here, however. If he doesn't show up, I'll happily harass him about it for weeks.

Jaslene and I stand near the door and survey the bustling scene. Not long after, a group of approximately twenty people of different ages, genders, and skin colors file out of a side door, settle onto chairs along the back wall, and warm up their instruments, including the single-string berimbau that drives a capoeira circle. I repeatedly tap Jaslene on the arm. "They have a real bateria. Tell me you're not impressed."

Jaslene gives me a grudging smile. "Okay, yes, that *is* impressive, but that doesn't mean their drumbeats are going to magically turn me into an acrobatic phenom. I'm going to look like a pendeja out there. And Max hasn't even shown up yet."

Before I can respond, a man in white pants, bare feet, and a T-shirt with the studio's logo on it motions us over to him. "Olá, meus amigos."

"Olá, estamos aqui para a aula inicial de capoeira," I say, hoping he doesn't notice my Portuguese language skills are intermediate at best.

His eyes brighten, and then the words flow from his mouth as though they're riding a rapid. I'm only able to catch every third or fourth one before Jaslene puts up a hand to slow him down.

"Whoa, there," she says. "I'm Puerto Rican, not Brazilian, and I'm having trouble keeping up."

He draws back in surprise, plainly having assumed Jaslene was a compatriot. Hanging out with my family and me as much as she does, she gets that a lot, particularly because she's Afro–Puerto Rican and her complexion is deep brown like mine. The man turns to me. "E você? Brasileira?"

My cheeks warm under his inspection. I'm always a tad embarrassed when I'm put in the position of explaining that I'm not fluent. "Sim, meus pais são brasileiros, mas eu não falo português fluentemente."

"No problem, friends. I'm Raul, your instructor for today. Welcome." He leans over and covers his mouth in a faux whisper. "I went to college and grad school here, and I'm losing my accent. But don't tell anyone."

Smiling at Raul's effort to make us feel comfortable, Jaslene and I introduce ourselves and exchange handshakes with him. We explain that we're new to the class and that it was recommended to us by someone who takes it.

"Max Hartley," I say. "Do you know him?"

Raul furrows his brows. "Not sure. But the membership is pretty fluid. I'll know him when I see him." Smiling broadly, he rubs his hands together. "Well, anyway, you're going to have a great time." He twists his upper body and scans the area around us. "Just drop your belongings in a cubby and find a spot to stretch. Restrooms are in the back. We'll start in five minutes."

After we set our belongings down, Jaslene plops onto the floor, dramatic in her resistance to being drawn into my and Max's skirmish. With a sigh, she reaches for her toes. "May I make an observation?"

I step next to her and slip into a standing calf stretch. "Of course."

"When I said you should be petty," she says, "I was thinking you'd be more subtle."

I grimace and drop to the ground. "The peppers were too much?"

She snorts. "Yes, Lina, yes. It's as though someone told you to flirt and you decided to flash your tits instead."

I snap my brows together and pretend to be confused. "Flashing your tits isn't flirting?"

Max's head appears in the space between us. "Hey, there!"

Jaslene and I both yelp and shrink away from him.

He falls back on one knee and gives us a wry smile.

"What the hell, Max?" I say.

Yes, he surprised me, but I'm embarrassed more than anything else. Figures I'd be talking about flashing tits when he showed up.

"Sorry about that," he says. "Didn't mean to interrupt. Just wanted to say hello."

Okay, he doesn't appear to have heard us. Small miracles.

"Hi," Jaslene says, her voice traitorously cheerful.

"Where'd you come from?" I ask.

"I was in the restroom changing into this," he says, pointing at his white sleeveless compression tee and track pants. "Can't do capoeira moves in a business suit."

He pushes himself to a standing position, and I'm forced to face some uncomfortable truths: Max has a chest. A sculpted chest. The kind of chest I can easily picture in bare form. Also, he's sporting ripples in the area where the average person's belly should be. His ab muscles are so obnoxious they show through his clothes. And Mother of God, the definition in his forearms suggests either he's a workoutaholic or masturbates frequently. Now that I think about it, his right forearm *is* more developed than the left one.

Where the hell did Hartley the Hottie come from?

I'm going to get a crick in my neck if I don't move my head soon, but my brain is having trouble processing the onslaught of information. It's too hard to digest. For everyone's safety, data as volatile as this should be doled out in carefully scheduled increments; to do otherwise would be irresponsible. *Shame on you, Max.*

At Raul's signal, the bateria begins to play an Afro-Brazilian rhythm. The people in the class shuffle around and find their places as I will my brain to forget everything it just saw.

Max takes a spot next to me and leans close to my ear. "Unless someone requests it, flashing your tits is just as bad as sending unsolicited dick pics."

Oh God. I hate him. And if there's any justice in this world, this class will teach me how to kick his ass.

After leading us through a series of warm-up stretches, Raul glides to the front of the class, the bateria still playing in the background. "Capoeira's precise origin isn't exactly clear. There are many theories about its inception. But what we *do* know is that this martial arts form was heavily influenced by enslaved Africans brought to Brazil in the sixteenth century. Are you aware that Brazil didn't abolish slavery until 1888, and that almost four million enslaved persons were brought to the country during the slave trade?"

A few classmates shake their heads, while others, plainly familiar with Brazil's history, nod as though what he told them is old news.

"Some believe that it started in the quarters of enslaved people," Raul says, "or in the quilombos, which were the settlements founded by those who escaped slavery. The idea being that the people battling could hide this form of training by making it look like a game or a dance. Today, we know it as a martial arts form, and as a symbol of Brazilian culture."

Raul plants his feet shoulders' width apart and places his hands on his waist. "This evening's class is all about the ginga. You can't perform capoeira without it, so we're going to focus on this move. Then we'll add a little fun with the meia lua de frente, which is a type of front kick." He puts a finger in the air. "Oh, I almost forgot. Do we have anyone who's returning? Because you all should be first-timers. The class in progress starts after this one."

Expecting Max to raise his hand and sheepishly make his apologies, I turn in his direction and smirk at Jaslene, who's on his other side. He just stands there, though, dutifully listening to Raul and smiling at his classmates.

"*Psst,*" I say to him. "Wrong class, buddy."

He stares straight ahead. "No, it's not. I'm a first-timer, too."

Jaslene groans. "You two are a mess."

I fire off my questions out the side of my mouth. "What do you mean? Didn't you tell me you were taking this class already? Are you kidding me right now?"

He whispers his response: "No, I said I take a class. I'm here. It's a class. And I'm taking it. All true. Just so happens that I'm as much of a novice as you are."

I flick my gaze to the ceiling and count to ten. My choices are clear: I can get mad, or I can get petty. It's not a difficult decision. I choose to be petty. Now I just need to figure out how.

Max waves a hand in front of my face. "Hey, no need to go glassy-eyed. Truth is, I've been wanting to take this class for a while. It's right around the corner from my place. And since you mentioned that you were stressed, I figured I could check out the class and you could benefit from it as well."

That pacifies me—but only a little. I'm still annoyed that he got me here under false pretenses, so retribution is in order. "It's fine, Max. We're here. Might as well make the most of it."

"Okay, everyone, pick a partner," Raul says. "That's the person you'll face off with as you practice the ginga." He turns to Jaslene and gives her a sweet smile. "I know you're nervous, so you're welcome to work with me."

Sure, Jaslene may be nervous, but I suspect Raul's offer isn't solely motivated by that fact.

My best friend looks to me for my okay, and I nod.

Seeing that everyone's quickly pairing up, I tip my chin up in Max's direction. "What do you say? Want to ginga with me?"

Max pretends to clutch his nonexistent pearls. "Don't you

think that's being a little forward? I mean, we barely know each other. Shouldn't we go on a date or something first?"

I hiss at him and he straightens.

"Okay, okay," he says. "Let's do it."

We follow Raul's instructions as he guides us through the footwork, a series of easy steps that incorporate the familiar rocking motion capoeira is so well known for. Max and I face each other, our bodies swaying as we step back, move from side to side, and swing our arms to protect our faces.

"As you get more comfortable with the ginga, you should feel free to add your own expression," Raul tells the class. "A little more movement in the hips. A little playfulness in your legs. Next, you can try the meia lua de frente, which is basically a front kick with a transition to a ginga, and a second front kick with the other leg back into a ginga." Raul demonstrates the kick several times. "Just repeat the steps and get comfortable with the movements."

The bateria slows the pace of the music, and as I repeat the steps in time with the berimbau's rhythm, the ginga begins to take on a surprisingly soothing quality. But as I wait for a sense of total peace to blanket me, my mind replays how I got here. Max isn't even a regular in this class. *What an asshat.*

"This is great, isn't it?" Max asks as he sways in front of me. He's sticking to the ginga, choosing not to incorporate the kicks Raul encouraged us to practice. "I think I'm getting the hang of it."

"You think so?" I ask. "Well, let me try a meia lua de frente on you, then. Can't be that hard, right?"

Max grins. "Go for it."

We continue the ginga movement several times, and then I

spring into action, sweeping my leg back and over in an arc right in front of Max's face—just like my brother, Rey, taught me.

Max, who's unprepared for the kick, jerks back and falls on his butt. Grumbling about vindictive people, he struggles to his feet as Raul walks over to us.

"That was excellent," Raul tells me. "You've done this before?"

I nod. "At home only. My brother took a class a few years back. Used me as his practice buddy."

Max rubs his butt as he straightens. "Funny that you never mentioned that."

I give him a smug grin. "My brother wasn't an instructor. We did it just for fun. It wasn't a class. So, yes, I'm still a first-timer. Would you like to go again?"

Max ignores me. "Raul?"

"Yes, friend?" Raul says.

"May I have another partner, please?" he asks.

"Come," Raul says with a grin. "Lina and Jaslene can pair up while you and I work together."

I snort at Max and wave goodbye to him as he walks (escapes) across the studio floor with Raul. Max was right: Capoeira *is* an effective stress reliever. I'm feeling better already.

Chapter Nine

MAX

$\mathcal{L}$ate for the firm's weekly staff meeting, I enter the conference room and take the first available chair. As I lower myself onto the seat, I'm reminded that my right butt cheek's still sore from the ass-whooping Lina treated me to last night.

Seconds later, my mother sweeps into the conference room as if she's an army general making a rare appearance among her enlisted soldiers.

She settles in at the head of the table and leans back to read a sheet of paper her assistant is holding in his hands, then her gaze jumps from person to person, until she's made eye contact with everyone in the room. "Okay, folks. Let's talk developing business first." She whips her head in Andrew's direction. "What's going on with the Cartwright Hotel Group?"

This is one of those rare moments when I don't mind that she's inclined to check in with Andrew first. We wouldn't be in this mess if it weren't for him.

Brother dearest loosens his tie as he stalls for time. "The Cartwright account?" He clears his throat. "Um, well, let's see, things are going great. Wouldn't you say so, Max?"

I glare at him across the table. He's the emperor of his own prickdom. A master at burdening others with his bullshit. Lina is his ex-fiancée, not mine, and yet he wants *me* to tackle the unenviable task of hiding her involvement in this project. But as usual, I clean up his mess.

"We're covering new ground with this assignment," I begin. "In essence, the client's designed a long-term interview for two people vying for the position of wedding coordinator. I'm working with one. Andrew's working with the other. We're each due to present our pitches in five weeks."

"That's interesting," my mother says. "It'll be a great way to home in on your different approaches to the same mission."

Yes, exactly. Glad to know she sees this, too.

Her gaze sways between Andrew and me. "Just remember the goal is to ingratiate yourself with the client, too. We want *all* of the Cartwright's marketing work if that's possible."

"We're on it," Andrew says unhelpfully.

The rest of the staff report on their work, and we break just before eleven. I'm checking my phone for new emails as everyone shuffles from the room. When I look up, Andrew's still sitting there, eyeing me pensively.

"What?" I ask.

He smooths his tie as he speaks. "I chatted with the other candidate this morning. His name's Henry. Sounds like a good guy. We're meeting tomorrow to discuss our plans. How's it going on your end?"

Not well, but I'm not sharing that morsel of juicy information with Andrew. "Lina and I had a working lunch yesterday." I consider whether to tell him about last night's capoeira class, then decide it's not work related, which is a revelation of its own. That outing served no purpose other than to give me an excuse to spend more time with a woman who's irritable, unforgiving, and maddening to the extreme. None of this is Andrew's concern. "We talked about a game plan, and I'm hoping to finalize the details this week."

That's assuming she'll answer my calls. I'm probably blocked by now.

Andrew presses his lips together and nods, looking suitably impressed that Lina and I have connected. "How is she? Is she dating anyone?"

Oh, hell no. I'm not going to be his spy, or worse, his rematchmaker. "Andrew, if you need to know anything about Lina, I suggest you go directly to the source. I refuse to be the middleman."

He waves me off. "Yeah, okay. I get it. It's no big deal. I thought I'd feel differently when I saw her again, but no, I'm sure we weren't meant to get married. She's a great woman, though. I wish her well."

"And now you're trying to help someone else get the job she desperately wants."

He shrugs. "It's unfortunate that doing my job means she'll lose hers, but Lina's a professional. She'll handle it with class."

Jesus. The last time he said something like that he was asking me to break the news that he wasn't going to marry her.

"You're forgetting something, though," I say.

"What's that?" he asks on a yawn.

As he waits for my reply, he leans forward, just an inch, and that tells me he's only pretending he couldn't care less about what that *something* might be.

I rise from my seat and swipe my phone off the table. "Lina and I are now the team to beat. And I have a feeling we're going to be unbeatable together."

Probably.

Okay, maybe.

Shit. Who am I kidding?

———————

I'm at my desk drafting a client newsletter mock-up when my phone buzzes in my back pocket. I absently pull out the phone as I read the last paragraph of the work I've written so far. When I glance at the screen, I see that it's a text from Lina, and it turns out to be the answer to my prayers.

Lina: Hi Max. Let's call a truce, okay? There's really no point in holding a grudge. I'm meeting a client this afternoon for a cake tasting. Figured this was as good a time as any for you to see me in action. What do you say?

Holy shit, this is everything I've ever wanted in a single text: forgiveness and cake. Sweets are my weakness, and I'm not ashamed to admit that I'd subject myself to unspeakable abuses—giving up Netflix, for example—if it meant I could eat my favorite flavor of cake every day: the incomparable marble with buttercream frosting. I've never been to a cake tasting, but I imagine I'll be able to, you know, taste cake, and that, quite frankly, sounds like the best afternoon of my life.

Me: Cake makes for a great fresh start, so I say yes. Where and
when?

She sends me the bakery's address, and we agree to meet a
few minutes before the appointment so she can give me a little
background. Lina's already given the client the heads-up that I'd
like to attend, and they're cool with my joining them.

An hour and a half later, I stride into the Sugar Shoppe in
Georgetown. For a minute, I simply take in the sweets that
seemingly cover every available surface of the bakery: pies, cakes,
eclairs, and chocolates. For another few seconds, I consider dropping to my knees and praying at this altar of sugary perfection.
The space is cheerful, with bright white walls and several bistro
tables set in soft pastels. And the smells. God, the smells. It's as
though I dabbed cake-scented cologne on my wrists. How did I
not know this place existed? Does it deliver? Can I get a job here?

Someone bumps my shoulder, clearing the visions of sugar-
plums in my head. The person interrupting my daydream is
Lina, and her brows are furrowed as she looks at me with suspicion. "Are you all right?"

"I'm fine." I sweep my hand in an arc. "Just appreciating the
view."

She smiles. "It *is* something, isn't it?" Leaning over to survey
the area behind me, she says, "We should have a reserved table.
Let me check in."

She strides to the counter, then speaks with the woman at the
register. Not long after, she motions me over to a table in the
corner. "This one's ours."

We sit across from each other at a table so tiny we may as
well be sitting in each other's lap.

"Cozy," she says.

I snort. "Your cozy is my awkward."

She grins. "Oh good. It's not just me."

Her hair's pulled back in a ponytail, and my gaze is drawn to her facial features. Until today, I never noticed how expressive her face can be if she's not scowling. When she walked in, her befuddlement was apparent in the crinkle of her brows. And even now, the humor in her eyes is hard to miss.

The woman at the counter arrives with a pitcher of water and three glasses. "We're waiting for Mr. Sands, right?"

"Yes," Lina says. "Do you mind if we move this seat out of the way? The client uses a wheelchair."

"Sure," the woman says. "I'll put it in the back."

I suppose I should throw away all my preconceived notions about Lina's clients. I'd been expecting a bride, but I can now see how antiquated my default thinking is. "So, tell me about Mr. Sands."

"Mr. Sands—Dillon—is the groom, and we're here to select his groom's cake. His bride refused to attend because Dillon's the most indecisive person on the planet, which means this is sure to be an exercise in patience. Dillon is also the most self-aware person I've ever met, so he'll readily admit to his flaws."

I settle back into my chair. "That's a useful summary. Is this something you regularly do for your clients?"

"Cake tastings? Absolutely. I'm here to remind them that their guests might not appreciate a jelly-filled concoction with peanut crumbles and key lime frosting. You wouldn't believe what people would offer if I didn't point out that berries are seasonal or that many people have allergies."

"Why does a groom need his own cake anyway?"

She shakes her head. "Because at some moment in time a groom felt slighted by all the wedding traditions focused on the bride and decided that even in the context of marriage, he was duty-bound to carve out a new tradition that catered solely to him."

I raise a brow at her succinct explanation. "Tell me how you really feel, why don't you."

Lina presses her lips together to avoid smiling. "I can't. I left my PowerPoint on the injustice of the wedding patriarchy on my office desktop."

She's teasing—and I like it. More than I should, probably. I get the sense there's a whole other person to discover, and I'm intrigued by the flashes of personality peeking through her no-nonsense exterior.

"Oh, there's something else you should know," she says.

Get back on track, Hartley. "What's that?"

"Dillon won't be able to decide on a cake flavor without a second opinion, but I can't really help him. Lactose intolerance is such a pain. If you're up for it, maybe you could offer to be his second taste tester?"

I make a big show of cracking my knuckles. "You've picked the perfect person for the task. I can eat cake all day, every day."

Her eyes narrow. "I was hoping you'd say something like that."

Before I can think too hard about the message in those expressive eyes of hers, Dillon Sands arrives, reminding me that in a few minutes, I'll be stuffing myself with cake as part of a work assignment. How fucking cool is that?

Chapter Ten

LINA

I don't know, Max. Marble's not my favorite," Dillon says. "What do you think?"

Max's head snaps back as though my client slapped him. "How could you not like marble? It's perfection on a plate." To emphasize his point, he cuts into his slice with a fork and brings the piece to his mouth as if the fork's riding a roller coaster.

He's having way too much fun with this—and that was never the goal.

These men have tried eight different cake-and-frosting combinations and are showing no signs that the tasting is getting to them. *Note to self: Men are pigs.*

"Hey, Dillon, guess what I'm doing?" Max asks. His eyes are droopy and he appears cake drunk.

Dillon isn't much better off. His left arm is carelessly draped against the back of his wheelchair as he fans himself. "What are you doing, dude?"

Max devours another forkful of the marble cake. "I'm having my cake and eating it, too."

Dillon stares at him, until he doubles over in silent laughter, probably because there's frosting stuck to his vocal cords.

I fail to see the joke. Is this a guy thing? Or does overconsumption of cake negatively affect your brain cells?

"I'm going to use the restroom," I say, rising from my seat in a huff. "Excuse me." After exiting the stall and washing my hands, I take a quick look in the mirror above the sink and reapply my lipstick as I ponder what went wrong. This was supposed to go one of two ways: Behind door number one, Max would decline to taste-test the cakes, in which case watching Dillon try more than a dozen cake-and-frosting combos would annoy him to no end. I was there when Dillon selected a style for the groomsmen's boutonnieres, and it took three hours; I wanted that experience for Max. Badly. Behind door number two, Max would eat his body weight in cake and forever regret the day he walked through the doors of the Sugar Shoppe. But he's happily shoveling cake into his mouth, completely undisturbed by the sugar and fat he's consuming.

He's depriving me of either of the outcomes I'd hoped for, and I want to stamp my foot at the injustice of it all. Maybe I'm not cut out for wicked games. Fair enough, then. I'll find some other way to extract my petty revenge on Max Hartley.

When I return, Dillon's slumped back against his wheelchair, and Max's forehead is resting on the table. The tablecloth is riddled with cake carcass.

"Are you guys okay?" I ask. "What did I miss?"

Max groans. "He bought a few cakes and challenged me to a cake-eating contest."

I stare at the disheveled heaps in front of me. "You both lost, I see."

Dillon opens an eye. "On the contrary, I won. Full disclosure: I hold the record in college for eating the most hot dogs in a three-minute period."

With his head still pressed against the table, Max whimpers. "That's information I could have used three minutes ago."

I mentally give myself a fist bump. This is *not* how I expected Max's suffering to come about, but I'll take it. Felled by his own competitive spirit; that'll teach him.

"Did you at least settle on a flavor-and-frosting combo?" I ask Dillon.

With his head thrown back, my client tries to nod. "I'm going with the chocolate cappuccino torte. And the butter pound cake for guests who don't eat chocolate."

"That sounds fantastic," I say. "Tricia will be so pleased."

"Well, if that's all you need from me," Dillon says as he rubs his belly, "I'm going to head back to the office."

Max raises his head long enough to shake Dillon's hand. "Great to meet you, man. I hope your wedding is everything you and Tricia want it to be."

Dillon smiles. "Thanks. With Lina at the helm, I have no doubt it'll be amazing."

And with my client gone, I'm free to needle Max. Humming my contentment, I take the seat next to him and lean toward his ear. "How you doin' over there, champ?"

Max falls back over and rests one cheek on the table, his face in my line of sight. "I'm so warm. So full. So bloated." He ekes out the words in a scratchy voice. "I don't think I want to eat another piece of cake ever again."

"Not even marble with buttercream frosting?" I say, unable to hide my amusement.

He shuts his eyes tightly and pretends to cry. "Not even that one."

He's adorable. Absolutely adorable. *No. Wait.* I'm trying to torture him. This isn't supposed to be cute. But it is, dammit. How could it not be? He looks like a drunk chipmunk. A stunningly handsome drunk chipmunk, but still.

"Should I order you a Lyft or something?" I ask. "Or call 9-1-1?"

He slowly raises his torso and rakes a hand through his dark hair, scrunching his nose as he tries to get his bearings. "Nah, I'll live. I've survived malagueta peppers, remember?" Then he swings his body to face me and wipes his mouth. "Do I look like I just ate five pounds of cake?"

"Yeah," I say. "Actually, you do. There's also cake in your eyebrows and on your cheek."

"Shit, I'm a mess," he says, fussing with his brows to shake out the crumbs burrowed in there.

"Here, let me," I say, flicking at his brows with my pinkie fingers. When he juts his chin out to give me better access, I can't help noticing the gold flecks in his brown eyes. And that's when I realize he's a little too close, and my hands are on him, and this isn't how we're supposed to interact with each other. But I don't stop. Because all I want to do is trace my fingers across his brows, down the sides of his face, over his lips, and this is the closest I'll come to doing any of that without him thinking I'm a creeper.

He licks off a crumb at the corner of his mouth, and my gaze snaps to his. His intense stare isn't hard to read.

Do it, his eyes say.

I want to. I could. Just a few inches separate our mouths.

But wait. What the hell is going on? Why am I even contemplating this? I immediately scoot back, the scrape of my chair echoing through the bakery as though it's warning me that I nearly crossed an invisible line.

"Everything okay?" he asks, his voice strained.

"Of course." I brush off my hands, and when I'm satisfied they're crumb-free, I continue to avoid Max's probing gaze by fishing through my purse. "I just remembered another appointment. If I'm going to make it there on time, I should get going."

He shakes his head. "Right. I, uh, I should get going, too."

Using my peripheral vision, I watch him smooth his hands down his thighs and give them a hard pat before he slowly rises from his chair.

"You're probably leaving this place ten pounds heavier," I quip, hoping to break the growing tension between us. Frankly, I want it to go back to wherever it came from. It isn't welcome.

"I wouldn't doubt it," he says, his eyes flickering with good humor.

"Oh, before I forget," I say, snapping my fingers. "I can't leave here without getting a few of their milk chocolate truffles. They remind me of the brigadeiros my mother and aunts sell at their store."

He walks with me to the counter, his steps less bouncy than they were when he first arrived. "They own a store?"

"Yeah, mostly Brazilian goods. But it's a mishmash of items. I used to kid them about it all the time. Jokingly renamed the place Food, Flip-flops, and Flooring. They were not amused."

To the woman at the counter, I say, "Four milk chocolate truffles, please."

After I've paid and she's handed them to me in a small white bag, I eagerly remove one of the truffles and bite into it. I roll my eyes as I chew, not bothering to finish before I speak. "So good."

Max studies me as I eat, rubbing his chin thoughtfully. "Wait a minute. I thought you said you're lactose intolerant."

I finish the truffle and lick my lips. "I never said I was lactose intolerant."

"Yes, you did," he says, his eyes widening as he stares at me incredulously. "That's why you asked me to be Dillon's second taste tester. And that's why I'm feeling like someone's kneading my stomach with a rolling pin as we speak."

I shake my head. "No, all I said was that I couldn't help him choose a cake. And I mentioned that lactose intolerance is a pain. And it is." I shrug. "For the people who suffer from it, I suppose. Besides, you watched me eat a ton of chocolate for dessert when we met for lunch. I can't help it if you jumped to a conclusion."

With his head cocked, he licks the front of his teeth and nods as though he's seeing me with fresh eyes. "I don't know what you're playing at, Ms. Santos, but let's not lose sight of the big picture. If we get this pitch right, by working *together* rather than at cross-purposes, a dream job—your words, not mine— awaits. It'd probably do you some good to remember that fact if you're still hell-bent on pranking me."

He isn't telling me anything I'm not fully aware of. But I must admit, I haven't had this much fun doing my job in a long time. Besides, preparing the pitch and pestering Max needn't be mutually exclusive. I can see Natalia's point now. What's he going to do anyway? Tell on me? And to whom? Giving him the broadest smile imaginable, I roll up my bag of truffles and wink at him. "Thanks for the reminder, Max. But don't worry. I'm in full control of the situation."

As I precede him through the door, he says, "Some people eat cake. Others eat their words."

I turn my head and pin him with a humorless stare. "Is that a threat of some kind, Max?"

He places a palm on his chest and scoffs. "I'd never."

The haughty tone he injects into his voice is a nice touch, I'll give him that. But he's wrong. There's no way I'm eating my words. I *will* retain control over the situation. Neither of the Brothers Karafuckoff will *ever* get the best of me again.

Chapter Eleven

MAX

"Heads up, dude!"

Too late. The basketball hits the back of my head with a *thwap* that makes everyone on the court turn in my direction and wince sympathetically. "Fuck." I lean over, clutching the spot I already know will be sore the rest of the week.

My best friend, Dean, jogs over to me. "Damn, man, you okay?"

I straighten and shake out my limbs. "I'm fine."

Dean angles his head as he scrutinizes me, a look of suspicion dominating his sweaty face. "What's going on with you today? You've been in your head this whole time. These guys will smoke you if you're not on top of your game, and you're at the bottom. *Way* bottom."

He's right. My brain's so scattered I'm useless on the court. "I'm calling it quits."

Dean walks over to the guys hovering nearby and lets them know we'll no longer be playing. They readjust to a four-on-four game before we even leave the gym. We're at the Columbia Heights Community Center, a place we frequent when we're in the mood for a quick pickup game. I'm not the best player, but I've never performed as poorly as I did today.

After a brief stop at the restroom, I meet Dean outside, where we squint at each other before we both throw on our sunglasses. Physically, we make an interesting pair. His dirty blond hair is never out of place, whereas my dark hair exists in organized chaos. I try to get away with a five o'clock shadow as often as possible; Dean carries a travel shaving kit in his briefcase. He's fucking tall as hell, too, towering over me by at least three inches, an asset we typically use to our advantage on the basketball court—when I'm not playing like a scrub, that is.

"You want to stop by my place and hang?" Dean asks. "The shower's all yours if you need it." He inches closer and sniffs the air. "And you definitely need it."

I shove him away. "Nah, I should get going. Tomorrow's going to be a busy workday."

Dean lives nearby, in a renovated loft that he purchased with his ridiculously comfortable salary as a law firm associate. His house has more bells and whistles than mine—and a high-tech television that's so advanced I'm sure it's going to kill my best friend in his sleep one day. I should be disgusted with his excess, but Dean deserves his toys. The man works about sixty hours a week, evenly splitting his time between private and pro bono work in a sweet arrangement with his firm.

"That's a half-assed no if ever there was one," he says. "Just bring your butt to my place. You know you want to talk about whatever's got your brain fuzzy."

I can't argue with that. My brain *is* fuzzy, and Dean's probably the only person in the world I'd feel comfortable talking with about the source of my confusion. We met in college, didn't see each other much for a few years—I was in New York and he was in Philadelphia for law school—but then picked up where we left off once we were living in the same area. He's that friend you always find your way back to, the one who knows all your secrets and doesn't care that you're flawed, the one who's seen your "before" pictures because he's in them. "Okay, I'm biking over. Meet you there in ten."

Fifteen minutes later—I'm more out of shape than I thought—Dean buzzes me into his building. I lock my bike in a storage area past the elevators and climb the three flights of stairs to his condo.

I arrive at the threshold and find the door open, so I stroll inside. Dean's at the fridge guzzling a gallon-size container of water. He wipes his chin. "Took you long enough."

I ignore the dig and point a thumb in the direction of his guest bathroom. "I'm showering. Back in ten."

As I let the hot spray of water work its magic on my sore muscles, I consider how much I should share with Dean. Maybe it's nothing. Maybe I'm just imagining this. Maybe I'm an asshole who's subconsciously seizing on another way to compete with my brother. Jesus, this is all kinds of fucked up.

When I'm done showering, I dress in the extra set of clothes I always keep in my gym bag, throw my balled-up towel in the hamper, and join Dean on the gray leather couch in his living room.

He clicks the remote and turns off the TV. "Leftover pizza's warming in the oven. In the meantime, tell me what's going on."

I spend the next few minutes telling him about the assignment with the Cartwright Group. He doesn't react much, but his jaw drops when I mention that Lina's one of the two wedding planners we're working with.

"Dude, this is wild," he says. "I get why your head's not on straight. You're trying to get more responsibility at the office, disentangle yourself from your schmuck of a brother, and now you're stuck working with his ex-fiancée and lying about it."

I'm astute enough to know my troubles aren't confined to those issues. My worries stem from all that *plus* the thrill I got from tussling with Lina at lunch, *plus* the effort I made to get her to a capoeira class I'd never taken before, *plus* the moment in the bakery I can't get out of my head—the moment when she brushed cake crumbs off my face and jumped away as though my skin had singed her. "It's even more complicated than that."

Dean fixes his gaze on the ceiling and sighs. "I'm going to need a beer for this. Want one?"

"Sure."

As he roots around in the fridge, I lean forward, place my elbows on my knees, and make a steeple with my fingers, trying to muster the courage to speak the words out loud. *Just say what you're thinking. He won't judge you. Never has. And he'll set you straight. No bullshit.*

He returns with two uncapped bottles and hands one to me. "Okay, you were saying . . ."

There's no use in stalling. Dean will get it out of me eventually. "Lina and I met this afternoon, so we could help one of her clients with a cake tasting. Long story short, she wiped a bit of cake from my face and I felt . . . something. I don't know what the hell it was, but she seemed to be leaning into me, but then she jumped, like being close to me threw her off . . . It made me think she felt it, too. And it's not the first time I've felt something, either. Ever since we reconnected at the Cartwright, I've been noticing things about her I probably shouldn't." I take a long pull on my beer. "Tell me to disregard all of it and move on."

He slaps a hand on my shoulder. "Disregard all of it and move on."

I lean back and look at him. "As simple as that?"

He stares at me, his expression somber. "It's that simple. Do you want me to list a dozen of the million reasons why?"

"I think I need to hear them," I say.

Dean stands and paces the length of his living room. "One, she didn't just date Andrew, she was going to marry him. Isn't that reason enough? Two, your mother would kill you. If she knew Lina was back in the picture, she'd be telling Andrew to get her back *pronto*. Three, you'd wreck your already tenuous relationship with your brother. Now, maybe that's not a big deal, but it could make for some uncomfortable times in the Hartley family. Four, you're trying to escape your brother's shadow. Pursuing his old girlfriend is exactly the opposite of that. Does the name Emily ring any this-is-bound-to-be-fucked-up bells? Five, as much as you compete with your brother, would you ever be able to satisfy yourself that you're not pursuing her because of some messed-up notion that you could win her? And what about Lina? Wouldn't she wonder the same thing? And finally, maybe it's all in your head and she freaked out because it's an awkward situation. I'm saying this as your best and most intelligent friend. There are hundreds of women in this city who'd be happy to marry, date, or one-night-stand you. Pursue them instead and leave this particular woman alone. I'm begging you."

I agree with every point he's making. Hell, he's echoing the thoughts I had on the bike ride over. But I'd prefer a longer bulleted list. Pocket-size and laminated. A handy guide I can pull out if I'm ever foolish enough to let Lina take up too much of my mental real estate. "What else?"

Dean's eyebrows shoot up. "Excuse me?"

"You said you'd give me a dozen reasons."

He whistles. "Damn, if you need more reasons than the ones I gave you, San Antonio, we have a problem."

Now I'm the one furrowing my brows. "You mean 'Houston, we have a problem.'"

"Nah, my last girlfriend was from that city. Refuse to say it on principle."

I bark out a laugh. "Just when I decide you're the brightest person I know, you say some ridiculous shit like that."

Dean shrugs and takes another swig of his beer. "Anyway, don't think I haven't noticed that you didn't respond to my compelling case for dismissing whatever you *think* you felt while you were coming down from your sugar high."

Okay, that's a good point. I wasn't thinking clearly earlier, and whatever spark of attraction I felt was probably influenced by cake-induced pheromones. I need to let this go and focus on the tasks at hand: helping Lina make her pitch and gaining Rebecca's favor. "You're one hundred percent correct on all fronts. I'm deleting that data from the mainframe."

Dean clinks his bottle against mine. "Excellent. Now tell me how I can help. Do you want me to set you up on a few dates?"

I shake my head vigorously. "No need. I go on plenty of dates."

"A hundred first dates isn't dating, Max. It's hiding."

"I'm not hiding. I'm just not tying myself down with any one person. You can't force a match, you know."

Dean sighs. "Emily's got you thinking you're not long-term

material. You think a woman's going to always choose someone else over you, is that it?"

I chuckle at Dean's poor attempt at psychoanalyzing me. I'll admit Emily's reason for breaking up with me messed with my head for a while, but I'm over it now. Sure, she thought Andrew was the better catch, but honestly, if she preferred my brother over me, then that was her problem, not mine. "Buddy, it's not that deep. I'm just not in a rush to get serious about any one person, that's all."

"Because if you don't get serious with anyone, then you don't have to wonder if they're stringing you along until another person enters the picture."

Fucking Dean. Always focusing on the shit I'd rather not think about. I bend over, rest my forearms on my thighs, and clasp my hands together. "This is probably why I should steer clear of Lina, right? If there's anyone who's going to make me wonder if I'm just a poor substitute for my brother, it's her."

"Actually, I'd give Lina more credit than that. This is about you, not her." He peers at me, his expression unreadable, until the oven timer goes off and saves me.

"Pizza's ready," I say.

We both jump up from the couch and make our way to the kitchen. Dean's throwing on an oven mitt when my phone buzzes in my front pocket. I pull it out and unlock the screen, my smile widening as I read Lina's text:

Lina: Hey, there. Meeting clients for a wedding rehearsal Friday evening. Another opportunity to get a feel for what I do. These folks are putting everything on social media. You could probably record it. Game? There won't be any cake, I promise.

The idea that Lina's somewhere in the universe thinking about me—even if it's just for the few seconds it took her to fire off this text—improves my day a fraction. And there's no earthly reason why that should be the case. Damn, I'm in trouble.

"Hang on," I tell Dean. "Let me just shoot her a reply real quick."

With one hand constrained by the oven mitt, Dean uses his other to snatch the phone away from me. He glances at Lina's text and rolls his eyes. "Don't respond. It's after-hours. Wait until tomorrow."

I tackle him, attempting to get my phone back, but he holds it above his head and out of reach. "Pull yourself together, Max. Desperation does not become you."

I plop onto a stool at the kitchen island. "I'm not desperate. Just being professional."

"It's not *unprofessional* to wait until business hours to respond to a colleague. Try again." He places *my* phone in *his* back pocket. "And just in case this pizza and my stimulating company aren't enough to distract you, I'll keep your cell until you leave. Deal?"

"Deal."

Still, I'm itching to reclaim my phone and reply to Lina's text. Which is precisely why I won't. Not until tomorrow morning, at least. Whatever "this" is, it ends now.

Chapter Twelve

LINA

I cover the phone receiver and clear my throat to get Jaslene's attention. "I think I may have found a promising lead."

She mouths *yay* and pretends to high-five me.

We're both on the phone, investigating potential office space, before the city's business districts shut down for the weekend. The realtor I'm speaking with now, who's put me on hold to grab the details of the listing, says their client's just reduced the price per square footage, and I'm anxiously awaiting more information about the amenities. If I had a choice, I'd move my and Jaslene's belongings to the Cartwright today, but there's no guarantee I'll get the job, so I need to investigate alternatives.

The agent returns to the phone and mutters to himself as papers crinkle in the background. Why isn't the info in a computer database, for God's sake?

"Let's see, let's see," he says. "Ah, here it is. This is class B space just off New York Avenue. Very close to the convention center. Two hundred and fifty-three square feet. Possibility of changing the floor plan to accommodate two lessees. Includes a restroom adjacent to the space. Working sink. You've seen the pictures?"

"Yes," I say. The possibility of sharing the space, and thus the rent, is key. But he hasn't told me the price per square footage yet, so I'm trying to temper my excitement. "And the PPSF?"

"Forty-two dollars for a one-year lease. Thirty-eight dollars if you agree to a three-year lease."

My shoulders drop and I squeeze my eyes shut. No way can I afford that *and* my own rent. I suppose I could move in with my mother and aunts, but that still won't be enough to pay the lease and have any disposable income. Securing more clients would be another route, but I'm already busy as it is, and since many weddings are scheduled on weekends, that's only fifty-two weekends a year to work with anyway.

"Oh, there are a few things you should know," the agent advises. "The sprinkler system and one of the office doors are noncompliant. You'll need to make those changes as part of the lease agreement. Would you like to tour the space?"

Well, this one's another dud. I'm not signing up for a lease I can't afford *and* agreeing to make renovations on my own dime. "Thanks for the info. I'm going to make some more inquiries before scheduling any tour appointments."

After I hang up, I look at Jaslene, who's massaging her temples.

"That bad?" I ask her.

She nods. "Class A. Fifty-seven dollars per square foot."

I wince at the thought of spending that much money on an office for my business. The situation's looking direr with each passing day. If I can't convince Rebecca that I'm the superior person to act as wedding coordinator for her hotels, I'm screwed.

"We're not going to resolve this tonight, though," Jaslene observes. "And you're due across town in thirty minutes."

I jump up from my chair. "Shit. Time flies when you're getting your ass handed to you by DC's commercial real estate market."

"The Lyft should be arriving in five minutes. The Josephine Butler Parks Center, right?"

I nod and grab my purse. "What would I do without you, Jaslene?"

She blows me a kiss. "Shrivel up and die, probably."

Twenty minutes later, I arrive at the center, a historic house in Columbia Heights with breathtaking grounds, elegant staircases perfect for wedding photos, and indoor accommodations in case the weather doesn't cooperate. The couple, Brent Sales and Terrence Ramsey, met in medical school. They're low maintenance, easy to please, and focused on two goals: making their special day festive and serving scrumptious food. Clients like Brent and Terrence make my job a breeze. It doesn't hurt that they're also the nicest couple I've ever worked with. Oh, and they're striking, both tall and broad-shouldered and too cute for words.

The wedding party is small, consisting of three of their closest friends and Brent's younger sister. The couple, their officiant, and all but one of their attendants are standing in the garden when I arrive.

"Fingers crossed we have weather like this on the actual day," I say by way of greeting.

Brent and Terrence cross their fingers; the officiant, a friend who applied for a license to perform weddings solely for this occasion, raises her hands in prayer. After we all exchange hellos, the couple and I stroll to the top of the cascading walkway, where the procession will begin.

"Fair warning," Terrence says, waving his pager in the air. "I'm the on-call hospital doc for my practice this weekend, so I might be pulled away through no fault of my own."

"Oh, it's your fault, all right," Brent says with a smile. "You're just so skilled at what you do, people need your advice at all times."

"That's no problem," I tell them. "We'll work around your schedule if need be. The photographer and videographer should be here soon to get the lay of the land. They'll want to see where you'll be standing during the ceremony so they can plan their shots and figure out the best location to set up shop. In the meantime, let's gather everyone and work on the procession. The band will be here for the actual ceremony obviously, but I've got your song cued up on my phone."

Brent and Terrence have decided to walk down the aisle side by side, preceded by their attendants, who will each walk alone. We're a few minutes into our first practice round when Max and the vendors arrive.

Max is wearing black chinos and a gray merino V-neck sweater over his button down. There's no tie to be found. There's also no way to ignore that he looks damn good, and because I wish I hadn't noticed, I'm now hyperaware of him.

I speak briefly with the photographer—I suppose he's wearing clothes, too—and then he shuffles off to examine his eventual workspace, the videographer following closely behind him.

Max stands off to the side, waiting for us to finish. The shades he's wearing aren't dark enough to hide that he's gazing directly at me, and I busy myself instructing everyone on the finer points of walking—yes, walking—to prolong the moment when I'll be forced to talk to him. I shouldn't be thrown off by his presence, but I am.

Brent and Terrence, in keeping with their personalities, draw Max into a friendship circle and introduce themselves, while I throw up a weak hand to acknowledge that he's here. I can't help noticing that Max is just as tall and broad-shouldered as Brent and Terrence. They're casually standing around and laughing as though they're shooting candids for a spread in *GQ*; it would be nice if I could photoshop Max out of my mental image, but no, he's there to stay. Ugh.

The photographer emerges from behind a set of bushes, making me yelp in surprise and causing everyone else to search for the source of the sound.

My ears grow hot and I seriously contemplate jumping behind the same bushes the photographer just came from.

"Sorry about that," he says, camera in hand. "Can we get the happy couple in the exact spot where they'll be exchanging vows? I want to see where the sun hits and figure out my angles."

I eagerly take the opportunity to do something other than stare at Max. "They'll stop at the end of the walkway," I explain to the photographer, "and then they'll land here and face each other. The chairs will be set up so that the guests will watch them descend."

Brent and Terrence take their places—and that's when Terrence's pager goes off. He pulls it out and walks off, apologizing but also telling everyone he needs to take the call. After a minute, when it's clear from Terrence's apologetic grimace that the call won't be quick, the photographer sighs and turns to me. "Lina, can you stand in for him? It'll be only a minute. It's just . . . I have another engagement after this."

I don't think twice about it. Of course I'll help my clients get the best photographs possible. That's in my job description. "Sure. Tell me what you need."

The photographer points at my hands. "May I?"

I nod.

He arranges Brent and me so that we're facing each other and holding hands. "Okay, this should work out fine."

The videographer walks up to us. "Can you two maybe say something so I can check the sound?"

"I can recite my vows," Brent says. "I know them by heart."

The videographer nods as he adjusts the camera's tripod. "Perfect. Just keep talking. And Lina"—he points at me—"don't be afraid to talk as well. I'll need to hear you both."

Brent fixes his face into a serious expression, then gazes at me adoringly. "So this is it. The big day. We're finally getting married. I'd begun to think this day would never come, but then I met you. I never imagined I'd find the perfect person for me, but that's exactly what I found in you. I never dreamed anyone would want me as much as I want them, but you do."

My client's speaking from the heart, his words simple but wonderfully impactful, and I can't help remembering the vows I'd written for my own wedding—the ones I never shared because the groom decided I wasn't what he wanted. It's not that I'm still pining for Andrew. Getting over him was extraordinarily easy. It's not even about a wedding. Or marriage. Those aren't necessary precursors to fulfillment. But I want companionship, the security of knowing someone has my back, the ability to comfort and be comforted. Friendship. Vacations. Maybe even kids one day. Someone solid. Predictable. A person who doesn't need passion and sparks to build a lasting relationship. I don't know that I'll ever find that individual—and that makes me extraordinarily sad.

I can feel the tears welling up, and to my horror, I realize it's too late to will them away. If only I were stronger than this. If only my stupid emotions didn't get the best of me every damn time.

A hand holding a handkerchief appears in front of my face. I look up to find Max staring at me. There's empathy in his gaze as he waves the cloth.

"Allergies?" he asks. "It's a brutal time of the year. I can hardly keep the tears out of my eyes, too."

I take the handkerchief and dab at my eyes. "Yeah. I'm always a mess in the spring."

He nods. "That's what I thought."

We stare at each other. *He knows.* Somehow he knew I was overcome with emotion and stepped in to help me save face. I really don't want to like the man, but he's giving me no other choice.

Max turns to the photographer. "I think she needs a second to collect herself. How about I take her place? You just need me to hold Brent's hands and pretend to be smitten, right? I can do that. Easily."

I'm floored by his offer. He's here to shadow me, yet he's willing to jump in so I don't embarrass myself. I don't want to appreciate the gesture, but I do. More than I could ever tell him.

The photographer nods enthusiastically. "That'd be even better. You're the perfect height."

"Let's do it, then," Brent says.

I shuffle off to the side as Max and Brent turn to each other and hold hands. They're grinning as though they're in on a secret, and Brent and Terrence's attendants are goofing around as they watch them.

Brent gives Max a smoldering look that makes Max double over.

"Children . . ." the photographer says with a good-natured smile.

Max cracks his neck. "Okay, okay. I can do this." He clears his face and stares at Brent.

"I knew you were the one the day I was sick and you came over with soup," Brent tells Max, staring into his eyes. "You said you couldn't imagine not checking on me."

Max bats his eyes. "Aww, that's sweet."

The videographer asked them both to talk, but I suspect he didn't have *this* in mind. It's entertaining nonetheless, and I'm smiling into my hand as I watch them.

"I'd never been in love, so I didn't know what to look for, what to expect, how to accept it," Brent continues.

Max takes a long breath. "Me, neither. I've only had one long-term relationship, and that was several years ago."

"Why'd you break up?" Brent asks.

Max shrugs. "She met my brother and told me she realized there were bigger and better fish in the sea. Wasn't crass enough to drop me for him, but she made it clear he was the superior alternative."

Oh no. She said this to his face? What kind of person would do that? I couldn't imagine being told that I didn't measure up to my sibling. It'd be even worse if the comment came from someone I thought cared for me. Does he resent Andrew because of it? Is that the source of their rivalry?

"I'm sorry," Brent says to Max. "How'd that make you feel?"

My client's a psychiatrist and can't help himself. We may be here for a while.

"Honestly?" Max says, his eyes clouding with sadness. "Made me feel like shit. I'm used to comparing myself to my brother. He's older than me. We compete all the time. That's expected. But when my girlfriend essentially told me I was the off-brand version of my brother, well, I'm sure you can imagine that was a difficult thing for a guy in his early twenties to hear." He straightens. "But I'm over it now."

Yeah. No. I'm thinking that's not entirely true.

"She obviously didn't deserve you," Brent says. "People like that—"

"Brent, it's okay," Max says on a chuckle. "This isn't the time or place. Let's focus on your vows."

Brent nods. "Right." He rolls his shoulders and puffs out his cheeks before he begins again. "Anyway, because this was all new to me, I didn't trust it, so I ran from our relationship, told you I wasn't ready to be tied down—"

Max shakes his head, a cheesy grin on his face. "No, it's important to know you're ready. There's no going back. You need to be certain this is *who* and *what* you want."

The amusement in his tone pushes me out of the moment and pulls me back in time again, to the night before my wedding. I can easily imagine Max saying these very words to Andrew—about me. And if Max was telling Brent the truth about the extent of his own romantic relationships just now, at the time of my wedding Max was giving his brother advice on a topic about which he had no frame of reference. For whatever reason, he chose to meddle in my affairs when he knew very little about me. And I still don't know why.

Brent, meanwhile, is undeterred, continuing to recite his vows despite Max's interruptions. "But in the end, I couldn't fight your love, your dedication to building something true and real with me. And I'm so glad I lost that battle."

Terrence returns and jostles Max out of the way. "That's enough of that. Those words are meant for me. You're lucky I've heard them already. Otherwise we'd be fighting."

Max backs up, wearing a good-natured smile and throwing his hands up in surrender. "He's all yours. You're a lucky man."

When Max turns to catch my eye, I let him, my face relaxed into what I hope he'll read as a neutral expression.

"Thanks for your help today," I say. "I'm going to finish up with them and head out. I'll contact you when I have another appointment that might be helpful."

He tilts his head back as he appraises me. "We're done here? You don't want me to hang around a little longer?"

I shake my head, my gaze focused on the joyful couple a few feet away. "There's not much else to do. We'll go over the procession once more and then I'll let them go. I didn't realize Terrence was on call, and I don't want to take up any more of his time."

When I chance a glance at Max, I see that his gaze hasn't strayed from my face. Somehow he manages to look both studious and aloof, as though he's trying to figure something out but wishes he didn't have to. "What about if I stand quietly over here and record some footage of you in action? You've already cleared it with them, right?"

I nod. "I did. And you're free to do whatever you want. Enjoy the weekend." And then I'm striding in Brent and Terrence's direction. Head high. Shoulders back. A power walk for the ages. It's exhausting but necessary. I don't want Max to know how he's affecting me. I'm not even happy about acknowledging it to myself.

Jaslene's right. I *do* need closure. Because every time I convince myself I'm not holding a grudge against Max, something happens to remind me that I actually am. Still, I can't just ask the man why he discouraged his brother from marrying me. Not outright. I'd be admitting that his answer matters, and I'm not prepared to do that, either. It's a conundrum—where to go from here. But when I reach my clients and catch the tail end of a comment about Brent's intimidating mother, the solution comes to me. My relatives are a potent weapon that I don't use often enough. It's time to sic my family on Max.

Chapter Thirteen

MAX

From: MHartley@AtlasCommunications.com
To: CSantos@DottingTheIDos.com
Date: April 16 - 9:32 am
Subject: Next Steps

Hi Lina,

As part of the process of helping you prepare for your presentation on Tuesday, May 14, I would like to speak with a few of your clients about their impressions of you and your services. At your convenience, could you send me the names and phone numbers of three client references? It would be helpful if you could include the approximate date and location of the event you helped plan for each client. Looking forward to hearing from you.

Sincerely,
Max

From: CSantos@DottingTheIDos.com
To: MHartley@AtlasCommunications.com
Date: April 16 - 9:37 am
Subject: Re: Next Steps

Sure.

Anthony & Sandra Guerrero
443-555-3334
Wedding on the National Mall; May of last year

Patrice Bell & Cynthia Stacks
202-555-3293
Reception at Meridian House; June of last year

Bliss Donahue & Ian Grey*
215-555-8745
Wedding and reception at the Savoy Inn; April of this
year
    *Note that Ian is Rebecca Cartwright's first cousin.

Best,
Lina

p.s. If you're free this Thursday evening, I have a wedding
consultation in Maryland you could attend. I also have a rare
day with no event scheduled this Saturday, so I'm scoping out a
venue for a client. It's in Virginia, about two hours away. You're
welcome to join me.

From: MHartley@AtlasCommunications.com
To: CSantos@DottingTheIDos.com
Date: April 16 - 9:41 am
Subject: Re: Next Steps

I'm free for both. Send me the address for Thursday's meeting and I'll be there. We can chat about Saturday then. Thanks.

I spend the next ten minutes leaving messages for the references Lina provided. In theory, her former clients will provide some insight into Lina's unique skill set. But what I'm really looking for is some insight beyond her planning abilities. A poignant anecdote. A save-the-wedding moment. A memory about Lina rather than the wedding. Clients don't hire companies, they hire people. So essentially, I'm digging for that elusive *something* that goes beyond Lina's unquestionably impressive résumé.

She certainly won't share that information herself. Not with me, at least. Every time I think we've taken a few steps along a smoother path, she drags me back through the underbrush. Maybe we're just destined to be uneasy allies. I suppose I should be thankful for even that, given our history. Lina doesn't owe me anything, and I need to stop acting as though she does. If there's any crucial information to be gained, I'll get it from her past clients. End of story.

With my self-issued marching orders in mind, I leave a message for the last person on the reference list, Bliss Donahue.

Less than a minute later, my phone rings. "This is Max Hartley."

"Mr. Hartley, this is Bliss Donahue. You just left me a message?"

"Yes. Thanks for getting back to me."

I explain the project without referencing that it's connected to a position Lina's interviewing for. "So what I'd love to hear from you are your general impressions. Anything you wish she'd done differently? All in all, would you recommend her?"

"Oh, wholeheartedly," Bliss says.

There's conviction in her voice, and that's good to hear.

"Lina knows what she's doing," Bliss continues, "from the big stuff, such as venues, to the small stuff, like which rental folding chairs are least likely to pinch your guests' fingers. It's dizzying the amount of information she has a handle on. She didn't stifle me. I wore a green dress despite what I'm sure were Lina's many misgivings about it. In the end, my day was just what I wanted. Well, except for my husband's shaved eyebrows."

"What's that, now?"

Bliss lets out an exasperated sigh. "His groomsmen shaved off my husband's eyebrows the night before our wedding. I swear, they're like extras from *The Hangover*. You know, that movie with Bradley Cooper? Anyhow, Lina handled it like a pro. Somehow he had eyebrows for the wedding."

"This is really helpful. Anything else?"

"Well . . ."

"It's okay, Bliss. My goal is to help Lina, so if there's something that would have made your experience even better, we'd love to know."

She releases a breath. "Okay, it's just . . . I'm not necessarily *entitled* to this, but I kind of wish that Lina were more enthusiastic about weddings. I don't know. I wanted her to squee with me when I found the perfect flowers. Or when Ian and I practiced our vows. I got the impression that Lina isn't a big believer in happily-ever-afters. It never affected her work, but it was something I picked up on. Don't hate me for saying so, okay?"

"No, no. I asked you to give me your honest opinion, and you did. Thanks for taking the time to speak with me."

"Sure," she says in a bubbly voice. "Good luck with the project."

And there's the information I was hoping for. An aspect of Lina's brand that could be affecting her success. A part of her business model that I can potentially affect in a positive way. Helping her play to her strengths also means discovering her perceived weaknesses. But I'm also wondering if Bliss is right. Maybe Lina's experience with Andrew left her jaded. Or maybe she was jaded even before she met Andrew? Everywhere I turn I find another mystery about Lina I'd like to unravel.

My mother's signature *rat-a-tat-tat* alerts me that she's making her weekly rounds. She pokes her head in. "Got a minute?"

"Yeah, come on in."

She lowers herself onto one of the guest chairs and sweeps her gaze over the walls, my desk, then me. "I just wanted to check in with you about the Cartwright account. Since you and Andrew aren't working together, I can't call you both in for a meeting. I don't really have a handle on what's going on, and I'm finding that unsettling."

My mother never owns up to feeling anything less than fully confident. It's what I love most and least about her. Her admission loosens the tension in my shoulders.

"We're at the information-gathering stage," I say. "I'm checking references. Getting a feel for what the wedding planner does for her clients on a day-to-day basis. Doing some research on the target customer as well."

She nods approvingly, then knits her brow. "Your brother's

former fiancée was a wedding planner. Carolina." My mother's face takes on a wistful quality that I'm not used to. "I wonder what she's up to now."

I shrug. I'm not saying a word in response to that. A bolt of lightning would strike me on the spot.

"What kind of pitch are you considering?" she asks. "Mixed media?"

I'm eager to move the conversation along, so I dive into my preliminary ideas. "We haven't gotten that far yet, and I'm taking my cues from her. But I'm going to suggest a video component and—"

The intercom buzzes, and my assistant's voice echoes in the room: "Max, Patrice Bell is on line one. Says she's returning your call about a reference for Carolina Santos and Dotting the I Do's. Are you free?"

Why, God? Why?

My mother's brows snap together and she leans forward in the chair.

I clear my throat. "Sammy, please tell her I'll ring her back in a minute."

"You got it," Sammy says cheerfully, unaware of the years she's just shaved off my life.

My mother rubs her temples and stares at her lap. "Let me see if I have this right. The wedding planner you're working with *is* Carolina Santos?"

"Yes."

Her head shoots up and she scrunches her face. "And neither you nor your brother thought it was appropriate to share that tidbit?"

"We didn't want to worry you."

That gets me an icy look. "Why would I be worried?"

"Because we didn't share that tidbit with Rebecca Cart-wright, either."

Silence can be as intimidating as a Mob gangster. This moment is proof of that. If I can figure out a way to black out now, I'll avoid the excruciating conversation to come. I look around my office for an object heavy enough to engineer a nonfatal blow. But after several more seconds of silence, and much to my surprise, my mother merely rises from the chair and shakes her head. "I'm disappointed in you both, but I'm not going to get in the middle of this. I'm not going to tell you what to do, nor am I going to sweep in and save you. But keep this in mind. If you want more responsibility here, you need to earn it. And if you screw this up, you *and* your brother should polish your résumés."

She's not joking. With that scathing soliloquy behind her, she strides out of my office and turns right. There's just one office down that hall. Andrew's. I could warn him, but I won't. He deserves to be the target of her wrath, too. I mean, c'mon, Lina's *his* ex-fiancée. I'm just an innocent bystander. Sort of.

I can't say that I blame my mother. If another employee pulled the shit we've pulled, they'd be out on their ass if they didn't fix their mistake. I knew when I came here she wouldn't coddle us. But more to the point, she's right. If I want more responsibility, I *do* need to earn it. And I will. No more distractions. No more detours. No more games.

———————

Thursday evening, I drive to Wheaton to meet Lina at her family's grocery store. At her suggestion, we'll travel together from there to her client appointment. After parking in the strip mall where the store is located, I walk to the entrance and pull on the door. Nothing happens—because the door's locked. The lights inside are on, though.

I lean against the door, poised to pull out my phone and text Lina, but then the woman of the hour appears on the other side of the door and unlocks it.

"Hey, there," she says cheerfully. *Too* cheerfully. "Come on in."

When I slip inside, I'm shocked to see many sets of eyes staring at me, Natalia's unwelcoming pair among them.

"Max, this is everyone," Lina says with an enthusiastic sweep of her hand. "Everyone, this is Max. He and I are working together on a project to help me get that wedding coordinator position I told you about."

A guy behind the counter straightens as his eyes narrow on me. He looks familiar, but I can't place him. His coloring and features favor Lina. Except he's also big. Burly as hell. Way taller than I am.

"I've seen you somewhere before," he says, his eyes squinting as though that'll help him recognize me.

"You're right, Rey," Lina says.

Rey. Short for Reynaldo. I remember him now. He's Lina's older brother. We talked briefly during the rehearsal dinner— two days before my brother canceled the wedding.

Lina gives me a wicked grin before she addresses her family again. "You remember Andrew, right? The guy who dumped me on our wedding day? Well, this is his brother. The one who encouraged him to do the dumping. Anyway, let's all sit. We have a wedding intervention to attend to."

Everyone's attention shifts to me, the schmuck who's un-steady on his feet.

She shoots. She scores. I'm dead.

I can picture my single-sentence epitaph now: *He never saw it coming.*

Chapter Fourteen

LINA

Negotiate a peace treaty among my family members about the scope and details of Natalia and Paolo's wedding? Or get some intel on Max by throwing him into the lion's den? Who says I can't do both?

"Why is he here?" Rey asks as he glowers at Max.

Tia Izabel, who's standing next to Rey behind the counter and who's fond of watching fireworks but never wants to cause them, elbows him in the side.

Max silently slumps into the chair behind me. I'm his shield, apparently.

"Like I said, he's helping me prepare a presentation for the position I'm applying for," I say. "Part of what he needs to do is see me in action, so I figured this would be a good way for him to watch me handle a delicate situation."

Natalia and Paolo join me at the table, while my mother takes a seat at another one nearby. Tia Viviane, the mother of the bride and the main reason for this meeting, swings her chair around and straddles it, positioning herself in her own space. She needs attention, and she shall have it. "Why is the situation delicate?"

I flick my gaze toward Natalia and Paolo. The groom, who's a sweetheart of a guy, will say next to no words tonight. He's not messing with his future mother-in-law. The former is a badass—except when it comes to her mother. I'm here to be the badass in her stead. "We need everyone to be on the same page about certain aspects of the wedding, and there are so many ideas bouncing around, it's getting overwhelming. We want to respect the couple's wishes and tastes, and that may not always be in line with yours."

"Talk specifics, please," Viviane says.

"Let's start with your dress," I say.

Everyone who's sitting—and I mean everyone—straightens up and leans back as though they want no part of this conversation. *Traitors.*

Viviane throws her hands on her hips. "What's wrong with my dress?"

I gulp before I speak. "It's a little . . . loud."

And that's an understatement. It's a purple Lycra glitter bomb with flesh-tone mesh panels along the waist and hips. Think *Real Housewives of New Jersey* meets *Dancing with the Stars* meets the ladies of World Wrestling Entertainment. My mother and Izabel, for their part, are wearing neutral-toned dresses that complement the wedding palette.

"It's perfect for the reception," Viviane counters. "It's going to look great under the lights when I'm on the dance floor."

Natalia groans. "With the amount of sparkle on it, that dress will *be* the lights on the dance floor. Disco lights, more specifically. We'll certainly save money on energy costs, at least."

Max chuckles.

Viviane's head nearly snaps off her neck as she swivels it in his direction. "You never get to laugh around here." She slides a thumb across her throat, her expression menacing. "Nunca."

I lean back and look at Max over my shoulder. "That means 'never.'"

A muscle in his jaw twitches, and he casts a veiled glance my way. "I figured that out on my own, thanks."

I want to giggle so badly, but if my family sees us getting along, they might ease up on him, and this is way too much fun not to let it play out a bit more and see what they're able to draw out of him.

"Listen, Tia," I say to Viviane, "you're the mother of the bride, so you're going to be a big part of Natalia and Paolo's day, but the focus should be on them. As lovely as it is, your dress is a distraction."

"Is that how you feel?" Viviane asks Natalia.

She nods. "Yes."

"Why didn't you just say so?"

Natalia sighs. "I did. On, like, five different occasions."

Viviane fusses with a napkin in her hand. "I must not have heard you." After a few seconds, she says, "Fine. I'll wear a different outfit."

I look over at my mother. "Mãe, you'll help her?"

"Sim, filha. I'll take care of it."

I slap my hand on the table as if it's a gavel. "Okay, next order of business. The strogonoff de frango on the menu."

"The stroganoff de what?" Max asks behind me.

Rey bangs his hand on the counter and points a finger at Max. "Hey, you. Don't talk. Observe."

Max crosses his arms over his chest and grumbles under his breath.

Poor Max. I bet this is unfamiliar territory for him—taking a back seat and being forced to remain quiet. He probably hates it. As for me, I love, love, love it. "How you hanging in there, champ? Doing okay?"

"How sweet of you to ask, ISTJ."

His reference to the fake Myers-Briggs personality type he assigned to me elicits the laughter he was probably shooting for. I turn my head over my shoulder. "A sense of humor even under pressure. I'm impressed. And just for that, I'll help you keep up. Strogonoff de frango is chicken stroganoff. Brazilian-style stroganoff is very pink—from the tomatoes—and prone to stain your clothes."

"What's wrong with the stroganoff?" Viviane asks, her forehead puckered in confusion.

I can't be around to mediate every situation between Natalia and my aunt, but I *can* show Natalia that it's possible to do it on her own. "Nat, if you could ask the family for one thing that would make the process of planning your wedding easier, what would you ask for?"

Natalia meets Paolo's gaze, and he gives her a small nod.

"I'd ask that everyone not add to our stress. That's it."

I nod encouragingly. "Okay, and how is the stroganoff stressing you?"

The words rush out of Natalia's mouth like the release of steam from a pressure cooker. "It's messy. And so I'm envisioning a disaster. Wedding photos with big pink splotches on everyone's clothes. That stuff is like spilled ink in your purse, you know? It explodes everywhere. I just don't want to worry that the flower girl is going to want a taste, or that a guest hugs me and gets it on my jumpsuit. It's just a headache I don't need."

"But it's tradition," Viviane whines.

My mother stands and motions for my aunt to zip her mouth shut. "Pare de choramingar, Viviane. Ela não quer strogonoff de frango no casamento, então não vai ter. Ponto final!"

Oh. Go, Mãe.

Max leans forward and whispers in my ear, "What'd she say?"

He's way too close, the puffs of his minty breath floating against my neck like a dozen butterflies. I scoot forward and clear my throat. "She said Natalia doesn't want stroganoff at her wedding so it won't be there and that's final."

"I love your mother," Max says.

Although I don't want to, I smile at his earnest—and ridiculous—pronouncement, then quickly return to business mode. "Next, let's talk about a Brazilian tradition we can incorporate into the wedding. Any ideas, Tia?"

Viviane rubs her chin. "We could pass out bem-casados as people leave." She juts her chin out at Max. "Before you ask, they're sponge cake cookies. For good luck."

"Perfect," I say. "Now we're getting somewhere."

Thirty minutes later, we've ironed out a host of differences and saved Natalia and Paolo's wedding. "Okay, I think we're in pretty good shape. The wedding's only a month away, so if you have to-dos, please complete them as soon as you can." I rise from my chair and stretch out my arms.

"Not so fast," my mother says. "We need to talk to that one over there."

Max, who's still sitting, turns from side to side and looks around. "Who? Me?"

"Yes, you," my mother says.

Izabel tuts at her. "Mariana, this isn't necessary."

"I think it is," my mother says stubbornly.

Bahaha. This is perfect. My family will take it from here.

MAX

Why don't I just tell Rey to knock me out and be done with it? That would be better than having to answer to Lina's mother.

I stand and cross my hands in supplication. "May I remind you"—I glance at Rey, then look at Lina's mother—"respectfully, of course, that *I* wasn't the one to leave Lina at the altar? That was my brother, in case there's any confusion on that point."

"But you encouraged him to?" Lina's mother asks.

"I suppose. Maybe this won't make sense, but I was a jack—*jerk*, I was an immature jerk back then. Listen, let me say my piece and then you can pick me apart all you want. I'll take it."

She nods and motions for me to come forward with a flick of her fingers, as though she's a character in a martial arts movie challenging her next opponent. The gesture confirms what I suspected: If I don't talk my way out of this, she *will* kick my ass.

I take a deep breath and do what I do best—identify a theme and sell it. "I don't see any point in rehashing the past. Suffice it to say that if my brother truly loved Lina, he either wouldn't have left her at the metaphorical altar or he would have found his way back to her." I swivel around to speak to Lina directly. "Assuming you would have wanted him back, that is."

To her mother, I say, "But here's what I know *today*. My brother's a decent guy. He isn't mean, he's rarely rude to anyone except me, and he doesn't fuss. I expect he'll make a fine father and husband one day. But being in this family's presence for less than an hour tells me that my brother wouldn't have been Lina's perfect match. You'd want her to have someone full of life like all of you. You'd want someone who would absolutely adore her. Who'd make her take down her bun and forget herself even for just a few minutes. Who'd make her cry, but only for the sappiest reasons." I take a deep breath and shrug. "All I'm saying is, I'm sorry for the role I played in their breakup, but I don't think my brother was right for her anyway."

Slowly, so as not to be obvious about it, I turn around to gauge Lina's reaction to my monologue. Surprise, surprise, her face is blank. I'm gearing up to make a joke to ease the tension, but she excuses herself and brushes past me, heading to an area beyond the store's front counter.

Lina's mother claps her hands together and smiles at her sisters.

Rey rounds the counter and approaches, the bulk of his upper body propelling him to where I'm standing.

I close my eyes. "If you're going to deck me, do it quick and knock me unconscious. It's the humane thing to do."

"I'm not going to hit you," Rey says as his bear paws land on my shoulders like feathers. "Any man who speaks about my sister the way you just did can't be all bad." He gives my shoulders a light squeeze. "I'm a big believer in second chances. And the way you and Lina have been getting along, looks like she agrees. That's enough for me."

It's not enough for Natalia, though. Lina's cousin shakes her head at me, a scowl on her face.

"What did I do now?" I say, unable to moderate the frustration in my voice.

"That hypothetical individual you described?" Natalia says. "The perfect person for Lina?"

"Yeah? What about him? Or her. Them." I shake my head. "You know what I mean."

Natalia gives me a sympathetic pat on my shoulder. "You just described her worst nightmare."

I can't even begin to wrap my head around what that means. But this is Lina we're talking about, so I shouldn't be surprised. Another part of her personality that confounds me? Eh, sounds about right.

I frown at Natalia. "Care to explain?"

She shakes her head. "That's the most you'll get from me, friend."

"We're friends now?" I ask, raising a brow.

Natalia winks at me. "Correction. We're acquaintances."

"I can live with that."

"You don't have any choice *but* to live with that," she sing-songs as she pulls Paolo up from his chair and spins him to the beat of the music suddenly filling the store.

If the universe liked me, I would fall for someone like Natalia. Someone who's open and unafraid to say exactly what's on her mind. But I'm thinking about the woman no longer in the room. Wondering if she's okay. Wanting to see her reluctant smile again. I don't know much, but I know this: The universe hates me.

Chapter Fifteen

LINA

My elbow connects with the corner of the medicine cabinet as I try to splash water on my cheeks. Damn, this bathroom's tiny. I'm probably only realizing it now because I have no reason to be here other than that it enables me to avoid everyone out there.

How the hell did this evening become a guest lecture on The Man I'm Meant to Marry 101? Oh, that's right. Max Hartley, visiting Distinguished Professor of Talking Out Your Ass, is in the building. Max doesn't *know* me. He has no idea what makes me tick, and he'd never understand why I am who I am. And still, he has no problem mansplaining *my* love life to *my* family.

Little does Max know, I once found that mythical creature he described. His name was Lincoln, and in my third and fourth years of college at UMD I believed we were destined to be together. I mean, even our nicknames—Linc and Lina—*proved* that fate was involved.

Lincoln pursued me for months, but I was wary of getting serious with anyone, especially when most of my classmates switched partners as easily as they dropped early morning classes. Wasn't that what college was all about? Shouldn't I have been doing the same? Lincoln was persistent, though. He made me feel special. Doted on me in ways I'd never experienced. And so I fell hard.

Which, coincidentally, is exactly when Lincoln decided I was no longer special. He began to play games. The kind that made me cry and scream. He'd disappear for days, forget my birthday, periodically ask me for space, then reappear when I gave him too much of it. I was a volatile person back then. And Lincoln loved it. Said my passion showed how much I cared and kept our relationship fresh.

It took me a long time to realize Lincoln enjoyed provoking me; eventually, he even lost interest in doing that. He distanced himself in stages, until the day I entered a crowded campus dining hall and saw Lincoln kissing and caressing another woman. If I'd been a stronger person, I would have stormed out and never looked back. But as I stood there watching him make someone else feel special, my insides squeezing my heart until I thought it would pop out of my chest, I was overwhelmed by profound sadness. Not eat-my-weight-in-chocolate sadness. Or even lie-in-bed-and-stare-at-the-ceiling sadness. No, this was far worse. It was I-can't-contain-any-of-this-inside-me sadness. So I crumbled. Made accusations as tears ran down my face. Wailed. Dropped to my knees like a melodramatic actress auditioning for a part as an extra in a B movie. It was ugly. And awkward. *Painfully* awkward. And when I looked up at the faces of my schoolmates, all I saw was pity. A loss of respect I'd never regain. And all because I couldn't control my emotions. I vowed in that moment that I'd never let anyone or anything reduce me to that embarrassing state again. I've only experienced one slipup since then—which also happens to be the incident that got me fired from my job as a paralegal—but I can confidently say that I now control my emotions whereas in the past my emotions controlled me.

It isn't fair to expect Max to understand any of this. He's uninformed. Still, I see no point in enlightening him; he can believe what he wants to believe.

I leave my miniature sanctuary and return to the front of the store, where the air's filled with laughter and the driving percussion of samba music. My gaze immediately lands on my mother, who's popping a brigadeiro in Max's mouth. He moans and rolls his eyes as he chews; my mother happily looks on as if meeting Max's dietary needs is her priority in life. Rey shuffles over in search of water and playfully pokes Max in the ribs on his return. Everyone else is dancing samba in the center of the room. It's official: They're throwing Max a welcome-to-the-family party. Honestly, I can't blame them. I've secretly enjoyed being with him, too.

Tia Izabel gestures for me to join their dance circle. I've done it countless times, just not with Max around. When I realize I'm stalling, I strut over so I can prove to myself I'm not hesitating because he's here. Rey and Natalia, always the loudest at any gathering, throw up their hands and shout their approval. My body eases into the familiar rapid-fire steps that require my feet, calves, butt, and hips to work together seamlessly. It took me years to perfect it, and now the dance comes to me as easily as walking does. I'm so lost in the music that I close my eyes and let my body swing and sway to the tempo, my arms above my head as I shimmy my torso.

The next song is slower, but I make the necessary adjustment, rocking my hips in smaller circles, until I lift my lids—and spy Max standing by the counter watching me, his gaze traveling over my body and eventually resting on my face. My breath quickens, and my heart is banging around in my chest. I don't look away. Neither does he. If we were alone, we'd close the distance between us—the pull is *that* strong.

Natalia bumps me with her hip, throwing me off-balance. Before I can even right myself, Max leaves the store.

I meet my mother's gaze, a question in my eyes, but she merely shrugs and turns away, a hint of a smile tugging at her full lips. Since I asked him to join me this evening, I feel compelled to go after him and make sure he's okay, so I push open the front door and peek outside. To my relief, he's a few feet away, pacing between two parked cars.

"What's going on?" I ask, rubbing my arms to ward off the chill in the air.

His head shoots up, but he doesn't stop pacing. "I could use a smoke."

"What do you smoke? Cigarettes? Weed?"

He shakes his head. "Neither. But tonight I'd reconsider. I'm just feeling a little off."

"Well, you're welcome to go if you need to. We're done here."

Max turns to face me and rests his hands on the car between us. He looks a little paler than usual, but otherwise seems okay.

"I think that's a good idea," he says. "Can you tell everyone I said goodbye? Explain I wasn't feeling well?"

"Of course. Don't worry about it. Do you think something my mother gave you is messing with your stomach? The brigadeiros have condensed milk in them."

He shakes his head, but he doesn't meet my eyes. "No, no. It's nothing like that. I'm tired, that's all. Makes it difficult to think clearly." His gaze darts to mine, then it rests on a spot behind me. "Your family's great, by the way. Intimidating but great."

I grin at him. "That's a perfect description."

"Your dad?"

"Not in the picture," I say, shrugging. "We're okay with that."

He nods, then lightly bangs his fist on the hood of the car. "Listen, about the things I said earlier: I'm sorry if I made you uncomfortable. Your family knows how to put on the pressure, and I just said what I believe. I realize what I believe doesn't mean jack shit, though, so let's pretend I never said anything. Deal?"

I could easily accept his peace offering, but my instinct is to reject it outright. Does that make me a bitch? God, I hope not. Even so, I give him a toothachingly sweet smile. "There are no do-overs in life, Max." *Wow, I am a bitch.*

He purses his lips as though my answer doesn't surprise him. "Right."

What's wrong with me? Why am I pushing him away when he's obviously trying to fix the rift between us? I set out to get closure this evening, and now that it's within my grasp, I'm lobbing it back at him as though it'll burn me. Maybe it's because I *need* this rift between us. Without a grudge to hold on to, what will I rely on to keep Max at arm's length? I'm too aware of him for it to be good for me. Still, I can't make him out to be the bad guy if he isn't. It would be convenient, but it wouldn't be true.

I stare at him as he fidgets with his key fob. He wants to bolt, and I'm standing here preventing his escape. I should say good-bye, but I don't want to end the night this way. "Max, it's true there are no do-overs in life, but we can move on from here. I'd like us to be friends."

He exhales a deep breath and taps the roof of the car. "I'd like that, too."

Before I can think better of it, I blurt out, "And I hope there isn't any doubt about this, but your ex-girlfriend was wrong. You're a great guy—in your own right. Don't let anyone tell you differently."

"Thanks for saying that." He runs a jerky hand through his hair. "But I still need to head out. I'll call you about Saturday."

He doesn't wait for my response. Confused by his impolite behavior, I watch him walk to his car and slip inside. Within seconds, he's speeding off—as if his own demons are chasing him and he's determined to outrun them.

MAX

*I*t's been two hours since I left Rio de Wheaton and I'm still unsettled. I'm also itchy and jumpy as hell. Not even a cold shower made a difference. And if all that isn't enough, Dean's ignoring my texts.

A beer would help, but I'm holding off on drinking one, because if Dean ever answers, I'm driving over to his place. He'll know what to say to get my brain in proper order. As of now, synapses are misfiring and my lobes are working against each other.

I scramble to grab my phone when I hear the text alert.

Dean: Sorry, man. Was on a date. What's up?

Me: Got someone with you?

Dean: Nope. Weren't feeling each other. The search for my
perfect partner continues.

Me: Can I stop by? Need to talk.

Dean: We're talking now.

Me: We're texting.

Dean: R u ok?

Me: I'm fine.

Dean: Is this a booty call?

Me: Fuck you. Can I come over or not?

Dean: Sure, come on over.

I'm there within fifteen minutes.

When Dean opens the door, he crowds the threshold. "What
the hell is that?"

I raise the items in the air. "An overnight bag and a pillow.
Just in case."

Dean scratches the side of his face and lets out a heavy sigh.
"Get your ass in here." He stalks away, then plants himself on a
stool in his kitchen, watching me set my stuff down in a corner.
"It's late, and I need to be at work bright and early. What's going on?"

I pace the length of his living room, trying to formulate my
thoughts. "I need to hear those reasons again."

I'm not sure how long he stares at me, but it *feels* like a long
time. A minute, maybe?

"What happened?" His voice is resigned, as though he has his
suspicions and only wants me to confirm them.

"Nothing happened. I'm trying to make sure that remains true."

He stands. "Don't bullshit me, Max." Shaking his head, he gestures in my general direction. "This is not what 'nothing happened' looks like. What'd you do?"

I slow my steps and face his skeptical gaze. "I had inappropriate thoughts about Lina."

"*Just* thoughts?"

I nod. "Just thoughts."

He throws up his hands and plops back onto the stool. "What's the problem, then? We all have inappropriate thoughts from time to time. It's called being human."

Dean's not getting it. I've been thinking inappropriate thoughts about Lina for the past two and a half hours. I'm having them *now*. And I don't want to get in bed because I'm worried about where those thoughts will take me. It would be a slippery slope—literally and figuratively. "Thoughts are one thing, but what if I do more?"

He blows out his cheeks, then releases them, peering at me with a puzzled look on his face. "What does that mean?" Several seconds later, his jaw goes slack and he falls over in laughter. "Oh damn. You're scared you're going to think about her as you jerk off?"

Hearing him say it out loud sounds so much worse than I imagined. I pull on my hair, zigzagging across his living room like a Ping-Pong ball. "It's not funny. I'm trash. Complete trash."

"What set you off this time?" he says on a chuckle.

"She was dancing at her family's shop, oblivious to the fact that I was watching her. And Dean, I'm telling you, I was fucking mesmerized." I whimper at the memory of the way she moved her ass and hips in the middle of that store. "Christ, she was going to be my sister-in-law at one point."

Dean purses his lips at me. "But she isn't your sister-in-law now, so calm the fuck down."

"Tell me what to do," I say.

He ponders my request, and then he asks, "Is she showing any signs that she's feeling the same way? Is this a two-way thing?"

"I'm not even sure she likes me. As a person, I mean. She said we could be friends. Said I was a great guy. I felt like I'd won the lottery. Freaked me the fuck out. To her, though, it's nothing. She tolerates me, probably for the sake of this big-deal job she wants to get. I mean, she wanted to marry my brother. She couldn't possibly be interested in me."

"Then tie your hands behind your back and go the fuck to sleep. My couch is your couch. Sheets and blankets in the hall closet. We can talk more tomorrow." He ambles toward the hallway leading to his bedroom. "Good night."

Grumbling at Dean's lack of support when I need him the most, I stomp to the bathroom, where I brush and floss my teeth. Still pissed, I throw a sheet on the couch, turn off the hall light, and dive under the comforter I grabbed from the closet, one that smells like a woman's perfume. *I don't even get fresh linens. Some host he is.*

And with nothing else to do, I settle in to consume the images of Lina that won't stop flashing in my restless brain. The way she moaned her appreciation for her lunch. The moment she brushed crumbs from my face. The dance of torture.

She's always in control. Detached. Not mean, exactly, just reserved. Face blank, voice even. Everything and everyone has a place. That's the planner in her, I suppose. But God, I want to disorganize her to within an inch of her life. Disorient her so thoroughly she throws on her clothes inside out afterward.

Extra points if I can get her to a state where she's incapable of telling the difference between a button and a boutonniere.

I picture us together, in high-definition resolution with surround sound and memory-on-demand playback capabilities. It's only a vision of my hand slipping underneath her pencil skirt as she squeezes her eyes shut and gasps, but it's enough to make me jump off the couch, drag the lavender-smelling comforter down the hall, and knock on Dean's door.

"What?" he barks.

I peek inside. "Let me stay in here tonight. Your bed is huge. It'll guarantee I won't . . . you know . . . and I promise to stay on my side."

He slaps a hand on his forehead. "Jesus Christ. Are you incapable of self-control?" After a few seconds more, he says, "Anything I've ever owed you is repaid tonight. Understood?"

"Yeah," I say, relieved he's not tossing me out.

"And if I sense any rocking motion, I will shove your ass onto the floor and permanently ban you from visiting me."

"No problem." I jump on the bed and fall onto my back, rearranging the comforter over my lower half. "Thanks, man."

"Fuck off," he says, turning to his side. "You need to figure your shit out, because this is not going to be a regular thing."

"I know."

I'll worry about that later. For now, I can rest easy knowing I'll be able to look Lina in the eyes the next time we're together. That's something, at least.

Chapter Sixteen

MAX

From: MHartley@AtlasCommunications.com
To: CSantos@DottingTheIDos.com
Date: April 19 - 11:17 am
Subject: Saturday

Hi Lina,

Just following up about the trip tomorrow. A few questions:

(1) Should we drive down together?

(2) What's the name of the place we're visiting?

(3) Do I need to bring anything?

It would be great to discuss our strategy about the presentation at some point, which is why I vote yes on Question 1.

Hope you're well.

Max

From: CSantos@DottingTheIDos.com
To: MHartley@AtlasCommunications.com
Date: April 19 - 1:13 pm
Subject: Re: Saturday

Hello Max,

(1) That's fine, but I'm driving my car there.

(2) Surrey Lane Farm, Raven Hill, VA

(3) I checked the weather forecast, and there might be a passing shower. Since it's a farm, weatherproof boots would be a good idea. And a change of clothes is always wise (in case the grounds are muddy).

I can pick you up at your place Saturday morning, or you can meet me in College Park and leave your car there. You'd be backtracking if you come my way, though. It's up to you.

Best,
Lina

I'm typing a reply when Andrew knocks on the door and waltzes in without waiting for my invitation.

"And hello to you, too," I say without looking up from my screen.

"Hey, got a minute?" he asks, sitting down in a guest chair.

"Let me just finish up this email."

I type. He waits. There's no chatting in between. After I hit *send,* I lean back in my chair and place my clasped hands on the desk. "What's up?"

"Two things," he says. "One, the Virginia Real Estate Consortium wants to discuss marketing for the third quarter. Within the next couple of weeks, if possible. When you get a chance, can you send Sammy the days you're free for lunch?"

I scribble a note to myself to do just that. "On it. What's the second thing?"

"For the presentations to Rebecca Cartwright, have you thought about what A/V equipment you're going to need? Will a computer suffice? PowerPoint on a projector screen? Just trying to figure out if we need to make any special requests."

Is he, now? The equipment he needs is always where it's supposed to be because I make sure it's there. Truth is, he's never concerned himself with these issues before, which immediately puts me on high bullshit alert. It doesn't take a genius to figure out what's going on here. My big brother's snooping and doing a piss-poor job of masking it. "Haven't given it much thought yet. Lina and I still need to talk about the specifics of the presentation. Right now I'm in the due diligence stage."

Andrew tips his head back slightly. "Really? The pitch is less than four weeks away. That's not a lot of time to prepare."

I shrug. "We're preparing. Believe me, everything we're doing will inform the pitch in some way. How's your guy? Henry, right?"

Andrew nods. "He's an organizational guru. Scarily put together. I'm excited to show Rebecca what we've come up with."

"I guess that's why they're planners. Organization comes easy to them."

"In Lina's case, she had other options," Andrew says, tapping his thigh. "Did you know she was a paralegal before she became a wedding planner? You should ask her about it sometime." He rises from the chair.

It irritates me that Andrew knows more about Lina than I do. Then I remind myself that he's Lina's ex-fiancé. He *should* know more. That irritates me, too. Wearing a self-satisfied smile, I look up at him. "Maybe I'll do that. We're heading to Virginia this weekend. Work-related. I could ask her during the two-hour drive."

Andrews stiffens, a muscle in his jaw clenching in response to the news.

Fuck. That was uncalled for. I can picture Dean pointing at us now and saying, *This. This is what I was talking about, man.* I'm ashamed of my small-minded behavior, and I wish I could retract the statement, but that's not how these things work. As Lina said, there are no do-overs in life. And she's right. There are only do-betters.

"Anyway," I say, mentally scrambling to clean up my shit, "we're looking at a potential wedding venue. I hope we don't kill each other before we get there."

His body goes lax again—well, as lax as Andrew will allow it to go—and he rocks back on his heels. "Good luck. You're probably going to need it."

He's so right. But not for the reason he thinks.

———

"This is your ride? A ninety-nine Volvo? It's yellow."

Lina huffs at me as she tries to jiggle the trunk open. "It's a 2002, okay? And anyone with a discerning eye can see it's Maya

Gold." She grits her teeth as she pulls on the latch, until the trunk pops open with a loud *kerplunk*. "That's just a minor jam. The car is sound."

I slip her a wary glance, unsure whether it's wise to put my belongings in the back of this behemoth masquerading as a vehicle. "I have a decent Acura less than a hundred feet away. It's not too late to hop in that one instead."

She rolls her eyes at me. "Listen, car snob, I'm driving, and I drive well in *my* car. Let's not alter any variables unnecessarily." Muttering to herself, she rounds the back of the banana cab and slides into the driver's seat.

She's wearing jeans today, and I honestly don't know if I'll be able to look at another pair without envisioning Lina in them. Who knew there was such a thing as a denim fetish? She's paired the pants with a black collared shirt that's partially tucked into her waistband, resulting in a look that once again throws my perception of her out of whack. This trip is already off to a shaky start, and we haven't even used an ounce of gasoline yet.

Knowing I need to extend an olive branch to make up for the dig about her car, I climb into the passenger seat and hold up the paper bag and thermos in my hands. "I brought snacks."

She twists her head in my direction and peers at me, the corners of her glossy lips lifting in a lopsided smirk. "It's nine in the morning. I think I can hold off on eating until we get to the farm, but if you're hungry, don't let me stop you."

I shrug. "Suit yourself. But give me a minute to get situated." Then I place the thermos between my legs so I can put on my seatbelt. After strapping myself in, I uncap the thermos and pour coffee into my reusable travel mug. The drink is sweet and creamy and probably has more grams of sugar in it than an entire bottle of maple syrup, but I like it. A lot. "Your mother makes a fantastic cup of coffee."

She wrinkles her nose but keeps her eyes trained on the road as she eases into traffic. "My mother?"

"Yeah. I stopped by Rio de Wheaton this morning. She gave me cafe and"—I shake the bag—"pão de queijo."

Her mouth falls open. "You didn't."

"Ah, Ms. Santos, I did. I knew I'd never be able to earn brownie points with you, so I figured I'd try for pão de queijo points."

She grins. "What do you need points for?"

"Insurance. If my past conduct is any guide, I will most definitely screw up in the future, and I'll need to cash in on any credits. I'm working on building a reserve now."

"Smart man," she says, still grinning.

A few beats of silence pass, during which she blinks so excessively I wonder if a lash is trapped in her eye, then her shoulders drop in resignation. "May I have one, please?"

"A cheeseball?"

She grimaces. "If you want to earn points, don't call it a cheeseball."

I scoff at her. "That's the literal translation."

"No, it isn't. The literal translation is cheese bread. And anyway, it's so much more than a ball of cheese. It's this morsel of goodness that's flaky on the outside, and gooey and warm on the inside, and when you break it apart, the cheese stretches for miles."

"Do you want it or not?" I ask.

"I want it," she says breathily, sticking out her hand.

"*Ah-ah-ah.* Safety first. Both hands on the steering wheel, please."

Her mouth twitches, but she does as she's told. I need to keep her in the driver's seat. She's much more agreeable in this position.

Despite the limpness of her expression, she opens wide as my fingers approach, then she takes the entire ball in her mouth. I will not make a smart-ass remark here, and to ensure it, I bite down on my bottom lip hard enough to make a small tear in the skin.

"It's good," she says as she chews. "But it'd be a thousand times better fresh from the oven."

"That's what your mother said. Luckily for me, I had a few at the store that were still piping hot."

She grumbles a few unintelligible words and says more clearly, "You're losing pão de queijo points here."

"Want another one?"

She nods. "One more."

I feed her another, then pop one in my own mouth, relaxing into the seat in preparation for the long drive. When she gets on Rock Creek Parkway, I twist in my seat to face her. "Sure you don't want me to drive a leg of the trip?"

"I like driving. It's actually a stress reliever for me, so if it makes no difference to you, I'd prefer to stay at the helm the entire way."

I shrug. "Makes no difference to me so have at it. What about music?"

She bares her teeth as though she's anticipating a negative reaction from me in response to whatever she's about to say. "I rarely listen to music in the car. That stress relief I mentioned? It comes from sitting in the driver's seat, watching the road, and working through my thoughts. But I'm not a car hog, either. If you want to listen to music, be my guest."

"No, no. I was just wondering. I'm comfortable with silence."

She nods. "Great."

We've finally reached a point when there's no animosity between us. It's a welcome change, and I figure now's an ideal time to ask her about her former job. "So Andrew mentioned that you were a paralegal before you became a wedding planner. Why'd you decide to make the switch?"

In the span of seconds, her expression hardens like quick-setting concrete. If she tried to crack a smile in her current state, her face would probably splinter into a thousand pieces. "Hmm. You and Andrew have been talking about me?"

Whoa. Okay, I didn't think I was going to need those pão de queijo points so soon. And sure, out of context, I can see why she wouldn't appreciate that revelation, but I can easily explain this away. "Not really, no. He made an offhand comment about wedding planners and their organizational skills and suggested that some of your skills come from your experience as a paralegal. He said I should ask you about it."

Staring straight ahead, she grinds her teeth a bit, then she sighs. "I didn't choose to make the switch from paralegal to wedding planner."

"You didn't?"

She shakes her head. "No, Max. I was fired."

Dammit. We were doing so well. Now I've raised a topic she obviously doesn't want to discuss. I squeeze my eyes shut, mentally cursing my brother for suggesting that I ask her about her old job. Even when Andrew's not around he's wreaking havoc in my life.

Chapter Seventeen

LINA

I'm not mad at Max for posing an innocent question at Andrew's suggestion; I'm annoyed that Andrew fiendishly encouraged his brother to ask it in the first place. Andrew doesn't understand how that experience impacted my life—because I never explained it to him—but he knows I don't like to talk about it. No purpose could possibly be served by rehashing that drama. Andrew's goal was to undermine Max, plain and simple.

I sneak a glance at Max, my heart twisting at his stricken expression. I'm feeling surprisingly protective of my travel companion, and I never imagined I would. "It's old news, okay? But yes, wedding planning is my do-over."

He clears his face of any evidence of his agitation. "*Do-better*, you mean."

"What?" I ask, frowning.

"You told me there's no such thing as a do-over, remember? So this is your do-better. I think the term fits perfectly. And I'm . . . I'm sorry if my question brought up bad memories."

I shrug off his apology. "Don't sweat it, Max. It's not a big deal."

He fidgets in his seat, then reaches for his travel mug, changing his mind mid-stretch. "How can it not be a big deal? It played a part in the person you are today. That matters." He shakes his head as he taps on the passenger window.

I understand why he's frustrated with his brother, but I also get the sense he's frustrated that he doesn't know this part of my background. It's puzzling—and a weightier subject than I want to tackle during a quick excursion to Virginia farm country. Unable to bear the silence any longer, I reach out to turn on the radio. Before my finger hits the dial, though, Max swings around, startling me.

He scrapes a hand through his hair and clears his throat. "I'm going to be honest here and tell you I fucking hate that Andrew knows your secrets. He doesn't deserve to."

Okay, then. I guess we're talking about this whether I want to or not. "So, what? You think you do?"

"I'd take better care of them," he says softly.

I believe him—and that scares me. Max would never use my past in an immature attempt to outwit his brother. But as much as I'd like to take his words at face value, I can't ignore their problematic nature. Because even though Max can't see it, I can: Neither he nor his brother knows how to exist without the other as a benchmark. Despite their efforts to resist their bond, it's there nonetheless—the good, the bad, and the annoying.

"No one gets anywhere with me by diminishing someone else. You want my secrets? Earn them." I give him a sideways glance to emphasize my meaning. "All on your own."

I wish I could see his reaction to the gauntlet I've thrown, but it's more important that we get to our destination without incident. I hear it, though. Boy, do I hear it.

"I'll earn your secrets," he says, his voice serious and steady. "I promise."

It doesn't surprise me that he wants to try. What surprises me is that *I* want him to. Unsettled and on edge, I scramble for something else to talk about. "Why don't we discuss a plan for the presentation? That seems like a productive way to spend the next couple of hours."

He blows out a slow breath and nods. "Good idea." Then he quickly pulls a bag from the back seat and produces a notepad and pen, as though he's just as eager as I am to move on. "So, I'll confess that I didn't have a good grasp on what wedding planners do on a day-to-day basis, but watching you in the past couple of weeks has been eye-opening. I'm thinking an approach that focuses on the different roles you play could be compelling. I mean, apart from making sure the actual wedding day goes off without a hitch, you wear so many hats: vendor intermediary, a location scout, a fashion consultant, a nutritionist, even a family counselor, and I'm sure there's lots more. The trick is that when a couple starts to think about doing all those tasks on their own, it'll sound overwhelming and rightly so. That could be one hook for your branding strategy."

It's gratifying to hear him speak about my work in such complimentary terms. People often assume wedding planners deal with trivial matters, but the weddings I handle involve complex family dynamics, test the strength of relationships, honor cultural customs and traditions, and embrace love and partnerships in all their iterations. It's hardly fluff, and I would side-eye anyone who claimed otherwise. I'm glad to know Max doesn't fall in that camp. "I like where this is headed. I'd like to focus on the practical ways I can help a couple. The types of tasks you can take off your to-do list if you hire me. That's how I came up with the name Dotting the I Do's."

He chuckles. "That name's perfect. In marketing parlance, we'd say that's a great way to build brand recall. The name stands out in a crowd. But keep in mind that if you want your strategy to hit your target audience, you need to address the emotional aspect of wedding planning, too. Case in point, I talked to a few of your references and a common theme that emerged is . . ."

The hesitation in his voice is no surprise. "Let me guess: I'm not as friendly as they'd like me to be."

He takes a deep breath and drops his chin. "Yes, something like that. Let me add, you got stellar reviews across the board, but if there's one place that could use a tiny bit of improvement, it's your perceived approachability."

Ah, there's that word again. The one that reminds me I'm never going to win any congeniality contests. My no-nonsense persona comes at a cost. I know this. Some people read it to mean more than it is. Words like *unrelatable, unapproachable,* and *unlikable* get thrown around. It hurts, but I can't fault people for not seeing what I don't show them. Plus, some will label me with those terms without knowing a single thing about me.

The irony of all this isn't difficult to see: I need to make myself more palatable to counteract the effects of the persona I developed to hide the *less* palatable aspects of my personality. The notion makes my head spin; I mean, it's not only a tongue twister but a mind twister, too.

"I'm sorry," Max says. "It can't be easy to hear that. Please know this is a *marketing* issue, not a *you* issue."

I glance over at him. His eyebrows are drawn together as he doodles on his pad.

"Max, I get it. I'm a professional working in an industry that treats emotions as currency. I don't gush or swoon or squee with my clients. That's just not me. But if the perception that flows from not being touchy-feely is hindering my brand, then I'm willing to address it for the sake of the pitch. I owe it to my family to give it my best shot."

"Your family?" he asks.

I drum my hands against the steering wheel. "Yeah, my family. My mother and aunts helped me start my business. Made a lot of sacrifices before then, too. I don't want to let them down."

"I'm sure that'll never be the case."

I wish I could say the same, but I can't. I let them down once already. "So, I suppose you want to adopt a marketing hook that'll soften my image. Is that the idea?"

He taps his pen against the pad again. "I wouldn't exactly put it that way. See, it's all about adopting a shorthand that will resonate with potential clients. An identity that'll do the emotional work for you. I'm not suggesting we film you running through a field of daisies as wind whips through your hair, but I bet we could put our heads together and settle on a concept we'd both be happy with."

I nod. "Now's as good a time as any, right?"

"Right," he says.

We spend the next hour brainstorming—and rejecting each other's ideas.

"What about 'the Wedding Whisperer'?" he asks.

I cringe, recalling my own nickname when dealing with Natalia. "Feels too hokey to me. Makes me think we're playing into the stereotype of bridezillas who need to be tamed. And what would the logo look like anyway? A silhouette of me putting a bride in a choke hold?"

Max barks out a laugh. "Okay, okay, fair point."

"How about a play on *maid of honor*? 'Planner of Honor'?" I shake my head. "I don't know. I'm so bad at this."

"Don't be discouraged. Trying and discarding ideas is part of the process."

I spy a rest stop ahead and prepare to pull in. "Okay if we take a break? I need to use the restroom."

He drops his pen and pad into his bag. "Of course."

As I'm parking, he abruptly shifts in his seat and snaps his fingers. "I think I've got it. A play on the fairy godmother character. Instead, you're the wedding godmother. You turn ordinary things into the stuff of dreams. Just when things seem hopeless, you sweep in and ensure a magical day. I'd need to massage the verbiage, but I think it could work. The key is that a godmother is that kind, helpful figure in your life. The person who'll be there for you when you need a bit of comfort as things get hectic. It'll make prospective clients envision that you'll be there for them, guiding them every step of the way."

I turn off the engine. "I like it, actually. Just as long as we emphasize that I do way more than pass out glass slippers. Oh, and if we need a tagline, I vote for 'Bibbidi-Bobbidi-Bitch.' A little truth in advertising never hurts, and it has a nice ring to it, don't you think?"

Max just stares at me.

"What's wrong?" I ask.

The corners of his mouth quirk up, then he says, "Who *are* you?"

I exit the car. Before I close the driver's-side door, I bend down and wink at him. "Ah, Max. That's for me to know and for you to find out."

Not to be outdone, he winks right back at me. "You have no idea how much I'm looking forward to the search."

On that note, I shut the door and scramble to the restroom. *Oh my.* This truce may be more than I bargained for.

When I return a few minutes later, Max is sitting in the passenger seat with his eyes closed. I don't want to notice that the skin above his five o'clock shadow is smooth, or that his lips are plump, or that his jaw is strong and bears a small bean-shaped birthmark on the left side, but in a ten-second visual sweep of his profile, it's hard not to. If I'm a little disoriented when I try to fit my key in the ignition, it's only because I've been driving for nearly two hours and the trip's taken a toll on me. And when I turn the key and nothing happens, it must be because I'm hallucinating.

Max turns his head and peeks at me with one eye. "What's wrong?"

"It's not starting. Not even cranking." I peer at the dashboard. "No lights, either."

He sits up and surveys the dashboard, as though *his* set of eyes will help solve a mystery that's already been solved. "Battery's dead."

"No shit, Sherlock."

He points a scolding finger at me. "You're the one who insisted on taking the banana cab for its last hurrah, so don't get snippy with me, woman."

And just like that, the truce is over.

I caress the dash and steering wheel, begging my car to wake up. "Come on, baby. We just need to go a few more miles and then we can get you checked out."

Max groans. "This is ridiculous." He climbs out of the car and whips out his phone.

I climb out as well and stare at him over the roof of the car. "Who are you calling?"

"A tow service. Got a better idea?"

I scrunch my brows at him. "We can just get a jump. I do it all the time."

He lifts his chin and narrows his eyes at me. "I thought you said the car was sound. How many times have you gotten a jump?"

What does it matter? And why is he interrogating me? I shrug. "Three times, maybe? It's really no big deal. Most manufacturers only recommend battery replacement after six or seven jumps."

He puckers his lips in disbelief. "That's not true."

"Well, it should be."

"For someone who plans everything, you're pretty lax about car maintenance."

"Car maintenance requires money, and I'm not rolling around in a bed full of cash, okay? Besides, I *do* maintain this car. I just thought the battery had a few more lives left."

He smacks his forehead. "Okay, never mind. Let's find someone with a working battery."

Hands on his hips, he spins around, searching for a person who can give us a jump. The only problem is, we haven't seen anyone drive past us in the ten minutes we've been parked at this stop.

After a few minutes of waiting in silence, I admit defeat. "I'll call a tow."

He widens his eyes and throws up his hands. "That's a brilliant idea. Why didn't I think of that?"

"Your sarcasm lacks imagination," I say, the phone at my ear. "You need to kick it up several notches."

He rolls his eyes at me. For someone who claims to be inherently low-key, he sure does hit all his high notes around me.

"Just get a tow, okay," he says. "In the meantime, I'll pop the hood and take a look. Make sure there isn't something else going on."

He untucks his blue button-down and unfastens it, slowly revealing the white T-shirt underneath.

My eyes almost pop out of their sockets. "What are you doing?"

The customer representative on the other end of the line clears his throat. "Excuse me?"

Shit. "Sorry," I say into the phone. "I was talking to someone else."

Max cocks his head at me, his eyes flickering with amusement. "I'm not going under that hood without taking this off. I don't want to mess it up."

"I'll do it, then," I whisper. "My shirt's black, so even if I mess it up, no one will be able to tell."

He ignores my offer. "You're making the call. I'm looking under the hood." Then he slips out of the shirt, opens the passenger door, and carefully drapes the shirt on the front seat.

Ugh. It's the return of Hartley the Hottie. I'm entertaining inappropriate thoughts about the man who would have been my brother-in-law, and it's making me crabby. I grimace at the enticing view, compelled to lash out at the person who's suddenly got me rattled. "Why are you just standing there? Will you get under the hood already? Chop, chop."

"I'm going, I'm going," he grumbles. "There's no need to be so rude. Sheesh."

He stomps off, and I find myself peering at his back to see if he's ripped there, too.

Dammit. He is.

———

"Yep, battery's dead," the tow truck operator—"TJ" per his nameplate—tells us. "But you're in luck. I can tow it to my shop, call around for a new battery, and get that sucker in by tomorrow morning."

"Tomorrow morning!" Max and I shout in unison.

TJ takes off his baseball cap and wipes his brow. "Well, yeah. We're not in the District, Dorothy and Toto. There isn't a parts distributor on the next corner. Hell, there are no corners round here. And it *is* a 2002 Volvo."

"We can hire a Lyft," Max says.

TJ laughs. "Good luck with that. This isn't exactly hired car service country, either. Most people have trucks. Or their own cars. Plus, you'll need to get your vehicle in the morning."

This trip will be a total bust if I don't make our appointment, so I'm determined to at least accomplish that. As for the rest, I'll deal with it later. "TJ, we're heading to Surrey Lane Farm. According to Google Maps, it's only 2.7 miles away. Can you take us there before you tow my car to your shop?"

He throws his cap back on. "I'd be happy to."

"Do I get a say in what we do from here?" Max asks. "Considering I'm the one being inconvenienced by your failure to prepare for the high probability of a breakdown?"

I shake my head at him. "Nope. You just used up all your pão de queijo points. Sorry." As I climb into TJ's truck, I hear the unmistakable grumbling sounds of a pissed-off Max behind me. That's music to my petty ears.

Surrey Lane Farm boasts the kinds of pastures and lush fields I'd expect to see in B-roll movie footage. With the Blue Ridge Mountains in the background, the farm's picturesque views are, in a word, breathtaking. My clients, who are planning to renew their vows, spent a weekend here for a couples retreat when they were experiencing problems in their marriage. They feel a sentimental attachment to the place, and now that they've decided to rededicate themselves to their relationship, they'd like to host their celebration where their second chance began.

Max and I are squeezed into the cab of a pickup truck as we tour the acres and acres of land reserved for sustainable farming and raising livestock. Hannah, our guide and the farm's resident event planner, handles the uneven terrain like a pro; my ass, however, is handling it like an amateur. Worse, my thigh and Max's are pressed so tightly together we might as well strap a rope around them and run a three-legged race. Earlier today I made a mental checklist of questions to ask Hannah, but with each bump in the dirt road, my body's tossed against Max's and I can't recall any of them. Each time my soft parts connect with his hard parts, I'm tempted to groan.

Max doesn't appear nearly as affected by our closeness as I am, although every so often he snaps his eyes shut and grits his teeth.

"I'll drive you over to the Starlight Barn," Hannah tells us. "That's a popular spot for receptions, and there's an area next to it where we conduct most of our outdoor ceremonies."

"That would be great," I say.

Judging by Max's knitted brows, *nothing* about this trip could even remotely be described as great. I'm sure he's still annoyed about the car debacle, but it's not as though I engineered the whole thing. "Hey, Hannah, any chance the inn has vacancies tonight?"

She bites her lip apologetically. "Oh dear, not a chance. The inn's completely booked. We're hosting a couples retreat this weekend. Sorry about that."

"Is there another place we could stay until morning?" Max asks. "Somewhere not too far away?"

"Not within an hour from here, no. But we can always put you up in the barn. You'd be surprised how comfortable hay can be."

"I'm sure that's why so many people roll in it," Max says under his breath.

I elbow him in the side. "Quit it."

A particularly brutal bump in the road suddenly sends me careening against Max. Scrambling to soften the impact, I brace one hand against Hannah's headrest and grasp onto Max with the other. Unfortunately, Max's crotch is the body part I inadvertently grab. My body locks into place, as though my traitorous brain knows an opportunity when it feels one. I can't look. I can't move. I can't breathe. Neither can Max apparently, because he's still as a stone, too.

The truck rolls to a stop and Hannah jumps out. "Here we are, folks. I'll give you a few minutes to look around while I check my messages."

Now that the engine's turned off, Max's breathing is audible. And it's labored. For that matter, so's mine.

"Um, Lina, can you unhand me?"

He whispers the question; it's no less embarrassing at a lower decibel.

Slowly, as if a lack of speed will somehow make the movement undetectable, I turn my head to meet Max's questioning gaze. My hand is on his crotch. My. Hand. Is on. His crotch. But I'm incapable of doing anything about it.

"Lina," he repeats sharply, the last vowel ending with a tortured moan.

I gasp, yelp, and unhand him—in that order—and then I scramble to exit the car on the driver's side. From Max's perspective, I'm sure it's just ass and elbows flailing, but at least I manage to get out physically unscathed. Mentally, though, I'm a big ol' mess. If another disaster strikes during the remainder of this trip, I'll know it was cursed from the outset.

Chapter Eighteen

MAX

I already know what I'll be dreaming about tonight: hand jobs. Quick ones, slow ones, surreptitious ones, urgent ones. And because the universe hates me, the featured guest in my subconscious will be Lina's hand. I didn't set out for this to be the case, but here we are.

Stomping after Lina, who's power walking toward the barn, I try to talk myself out of my unruly thoughts: *There's nothing to see here. It was an awkward mistake and nothing more. She doesn't think of you in that way. You shouldn't be thinking of her in that way, either. Remember all the reasons Dean laid out for you? Jot them down on a Post-it and staple that shit to your forehead.*

When I enter the barn, Lina's circling the space, pausing every few feet or so to ask Hannah a question. No one would ever suspect that she had her hand on my crotch only a minute ago. If she can put the episode behind her, so can I. Maybe.

"How many seventy-two-inch round tables can we fit in this area?" she asks Hannah.

"Comfortably?" Hannah says. "Sixteen. We could squeeze in two more, but that wouldn't leave much room for a dance floor."

Lina points up at the roof. "Rainproof?"

"Rain-resistant," Hannah says. "It's metal, and the panels are raised so runoff is good."

"What about gutters?"

"Gutters and leaders replaced just two years ago."

Lina's gaze darts from one end of the barn to the other as she ticks off her mental checklist. Her inspection is systematic and thorough. She even leans against a post to test if it creaks. Hannah takes it all in stride. I bet she knows a professional when she sees one.

"And do you have a liquor license?" Lina asks.

Hannah laughs. "Babette—she's the owner—wouldn't have it any other way."

Lina ambles past me; she doesn't even glance my way. Her uncompromising focus is one of her many strengths, and as I watch her, I try to imagine the marketing copy that would convey this particular benefit of hiring her. I easily picture the visual: Lina attending to her tasks and ignoring two families in formal wedding attire brawling in a working fountain.

"How's the barn powered?" Lina asks. "Generators?"

Oh, right. A wedding needs electricity. I'd be so bad at event planning if someone put me in charge.

"A couple of years ago, we ran power lines out to the barn, so it's on the grid," Hannah says. "What date are the Jensens contemplating?"

"May of next year," Lina says.

"You're in luck, then. We're switching to solar power by the end of March. We'll be able to run everything—lights, heat lamps, A/V equipment—courtesy of the sun."

Lina, plainly pleased with that news, nods enthusiastically. "The Jensens will love that. An environmentally friendly venue would be a huge plus for them."

Hannah checks her watch. "If you don't have any other questions, I'm going to head back to the office before I leave for the day. When you're ready to tour the inn, just head on out there. Someone will be able to show you the common areas, kitchen, and powder rooms."

Lina gives her a polite nod. "Thanks so much, Hannah. You've been incredibly helpful."

When we're alone, I turn to Lina with what I'm sure is awe in my eyes. For people looking to plan a wedding, hiring Lina *should* be a no-brainer. "Confession: Many of those questions wouldn't have occurred to me."

"Wouldn't have occurred to my clients, either," she says. "That's why I include location tours as part of my services." She motions for me to follow her. "Let's head outside. I'd like to snap a few pics of the ceremony area. The website has a photo gallery, but I didn't get any sense of scale."

The area's a swath of grass surrounded by a circular stone path with a mix of pine and oak trees dotting the perimeter. "What if it rains?" I ask her.

"We either move the ceremony inside or rent a tent as our Plan B." She spins to face the inn behind us. "It's nice that the dressing and sleeping areas are so close."

"It'd be nice if we could stay in one of those rooms tonight," I say.

True to form, she ignores me and takes photos with her phone. A few clicks in, it rings. She looks at the screen and breathes a sigh of relief. "It's TJ. I hope he has good news."

I do, too. The possibility that we'd have to spend a night in the barn, even with a dozen comforters and heat lamps, doesn't thrill me, and I have no doubt it would be awkward.

Lina nods as she listens to TJ. "Okay, TJ. That's great. So you'll tow it here at what time?" She smiles at his response. "You're the best. Thanks so much." She ends the call and does a little celebratory dance. "A friend's hooking him up with the new battery, and he'll have it early in the morning. We should be able to get out of here no later than nine-thirty."

That's lots and lots of hours in a barn. With Lina. Alone. "So what's the good news?"

She sticks her tongue out at me. "Goodness, you're a ray of sunshine today. I know this isn't an ideal situation, but I'm try-ing to make the best of it. At least we were close to the farm when the car broke down. We could have been in no-man's-land and that wouldn't have been fun."

Her casual observation sets off a chain of unwelcome thoughts. Imagine if I hadn't joined her? She would have been out here alone. I picture her stuck on the side of the road waiting for someone to give her a jump. *Jesus.* I know she prides herself on being self-sufficient, but she's taking risks with her safety when she travels. I don't like it. Worse, I'm mad at myself for *how much* I don't like it. "That banana cab needs to be put out of its misery. First, it's the battery. Next, it'll be the alternator. Or the engine. If you're going to drive long distances, you should get your car checked out first. We wouldn't be in this mess if you'd done that."

Phone still in hand, she throws her arms over her chest and gives me a no-nonsense stare. "I get it checked out regularly, but I can't predict car problems."

"Then you need to get a better mechanic."

"What is your problem?" she shouts, her eyes narrowed to slits of doom.

The volume of her voice surprises us both, and it only adds fuel to the inferno burning in my chest. I respond in kind, not caring if anyone hears us. "*You. You* are my problem. And I wish to God that wasn't the case."

"Everything okay, friends?" a tall, Black man standing in front of the inn asks. He's wearing chinos, a white collared shirt, and a V-neck sweater complete with a tie. Any minute now, he's going to ask us to please be his neighbor—or have a chat with a miniature trolley.

"We're fine, sir," Lina says, swatting at the hair blowing in her face. "Just a little disagreement about a *minor* inconvenience."

"I wouldn't call it minor," I say, "but I suppose you're free to interpret the situation as you see fit."

Chuckling, the man descends the steps and strides toward us. "Oh boy. You two need to hang out at the inn this weekend."

"We wish," Lina says. "Unfortunately, we don't have a room."

He comes closer, cupping his hand over his mouth as though he's working out a solution in his head. "We always reserve an extra room, in case one of our couples needs a time-out. I wouldn't fork it over for just anyone—everyone's more comfortable when we're the only guests at the inn—but for a couple that obviously needs to join our sessions, I'd certainly consider it." He puts out his hand. "I'm James, by the way."

Lina takes it. "It's nice to meet you, James, but he and I aren't—"

"Too sure about joining your retreat," I say, throwing my arm over Lina's shoulder. "What exactly would that entail?" I can sense Lina's questioning gaze on me, but I'm hoping she'll catch on quickly, because this . . . this is a gift.

"The retreat's already in full swing, but we could bring you up to speed," James says. "We do a few exercises. One exercise is called I Wish and aims to get the couple talking about what's holding back their relationship. We do physical exercises, too. It's fun and challenging. Sometimes it gets heavy, but my wife and I have been doing this for more than a decade, and nothing surprises us anymore."

"How much does it cost?" I ask.

"Four hundred for the entire weekend. Two hundred for today only. Plus the cost of the room usually, but since it's already paid for as part of our agreement with the inn, we could waive that amount. I'd need copies of your driver's licenses and you'd have to sign a nondisclosure agreement promising not to share what you learn about the other couples."

Two hundred dollars not to sleep in a barn overnight? Is there any decision to be made here? "Can you excuse us for a minute? I'd like to speak to my . . . her about the idea?"

James salutes us. "Good thinking, young man. It's always wise to make decisions as a couple when they affect you both."

"Right, right," I say, pulling a dazed Lina away so James won't be able to overhear us.

We find a spot under the canopy of a weeping cherry tree, where Lina spins to face me, whispering her confusion through gritted teeth: "What are you up to, Max?"

"Isn't it obvious? I'm getting us a room. With a bed."

"But we'd need to pretend to be a couple."

"For just one night." I cock my head at her. "How hard could it be?"

"Very hard, I imagine," Lina says, a deep line etched between her brows. "We'd be lying to these folks. They'd be sharing stuff about their personal lives, and we would be eavesdropping. It's wrong."

She has a point, but we're smart people. We can figure out a way not to be around when other people are sharing. "What if we make excuses to miss most of the events? Or when other couples are doing whatever they're supposed to do? If it gets to be too much, we can always skip out and spend the night in the barn. But for the possibility of being in a room, I say we go for it."

Lina chews on her finger as she considers the proposition. "What are we going to do about having only one bed?"

"Easy," I say. "I'll sleep on the floor. Or we can split our time between the bed and the floor. Or put pillows between us. Whatever. And we can share the cost, too."

She bounces on the balls of her feet as she considers what to do. I've never seen her this indecisive. And I'm not above using any weapons at my disposal. "Let me ask you this, because I can't remember if this came up earlier when you were talking to Hannah: Where are the bathrooms in the barn? Oh, and did you happen to bring bug spray?"

Her head snaps back and her eyes go wide. "Shit."

"Exactly," I say with a nod.

In answer, she throws her arms around my neck and gives me a wink. "I'm going to be the best damn girlfriend you've never had."

The hair on the back of my arms stands on end as a shiver runs through me. Yeah. That's exactly what I'm afraid of. But hey, at least we won't be sleeping in a barn tonight.

"It's . . . cozy," Lina says, spinning around and surveying the room. "That has to be a California King. Plenty of room for us to share."

"You think?"

She puckers her lips and nods. "It'll be fine. Much better than a barn floor, that's for sure."

Yes, the bed's big, but Lina's glossing over the obvious: It's a four-poster, complete with a gauzy canopy and silk drapes at each corner. There's no question the bed is the room's main attraction, everything else in it, from the small antique dresser to the plush matching armchairs, serving as accessories for the outfit. If I were working on marketing copy for this room, I'd use words like *sensuous* and *decadent* to describe this bed. Basically, it's not helping an already tension-inducing situation.

Lina hops on the bed, testing its firmness, then she falls onto her back, stretching her arms above her head. *She's* not helping, either.

"It's so big, I can make snow angels," she says, waving her arms up and down across the bedspread. "This is nothing like the twin bed I slept in when I was a kid."

Okay, you know what? She's killing me. On the one hand, that's fucking adorable; on the other, it's torturous. Obviously we need to minimize our time in this room. I plant myself at the foot of the bed and catch her arms on the downswing, pulling her up to a sitting position. "Snow day's over, Lina."

She lets out a surprised *oh*, glances at our joined hands, then jumps off the mattress, nearly toppling me in her rush to put distance between us. I stumble back, but it's Lina who grabs my arms and draws me toward her so I don't fall, and as a result every soft curve along the front of her body is pressed against the hard planes of mine. My apology gets trapped in my throat when I look down at her face and see the flare of awareness in her heavy-lidded gaze. She licks her lips, and my heart gets thrown out of its regular rhythm, pumping fast and then slow and skipping a few beats in between. If she tips her chin up, bringing her mouth closer, I may very well flatline.

A loud, rapid knock on the door drags us out of the moment, and we spring apart like boxers rushing to our respective corners at the end of a round.

"The retreat will be resuming soon, folks," a voice outside the door says. "Be on the field out back in ten minutes."

Her gaze downcast as she riffles through her bag, Lina says, "I'm going to freshen up a bit. Meet you out there?"

I nod even though she's not looking at me. "Yeah. That's a good idea."

And frankly, we need all the good ideas we can get—mostly to counteract the reckless ones swirling in my head.

Chapter Nineteen

LINA

I'm sure I misheard him, so I raise my hand. "Excuse me, James?"

He spins around and gives me a cheerful smile. "Yes, Carolina?"

"I think the heat's gotten me all"—I cross my eyes—"loopy. Did you say we're playing ball? Like basketball? Baseball?"

Before he answers, a large transparent inflatable ball with human legs appears from behind the barn and comes charging toward us. Everyone scrambles out of the way.

"It's the Kool-Aid Man!" someone yells.

"Wanda, quit playing," James shouts, his eyes crinkling with laughter. "We're supposed to be the grown-ups here."

Wanda, James's wife, bumps him and cackles when he stumbles back. James straightens to his full height and looks at me. "To answer your question, Carolina—"

"Lina's fine."

"To answer your question, Lina," James says, "we're playing bumper ball, and all that means is, you're going to be the ball and you're going to do the bumping." He directs his attention to the rest of the couples—there are seven of us in all—and rubs his hands like an evil villain. "The goals are to have fun, let out some aggression, and work as a team. The object of the game is to stay within the orange cones. If you get bumped out of bounds, you're done. The last couple remaining within the cones at any point in the game will be crowned the winner. Simple enough?"

Everyone nods.

"Oh, one more thing," James says. "Your hands must remain in the ball at all times. If you use your hands in any way other than to hold on to the straps on the inside of the ball, you're disqualified."

I turn to Max. "Do you see what you've gotten me into?"

Max gives me a self-satisfied grin. "I know. Isn't it great?"

"All right, folks," Wanda says. "Let's suit up."

This seems like a lot to put us through for the privilege of not sleeping on a barn floor. Especially when I consider that some of these couples aren't smiling and may have missed James's "have fun" part of the speech.

"Okay, what's our strategy?" Max asks.

He's taken off his button-down, so he's returned to Hartley the Hottie status, and I want to bump the shit out of him just for that. If I'm subjected to one more that-was-close moment like the one we just had in the room, a cold shower won't be enough to cool me down.

I see ice baths in my future. Lots and lots of ice baths.

Wanda, who's a sweetie with a wicked streak, was nice enough to give me early access to the T-shirt each participant is supposed to receive at the end of the program. I've paired it with boxers I borrowed from Max. "Let's just run over everyone."

Max purses his lips appreciatively. "That works."

I slip into the shoulder straps, pushing through the momentary bout of claustrophobia that assaults me.

"You okay in there?" Max asks.

I grasp the handles and lean over, so I can see him from the top of the ball. "I'm good. You?"

"Excited. I tried to convince my best friend, Dean, to do this at a local rec center we go to, but he refused."

"Dean sounds like a smart man."

"Yeah, you two would get along well. He's practical, just like you. A little more animated, though, I'd say."

I flutter my eyelashes. "Dean must be the perfect person. Ever consider dating him?"

Before he can respond, James blows a whistle and motions for us to gather around him on the field of play. Because we joined the group late, we don't know the other couples, and they don't know us. I suspect that as the newcomers who didn't show up on time—or so they think—Max and I will be targeted first. On the outside, I'm all polite smiles and chummy camaraderie. On the inside, I'm thinking, *Bring it, suckers.*

I bump Max a bit to get his attention. "Hey. Walk with me over here."

Max follows. "What's up?"

"So now I'm thinking about strategy. Let's split up. Together, we're a bigger target, but if we're separated, we'll attract less attention. We can let the others duke it out until we're the last ones standing."

Max indicates his disagreement by shaking his body, and thus the ball, back and forth. "We should stick together. Show a united front. They're going after us first, but if we present a strong defense, they'll quickly scatter and attack someone else."

I pause. "Wait a minute." I call out to our host. "James, is there a prize for the winning couple?"

"Bragging rights," James yells back.

Max and I look at each other.

"Okay, so the stakes are low," he says. "Why don't we try it your way and see how it goes. If that strategy doesn't work, we'll try it my way. Deal?"

I shake my whole body up and down to indicate my agreement. "Deal."

James blows the whistle, and everyone scatters on the field. I run to a far corner, careful not to stand too close to the perimeter of the game box. Before I can even get my bearings, a muscular guy with very hairy arms clips one of my legs with his own, a move that sends me tottering toward the edge of the field, until I lose my balance and fall over. My legs are dangling because they have no support, and I have no clue how to get up. I'm stuck. Dammit, Max was right: We should have presented a united front.

My teammate finds me writhing on the ground and can't resist teasing me. "If I could reach my phone and take a photo of this, I would. I never imagined I'd see you like this. Never."

That's rich. He's chuckling at my predicament, unaware that he looks almost as ridiculous as I do. "Need I remind you, Max, that you're standing in a big plastic ball?"

He leans over and looks at me from the top of the contraption. "The operative word here is *standing*. Which isn't what you're doing right now. Just so you know, you look like a T. rex that's been tipped over. I'd help but—"

Through the ball, I see Max run away, another player on his heels. He yells over his shoulder, "I'll . . . be . . . back."

I can't help laughing as he tries to wobble across the field. *How is this my life right now?*

In the meantime, I twist back and forth, hoping to get enough momentum to propel me to an upright position. It doesn't work. I'm doing a spot-on impression of what Humpty Dumpty would have looked like if he hadn't cracked after the fall, and I cackle when I imagine what I must look like to everyone else.

With considerable effort, I manage to flip around so I can see the field, my gaze finding Max in the chaos of plastic balls bouncing on the grass. In a jaw-dropping move, he launches himself at Hairy Arms Guy, which forces my nemesis past the orange cones. "Yes!" I yell.

Max dodges and weaves his way back to me, panting like a furry dog who's been out in the sun too long. "I . . . have . . . an . . . idea."

"Well, I'm a captive audience, and I'm all ears."

"Okay, if I sit behind you and we both bend our knees, we can try to use each other as leverage to stand. It won't be pretty, but I think it'll work."

I squint up at him and shift around to avoid the sun's blinding rays. "At this point, I'll try anything."

We do as he suggests, and after several tries—one try having been sabotaged by a woman unsuccessfully seeking retribution on behalf of Hairy Arms Guy—we manage to stand. My sense of triumph is disproportionate to my achievement, but after squirming on the ground for five minutes, I'm glad to be back in the game.

"See?" Max says. "We're better as a team."

Thinking back to our brainstorming session in the car, I'm starting to agree. And though sparring with Max is satisfying in small doses, horsing around with him like we are today is way more fun.

This time, Max bumps me to get my attention. "Okay, let's walk nonchalantly over to that couple and then charge them. We'll knock each and every one of them on their ass. And let's scream when we go after 'em."

I give him a blank look. "Why would we do that?"

"To intimidate them. You know, put them on the defensive. It'll throw them off their game." He leans over so I can see his face. "Plus, it'll *feel* good."

His emphasis on the word *feel* takes me somewhere he probably didn't intend. I can think of dozens of ways to feel good, and all of them involve Max. *Focus, Lina. Focus.* "I'm not so sure yelling's going to win anyone over."

"Who cares about winning them over?" he says, his brows furrowed. "We're trying to beat them. Besides, you'll never see any of these people again. You have nothing to lose."

Well, he's right that I'm unlikely to see any of these people again, so why the hell not? Nothing about this day is panning out the way I expected it to anyway.

I look up and notice four players beyond the cones. That means there are only four couples we need to eliminate. I switch to beast mode. "Okay, Max. Let's do this."

Max and I stumble over to our targets, whistling as if we're simply meandering across the field. When we're within striking distance, he shouts, "One, two, three!" and then we're slamming into everyone.

"You can't defeat us," Max yells.

I shout at our opponents, too. "This is our house, bitches. Ahhhhhhhh!"

Max freezes in place. "Too far, Lina. Too far."

I grimace apologetically. "Sorry."

Two minutes later, my voice is scratchy from all the yelling. Max was right—it *does* feel good to scream with abandon knowing no one's going to look at you askance for doing it. Well, except when you call them bitches.

Now it's down to us and a hippie couple wearing matching Birkenstocks. With socks.

"We got this," Max says. "They're probably high on weed anyway."

I'm mortified that he's made that comment out loud, but I'm laughing so hard my belly's aching.

One of the women says, "Ha. You're right about that, cupcake."

Before we can get out of the way, both women drop to the ground and lean all the way forward, instantly transforming themselves into human bowling balls bouncing and rolling in our direction. When Max and I realize we're the bowling pins, we look at each other in horror through the plastic separating us, but it's too late to do anything about it.

We're out.

Bad news: We won't get the bragging rights we were aiming for.

Good news: I'm having the time of my life.

More bad news: I'm 100 percent positive it's because I'm spending the day with Max.

———————

"Kudos to Lina and Max on a well-played game," James says. "Now that we've gotten any bad energy out of our systems, we're moving on to our next exercise. It's called I Wish You Would,

I Wish You Wouldn't, and it's very simple. One person in each couple is going to share three things they wish their partner would do or would do more of. The other person will share three things they wish their partner *wouldn't* do or would do less of. Partners, there's no need to get defensive. Everyone gets a turn. But the important point is this: The person sharing needs to explain *why* those are your three things so that your partner can try to understand where you're coming from. Additional rule: Your partner's allowed to ask questions to gain that understanding. Make sense?"

We're sitting in a circle of chairs in the inn's living area, a room with heavy brocade drapes, cherrywood furniture pieces, and yellow walls that counteract the darkness of the space. Despite a bathroom and snack break, the group's looking run-down and wary. I can't tell if we're noticeably less enthusiastic about this exercise than we were about bumper ball because we're just tired or because we're not looking forward to the subject matter. It's about to get personal, and I don't envy the couple that goes first.

Wanda claps once. "Okay, friends, who wants to start us off?"

Max shoots his hand up in the air. "I'll go."

My stomach knots as a few people look at me to gauge my reaction. Per usual, I'm wearing a poker face, but in my head, I want to poke *him* in the face. What is he doing? We're not dating, so what could he possibly have to say? And why the hell would he want to make us the guinea pigs for this relationship experiment?

I lean over to whisper in Max's ear. "Why would you want to go first?"

He throws an arm around the back of my chair and whispers his reply: "I'm trying to deal with your concern about hearing other people's personal information. If we go first, we can make our excuses and leave. Plus, we didn't eat lunch, so I'd like to go forage for food."

Oh, okay. I appreciate that he's being mindful of my concerns. Pão de queijo points unlocked. Besides, he'll say a bunch of bullshit that won't matter, I'll do the same, and then we can go off and find some food. *Excellent.*

"Max," Wanda says. "You're up."

"Should I sit or stand?" he asks.

Wanda shrugs. "Whatever's comfortable for you."

"Okay, I'll stand," he says, rising from his seat. "That way, I can give Lina some breathing room."

"Or protect your jewels," Hairy Arms Guy says on a laugh.

His partner smacks him upside the head so I don't have to.

Max blows out a breath and wipes a hand down his face to produce his serious expression. "A little background here. Lina and I haven't been together very long, so a lot of this could just be the newness of the relationship. That's what I tell myself, at least."

Oh, that's good, Max. Way to give the proper context for the made-up stuff you're about to share.

"Anyway," he says, rubbing his hands and pinning me with a clear-eyed gaze that's more serious than the moment warrants. "I wish you would open up to me. I get the sense that you keep yourself closed off from everyone, and I'm not sure why. I want to know what you're thinking, but I almost never do. I mean, do you ever get angry? Like, *really* angry? What makes you sad? What's your worst fear?"

I'm squirming in my seat as I listen to him, but I keep my face impassive. Either Max is speaking from the heart, or he's a skilled actor who knows exactly how to unsettle me. I'm hoping it's a performance; after all, he easily slid into the role of a stranger when we were reunited at the Cartwright a couple of weeks ago. But he looks so earnest. And if this isn't just for show, then he's asking questions that never occurred to any other man in my life, not even Andrew. And dammit, I don't want to get emotional. Not in front of these strangers.

"Lina, would you like to respond to that?" James asks.

It's too soon to tell what's going on here, so I inspect my nails to emphasize my (fake) boredom. "Nope. I'm good for now."

Max nods, then curls and uncurls his fingers as he presses ahead. "Okay, number two. It's related to the first. I wish I knew how you feel about me. As a person. Are you still angry with me? Can we get beyond what happened? Because I want to. I'm not the person I was back then, and I don't think you're the same person you were back then, either."

Shit. I could clobber him. Or hug him. He's using this charade to talk to me. *Truly* talk to me. And I don't know how much I can say without revealing feelings I should probably keep to myself. Max doesn't need to know that I'm attracted to him. Or that he's slowly chipping away at my defenses by trying to get to know the real me. Or that I like the person I am when he's around. But maybe if I answer his precise questions, I can keep those facts from surfacing.

James looks over at me. "Anything to say, Lina?"

I push past the knot in my stomach and take a fortifying breath. "I like you, Max. As a person. A lot. I didn't expect that I would, but I've been doing quite a few things out of character for me these past two weeks, and I'm okay with that. I'm not angry with you. Not anymore. I'd like us to focus on the people we are today and remember the goal we're both working toward."

He purses his lips and sighs. "The pitch. Of course. How could I forget."

He's disappointed in my answer. Is it because he wants me to dig deeper? Reveal more? "No, it's not only about the pitch, Max. Not for me at least." I lean forward. "But why does it matter so much to you? Whether we can move beyond our past?"

"This is good, really good," James says. "You're open to what he's saying. Asking your own questions. Everyone else, take notes."

Max hesitates, his mouth snapping shut then opening again. "Tell me," I say.

"It's related to the third thing I wish you'd do," he replies.

Wanda waves her hand at Max. "Tell us that one more thing, and then we'll hear from Lina."

Oh, no the hell we won't. I need to get out of here. Soon. If I don't, I'll surpass my daily emotional quota, then overheat and pass out.

"Okay," Max says, his gaze never wavering from mine, "this is the last thing, but it's an important one. I wish you would see the potential in us. I know it's hard to see me with new eyes, especially given our history, but there's *something* here. I don't know what it is exactly, but it's strong enough that I don't want to shut the door on it. It's a big ask, I know. And it's complicated. There are probably a dozen reasons why we shouldn't even try. And maybe you can't see yourself being with me. But I want you to know that if there's any chance for us, I'll take it."

One of the Birkenstocks ladies gasps. The other slides down in her seat. I'm afraid to move or blink or respond, but I'm inclined to follow suit. This exercise is tailor-made to push all my buttons, and it's all Max's doing. I should be upset that he's putting me in this position, but if I'm being honest—*totally* honest with myself—it's a liberating exercise. I don't need to curb my feelings here, and I can choose to share as much or as little as I want. Plus, I can't ignore the little flutter I felt in my belly when Max said he wants a chance to be with me. I shouldn't encourage him, not when I can't give him what he's looking for, but Max has put himself out there, and it's only fair that I do the same.

Wanda, probably sensing that I'm feeling vulnerable, speaks to me softly: "Lina, would you like to share your three things? You don't have to if you're not comfortable. We want you to have a turn, but we also want you to do what's best for you."

Looking up at Max, I let out a slow breath and stand. "Sure. I'm up for it."

Okay, Lina. Here goes everything.

Chapter Twenty

MAX

So this is what it's like to have an out-of-body experience, huh? I'm not a fan.

I can't believe I bared my soul in a room full of mostly strangers. If Lina's pissed, I wouldn't blame her. Because the blame in this instance is all mine. She gave me a tiny opening—said her feelings about me weren't only about the pitch—and I took that info and ran right into a fucking wall with it.

After clearing my throat, I slip her a meaningful glance and give her an out. "Um, Lina, didn't you have an important call to return?" I look at my watch. "Right about now? Maybe we should step out and find a quiet place for you to do that."

Lina studies me, her expression giving nothing away. After a few uncomfortably silent seconds, she says, "I forgot to tell you. The call was rescheduled. I don't have anywhere I need to be. I'm completely free."

I plop onto my chair. *Got it.* She's probably plotting my demise. Or she's planning to share an embarrassing fact about me. The cake incident, maybe? And I wouldn't be surprised if she makes up a few unflattering stories. I'd be powerless to defend myself. Frankly, given what I've done here, I deserve all that and more. So I sit and watch her—and wait for what's rightfully coming to me.

Lina's still wearing the couples retreat T-shirt, and she's knotted it on the side so that I can see a sliver of her stomach. It's as if I'm looking at a gift that's been on my wish list and I've finally made the first tear in the wrapping paper covering said gift. Only problem: Lina would deck me if I tore up the rest of her shirt.

She wipes her hands down the fronts of her thighs and clears her throat. "Three things I wish you wouldn't do or would do less of. Okay, here goes. First, I wish you would be less oblivious to what you're asking of me when you say I'm closed off. You want to know if I cry? If I ever get angry? Of course I do. But I need a safe space to do that, and there aren't a lot of those around. I'm a woman, Max. Afro-Latinx, too. Being emotional isn't exactly something I can do freely, not without repercussions."

"Girl, preach," Wanda says.

"A Black woman isn't justifiably upset, she's *angry*. A Latinx person confronts someone, they're fiery or feisty. I don't like raising my voice in public, Max. There's too much baggage associated with it. A woman gets emotional in the workplace, she's *irrational* and not fit for leadership. I was *fired* for being overly emotional in a male-dominated space."

This is real life we're talking about. She's plainly taking this exercise seriously, and there's no way I won't take it seriously, too. And because the urge to ask is overwhelmingly strong, I give in to it despite my reservations. "What happened, Lina? Why were you fired?"

She closes her eyes for a few seconds, opens them, then lifts her chin. "Before I was a wedding planner, I was a paralegal at a prestigious law firm." Her gaze travels over everyone's faces. "I loved that job. I was young, not even three years out of college, and all I wanted to do was prove that I deserved to be there. When I got my first chance assisting a partner during a trial, it was a big deal. Unfortunately, I screwed up. Royally. I numbered the exhibits incorrectly. I don't know if it was exhaustion or what. Anyway, the judge was confused. The partner was confused. *I* was confused. The jury didn't have any exhibits to look at. And all of that would have been fine. The judge would have given us time to correct the exhibits. But I was so overcome with emotion, so disappointed in myself that I cried. And I don't mean the pretty tears you see in movies. I mean the kind of big ugly tears that come with bawling your eyes out. And afterward, I was totally ineffective in fixing my mistake because I was embarrassed. I'm sure it comes as no surprise to anyone that the partner lost confidence in me."

It's hard to picture the version of herself Lina's describing to us, but I don't doubt her story. She's plainly changed since then, though.

"Getting fired isn't the worst thing that can happen to someone," she says. "I *know* this. But getting fired for being an emotional wreck was tough to swallow. Still is. Especially when I think about my mother's strength in difficult times. I *hate* that I couldn't rise to the challenge. Anyway, after that, none of my colleagues really wanted to work with me, so they eventually let me go. And without a glowing recommendation, I struggled to find a new job. My friend, knowing I was feeling down about the situation, asked me to help her plan her wedding, and the rest, as they say, is history. I just don't want to be the person who went through that ever again. So when you ask me to show you more emotions, it's not as easy as you're making it out to be."

Shit. I'm a White man, and I'm embarrassed to realize that none of this would have occurred to me if Lina hadn't forced me to see it. It's a privilege I take for granted—the ability to be *who* I want and say *what* I want no matter the space I'm in. How many times have I watched a male colleague get red in the face because of some perceived slight and stomp around in a conference room because of it? Did I ever look at him with derision? No. But a woman's tears in that same conference room? Yeah, I have to admit they made me uncomfortable. Is that why my mother insists that Andrew and I forget we're her sons when we walk into the office? So she's not viewed as our emotional caretaker? Or as a weak leader? It's hard to say. As for Lina, though, it all makes sense now. Lina's built walls around herself because she needs them. "I'm sorry you went through that. And I want to be a safe space for you. Whether as a friend or . . . something else is obviously up to you."

"That means a lot," she says, giving me a faint smile. "Thank you."

Wanda slaps a sheet of paper on her thigh. "You two are doing exactly what James and I hoped for. Being open. *Communicating.*" She reaches out and grabs Lina's hand. "And I'm proud of you, baby girl. You spoke your truth, and you made him listen. Anything else? If you want to stop there, you can."

Lina sighs. "Yeah, it's been a day, and I'm tired and hungry, so I think I'll wrap this up soon."

I collapse farther into my chair, exhausted for us both. If I could do anything to alleviate the emotional overload she's experiencing, I would.

"Another thing I wish you wouldn't do," Lina says.

I straighten in my seat, my gaze snapping to hers.

She ponders what she's going to say, as though she's trying to formulate a diplomatic way of approaching the subject. "I wish you wouldn't use other people as the yardstick for your own success. Even in the short time I've known you, I can see that you're an incredible person in your own right. Competing with someone else isn't going to help you find what you're searching for. You need to compete with yourself. When you're looking to improve, refer to the last and best thing you did and go from there."

She's talking about Andrew. We both know it. And she's unwittingly stumbled upon the issue that makes me wary of my feelings for her. Does she compare me to Andrew? Does she use him as the yardstick by which she measures *my* worth? I suspect not. Otherwise why would she advise me not to do the very same thing? Still, I'd be lying if I said it isn't a concern. "It isn't easy. I'm dealing with a lifetime of being compared with someone else. But I promise I'll work on that."

"Good," she says.

"Anything else?" Wanda asks.

Lina shakes her head and sits.

I can't deny that I'm disappointed. She ignored the part where I asked her to give us a chance. But what did I expect, exactly? That my brother's former fiancée would admit to being attracted to me? That she'd want to explore the possibility of more between us?

I can't recall any of the reasons Dean said Lina and I wouldn't make sense. But that doesn't matter. Lina's a levelheaded woman and won't entertain my ridiculous fantasies anyway.

LINA

*J*ames announces a fifteen-minute break. Before a single person files out of the room, Max and I pounce on him. Plainly, we've both had enough of this farce.

"We're wiped out—" I say.

"We're hungry—" Max says.

Max and I stop talking and exchange knowing grins.

James rolls his eyes. "Get out of here, you two. You've earned the rest of the evening off." He leans into us and speaks under his breath: "Rumor has it they're setting up a buffet dinner in the kitchen. You might be able to grab something there."

As we race to the sliding doors, James calls after us, "I'll still want your course evaluations in the morning."

"Sure," I say over my shoulder.

"Will do," Max adds, following close behind me.

While everyone else shuffles outside for fresh air, Max and I hoof it to the kitchen, where a man and a woman are covering aluminum chafing dishes with foil.

The man, who's middle-aged, looks up and smiles. "You're a little early, folks. Dinner won't be served for another half hour or so."

Max groans—or maybe that's his stomach. "Any chance we could grab a couple of pieces of bread? Porridge? A slice of cheese? I'm not picky."

The woman laughs. "Well, we can't let any of our guests go hungry, can we?" She hands us large white dinner plates. "We've got lemon pepper brined chicken, a tomato and green bean salad, a sweet potato hash, and warm rolls. You're welcome to start." She looks down the hall leading to the kitchen. "But don't eat in the common areas. I wouldn't want to start a stampede."

"That's very sweet of you," I say. "You're saving me from fainting."

Max and I work together to uncover the foil sheets and serve ourselves. After our plates are filled, we juggle our spoils— utensils, napkins, glasses of lemonade, and heaping plates of food—and tiptoe past the front door.

"Should we go up to the room?" I whisper.

Max nods. "Lead the way."

We settle into the armchairs by the fireplace and wolf the food down.

"Oh my God, this is hitting the spot," I say as I chew. "I'm sorry. I have no manners right now."

Max lifts a leg of chicken with his thumb and forefinger and bites into it like a dog attacking a bone. "S'okay. I'm not the picture of refinement, either."

Minutes later, after we've demolished dinner and taken turns using the hall bathroom, we find ourselves back in the armchairs, unable to resist their plushness.

Max's voice pulls me out of my food coma. "You know, there's no reason we couldn't take a nap on the bed. Unless you don't trust yourself. I mean, I know I'm hot as fuck, but if you can control yourself, we'd enjoy a firm mattress and I wouldn't get a kink in my neck."

I want to side-eye him so hard, but my brain disagrees and forces me to smile instead. "I'm not sure all three of us would fit on the bed."

"Three of us?" he asks.

I open one eye and wink at him. "You, me, and your ego."

He chuckles as he stands, then he offers his hand—which I take despite my reservations—and he pulls me up easily. This was the plan, so why am I suddenly hesitant to share a bed with him? His declaration of interest during the retreat doesn't need to mean anything unless I want it to . . . but maybe I want it to. I need space to think, and I can't do that with Max inches away. I dive for my travel bag as though it's a life jacket that'll save me from drowning. "I'm sweaty and grimy. I think I'll take a shower before everyone else decides to do the same thing."

"Good idea," he says. "I'll take one after you."

Knowing he's going to take a shower after me shouldn't spark dirty thoughts, but nothing's making much sense today, so of course it does. I picture him soaping up his body and stroking himself as puffs of steam swirl around him and water runs down his torso and legs. Squeezing my eyes shut, I try to erase the image in my mind, but it only becomes more vivid, as though I'm peering at it on a computer screen and the pixels are sharpening as the download progresses. *What the hell, brain? Stop it.* "Okay, I won't be long."

Once I'm safely inside the bathroom, I turn on the water and peel off my clothes. To my utter horror, I discover grass stains on one of my favorite pairs of panties, a La Perla limited edition I'd splurged on for the wedding night that never was. I probably should have tossed them years ago, but fuck that—these panties weren't cheap. Hoping I can remove the marks before they set in, I use a trial-size liquid detergent from my emergency kit and scrub them mostly clean, then I let them soak in one of the paper cups meant for guests of the inn. This is the upside of being a planner by nature: I'm always prepared.

Yes, the memory of Max barking at me about my car begs to differ, but whatever. No one's perfect.

I shower and freshen up in minutes, humming as I throw my bra back on—my breasts shall not go unharnessed with Max nearby—and then I search for underwear and Max's oversize retreat T-shirt, which he let me borrow because my own T-shirt is dirty. I find the tee in seconds, but after searching every nook and cranny of my bag for the one article of clothing always on hand, I face the fact that I forgot to pack a spare pair of underwear, at which point I walk to the sink and stare at the only panties I do have: a pair that's soaking wet and balled up in a cup. Channeling Eartha Kitt's Lady Eloise character in *Boomerang,* I look in the mirror and sum up my predicament in a breathy whisper: "I don't have any panties on."

Chapter Twenty-One

LINA

It'll be fine. The T-shirt ends just above the knee so it's not as though I'm going to flash anyone. Still, this isn't an ideal situation: I'm keeping a potentially sexy secret at the precise moment when I shouldn't be thinking about sex at all.

I puff out an encouraging breath and reenter the room.

Max pulls himself out of the armchair, his gaze hovering above my shoulders. "Good shower?"

With the traitorous travel bag hoisted on my shoulder, I tug at the hem of the shirt. "It was great. Really great. Never better. The best shower I've ever had."

He cocks his head, his right eyebrow shooting up. "Wow. That's quite an endorsement."

I'm rotating my head like a ceiling fan as gibberish spews from my mouth. "Yeah, just wait till you try it. So invigorating. Beyond refreshing. You're gonna love it. Gua-ran-teed."

He eyes me curiously. "Hmmm. Can't wait."

I salute him as he walks out the door, his own bag in hand. "Enjoy!"

When he's gone, I groan and fall back onto the bed. I should close my eyes and succumb to this heady mix of anxiousness and exhaustion. And I almost do—until I remember my panties are still in the bathroom.

Soaking in a cup.

And Max is in there, too.

That's when I shake out the blanket at the foot of the bed and throw it over my head. Apparently I don't even need sleep to conjure my nightmares.

A few minutes later, my heart trips when the room's door clicks shut. I slowly press my thighs together, my face still buried under the blanket; this way, I'll avoid Max's gaze and he won't be burned by the flames of embarrassment blazing across my cheeks.

The mattress shifts as he climbs onto the bed, but he remains silent, perhaps assuming I've drifted off to sleep.

"How was the shower?" I ask from under my anti-mortification cloak.

He laughs. "Wasn't sure if you were up." After a pause, he says, "It was decent. Good pressure. Not anything special, though."

"You must be a more discerning shower taker than I am, then."

"Can you breathe under there?" he asks.

I let out a soft laugh, come out from hiding, and turn on my side. *Oh Jesus.* Max is sprawled on top of the bed in the same jeans he was wearing earlier, his dark hair almost inky black now that it's damp. He's changed into a different T-shirt— same style, different color. And his lips are plumper and pinker than usual. A pleasant side effect of a steamy shower, maybe?

Regardless of the reason, he's exuding Big Lick Energy, and I'm into it.

"Sorry about the car," I blurt out, desperately needing to fill the silence with non–sexually related conversation, no matter how inane it is. "You're stuck here because of me, and I feel bad about that."

He turns on his side and peruses my face before he meets my gaze. "I'm not feeling stuck, so no apologies necessary. I do have an apology for you, though."

I lift my head off the pillow and lean on my elbow, raising a brow in surprise. "You do?"

He nods. "Yeah." Sighing, he drops onto his back and closes his eyes.

Taking his cue, I do the same.

"I'm sorry about what went down earlier," he says, his voice a level up from a whisper. "You didn't sign up to have your life dissected like that. I shouldn't have taken advantage of the situation. I can be impulsive from time to time, and the results aren't always pretty."

I snicker, recalling my own uncharacteristically impulsive behavior in the last two weeks. "Max, I pretended not to know you or your brother during a job interview and convinced you to go along with the ruse. I growled at you in a restaurant. I almost drop-kicked you in a capoeira class. I think I've got you beat on impulsiveness this month. Besides, you gave me an out, and I didn't take it, so obviously I wanted to talk about some of that stuff."

He doesn't say anything for a long while, then he asks, "But not all of it, right?"

I open my eyes and stare at the ceiling. He's right. I wasn't ready to discuss all of it. Not with an audience. Here, I can try.

He asked me to see the potential in us, but there isn't any. Max is the exact opposite of his brother in so many ways—and that's why we're incompatible. I don't want someone who makes me weak in the knees. I hate the idea of being with someone who'll poke and prod to get a reaction from me. I'm not interested in thinking about someone way more than I should. All that's happened with Max—and we aren't even dating. Besides, what future could we possibly have together? I can't imagine going to dinner with his parents and staring at my ex-fiancé's face across the table. I'd probably beat him with a baguette.

But maybe, just maybe, Max is the perfect person to have an affair with precisely *because* he's unequivocally the wrong person for me. If I already know Max and I can never build a long-term relationship, wouldn't that prevent me from falling hard?

Would that be unfair to Max, though? Yes—if he's looking for more than I'm willing to give. Part of the problem is, I don't know what he wants.

Before I can ask, he jumps off the bed.

I sit up and scoot to the edge of the mattress, making sure to keep my legs closed. "What's wrong?"

He grabs the hem of his T-shirt and pulls the fabric away from his body, fanning himself, as if it's suddenly too stuffy in the room. "I'm going to head outside. Take some time to enjoy the country air."

Then he reaches for the door handle. I spring off the bed and place my hand on his, preventing him from opening the door.

Max waits, but he doesn't meet my gaze, so I stare at his profile.

"I'm not interested in anything serious," I say, my voice breathier than I intended. "You, me, us. It wouldn't work, Max. Not long-term. There's just too much baggage to sift through."

He raises his head, looking up at the ceiling, and I'm transfixed by the way his Adam's apple bobs in his throat. Finally, he says, "In other words, you're not looking for a commitment."

"Right. But I *am* open to companionship. No promises."

He turns sideways to study me, his head and shoulder resting against the door. "And what if I told you I could live with that?"

I reach up and caress his jaw. Max's eyes shutter closed, then he snuggles into my hand, brushing his lips against it. Warmth gathers in the center of my chest and slowly spreads out like molten lava. My fingers ache to travel over more of his skin, but I force myself to focus on answering his question. "If you can live with that, then I'd tell you my one remaining 'I Wish You Wouldn't.'"

He opens his eyes. "Which is?"

"I wish you wouldn't leave this room."

His lips curve into a half-smile, as if he thinks the wish is promising but wants to reserve judgment until he hears how the rest of this conversation plays out. "Can I tell you more of my wishes, then?"

I'm on my toes, leaning in close but no longer touching him, the heady sensation of anticipation coursing through me all the way to my fingertips. "Tell me."

He straightens and brushes back a lock of my hair that's escaped its ponytail. "I wish I could kiss you. I wish I could touch you. I wish I could . . ." He shakes his head and peers at me. "No, you're not ready."

I immediately press him for more, not caring that it betrays how easily I can be baited. "What else? I can handle whatever you're going to say."

With his teeth digging into his bottom lip, he tilts his head and examines me for evidence that I'm speaking the truth. He's making an obvious effort to appear only faintly interested in the fruits of his inspection, but he's breathing heavily, and his pupils have hijacked his brown eyes, masking their true color. Max is aroused. *Because of me.* I don't even need to hear him say it anymore. Whatever it is, I know I'll want it, too.

"All right, then," he says on a sigh, as though I've finally, regrettably, forced it out of him. "I wish I could make you come so hard you'd cry out loud enough to shatter the windows of this ridiculously charming inn."

I take much-needed air into my lungs, my chest rising and falling with each gulp. That's quite a wish. The possibility that I'd reach that level of abandon worries me, but I can't deny that my hands are now clammy or that I'm purposefully contracting my sex because my need is so strong. If I could be certain it wouldn't frighten him, I'd rip his T-shirt apart, clear down the middle, and run my hands over his chest so I could see his bare muscles flex as nature intended them to. Oh, yeah, and I want specifics. Does he mean to drive me wild with his mouth? His fingers? His cock? All three? Not at the same time, obviously, but in multiple rounds, maybe?

"Have I rendered you speechless?" he asks, interrupting my stream of cocksciousness.

I shake my head. "No, no. It's just that I doubt that's even possible."

His face falls, as though he was hoping for a different, more meaningful answer.

"Still, I'd love to see you try," I add.

He jerks his head up and whispers my name—not Lina but *Carolina*—and then there's a flash of movement that ends with my back pressed against the door and his fingers entwined at the nape of my neck.

"Oh," I say. "You're agile."

"Too much?" he asks, his gaze roving over my face for signs that he's overstepped his bounds.

I grab onto his waist and pull him even closer, *wanting* him to crowd me. "No, just right."

Too right, in fact. It's an impressive start to an encounter I'd secretly prefer to be ho-hum. Because that would simplify this whole mess, wouldn't it? Bad sex is easy to dismiss; good sex is hard to forget.

Slowly and so carefully that I'm unsure of his intentions, he draws back, lifts my chin with his index finger, and pins me with a heavy gaze that makes me think of lazy Sunday mornings, rumpled sheets, and sunlight pouring in through delicate curtains fluttering in the breeze. Unable to wait any longer, I nip at his lower lip, tugging it until he brushes his mouth over mine, back and forth and up and down. He does this more times than I can count, bringing us to the edge but never tipping us over.

Just as I'm about to reach my limit and beg for more, he nudges my mouth open and swirls his tongue with mine, his hands sliding up above my head and caging me in. I don't want this to be good, but damn him, if this preview is any indication, it most certainly will be.

When we finally pull apart, he raises his head, undisguised need burning in his eyes, and then he examines my face for signs of . . . something. If he's looking for a reaction to the kiss, that's not where he'll find it. But if he lowers his gaze a few inches, he'll see the outline of my stiff nipples. And if he trailed a finger down my chest, he'd feel my heart racing. And if he slipped his hands between my thighs, he'd feel the heat there. Yes, this body's on board. My mind, however, is operating a few steps behind. Because there's no coming back from this. Once it's done, it's done. *Please* let it be mediocre. *Please, please, please.*

"What are you thinking?" he asks.

I shift my head and stare past him. "You don't want to know."

He dips his head and plants a single kiss along my jaw. "Tell me."

I shiver at the small contact. Again, damn him. "Honestly, I'm hoping you'll be epically bad at this. I want this to be the worst sex I've ever had. That would solve a mountain of problems."

He lifts his head and raises a brow. "Because then you can walk away easily?"

There's no point in denying it, so I nod. "Yes."

His lips quirk up at the corners. "So what you're saying is, if the sex between us is incredible, you'll be disappointed?"

I bare my teeth sheepishly. "Perverse, right?"

He raises a brow. "Then there's just one thing left for you to do."

"What's that?"

"Prepare to be disappointed."

Chapter Twenty-Two

MAX

Lina's unknowingly issued a challenge, and I intend to meet it. She's hoping for bad sex? Not on my watch. But *how* do I approach the task so that she's incentivized to work with me toward a common goal?

I take a step back and stroke my chin as I study her, searching for an angle custom-made to disarm her. She's still leaning against the door, her chest rising and falling as she waits for me to do or say something. Mentally rewinding through our last few minutes together, I pause at the moment when she initiated our first kiss; the memory gives me an idea that's either brilliant or witless. "I need you to give me a fair shot here, and I think I can help you do that. You see, I'm a lot like a dog. Not in the 'all men are dogs' way you may be thinking, but rather in the sense that I'm eager to please and highly trainable. So, I figure if you tell me how I can screw this up, I'll just do the opposite." I give her the thumbs-up equivalent of jazz hands. "What do you say, friend?"

She works her jaw as she considers my question. "In other words, you're putting the onus on me."

I wave my index finger at her. "No, no, no. I'm making us equal partners in the success of this joint venture."

Chuckling, she drops her chin and squeezes her temples. "You talk too much."

"True. And some people—otherwise known as the royal *me*—would argue that you don't talk enough. So how about it? Help me out here?"

After several beats of silence, she nods. "Okay, we'll do it your way."

I grin. "Which is really your way."

"Shut up, Max."

"Right."

She addresses me as though she's making a presentation, her hands gesturing for emphasis. "Here's what doesn't impress me. When a guy thinks his dick has all the answers. That usually means he'll rush through sex as though penetration is the ultimate goal. It isn't. A guy who doesn't take the time to explore my body is wasting a golden opportunity to bring me the kind of pleasure I'll daydream about for weeks."

"With that in mind, may I approach?" I ask.

She smiles. "You may."

I erase the space between us and slide my hands under her hair, massaging her neck. "How could anyone not want to caress this beautiful skin? It would be a fucking crime."

With her eyes closed, she drops her head back and exposes her neck to me. I trail my lips across her collarbone and up the side of her neck, until I press a soft kiss on her jaw. Her skin smells like an intoxicating combination of peaches and vanilla, and if

I make it out of this room alive, I'll be on the hunt for a dessert that reminds me of this scent.

My hand bunches the fabric of her T-shirt at the waist. "What's under here? Can I see?"

In answer, she lowers her head and slowly pulls up the tee, revealing her silky-smooth thighs. I'm primed to devour her with my eyes, but she hesitates.

"Show me, Lina."

She presses her teeth into the corner of her bottom lip and raises the fabric a couple of inches more. *Fuck me.* She's not wearing any panties, and seeing her bare pussy is more than my already overtaxed heart can handle. "Well, someone's efficient."

She giggles, and it's the sweetest sound I've ever heard. "That wasn't planned. It's a long story."

"It begins with the pair of panties I saw in the bathroom, doesn't it?"

She drops the T-shirt and covers her eyes. "Yes."

"Don't," I say, pulling her arms down. "I wrung them dry and brought them back in here. Didn't want to give any of the guests a heart attack. So now it's our secret, one I wish I'd been in on about a half hour ago. Would you take it off completely?"

"Sure," she says, reaching for the shirt again. In seconds, it's gone, tossed onto the armchair to her right.

My first look at her nearly brings me to my knees. "Lina," I breathe out, unable to say anything profound. With rounded hips and full tits encased in a sheer blue bra, her dark brown nipples erect and her rich brown skin glowing, Lina is everything that could possibly turn me on. My dick presses against the fly of my jeans, and I shift my own hips to alleviate some of the discomfort.

"I like being on display," she says, snapping me out of my trance, "but only when the person I'm with is on display, too. Don't just tell me you want me. *Show* me."

My T-shirt disappears in a flash. Next, I unbutton my jeans and pull the zipper down. Staring at her intently, I tug my pants over my hips, leaving them scrunched at the middle of my thighs, and then I free my erection from the boxers restraining it. It bobs a few times, stiff and high, until it settles in the air, standing at attention and waiting for direction. "Better?"

She nods, her dark eyes glinting with interest. "Much. With that as part of your arsenal, the chances of winning the war are high. Come here so I can touch it."

"Please?" I ask, a hint of a smirk undermining the affronted tone I'm faking.

"Pretty please," she says, as she removes her bra, revealing her heavy breasts.

Distracted by the sight, I step forward—and nearly pitch myself into the wall.

"You'll need to take off your pants first," she says on a laugh.

Grumbling to cover my gaffe, I strip out of my jeans and kick them out of the way.

"Another thing that's sure to make sex unimpressive is a person who doesn't know how to have fun with it," Lina says pointedly. "A bit of good-natured self-deprecation isn't necessarily a bad thing."

Catching her meaning, I lean over and slap the top of my thigh. "You saw that? Me stumbling in my jeans? Hilarious, wasn't it?"

"Get over here, Max," she says, her expression amused.

Enjoying her playfully bossy tone, I don't waste time getting

there, taking one giant step forward and placing my hands on her
hips as my mouth covers hers. We both moan our approval when
our bodies connect again. I'm surrounded by heat and softness
and curves, my new happy place in the flesh. Lina slips a hand
between us and strokes me, her grip sure and firm. I slide my
mouth away, unable to control the hiss that escapes my throat.
This is too much. She's fucking *too much*. I can already predict
that I'll want to do this with her over and over again. Now I
need to ensure she feels the same way by the end of the night.

I bend my knees and look up at her. "I'd like to spend some
time down here." Leaning forward, I breathe her in and lick my
lips. "Any tips before I begin?"

She grips the doorknob for support, her eyes glazing over. "I
don't enjoy it when men jab their tongue in as though they're
poking a bee's nest with a stick. Or when they munch on me
like a crunchy snack they can find at a concession stand. Cunnilingus is an art. It requires imagination and nuance. Oh, and
I love when a person talks dirty to me as they do it—in small
doses, of course, because I'd obviously want you to be focused
on the task at hand."

Does she have any idea that she's talking dirty to me now?
Does she realize what a tempting picture she's making as she
rubs her thighs together in anticipation, her back arched to emphasize her swollen breasts? If I can give her even half the pleasure she's giving me simply by standing here, the windows in
this room *will* shatter.

I tap her right leg. "Put this over my shoulder. Grab onto my
hair if you need to. I like that a lot."

She doesn't let go of the doorknob, as though it's her security
against collapsing, but she does swing her leg over my shoulder

and grip the back of my head. I bury my face between her thighs and lick her folds, groaning at the hint of wetness I find there.

"Oh God," she moans. "Yes, Max. Just like that."

I lift my head and look up at her. "Tell me what your pussy needs, baby. Whatever it is, I'll do it."

"My clit," she whispers. "I need you to suck on it. Scrape it with your teeth."

And so I do. Settling into an unhurried rhythm, I slide the flat of my tongue inside and lap at her with short and long strokes, then I roll my lips across her clit and suck it gently, my fingers separating her flesh so I can get where I need to be.

Minutes later, her grip on my head falters, but she rights herself, and grasps the back of my head even harder, her hips rolling in time to the slip and slide of my tongue. "Oh, I can't . . . it's . . . I need to . . . it feels so good, Max."

I can hear her voice rising with each word. In a perfect world, she'd tell me if she was close, because I refuse to leave this slice of heaven I've stumbled upon without good cause. Deciding to test her readiness using some of that imagination she asked for, I scrape my teeth against her clit and simultaneously slip two fingers inside her. She cries out as she detonates, her body shaking as if she's exploding from the center outward and her hand banging against the doorknob until her hold on it slips.

As she blinks herself back to consciousness, I wipe my mouth and sit on my heels to enjoy the view. She looks languid and disheveled, the band around her ponytail dangling at the ends of her hair and a sheen of sweat kissing the skin of her belly and thighs.

I could stare at her in this state all day, but not even ten seconds after she trembled under my tongue, someone knocks on the door.

"The kitchen's closing down soon, folks, but in the meantime you're welcome to join us for a nightcap in the parlor if you're free."

Wide-eyed, Lina snorts, then she slaps a hand on her mouth when she realizes her voice may carry beyond the room.

"Thanks for the invitation," I call out, "but I think we're staying in for the night."

Lina bends a little and wrinkles her nose at me. "Who needs a nightcap when you can have a night-come."

She was irresistible before, but discovering she has a wicked sense of humor and perfect comedic timing seals my fate: This woman's perfect for me. And that can only mean trouble. Pure, unadulterated, non–genetically modified trouble. But right now? I couldn't care less.

Chapter Twenty-Three

LINA

So far, Max is doing a superb job of disappointing me. I should have known he wouldn't cooperate. For that matter, my body won't cooperate, either. It thinks Max is a *very good boy*, indeed. And who could blame it, really? I told Max cunnilingus is an art, and he took it upon himself to create a masterpiece worthy of its own wing in the Louvre.

Damn him to a world with no cake in it.

The man who'll star in my daydreams for the next few weeks rises to his full height, his thick penis pointing to the ceiling. When he moves, more muscles than I thought any single human could possess activate and flex in rapid succession, the way I imagine the gears of a manual clock work together to mark the passage of time. It's fascinating—and disorienting.

I'm aware there's still an opportunity for him to screw up, but the odds are not in my favor, and as he's already pointed out, I'm just as responsible for the success of this endeavor as he is.

"Tell me something," he says. "Do you have a grudge against the bed?"

"Not at all," I say, lifting a brow. "Why do you ask?"

"Because I'm starting to wonder if your back's going to fuse with the door."

I push off said door, my cheeks warming under his amused scrutiny. I glance at the bed, its intricately detailed headboard and elegant drapery beckoning me. The bed's so . . . intimate. It will eventually lead to sleep, maybe even cuddling if we're feeling adventurous. And sleep leads to morning afters. Which are often filled with regrets and *oh-shit-what-the-fuck-did-I-do*'s. But thinking I can put all that off is silly, and I'm glad Max called me on it.

Just enjoy the moment and worry about everything else later.

I shake my head. "I've got no problem with the bed." To prove it, I glide past him, pull back the coverlet, and crawl onto the mattress. Lying on my side with an elbow on the bed and my chin in my hand, I ask, "Now, where were we?"

He slides in as well and lies on his side. "You were going to instruct me on the finer points of bringing you pleasure."

His statement doesn't sit well with me. Everything's not about me, and it's selfish to focus on my needs only, especially considering how attuned he's been to mine. "Let's flip the script and talk about what *you* like."

He pauses, his expression thoughtful, and then he scrunches his face. "You sure you won't judge me too harshly?"

"If it warrants my judgment, then it can never be too harsh."

Groaning, he rolls his eyes. "Fine. I'll risk it. Okay, let's just say I'm not a fan of possum sex."

I gawk at him. "Possum sex? What the hell is that? Don't tell me you're a shape-shifter."

He laughs. "No, possum sex is when a woman just lies in the bed, still as a statue, or as I like to think of it, when she plays dead like a possum. It's disturbing as fuck. Now, don't get me wrong, I'm not a total asshole. If someone's physically unable to ride me like a rodeo star, I'd understand. But barring that, I enjoy a little participation on the part of the person I'm having sex with."

My shoulders shake as I imagine what possum sex looks like. When I recover, I offer an alternative explanation. "Are you sure it wasn't a kink and you didn't know it?"

"If it was, I didn't sign up for it," he says.

"Or maybe you just weren't all that exciting. That's a possibility, too."

"You're heartless, and I'm not going to treat you with kid gloves just because your pussy's amazing." He casually sits up, and before I can guess his intentions, he grabs a pillow and socks me in the face with it.

I yelp in surprise as I scramble to my knees, and then I'm brandishing my own pillow, ready to strike, until someone knocks on the door—yet again.

"Everything okay in there?" the voice asks.

"I think it's James," Max whispers. Then he calls out, "We're fine."

"Just having a pillow fight," I explain in an overly loud voice.

"Okay, well, I think a few people are getting ready to retire for the night," James says.

"We'll be quieter," I say. "We promise."

Max slips from the bed and reaches for his jeans, fishing inside a back pocket. He returns with a few condom packets.

I gaze at him knowingly, my lips pursed in an "of course you did, you cocky son of a bitch" expression. "Just happened to have those handy, huh?"

He purses his lips, pretending to be insulted by my question. "Actually, I didn't. Found them in the bathroom medicine cabinet. Went rummaging on the off chance this would happen."

"Did you check the expiration date?"

"Yep."

"Give me one, please."

He moves on his knees to the center of the bed and offers one to me, his hand shaking slightly as he waits for me to take it. I don't want him to be nervous about this, but I wonder if all my sex talk—designed to help me build my own bravado—has put unnecessary pressure on him. If so, I want to correct that. I knee-walk to him and set the condom on the bed. Placing one hand on his shoulder, I lean in to kiss his chest, then his Adam's apple, then his jaw. When I straighten, I give him a penetrating stare. "It's been incredible so far, and I truly believe there's no way we're going to mess this up." I press a soft kiss to his lips and reach between us, stroking his cock slowly. "I just want us to make each other feel good."

He shudders against me, his lids falling to half-mast. "Ahh, Lina. I think we can check that off the to-do list already."

"Not yet," I say, nudging his shoulder and motioning for him to lie down.

Max sits on his heels, then slides his legs in front of him and falls onto his back. I look over his smooth skin, his broad shoulders, his stiff erection—all of that's waiting for me, and it's alarming how much I'm looking forward to this.

"Lina, I need you," he grounds out, his voice crackling like pebbles are churning in his throat.

The longing in his voice feeds my own hunger, powering it to another level and threatening to wipe out the grid. My nipples are puckered nearly to the point of pain, and I can feel the wetness at the apex of my thighs. I straddle him quickly, reaching for the protection with fumbling fingers and sighing in frustration when the packet doesn't open easily. Max kneads my breasts, tweaking the nipples with light, torturous flicks, while I wrestle with the condom packet that refuses to give. I finally manage to pry the resilient fucker open and slip a finger inside.

My eyes go wide and my stomach drops. "It's empty."

Max lifts his head off the bed. "What the hell? Let me get another one."

I study the packet and snort. "Don't bother. These are gag condoms, Max. The name's Nojans. The label says, *For the person who won't be getting any tonight.*"

Max's face flushes to a lovely shade of *Mean Girls* pink before he throws the pillow over his head, then he thinks better of it and peeks out. "Admit it, this *is* the worst sex you've ever had."

I shove the pillow away. "Not the worst, but certainly the most memorable." I climb off him and shift to the side, taking his thick shaft in my hand. Before I take him in my mouth, I say, "But don't worry. The best is yet to come."

Chapter Twenty-Four

LINA

Max's side of the bed is empty when I wake up. I stare at the ceiling and wait for the *oh-shit-what-the-fuck-did-I-do*'s to rattle inside my brain, but they're nowhere to be found. It's easy to figure out why. Andrew is my past. Max is my present. Besides, Max and I aren't interested in building a future together. We were both blindsided by our mutual attraction, and now we're just enjoying it for what it is. Neither of us has any reason to feel guilty, and there's no need to worry about the long-term consequences because there won't be any.

I snuggle into the coverlet, wanting to enjoy the peace and quiet a few minutes more. But seconds after closing my eyes, Max bursts through the door, his reusable travel mug in his hands. "Rise and shine and drink coffee, sweetheart. It's time to get on the road."

I sit up and smooth my curls down. "But we don't have a car yet."

He stands by the side of the bed, places the mug on the night-stand, and leans in for a soft kiss. As he pulls away, he takes my bottom lip with him, forcing me to get on my knees to prolong the sweet greeting. "TJ dropped your car off early. The bill's paid—I figure we can settle up later—and we're now free to go. It's Easter Sunday, so I need to get back to Vienna for an early dinner with the family."

"Oh shoot, I do, too," I say, climbing out of the bed and wrapping my hands around the travel mug. "I'm already going to get an earful about missing church." I take a few sips, the liquid warming my belly like comfort food. "I'll just throw on a fresh top and yesterday's jeans and we can be on our way."

"And maybe you should brush your teeth," Max says as he packs up his fancy phone charger.

I stare at his back until he turns his head and glances at me with a wicked grin. Grumbling, I chuck a pillow at his head. "I'll go freshen up."

He catches me at the door and wraps me in an embrace from behind. "I have a suggestion."

"What?" I ask, angling my head so he can press his lips against my neck.

"Why don't you stay in your T-shirt? It's long enough and it's actually cute. No one would ever know it wasn't meant to be worn in public. And it'll allow me to enjoy the sight of your fine-ass thighs on the drive home."

I playfully shake him off me. "I'll think about it as I *brush my teeth*."

In the bathroom, I decide his idea isn't a bad one and add a thin belt to the T-shirt so I can pretend it's a trendy outfit. It doesn't work, but if it means Max will be able to slip his hands between my thighs in the car, I'll suffer through this fashion crime. As I brush my teeth, I marvel at how easy we are together this morning. There's no awkwardness at all, and I attribute that to our being honest about our intentions.

When I reenter the room, Max is sitting in the armchair, a hardcover book and a sheet of paper balanced on his lap. "Don't forget to fill out the retreat evaluation. James is standing at the front door making sure anyone leaving early turns it in before they go."

I grab my evaluation off the dresser, plop onto the armchair next to Max, and read the first question. "'Did the retreat help bring you and your partner closer together?' Hmm. Considering we were minutes away from clobbering each other and ended up giving each other mind-blowing orgasms, I'm going to check yes."

Max chuckles as he scribbles intensely. "What a coincidence. I wrote the exact same thing in the comments section."

"You did not," I say, leaning over to read his paper.

He lifts the sheet and slaps it against his chest. "These are private, ma'am. Mind your own evaluation."

I roll my eyes and finish answering the questions.

When we're both done, we gather our belongings and prepare to go. I give the room a last, wistful glance before I close the door behind me. We take a quick detour through the kitchen to grab a few muffins for our road trip, then we meet James in the foyer. He puts out his hand. The evaluations are his top priority.

"Well, friends," he says with a smile, "it's been a pleasure getting to know you. I wish we could have spent a bit more time together, but I think you two got what you needed out of this experience."

I wink at Max and his mouth twitches.

"We certainly did," Max says.

James leans in between us. "I'll confess that in the years Wanda and I have been doing this, we rarely see new couples be so open with each other. It tells me that you two have the foundation to really make your relationship work." He points at Max's heart, then mine. "The tools are there. Now all you need to do is use them. Remember, communication is everything."

The first pangs of genuine guilt hit me. James is such a sweet man, and I hate that we lied to him about our relationship just to get a more comfortable stay. It's true, however, that Max and I experienced a breakthrough yesterday, and this knowledge soothes the sting of remorse lodged in my chest. I pull out a card from my bag and hand it to James. "Listen, if you and Wanda are ever in DC, look me up. I'd love to take you to lunch sometime."

James studies the card. "Will do. We only make it up there for special occasions, but Wanda's always harassing me about seeing a performance at the Kennedy Center. Maybe we can make a day of it."

I nod. "That'd be great. I can recommend a few places for dinner, too."

Max grabs my hand, raises it in front of me, and sweeps his mouth across my knuckles. "Baby, we need to get going. We've got a long trip ahead of us, and I want to take one last drive out past the flower fields."

My momentary shock at the casual way he kissed my hand is eclipsed by my confusion. He wants to tour the farm again? This is news to me.

"Well, don't let me keep you," James says. "It's a perfect day to be out there. If you drive out past where they grow heirlooms, you won't see another soul for hours. An excellent place for a morning picnic."

"Yeah," Max says. "Hannah mentioned yesterday that it's a great location for photos. Figured Lina would want to see that, too."

She did? When did she say that?

James raises a chin at Max. "Riiiight." He tips an imaginary hat at us. "Enjoy and get home safely."

Outside, I circle the car and inspect it with a mother's touch. "My baby's all right."

"For now," Max says under his breath.

"And TJ cleaned it, too."

He stares at the car, plainly unimpressed. "It needs all the help it can get."

"Okay, you know what," I say, pointing a finger at him, "this car is getting you home, so you may want to treat it with kindness."

He shakes his head at me, his lips curled in feigned disgust, but before he climbs into the car, I hear him whisper, "Sorry, banana cab."

Once I'm settled, I start the engine and place my hands on the steering wheel. "Okay, how do we get to this magical place you mentioned?"

He points at a fork in the dirt road; both paths are hugged by rows of trees spaced closely together. "Head out that way, and don't veer off. If we follow the road, we won't get lost."

"Got it." I let the driver's-side window down a bit—enough to listen to the early morning sounds on the farm but not enough to jack up my hair. I expect to hear a horse's neigh or an occasional cow moo, but I mostly hear birds chirping and heavy machinery churning in the distance. The sun is shining brightly, its rays casting a golden glow across the hayfields. "Beautiful out here, isn't it?"

Max nods slowly. "We couldn't have asked for a better day."

After a minute of travel, the fence surrounding the farm's livestock ends and the land blends into a mix of grass and trees followed by several fields, each with its own sign indicating the type of vegetable grown there. "You sure we're going in the right direction?"

The corners of Max's mouth quirk up. "I'm not sure, but with all this outside my window, who cares where we end up."

"Well, I—"

Before I can tell him *I* care, the scene that comes into view robs me of the ability to put even an ounce of snippiness into the world. "Oh my God, will you look at that." Rows and rows of tulips—yellow, red, and bright pink ones—blanket the land as far as I can see. "Can we stop?"

"I was hoping we would," Max says, his eyes soft as he takes in my reaction.

I park the car in a small clearing, and we jump out. I rush ahead of Max, running through the narrow paths between the rows as I let my fingers kiss the petals. I feel like a kid without a care, and I wish I could stay in this hidden corner of the world forever.

Max snaps a picture of me with his phone, and we turn it into a silly photo shoot, complete with goofy faces and clichéd poses. When we're done, I run ahead of him again, this time in the car's direction, but he quickly catches up to me and takes my hand, slowing us down to a leisurely walk.

"This is what you wanted me to see?" I ask.

"Yeah. Saw it in a customer review and thought you'd love it."

"I do," I say, resting my head on his shoulder. "Thank you."

He puts an arm around me and buries his nose in my hair. "You're welcome."

We're doing what couples do, aren't we? Well, couples in sappy movies, that is. Running through flower fields. Taking silly pics together. Strolling hand in hand. This isn't supposed to be us, but somehow it is. Obviously we need a course correction.

I pull out of his embrace. "Time to head back." Striding with purpose, I reach the car in no time.

Max tugs on my hand and stops me before I can slip inside. "Hang on a minute and turn around. This is your last shot to appreciate this view."

With my shoulders stooped, I relent and turn around. He studies my face as I gaze at the field, then he tugs me toward the hood of the car. "Sit. Relax. Enjoy."

I sigh, as if appreciating nature is off-putting. Chuckling and shaking his head, Max lifts me in his arms and gently deposits me on the hood.

"Kiss me," he says, his eyes glittering with seduction-on-the-brain fairy dust.

I shouldn't, even though I want to. Then again, wouldn't this be a course correction of sorts? Whatever happens here will remind us both that this is mostly sex with a side of tentative friendship. Armed with watertight reasoning, I raise the hem of my T-shirt—ah, so *that's* why he made the suggestion—and open my legs wide enough to make a space for him, which he fills easily, the palms of his hands resting on the outsides of my thighs. I slip my hands around his neck and pull him close, angling my head before our mouths meet.

This kiss is different. Harder. Messier. What it lacks in finesse it makes up for in enthusiasm. We're focused on results rather than execution, as though we want to crawl inside each other and the kiss is the gateway that will allow us to enter. A rumble builds in Max's chest and escapes his throat when I draw his hand between my thighs.

"Touch me," I manage to say between my own efforts to breathe in his scent and rub my nose against his cheeks and jaw.

"Fuck, Lina, you're . . . so . . . hot here," he says.

His voice is hoarse and uneven, but his fingers are certain as he swiftly pushes my panties to the side and slips two digits inside me.

"Oh, yes, that's it," I say. Unable to keep my head up, I throw it back, widening my legs even farther.

He strokes me over and over, his thumb feathering over my clit in an agonizing two-step that provides no relief. Desperate for release, I pull up and dig my fingers into his shoulders, riding his hand so I can chase the sensation of his thumb sweeping across my nub. I drop my head into the crook of his neck as I undulate against the hood of the car.

"I want to fuck you," he whispers. "Would you like that?"

"If only," I say on a sigh. "As soon as we get back, I'm getting us a bunker's worth of condoms."

He taps me on the shoulder, at which point I lift my head and see a foil packet—a real condom package—in his hand. I snatch it away and study it as though it's a new life-form.

"Where'd you get this?" I ask.

Max smirks. "The guy with the hairy arms? In our group? He hooked me up."

"Hairy Arms Guy came through for us," I shout. "Woot!"

I rip the packet open as Max unzips his jeans and tugs them down his thighs. Then I lift my ass so he can pull my panties off.

"Come closer," I say. "I'll put it on."

I scoot to the edge of the hood and sheathe him, my gaze never wavering from his. "Ready?"

He nips at my lip. "So ready I might spontaneously combust in frustration."

My hand dips between us as I center him at the entrance to my core. "We can't have that, can we?"

"No, we—"

He goes still as I take him inside me. "Fuck, Lina. I just . . . fuck . . . that's . . . I . . . *fuck*."

I stretch around him, slowly taking his cock inch by inch. The fullness is intoxicating, dulling my senses of sight, hearing, touch, taste, and smell while sharpening a new one: my sense of Max. If a bomb went off a foot away, I probably wouldn't notice. But if Max blinks, I'll know it without even having to see it. "So good," I mumble.

Max jolts, as if I've shocked him back into consciousness, wraps my legs around him, and slams his hands on the hood. He pumps into me slowly, testing the friction and studying my response. "How's that? Feel good?"

I squeeze my eyes shut so I can focus on formulating the right words. How do I explain that he fits me perfectly? That I want to do this with him every day for the foreseeable future? That my mouth is dry, and my breasts are heavy and aching, and my head might pop off because it's both too much and not enough all at once? I can't say any of that. *Nope, nope, nope.* So I say, "That's good. Really good." Then I open my eyes and catch his satisfied smile, and his expression nudges me to add, "It's so fucking tight I might burst."

"That's the goal," he says on a chuckle, and then his eyes grow serious, hooded with desire. "And this?" He pumps faster, each time grinding into my pelvis before he withdraws.

Slack-jawed, I clutch the back of his T-shirt, seeking leverage to meet him thrust for thrust. Max has other plans, though, and gently lowers me so my back rests on the hood. He scoops my ass and pulls me forward. I'm teetering on the edge of the hood, but the position allows him to press his chest onto mine and brings our faces within centimeters of each other. I shudder and close my eyes.

"Open them, baby," he says. "Please."

I don't want to. I really don't. I'm already overwhelmed by him. Staring into his eyes as he brings me this much pleasure will do something to me I'm unprepared for. I don't know what exactly, but I *know* it will. And it'll be irreversible.

"Lina, don't let me do this alone," he says hoarsely.

I don't know what "this" is, but the longing in his voice can't be ignored, so I open my eyes and meet his lust-filled gaze.

"There you are," he says.

He clasps my hands and squeezes them tightly. The tingling between my legs jumps tracks, rerouting to my heart, which is beating so rapidly Max might need to perform chest compressions on me before we're through. *No, no, no.* I shake myself loose, preferring to grab his ass instead. And that small adjustment does something to *him*.

"Fuck, Lina," he grounds out. "Yes." He lifts his torso and drags his hand between us, placing two fingers on my clitoris and rubbing in expertly targeted circles.

The need to release this unspent tension causes me to buck against him. I'll do anything to come. *Anything.* "Max . . . I'm almost there. I—"

I stiffen against him. He stills, too. And then he spasms above me, an incoherent stream of cussing and *oh, Jesus* filling the serene spring air. Despite his frenzied state, he doesn't forget me. "I want you to come so badly," he says. With a gaze that's fierce with determination, he moves his fingers in one gloriously slow circle and I fly apart, writhing underneath him and screaming like the fox that lived in the woods behind our house when I was a kid. If someone hears my cry, they'll think Max is murdering me. It's a distressing sound, not at all pleasant to the ear, and truly, irredeemably mortifying. But as the last of the tremors leaves my body, I know this: It was totally worth it.

Max wraps a lock of my hair around his finger and bends over to press his lips to mine. He doesn't move to lick his way inside. It's just one long meeting of our mouths. A period at the end of this lovely sentence. I should be calming down now. Instead, my heart is ratcheting up. I squirm underneath him, my gaze locked on the sky.

I can sense him staring at me, but I can't return the favor.

Finally, he pushes off the car and slips out. There's some rustling, and then I hear him zip up his jeans. Without a word, he tugs my T-shirt down and pulls me to a sitting position. I can't *not* look at him any longer. That would be rude.

He nibbles on his bottom lip as he studies me. Then he raps the hood of the car. "Forget I ever said anything unkind about old banana cab here. She *and* you just helped me scratch off the first item on my bucket list." He pecks me on the forehead and gives me a handkerchief. "Thank you."

It's the right thing to say to someone who's plainly having a tough time putting what we just did in proper perspective. But it *feels* wrong—and that's a problem.

Chapter Twenty-Five

MAX

I wake up groggy and disoriented. *Where the hell am I?* I open an eye and spy a dashboard. Oh, yeah. The banana cab is now the silence cab.

It's true that sex with Lina depleted my reserves so thoroughly that I would have fallen asleep anyway, but I dozed off within minutes of climbing into the car because it was clear from Lina's lack of engagement that she wanted me to.

If she needs space, she'll get it.

And if she's worrying about us, she's not alone. This weekend has been more intense than either of us could have predicted. But we're returning to DC soon, and the normalcy of everyday life will help us reestablish the casual relationship we've agreed to. If I know Lina, and I think I'm starting to, focusing on work will alleviate some of her distress and give her the confidence that we can handle a no-strings, no-future arrangement.

I sit up and readjust the seatbelt across my chest. "Sorry I fell asleep on you. You stole my mojo." *Dammit. How is that focusing on work, Max?*

A smile tugs at her lips nonetheless. "Totally okay and totally understandable. Some people have more stamina than others." She purses her lips in an obvious effort to suppress a smile.

Do not engage. You'll take it one step too far, and she'll go quiet again. I pull up the note app on my phone and clear my throat. "So let's discuss any specific ideas or concepts you have. On the ride here, we were both on board with the wedding-godmother theme. Any thoughts about the scenarios where we could explore that theme?"

She sits up straighter, her face brightening with excitement.

This woman's such a fucking cutie. If I'm not careful, I'll want to be around her all the time.

"I like the idea of being the calm among the chaos," she says. "I envision images showing mini-catastrophes with me at the center sorting it out. When clients hire me, they're concerned that mayhem will ensue without my services. I think it would be smart to convey that."

It's not a bad idea, but there's a flaw she hasn't considered, and spotting the issue is why I'm here. "You're used to working with various vendors at different venues and the like. But with the Cartwright, the hotel is your main vendor. It's supplying the location, the catering, the guest rooms, even the table settings, and more. I don't think Rebecca would appreciate the suggestion that her hotel is likely to be the center of chaos, even if her master wedding coordinator will ultimately save the day."

"Hmm," she says. "I see what you mean. Let me give it some

more thought, then." She grumbles playfully. "Some people just have to show off and expertly expert."

I crack a smile even though I'm trying to be all business. "We don't need to figure it out today. What about the hotel amenities?"

"What about them?" she asks.

"Have you tried them? A hotel suite? The restaurant? The spa where members of the wedding party might go for a day of pampering before a wedding?"

"I visited the restaurant last week," she says. "For lunch. I need to go back for dinner. And Rebecca said she'd arrange for me to tour the available accommodations at my convenience. I think I want to propose that the hotel knock down the walls between two rooms and create a dedicated wedding suite. Probably more than one. It'll solidify the hotel's brand as a wedding venue."

I nod as I start typing again. "You're right about that. We could add it to the wish list. We're clearly not going to have dedicated rooms before the presentation, but I think it would be smart to float the idea as part of your vision. I could go with you, by the way."

I can see a hint of a furrowed brow in her profile. Apparently I didn't slip in that suggestion smoothly enough.

"Go where?" she asks.

"Blossom," I say. "The hotel restaurant. For dinner. I mean, we should be able to enjoy a meal together from time to time, right?"

"Uh, sure. That would be nice." After a few beats of silence, she asks, "Do you enjoy what you do?"

The question comes out of nowhere, and I jerk my head up in surprise. I'm not sure if she's uncomfortable with the notion of going to dinner with me or if she's generally curious about my professional aspirations. Could be both.

She rushes to explain before I can answer: "It's just that Rebecca asked me this recently, and I realized how often people can be competent and even great at their jobs without having a passion for them."

"There are many aspects I love," I tell her. "Learning about the client's business. Researching the market. Devising a marketing strategy to achieve the client's goals. I like that my profession's currency is one part ideas and one part data. It feeds both my creative side and the part of me that needs to see results."

"So what are the aspects you *don't* love?" she asks.

"The ass-kissing," I say quickly. "Tons and tons of ass-kissing. The schmoozing. Plus, sometimes our clients have shitty businesses or fundamentally fucked-up strategies, and no amount of marketing is going to help them sell a shitty idea."

She nods thoughtfully. "What's it like working with your mother?"

I swing my head in her direction, my face deadpan. "A challenge. She's a good boss, but she has a hard time accepting that Andrew and I can't meld into a single, perfect human being. I'm trying to break out of the bubble wrapped around us, but my mother thinks everything's working out as it should."

"The assignment with Rebecca," she observes. "That's your opportunity to show what you can do on your own, I take it."

Exactly. I don't need to explain why I want to disentangle myself from Andrew. She gets it. "You're absolutely right. If I can impress Rebecca, then maybe she'll ask me to be the lead manager on the account."

She glances at me and returns her eyes to the road. "That's *if* you impress her more than Andrew impresses her, you mean."

"Well, yeah. It's kind of unavoidable. But think of it this way: By working with me, you're necessarily sticking it to Andrew."

Her brows knit in confusion. "That's never been my goal, though. That's yours."

I shrug. "Not a goal. Just a by-product."

"My bullshit meter says otherwise."

Damn. I thought she understood. Apparently not. This is the problem with being inextricably linked with Andrew: Even when I'm trying to escape living in his shadow for my own good, I get pulled back into competition with him. It's not my fault that my success necessarily requires him to fail. Knowing this conversation may not end well, I feign a big yawn, opening my mouth wide and stretching my arms out above me. "I think I'm going to need another nap. Do you mind?"

She purses her lips as she shakes her head. "Not at all. You know I enjoy the quiet. And like I said, some people have better stamina than others."

Somehow I don't think she's talking about my physical endurance, but if she is, I'd rather not confirm it.

And when I don't want to deal with an issue, sleep is always the answer. Always.

———

"Want to come up?" I ask. When she doesn't respond, I add, "Just to see the place."

We're double-parked in front of my building, a three-story

rowhouse the owner has split into three living spaces—which is the only reason I can afford it. The main drawback is that my housemates and I share a common kitchen. For the most part, though, we don't get in one another's way.

Lina grimaces. "I'd love to see your place, but I don't have an advanced degree in reading parking signs in the District, so I'll probably get towed." She peers down the street through the windshield. "Besides, I don't think there's an empty spot any-where."

"Parking's free on Sundays, but yeah, the street's looking tight." I look up and down the block and see nothing but occu-pied parking spaces. I reluctantly climb out of the car, the urge to prolong our time together slowing me down. "Okay, well, maybe we can try another—"

"Hey, Max," my housemate Jess says, half of his body hanging out the front door. He's a chief of staff for a DC councilmember and is almost never home. That's pretty much all I know about him. "I'm heading into the office." He glances at the car. "Need me to move?"

My man, Jess. We're going to be best friends someday. "Yeah, that would be great. Thanks."

"No problem," he says before disappearing back inside.

After Jess and Lina make the coveted DC-parking-space ex-change, she follows me up the short set of steps leading to the front entrance.

"Welcome to my humble abode," I tell her. "I'm on the sec-ond floor."

"You live in Adams Morgan," she says as she begins to climb the stairs. "How humble can it be?"

"Fair point," I say behind her.

She trails her hands along the banister. "So listen, I'm not going to stay long. I'm just going to take a peek because I'm curious, then I'm going to head out."

I slip past her to unlock the apartment door. "Fine, no problem. That's exactly what I expected you to do." Faking nervousness, I take a deep breath and open the door. "Here it is."

She glides inside and her jaw drops. "Whoa. It's a Crate & Barrel showroom. The bachelor edition."

Lina immediately focuses on my favorite part of the place: the exposed-brick wall that faces the south side of the apartment. More than two dozen black-and-white photographs hang on it. She spins around and looks at me, her thumb pointing behind her. "Don't tell me you took these?"

I shake my head. "No way. I'm just a fan of black-and-white photographs. I pick them up when I come across them. For some reason, wine festivals are excellent places to buy art."

She faces the opposite wall, her gaze settling on the mini home gym in the corner. "Ah, so that's how you get all those squares on your stomach."

I nod. "I have a personal rule: If I'm watching TV, I'm on that machine."

"How barbaric," she says, wrinkling her nose. "When I'm watching TV, my exercise consists of bathroom and fridge breaks." She holds up an index finger. "Before you criticize, know that I drink lots of water when I watch TV so I actually do take a few hundred steps as part of my plan."

I put my hands up in surrender. "I'm not saying a word."

"Smart man." She points down the hall. "Bedroom?"

It's a simple question, so why is the answer stuck in my throat? *Jesus. Get it together, Hartley.* "Yeah."

"Mind out of the gutter, Max. I just want to see if you're one of the few guys under thirty who actually use bedsheets."

I smirk at that one. Who knew she was such a smart-ass? I cup my mouth and lean over as though I'm going to share a secret. "*Psst.* I even have a bed skirt."

With that news, she marches theatrically to my bedroom door. "Oh, this I *must* see. That's gotta be as rare as the Hope Diamond."

Standing at the threshold, she leans in and sweeps her gaze over the room. I watch her from the hall. Is she imagining me sleeping in there? Even better, is she imagining us *not* sleeping in there? I can picture her lying against my sheets, her hair tousled and falling onto her face, as I brace myself in a push-up position and then sink into that sweet body of hers.

She claps her hands together loudly, the sound dousing the heat that was building in me. *Damn.* I can't even see a bed and not think about getting her in it. I'm a sad, sad man.

"Well, this has been great," she says. "Really great. Thanks for letting me see your humble abode. It's nice. Really nice."

So far, I've only seen this babbling side of Lina when she's aroused and doesn't think she should be. I thought we decided on a no-strings affair, but something about this morning's events seems to have taken us back to square one. I don't know what's going on in her head, but I'd like her to be at ease with me, and if that means I need to wait for her to work out whatever's spooking her, then that's how it'll be.

"Walk me to the door?" she asks.

As if there would ever be a question that I would. *C'mon, Ms. Santos. I hope you know me well enough to expect common decency as the baseline.* "Of course."

Before we get to the door, she turns and rests the palm of her hand on my stomach. "I've been acting weird, haven't I? You felt it, right?"

My mouth's going rogue, trying to curve into a smile, but I'm fighting it, not wanting to do anything to make her skittish. "Tell me what's going on."

She sighs. "I just . . . I think I was going off adrenaline and pheromones and spring-in-the-air-itis this weekend. And everything was fine until you took me to the flower fields and it felt like too much. And then once I was in the car, and all the adrenaline and pheromones and spring-in-the-air-itis was gone, the enormity of what we did hit me."

Only a person with his head up his ass would be surprised by her explanation. Glad to know that isn't me. "Honestly? I figured. But it doesn't have to be a big deal, remember? We'll play this how you want to play it. Eyes open. Zero promises. No need to make it more than it is."

"Yeah," she says, her lips pressed together as she looks off to an area behind me. Then she shakes out her arms, as though she's exorcising whatever's troubling her. "You're right. Well, I'm going to go. And maybe we'll see each other later in the week?"

I nod. "Was hoping you'd say something like that."

"Okay," she says, patting my stomach. "Good, good." She turns back toward the door, hesitates, then faces me again, her expression soft and her voice unsure. "May I kiss you goodbye?"

That fucking question. It has a pulse and fingers and is currently digging into my chest as though it wants to pull my heart out and hand it to her. *What. The. Hell.* I puff out my cheeks, trying to pretend I'm considering her request because I don't know what else to do with myself. "I'm thinking about it."

She pokes me in the stomach. "Yes or no?"

I gently take hold of her wrists and pull her toward me. "Definitely yes."

She leans into my side and places her right hand in my left one. It's a pose I've seen on dozens of special occasions, when the newly married couple dances for the first time. I wonder if she's seen it so often she's taken to mimicking it.

"Are we dancing?" I ask.

"No," she says, threading her fingers with mine. "I just like being tucked against you."

I bend and sweep my lips across her forehead. She seizes the opportunity to place her index finger against my chin and rotate it so our mouths meet. Her tongue leads, and mine follows. That single digit is now a five-finger caress against my cheek and jaw, and despite the many points of contact between us, it's that hand that makes me shudder. We slowly draw apart, both of us a little dazed, and now I'm the one rocked by the enormity of what we just did—because of all the things we've shared this weekend, this moment is the one I'll remember the most.

Chapter Twenty-Six

LINA

Rey lifts his palms in the air excitedly. "Turn it up. Turn it up."

My older brother's demanding when the remote control isn't in his hands. Knowing this, Natalia and I instinctively toss the device between us to keep it out of his reach.

"Y'all are such brats," Rey says as he tries to snatch it in midair. Eventually, Natalia and I stop horsing around and I increase the volume.

We're in the living room of the small home my mother and her sisters share in Silver Spring. Everyone except Jaslene and me is wearing their Easter Sunday best, and lest I forget it, my mother's periodically sucking her teeth to remind me that my outfit—a cream blouse and taupe slacks—is underwhelming. Jaslene, who sometimes spends special occasions with us because she lives alone and her family's in New York, is exempt from my mother's ire—for now.

Paolo's managed to get YouTube through the TV, and we're watching videos of this year's Carnaval celebration in Rio's Sambadrome. It's the culmination of an intensive and seemingly all-consuming effort on the part of dozens of samba schools to throw one of the most elaborately staged parades in the world.

"So which samba school is this?" Jaslene asks, a pastel de carne in her hand. It's essentially a Brazilian-style beef empanada but because Brazilians tend to do everything on a grand scale, this version is the size of a pizza slice.

"Estação Primeira de Mangueira," Natalia says from her spot on the armchair Paolo's sitting in. She throws her hands in the air. "Their theme this year was perfect, and now they're champions once again."

Tia Izabel groans. "I wanted Unidos da Tijuca to win."

Everyone except Jaslene boos at her.

"Wait," Jaslene says, her brows furrowed. "What's wrong with what she said?"

"Brazilian samba schools are really clubs tied to different parts of the city," I explain. "To many, a school is on the same level as a favorite professional sports team. So loyalties and rivalries are inevitable." I give my aunt a playful evil eye. "It's like saying you're a Phillies fan in a bar filled with Mets fans. It's not wise. And anyone in this house who isn't a Mangueira fan is suspect."

Tia Izabel huffs and joins my mother and Tia Viviane in the kitchen, while Natalia grins and high-fives me.

"Look at the flag," Rey says. "That must have caused an uproar."

He's referring to the fact that Mangueira reimagined the Brazilian flag, even changing its colors from green and yellow to pink, green, and white, to represent the forgotten ones in Brazilian society: Indigenous peoples, persons of African descent, and the poor.

"Look at that woman's costume," Jaslene says, cringing. "I think I'm having sympathetic butt-crack pains. There's no way that material should be up there."

To some, the outfits are outrageous, but to me, they're a whimsical symbol of our culture, and I'm in awe of the colorful and thought-provoking display they make. No matter how many times I see Carnaval, whether in person or on television, the samba school competition never fails to amaze me. They prepare for it for months, building elaborate floats, designing jaw-dropping costumes, and perfecting the songs and dances that will hopefully win over their fans and the competition judges alike. "I wish we'd been there this year."

"Talvez no próximo ano, filha," my mother says, sticking her head out of the kitchen's pass-through window.

"But next year's so far away," I say. "And it's hard to get time off in March since I'm always preparing for the onslaught of wedding season."

Natalia reaches over and smacks my thigh. "That reminds me. Mom said you were stuck in Virginia for work. What happened?"

My face is blank, but my brain is on high alert, and my stomach's churning. "Car conked out on me." I give her a dismissive wave. "It wasn't a big deal. The wedding venue I was touring was only two miles away. Stayed at the inn there." *Not bad, Lina. Informative yet succinct.* With any luck, she'll be satisfied with that answer and move on.

"Max must have *loved* that," Jaslene says.

Shit.

The women around me and in the kitchen all snap their heads in my direction. In fact, I'm almost certain the combined force of their movements caused the rush of air that just breezed past me.

I blow out my cheeks and massage my temples. "It really wasn't a big deal. We stayed the night and came back the next morning."

"Glad it worked out, then," Natalia says nonchalantly as she stands. "Well, since you and Jaslene are both here, do you think we could talk about some last-minute ideas for the wedding?" She motions with her googly eyes and exaggerated arms to the rooms upstairs. "Some of it has to do with what I'm wearing, so Paolo can't be around for the discussion."

I raise my face to the ceiling, well aware that she's planning to fish for information about the trip to Virginia. Natalia is my closest cousin, but she's also volatile and unpredictable. Plus, she's the member of my family most likely to divulge decades-old family secrets when she's tipsy, so it's always wise to tread carefully around her. Jaslene, on the other hand, is discreet and never judges anyone except herself. Her presence alone will make Natalia less jumpy, so I'm glad she's around.

I sigh. "Okay, let's head up to your old bedroom."

"Don't take too long," Tia Viviane calls out after us. "We'll be eating soon."

Natalia takes the steps by twos. Jaslene and I climb the stairs like well-adjusted adults operating at normal speed.

Inside the bedroom, Natalia jumps on her old bed, landing on her stomach and propping herself up on her elbows. "Spill. And make it interesting."

Jaslene sits in a desk chair and simply waits for me to talk. Before I can close the door, Rey slips inside and holds up the wall.

"I want to hear the gossip, too," he says, waggling his brows.

I blow a raspberry at him and claim my spot next to Natalia's head. There's no magic to sharing what happened, so I just open my mouth and pray for the best. "Max and I went to Virginia to check out a wedding venue, my car battery died, there was no room at the inn, we bickered, a person who was running a couples retreat overheard us and invited us to participate in counseling, we accepted, faking that we were a couple so we could take the only available room, and then we had sex. That's it. That's what happened." I gulp in air after spewing my verbal vomit. "Oh, we also might have agreed to continue seeing each other on a non-permanent basis. Questions?"

Rey rolls his eyes. "Straights make everything unnecessarily complicated. Good luck. Use condoms. I'm out."

He saunters out the door and shuts it behind him. We resume our discussion as if Rey never entered the room.

"Exclusively?" Jaslene asks.

I shake my head. "What?"

Jaslene takes my hand. "Did you and Max agree to see each other on an exclusive non-permanent basis?"

I ponder this as they stare at me. Natalia, for her part, is disturbingly quiet.

Now that I think about it, Max and I didn't really say all that much. It was enough to say what our relationship *wouldn't be* rather than what it would. "We didn't discuss exclusivity," I say. "I guess I should talk to him about that."

Natalia smirks at me, then says, "Unless there's another brother, in which case you'll want to keep your options open."

I give her my active bitch face. "You know, I can arrange to have a swarm of bees released at the end of your ceremony." I put out my hands as though I'm weighing options. "Butterflies. Bees. What's the difference, really?"

Natalia sticks her tongue out at me. "Whatever. Don't forget I'm paying you."

"At a deep, deep discount, so don't get too cocky," I say. "You get what you pay for."

I'm kidding, of course. Natalia's getting the same treatment I give to my regular, paying clients. The benefit to me is that I get to say things to her I'd never say to anyone else, which is more than enough to justify the reduced rate on my services.

Jaslene scoots forward in the chair. "Lina, do you think the pitch next month will be affected by the fact that you and Max are doing"—she waves her hands in front of her—"whatever you two are doing?"

I raise a brow at her. "In a negative way, you mean?"

She shrugs. "I don't know. In any way, I guess."

"If anything, I think it'll help," I tell her. "We were at odds from the beginning. I mean, I claimed I wasn't going to cooperate from the outset. But now? Now we're working together toward a common goal. That's actually the easy part."

"What's the hard part?" Jaslene asks.

I sigh. "Making sure Max and I don't get stupid and think this can be more than a fling."

Jaslene frowns at me. "But why can't it be? You and Andrew are no longer together, so what you and Max do is none of his business."

She's not wrong. Andrew and I parted ways a long time ago, and it was his choice, not mine. My current relationship shouldn't be any of his concern. Still, I'm not coming between two brothers whose relationship is already strained. Plus, I'd never sign myself up for a lifetime of needing to interact with my former fiancé. It would be so awkward—for Max especially. And his parents? My God, what would they say about all this?

Natalia expels a dramatic breath. "Goodness, could you imagine what dinners with your in-laws would be like?"

"Exactly," I say. "And even if Max weren't Andrew's brother, he'd still be too . . . everything. I'm off-balance when I'm around him. Prone to say and do things I usually never do. He's just not the man I envision spending my life with."

Jaslene narrows her eyes. "You don't want Andrew, but you want someone like him, right?"

"*Now* you're getting it," I tell Jaslene. "I need someone as far from provocative as I can possibly get. Anyway, I'm not sure why this conversation went as far afield as it did."

"I know why," Jaslene says with a secret smile.

"Look at you," Natalia says to Jaslene. "Sittin' there like some oracle and shit."

I stick my hand out and bob my head. "Well, care to share?"

Playing the role Natalia's cast her in, Jaslene straightens and waves her hands around, adopting a majestic voice. "Because despite all the reasons you and Max shouldn't be together, you yourself admitted that limiting your relationship to a fling would be—and I quote—the 'hard part.' What does it tell you when you already need to be reminded of that fact?"

Natalia tilts her head and nods. "She has a point."

I jump up and smooth my hands down the front of my pants. "It tells me I'm a careful person, that's all. You should expect that from me by now. So, I bet it's time to eat. Ready to head back down?"

Natalia and Jaslene grin at each other even though I don't recall saying anything amusing.

The front doorbell rings just as we're getting ready to dig into dinner. Rey returns with Marcelo in tow, and our family friend takes the empty seat next to Tia Viviane. He nudges her with his shoulder and she winks at him. Yeah, I'm certain those two have seen each other naked.

We pass bowls of food to one another in a feeding free-for-all. If during any part of this process the plates are passed counterclockwise, it's a fluke. I'm the last to receive the feijoada, and as expected, the vultures have stripped the dish of all the delicious pork and beef bits that make this bean stew one of my favorite meals.

"Seriously, people?" I say, pushing the serving spoon around. "There's no linguiça left." Feijoada isn't feijoada without spicy pork sausage, so now I'm ready to fight someone.

My mother, who's sitting to my right, slaps a piece of linguiça on my plate and continues to pass dishes as they come to her.

"Obrigada, Mãe," I say.

She smiles, delighted as usual when an occasional Portuguese word rolls off my tongue. "De nada, filha."

As we eat, Marcelo tells us about his daughter's home in Vero Beach, Florida. It's spacious, according to him, and he'll be living in the in-law suite.

"You could come visit me," he tells Tia Viviane.

"Or you could come visit me once you're gone," she replies with a lift of her chin.

"Maybe I will," he says, leaning into her.

"You're going to be one of those pervy men watching people on the beach, aren't you?" Natalia asks, peering at him with a smile.

Paolo groans. "Baby, don't. It's Easter Sunday—"

"No," Marcelo says, talking over Paolo and shaking his head. "When the women see me in my bathing suit, they'll be the ones checking *me* out." He crouches down and adds in a whisper, "And it's a Speedo."

Natalia sticks her finger in her mouth and gags; Rey cringes. Jaslene just blinks and stares at Marcelo.

Their jokes about his upcoming move gloss over the upshot: Soon I won't have business headquarters, and unless I get the position with the Cartwright Hotel Group, I'm going to be running my business from the front passenger seat of my car.

Perhaps I grimace as I think about the repercussions because Marcelo stops laughing and his expression grows serious.

"Any luck finding a new location?" he asks me.

"Not yet. But Jaslene and I have been devoting a couple of hours each day to scouting candidates."

"Your aunt tells me you're trying to get a new job," he says. "What would you be doing?"

I tell him about the position, even mentioning the potentially significant increase in income.

"*Cha-ching*," Natalia says between bites of her food.

"So if you get this position, you won't need to worry about the lease, right?" Rey asks.

"Exactly. It would definitely take the pressure off me. Plus, more money."

"But you'd be working for someone else," Tia Viviane observes. "Are you ready for someone else to tell you what to do? Even if it means more money?"

Am I ready? Hell, yes, I'm ready. Owning my own business is stressful—I get night sweats around tax time—and I'd gladly give it up if a better opportunity came along. But these women would laugh in my face if I told them my troubles. They came from another country, got married then divorced, learned the English language, and opened their own business. They don't have time to hear about my silly American problems. So I make light of Tia Viviane's question because it's easier that way. "Ha. I'm a wedding planner. People tell me what to do all the time."

"You know what I mean," Tia Viviane says.

"I wouldn't necessarily be doing it forever," I hedge. "It's a great opportunity."

"Sounds like it," Tia Izabel says, giving me an encouraging smile.

"Having options is never a bad thing," my mother adds flatly.

The tension holds me in place like a paperweight. I can't help thinking that they're disappointed in me, Viviane in particular. She's the eldest, and the reason my mother and Izabel were able to come to the States in the first place. They faced obstacles and overcame them—under circumstances far more challenging than mine.

The truth is, failure shouldn't be an option for me, but if neither Plan A nor Plan B works out, how will I avoid it? It's only then that I truly realize the extent of my predicament: I need a Plan C, but I don't have one.

Chapter Twenty-Seven

MAX

I start the workweek the same way I'm likely to end it: thinking about Lina.

I'd like to reach out to her, but I'm not sure how I should go about it. An email's probably too impersonal. A text might be too familiar. No, I should call her at the office. That way, I can start the conversation with business and test out whether I should end on a more personal note. After dialing Lina's business number on the speakerphone, I look down at my clammy hands. Damn, I'm in high school all over again.

A cheerful voice answers. "Good afternoon, this is Dotting the I Do's, where no detail is missed. How can I help you?"

"Uh, hi. This is Max Hartley. Is Lina . . . Carolina Santos in, please?"

"Max, this is Jaslene, Lina's assistant."

"Hi, Jaslene. Nice to speak with you under better circumstances."

She snorts. "Yeah, Natalia was in usual form that day. Sorry if we made you feel unwelcome."

"No worries. It's good that Lina has people who have her back."

"That, she does," Jaslene says. "Listen, Lina's already at the Cartwright, so you can catch up with her there."

"At the . . . Cartwright?" I sift through my mental calendar, wondering if I've missed an appointment. Then I check the calendar on my watch, which shows I'm free all afternoon.

"Weren't you going to be meeting her for the tour of the . . . Oh shoot. Never mind, Max. I must have misunderstood Lina's plans."

So Lina's at the Cartwright, touring hotel rooms in connection with our project, but she didn't invite me to join her. *Interesting.* "Thanks anyway, Jaslene."

"Max, wait," she says in a tone of voice noticeably less cheerful than the one she used in her phone greeting.

"Yes?"

"If you go over there, check in with her first. Don't show up without any warning. I already feel bad about telling you where she is."

"You have my word."

"Make that mean something, okay?"

"You got it," I say before hanging up.

Jaslene and Natalia are fiercely loyal to Lina. Jaslene carries that fierceness in an understated way, whereas Natalia carries herself as though she'll cut you. Either way, I'm glad these women are protective of her. If Lina let me, I'd be protective of her, too.

———

Me: Hi Lina. Just checking in to see if you wanted to get together to tour the rooms at the Cartwright. My schedule is pretty flexible this week.

I fully intend to disclose my sources, but I'm curious to see how she'll respond to my open-ended question.

Lina: I'm actually at the Cartwright now. Not much to see here. Took a few pics but most of the info is available on the hotel website.

Me: Maybe I'd see something you didn't. You know, two sets of eyes and all that.

Lina: Hmmm.

Me: Okay, you got me. I just want to see you.

Lina: How fast can you get here?

Me: I'm in the hotel lobby. A minute, maybe?

Lina: ???

Me: I'll explain upstairs if you still want me to join you.

Lina: Sure, come on up. Room 408.

Me: On my way.

The elevator isn't as fast as I thought it would be, so I take two minutes to get there. I knock on the door and smooth the sides of my hair as I wait for her to answer.

Lina opens the door and steps to the side to let me in. "This is high-level stuff we're doing here. Where's your security detail?"

"They're downstairs. Told them to make sure no one makes it upstairs." I enter the room and briefly scan my surroundings before my gaze settles on Lina. She's wearing a yellow dress with tiny blue flowers on the skirt. It's cinched at the waist and showcases her curvy figure. Her hair's down today, the front twisted and held back with two yellow hair clips. I suddenly have a craving for banana cream pie. "Hi there."

"Hi there, yourself," she says, her eyes twinkling. "How'd you find me?"

I put up my hands. "Now, don't count this against her, but Jaslene slipped and told me you were here." I furrow my brows. "She seemed to think we'd be doing the tour together."

Lina turns toward the windows. "I wasn't trying to box you out, if that's what you're implying."

"I'm not implying anything. Was just wondering. Anyway, I'd understand if you didn't feel comfortable being alone with me in a hotel room. We both know you lack self-control where I'm concerned."

She faces me and waggles her eyebrows. "You say that as a joke, but it's totally true."

"And that's a problem?"

She wrinkles her nose and puts her hand out in a so-so motion. "Sort of, but I'm starting to get used to it."

That's quite an admission, but I know better than to make a big deal of it. I sweep my arm through the air. "So, did you come up with any brilliant ideas about how to use the room?"

Lina presses two fingers to her parted lips as she studies me, her eyes glinting with mischief. "Absolutely."

My mouth goes slack and my heart bangs around like shutters in a storm. Still, I'm going to be the voice of reason because we're in what could one day be her place of business. "I like where your head is at, but I should point out the obvious."

She stalks closer. "Which is?"

I put up a hand. "You never know who might be around, or

even whether Rebecca will take a trip up here, in which case"—I bare my teeth—"awkward."

Dean thinks I have no control. I wish he could see me now. He'd be so proud.

She freezes in place, tilts her head, and purses her lips in thought. "But a kiss couldn't hurt, right?"

Lina gives the best kisses, so there's no way I'm saying no to her suggestion. I narrow the distance between us and draw her body flush against mine. She immediately throws her arms over my shoulders and threads her fingers through the hair at the nape of my neck, standing on her toes and angling her head in one fluid sequence. It's a succession of movements that seems instinctual, as though kissing me is part of her muscle memory.

This kiss is lazy and tender, so my eyes pop open when her hands trail down my back and land on my ass. I groan into her mouth and grind into her, unable to resist the possibility of creating enough friction to get her aroused with our clothes on.

Someone knocks on the door and we freeze.

"Shit," she whispers.

"Fuck," I whisper back.

"Lina, it's Rebecca. Just thought I'd stop by to say hi."

Lina looks up at me, her lips curled in mock disgust. "You summoned her."

I grit my teeth. "We don't have time for pointing fingers."

She shrugs. "Just play it off. We're in here working."

I look down at my crotch, which is sporting an erection of sizable proportions. "That doesn't suggest we were working. And I don't even have a jacket to cover it."

"Get in the shower," she says. "She'll never guess you're here."

So this is where my life is headed. I'm hiding in showers now.

She widens her eyes and shoos me away. "Go."

I tiptoe to the bathroom while she strides to the door. As silently as I can, I peel back the curtain and climb inside the tub.

"Hey, there," Lina says to Rebecca. "I'm almost done here."

"Didn't mean to disturb your work, but Bill in reception told me you were visiting, so I decided to swing by."

"Oh, that's nice."

"So what do you think of the room?" Rebecca asks.

"It's spacious. Huge. Massive. *Impressive.*"

If I didn't know any better, I'd think she was talking about my hard-on.

"You think so?" Rebecca asks. "I didn't realize it was larger than average."

"Oh yes. Yes, it is. And I should know. I've seen quite a few in my day, but this one definitely stands up. *Out.* Stands out."

Yep. She's talking about my dick. *Bravo, Lina. Bravo.*

"It's functional yet attractive. And it's sure to bring pleasure to whomever has the good fortune of using it. The best part, though, is that it's equipped for significant expansion if you use your imagination."

That it is, Ms. Santos.

"Well, I'm intrigued," Rebecca says. "Can't wait to see your presentation."

"I'm excited, too."

The room door opens.

"You coming?" Rebecca asks.

I squeeze my eyes shut.

"Unfortunately, not yet," Lina says. "*But soon.*"

"Okay, then. Good to see you again."

"Yes, great to see you, too."

After the door shuts, I count to fifteen, then jump out of the tub and leave the bathroom.

Lina's standing by the window wearing a wicked grin. "You're such a bad influence on me."

I pull her to my chest. Within seconds, her gaze grows heavy with anticipation.

"There will be consequences for your shameless behavior, though," I say.

She gives me a flirty smile. "Oh yeah? When will you apply them?"

I step back and tweak her on the nose. "'Unfortunately, not yet. *But soon.*'"

Lina drops her hands to her sides and stamps her foot. "When is *soon*?"

"When will I get to see your place?" I ask.

"Are you fishing for an invitation?"

Damn right I am. It'd be much easier to fantasize about Lina if I can picture her in her own bed. Or walking around in her underwear and a sheer tank top that hugs her breasts—

"Max," she says sharply.

"What was the question?"

She blows out her cheeks. "I asked if you were fishing for an invitation to my place."

Pretending I have a fishing rod in my hands, I throw out the line and reel her in. "Yes, I'm absolutely fishing for an invitation."

She touches a hand to her heart and licks her lips. "You are cordially invited to my place for dinner, then."

"When?" I say, knowing this is a big deal for her.

"How about Friday?" she asks.

That's four days away. I'm inclined to stamp my foot and ask to come over tonight, but since I was patting myself on the back about my self-control just a few minutes ago, I can't very well complain without being hypocritical as fuck. "Friday's fine."

"And we won't need to worry about waking up early"—she draws in a long breath—"if you want to stay, that is. Totally up to you. I'm used to sleeping alone, so you shouldn't feel obligated. It was just a—"

I take a step toward her and thread her hand with mine. "Lina, I'd like to stay."

She exhales. "Okay, great. It's a dinner date."

"Maybe we could watch a movie, too."

"Maybe," she says, shrugging. "If there's time."

If there's time? I definitely like the sound of that. "Since we've already established that you lack self-control around me, I'm going to head out." I spin away from her and walk to the door. Once there, I turn around and wink at her. "See you Friday."

Damn. Four days is going to seem like a lifetime.

Chapter Twenty-Eight

LINA

From: MHartley@AtlasCommunications.com
To: CSantos@DottingTheIDos.com; KSproul@
   AtlasCommunications.com
Date: April 24 - 9:37 am
Subject: Materials for Pitch to Cartwright Hotel Group

Lina, meet Karen.

Karen, meet Lina.

Lina, Karen is our in-house graphic designer. She'll be helping us prepare materials for the pitch to the Cartwright Hotel Group on May 14. Our initial thinking is that Karen could prepare mock website landing pages, social media graphics, and storyboards for any video elements. Let me know if that sounds good to you.

The wedding-godmother theme is a go, but I'm still working through the conceptual framework. Taking more time than I expected. If anything jumps out at you, feel free to send your ideas my way.

Hope you're well.

—Max

April 24 – 9:54 am

Me: I like it when you're in business mode. Makes me want to visit you in your office so I can role-play as your assistant. I'd take excellent dicktation.

April 24 – 9:57 am

Max: That can be arranged. I have a lot of dicktation to give you.

April 24 – 9:58 am

Max: Are you sexting me???

April 24 – 9:59 am

Me: Yes.

April 24 – 10:00 am

Max: Be still my beating cock.

From: CSantos@DottingTheIDos.com
To: MHartley@AtlasCommunications.com; KSproul@
AtlasCommunications.com
Date: April 24 - 10:03 am
Subject: Re: Materials for Pitch to Cartwright Hotel Group

Nice to meet you, Karen.

Max, I'm on board with using the types of pitch materials you identified, and if I think of anything, I'll definitely let you know. Maybe there's a reason you're taking more time than expected on the wedding-godmother theme? I'll think about that, too. In any case, I can't wait to see what you come up with.

All my best,
Lina

April 24 — 10:09 am
Me: Planning to cook for you Friday evening. A Brazilian dish. Any allergies? Foods you hate?

April 24 – 10:12 am
Max: No food allergies. Can't stand green peas. And just so you know, I've developed an aversion to spicy peppers. Will be on the lookout for those. Ahem. Can I bring anything?

April 24 – 10:13 am
Me: Dessert from the Sugar Shoppe?

April 24 – 10:14 am
Max: Done. Looking forward to it.

April 24 – 10:15 am
Me: Same.

———————

The intercom chimes just as I'm removing the empadão from the oven. I tried to make the recipe my bitch, but the pie's blackened surface and the acrid smell of burned pastry dough confirm that I'm the one who's fucked.

Muttering a year's worth of obscenities in under twenty seconds, I place the baking dish on the stove and fling my oven mitts across the room. The menu now consists of a green salad and roasted carrots. Apparently I'm expecting Peter Rabbit.

I press the intercom with more force than necessary. "Yes?"

"Lina, it's Max."

"Hey, there." I inject my tone with as much cheer as I can muster. "I'm glad you made it. Come on up." Then I buzz him in.

Remembering the state of my kitchen, I scurry to the door and open it wide. When Max steps off the elevator, a bakery box in hand, I'm swinging the door back and forth to air out the apartment. I give him a brief once-over, taking in his dark-washed jeans and untucked white button-down shirt. Whether in casual or business clothes, he always exudes confidence in his personal style, never appearing as if he's trying too hard. *I like what I see.*

His eyebrows shoot up as he approaches. "Technical difficulties?"

"That's putting it mildly." When he reaches me, I drop my head to his chest. "I ruined dinner."

With his free hand, he gathers my hair and pushes it to one shoulder, which deprives me of my natural hiding place. "Dinner would only be ruined if I couldn't spend it with you."

I look up at him. I'm making a valiant effort to suppress my heart-eyes gaze, but I probably look like the emoji personified. "Aww, that's sweet. I'd still recommend that you hold that thought until you see what's for dinner."

I should also tell him that swoony statements are wasted on a fling, but I can't bring myself to detract from his superb delivery. Maybe he doesn't need a reminder that this is a no-strings affair, but I do. *Note to self: Don't get any ridiculous ideas about a long-term future with Max.*

He follows me inside, places the bakery box on the kitchen island, and scans the area. Management calls it an open-concept design. In truth, they're too cheap to put up walls.

"Whoa," he says on a spin. "You mocked me about my Crate & Barrel living room. Now I get to tease you about yours. Do you have enough candles, Lina?" He makes jazz hands. "Planters, shaggy pillows, and tapestries, oh my!"

I playfully shove him toward the kitchen area. "How rude. Guests aren't supposed to comment on . . . I'm going to shut up now."

"Smart woman," he says, winking at me. He looks at the stove and points at the empadão. "Is that the patient?"

I snort. "Yes."

He walks over, a hand under his chin, then nods gravely. "What was it supposed to be?"

"An empadão de frango. It's basically a Brazilian potpie. The crust should be buttery and flaky. The chicken and vegetables inside should be moist and perfectly seasoned. Instead, we have this monstrosity."

"Is there any point in keeping it?" he asks.

"Only as a reminder that I'll never be able to re-create the dishes my mother makes. Otherwise, no." I blow out a harsh breath, holding back the tears that always threaten to fall whenever I get even a tiny bit emotional. "I can't even bake a fucking pie."

Max raises a brow. "Hey, hey. Watch an hour of *Nailed It!* and you'll see you're not alone. It's just a pie."

I plop onto a stool by the island. "It's not just a pie, Max. I wanted to make a special dinner. Share something from my culture. That didn't go well, obviously. I don't know how I'm supposed to pass on family traditions if I can't follow a basic recipe."

He takes the stool next to me and folds his hands on the counter. "Is it your mother's?"

I jerk my head up. "What?"

"The recipe," he says. "Is it your mother's?"

"God, no. She doesn't write anything down. Says the best way to learn is to watch and assist. I don't understand how it comes so easily to her. I ask how much I should add of something— flour, tomatoes, garlic, whatever—and she says, 'a little bit of this, a little bit of that.'" I turn to him. "Max, my mother doesn't even own measuring cups."

Most people might laugh off that fact, but in times like these I want my mother's recipe in printed form and I want things like a quarter cup of oil—not *eh, about this much, filha*—to be reflected in it.

"Maybe you could try forcing her to do it your way. You know, show up one day with measuring cups and spoons and a notepad. When she says, 'a little bit of this,' you say, 'show me using the cup.' Then write every step down so you can work on it here."

I tilt my head in his direction, envisioning how that would work. "You know, that's not a bad idea. And maybe I could re-cord her making a dish. Might be nice just to have it for poster-ity's sake." I briefly close my eyes, upset with myself for revealing how even the smallest things set me off. Max must be regretting this dinner as we speak. I wave my hands as though I can erase the last few minutes in one motion. "Anyway, enough about that. You didn't come here to listen to me talk about this stuff."

He turns his body sideways, placing his feet on the bottom rung of my stool, and then he gently turns my chin in his direction. I swivel my body to face him.

"I came here to spend time with you," he says, "and if that means we talk about something that's bothering you, then I don't have a problem with that. Keeping it casual doesn't mean I won't care about you as a person. That would be impossible. And I suspect it would be impossible for you, too. I mean, I get the sense you don't share what's bugging you with just anyone." He caresses the sides of my face and presses a kiss to my forehead. "So thank you for letting me be more than just anyone."

Is it possible for your heart to expand in your chest? I don't know enough about anatomy to say for sure. But it *feels* like my heart's making room for Max to come inside even though I don't want him there. *Well, heart, we certainly can't have any of that.* Obviously we both need to be reminded why we're here.

I take his hands in mine, lean forward, and kiss his neck, burying my nose in his skin and breathing him in deep. He smells like a mix of earth and citrus, as though an orange fell from a tree and someone plucked it up from the rich soil and packaged it on the spot. "The salad will keep, and the carrots can be reheated. Care to skip to the main attraction? I wore a skirt for the occasion."

His eyes darken as he considers my invitation. "Dinner wasn't the main attraction?"

Dinner *can't* be the main attraction. That's not what flings do.

Rather than answer his question, I rise from the stool and tug on his hands. "Come with me."

Max stands reluctantly, his gaze returning to the ruined pie on the stove. He opens his mouth, closes it, then opens it again. Whatever he was going to say is now tucked away, hidden behind the wicked curve of his lips. "You mean that literally, don't you?"

I nod as I lead him to my bedroom. "I absolutely do."

When we cross the threshold, Max says, "More throw pillows and candles, I see," and he gets a slap on the ass for that one.

He turns to me and puts up a hand. "Listen, I know you've been dying to touch my ass, but you don't need to pretend you're doing it to punish me for making a valid observation about the state of your room."

My gaze narrows on him. "I really hurt you when I mentioned Crate & Barrel, huh?"

He throws his hands over his chest and lifts his chin. "Maybe. It's just that it's where my mother shops, and I've always regarded her style as . . . nothing like mine."

"Aww, I didn't mean to make you self-conscious about it. Forget I said anything." Without fanfare, I pull my short-sleeved top over my head and toss it behind me. "Will this help with the memory loss?"

I'm standing before him in a highly impractical powder-blue bra. The demi cups are good for absolutely nothing other than making my breasts look like they're being presented on a platter. I call it my cosmetic harness, a scrap of material made solely to, one, enhance my cleavage, and two, be removed.

Max raises two fingers to his lips and takes a slow breath. "Who are you? Where am I? What year is it?"

I settle my hands on his chest and step forward, forcing him to retreat until the backs of his knees hit the bed and he drops onto it. I'm on him with the speed and dexterity of an Olympic athlete. Meanwhile, he fusses with the front clasp of my bra as though he's performing the "Itsy Bitsy Spider."

"Need help, partner?" I ask him.

He grits his teeth. "This is like picking a lock. Do you have a safety pin or something? Credit card, maybe?"

I slap his hand away. "Let me. Watch and learn. See, you need to flip the clasp outward and pull up."

His mouth drops open. "Genius."

I love that we're comfortable together. I love that I don't have to guess what he's thinking. We just fit. There's no artifice between us. We're just two people enjoying each other—in bed and out.

He raises his hands. "May I?"

I nod and he slips his hands under the bra straps and slides it off.

"And these are beautiful," he says.

"Go ahead. Touch them. You know you want to."

He cups my breasts, the tips of his fingers ghosting over my skin as he fondles me. He looks up, observing my reaction. But my face can only tell part of the story. I'm shamelessly undulating on his thigh, unable to remain still. And I want to speed things up because I know what awaits me near the finish line. When his thumbs brush against my nipples, I fall forward, rocking into him.

"Can I get a condom?" I ask. "Please?" My voice is low and urgent. Needy as hell.

He nods, his mouth opening but not forming words.

I scramble off the bed and grab a packet from the bowl of condoms on the dresser. I toss it onto the bed, slip off my skirt and panties, and dive for his jeans. Max, my trusty assistant, unbuttons his shirt and slips it off well before I'm done.

"You're fast," I say, stepping back to give him room to discard his clothes.

"I'm impatient."

He raises off the bed long enough to toe off his shoes and yank his jeans down, kicking both to the side of the bed. My gaze meets his when he puts his hand on his cock and strokes it—slowly. *Oh God.* My own personal sauna engulfs me, the heat originating inside me and spreading out to my arms, the backs of my knees, and the expanse of skin between my thighs. I'm unsteady on my feet and woozy in the brain. With shaky hands, I reach out to grasp the dresser behind me. He's watching me intently as he touches himself, making it easy to imagine I'm the one bringing him pleasure.

Still watching me and stroking his erection, he slides his free hand out to the side and pats the bed until his fingers find the condom. He rips it open with his teeth, the intensity of the movement speaking for him, as if to say, *This is what you do to me.*

He rolls on the condom based on touch alone, his gaze never straying from my face. I stare at him as he sheaths himself, my lips parted to ensure I remember to breathe and my hands resting on the dresser for support.

"I wonder if you want me as much as I want you," he says.

I don't know the extent of his need. If it's to a degree that muddles his brain and makes him ache everywhere, then the answer's yes. "I'm going to take a wild guess and say I do."

"Come here and take what you need, then."

I straighten and walk toward the bed, holding out my hands when I'm close enough to reach his body. He threads his hands with mine and holds me up so I can straddle his thighs. I use my body to tease, grazing his cock as I center myself, until our bodies are aligned just so and I sink onto him.

"Max," I say, squeezing my eyes shut and seeing spots.

We're an exquisitely tight fit. For a few seconds I sit still, simply experiencing what it's like to be stretched around him. Then I tighten my core and rise off him, reveling in the friction.

Max chokes out my name and grabs my ass, pumping up when I push down. "Can we just do this forever?"

My eyes pop open. Judging from his wide-eyed gaze, I gather the question startled him, too. I grind faster, focusing on the tingling in my body rather than any thoughts threatening to take root in my untrustworthy brain. He trails his hands up my back, caressing my shoulders before tracing his fingers over my nipples again. His touch leaves tiny sparks in its wake that heighten the pulsing between my legs. It's lazy and decadent and deliciously torturous. The faster I bounce the slower he moves, until he's touching me at a glacial place, as if he means to show me that everything isn't always within my control.

"I need to come," I say in a breathless rush.

"And you will," he says, his voice as ragged as mine. "Look at me, Lina."

I drag my gaze from the spot over his shoulder back to his face, slowing down to focus on him. "I'm here."

"Are you?" he asks. "Just let go of whatever you think should be the case and simply feel. I promise you, I'll be right there with you."

I could fall for him easily. Make a fool of myself with hearts in my eyes and glitter bursting from my chest. For so many reasons, Max shouldn't be the one for me. And certainly not for the version of me I need to be. I'm trapped in a maze, unsure where to turn, but somewhere in the distance, Max's voice calls out, and though I don't know where that voice will take me, I follow it anyway. Simply feel? I can do that. Am I with him? Yes, I want to be. So I nod.

With a triumphant gleam in his eye, Max pulls my torso against him and buries his face against my breasts. We rock against each other for several minutes, our harsh breathing and the slapping of our thighs the only sounds in the room. I pull away, searching for his lips, and find his mouth as eager as mine.

Through it all, I ride him hard, and when we come up for air, he nuzzles my jaw, peppering it with kisses as he tries to gauge whether my orgasm is near. "Lina, baby . . . are you . . . close?"

"I am," I manage to eke out.

And I can hardly keep my head up. The pleasure spiraling through my body is like an anchor, tethering me to this moment and leaving no room for anything else. "Max, I need your fingers."

He growls against my ear and snakes his hand between us, his thumb grazing my clit.

"That's it, yes," I say, still rocking against him.

Max looks up at me, his heavy gaze and swollen lips broadcasting that he's as tied up in knots for me as I am for him. "Squeeze around me, baby. Make it as tight as you can." His voice is laced with need, which only heightens my own.

As I contract around him, Max's fingers roam over me, until

he finds a glorious angle that produces the right amount of friction against my clitoris. All I can do in response is bear down on him and say his name: "Max . . . Max . . . yes, right there, Max."

"Christ," he says, his voice tinged with awe. "I can't believe we feel this good together, baby. How can you not want this over and over?"

I clench around him, trying to draw out the orgasm that's just out of reach, building and building. When Max alters his approach, using his middle and index fingers to draw tight circles perfectly centered on my nub, all my nerve endings seem to fuse together into one continuous loop of pleasure that flows through me like billions of fireworks going off at the same time. Crying out his name, I shake and shudder and writhe, a mass of vibration and movement that I can't control even if I wanted to.

I tremble for what seems like minutes, experiencing tiny aftershocks, and when I finally, just barely, regain my bearings, Max is shuddering against me, too, his arms pulling me into his tight embrace as he pumps into me. "Fuck, Lina. Yes, yes, fuck, yes, fuck." He stills, and then he lets out a long groan and slumps backward.

When our hearts are no longer racing, I press a light kiss to his forehead and smile against it.

"What's so amusing?" he asks, his warm breath teasing my neck.

"I was thinking we're an eloquent pair. All the *yeses* and *fucks* are a testament to the true depth of our vocabulary."

"Having range is important," he says on a chuckle, "and anyway, our bodies are communicating like they've mastered their own language. I'm good with that. You?"

I mimic his words because I can't do much more. "Yeah, I'm good with that, too."

Now that I'm capable of stringing coherent thoughts together, I remember that the point of this "main attraction" was to remind us—well, mostly me—that we're having a fling. But as I wrap my arms around him, I admit to myself that I came nowhere close to reaching my goal.

Chapter Twenty-Nine

MAX

Feeling Lina's backside against my morning wood ranks as my favorite wake-up call ever. Drawn to the peachy scent in her hair, I place my arm on her waist, scoot closer, and breathe her in. She moans and snuggles into the new position.

I don't know where we're headed, or even if we're headed anywhere at all, but I suppose the best approach is to take my own advice and not worry about what *was* or *should be* and concentrate on what *is*. Because I'm sleeping with the woman my brother almost married, and I have zero interest in changing my current status.

Lina stretches her arms and lets out a happy sigh.

"Good morning," I say against her ear.

She reaches behind her and strokes my jaw. "Good morning back." Then she lifts her head. "Ouch. Why is there a twig in the bed?"

"What?"

Frowning, she sits up and reaches under the covers, her hands searching for whatever's distracted her. Until she grabs my dick. "Oh. Sorry. I mistook that for a twig. Thought I might have gotten something stuck on me when I was gardening. Never mind."

With my mouth curved in amusement, I do nothing for several seconds—and then I pounce, wrestling her to the mattress as she screams and feigns outrage. Eventually I manage to pin her down and press my "twig" against the apex of her thighs.

Quite pleased with herself, she gives me a lopsided grin, her eyes bright with mischief.

"Are you ticklish?" I ask.

She shakes her head. "Not at all."

I watch her quietly as her eyes travel to a spot over my shoulder. That's her lying gaze, and I won't be fooled by it anymore. "Well, if that's the case, then you won't mind this." Growling, I dive under the covers and tickle the backs of her legs and the sides of her waist. Lina yelps, bucking against me like a bronco and throwing me off her in seconds.

I lie back against the mattress and stare at the ceiling, a smile that even *feels* goofy plastered on my face. If it were up to me, we'd spend the day together, feeding off these good vibes. But it's not up to just me, and Lina's still skittish about our relationship. Maybe there's a way to keep this day going without making her nervous. Knowing Lina, if her work figures into it, she'll be game. "Let's go to dinner tonight. At Blossom." I turn on my side and catch the way her eyes widen at the suggestion. "The pitch is a little over two weeks away, so we should probably get started on figuring out how to feature the hotel restaurant."

She sits up and tucks a few strands of hair behind her ear. "Yeah, thanks for the reminder. The presentation *should* be our priority." Letting out a heavy sigh, she rolls her eyes upward. "But I have tons to do today. Want to meet there?"

"I don't mind picking you up."

She shakes her head. "No, that's okay. I'll probably be near that side of town, so it'll be easy for me to order a Lyft straight to Blossom."

If that will make you feel better, sure. To her, I say, "That works. I need to run a few errands before then anyway." I lean over and kiss her cheek. "I had a great time. I'll use the bathroom and get out of your hair."

I can't say that I blame her for wanting to keep our relationship casual, but a part of me wonders why it requires so much effort on her part. This is me, trying to keep it casual. Why can't she do the same? Maybe her need to distance herself is a symptom of the push and pull that brought us together in the first place. Maybe this is just us. What I do know is that she's fucking precious when she's second-guessing me. Or am I second-guessing her? She could very well have a lot of shit to do today, and I'm just feeling unsure about my place in her life. *Christ.*

She drops her shoulders, probably surprised I'm not campaigning for more sex. "Oh. Okay, yeah. How about I make a reservation for six?"

I stand and stretch, yawning out the last of my sleepiness. "Perfect."

What's even more perfect? Keeping Lina off-balance. Because I don't want to be in this alone. *Welcome to the I'm-Into-You-and-Don't-Know-What-to-Do-About-It Club, Ms. Santos. We've been expecting you.*

"Welcome to Blossom, folks. My name is Camille and I'll be your main server this evening. Have either of you dined with us before?"

Lina nods. "For lunch only, though. Looking forward to trying something else on the menu."

Camille smiles. "Excellent. We're glad to have you back. Just to explain to the gentleman here"—she turns in my direction—"any staff member on the floor can help you, whether it's because you need more water or a utensil, or because I'm taking too long to bring the check." She leans over and drops her voice to a whisper. "That last one never happens."

A different server arrives to fill our water glasses and another places a basket of bread in the center of our table.

Camille hands us each a piece of delicate paper. "And this is our tasting menu. Very popular right now. Happy to answer your questions once you've had a chance to look it over. In the meantime, can I get you started on a cocktail?"

Lina orders a pomegranate martini. I order a Tom Collins.

When Camille's gone, Lina leans forward as though she wants to tell me a secret. "I've been dying to try the martini. I saw it on the menu when I came for lunch, but I didn't want to risk being tipsy during an afternoon appointment."

"Well, now you can be tipsy with me. This should be fun."

A smile dances on her lips as she opens the menu. I can't stop looking at her. The simple dress she's wearing hugs her curves, and its deep red color accentuates her glowing skin. Her hair falls to the side in ringlets, a gold barrette at her temple helping to hold some of it in place.

She meets my gaze over the edge of her menu. I straighten in my seat.

"What are you considering?" she asks.

Honestly, I'm considering how beautiful she is. As for the menu, I haven't even glanced at it yet.

"I'm thinking about their spin on paella," she says. "Rabbit, pork, rice, chorizo, *yum*—the list of ingredients goes on and on. It's for two, though. Any interest in sharing?"

I set the menu aside. "I'd love to go in on that with you." I scan the restaurant's main dining area, taking note of the decor. "So what do you think of the room design?"

Lina places her menu on the table and turns both ways in her chair before scrutinizing the area behind me. "Love the gray weathered shiplap walls. And the wildflowers below the sconces are the perfect touch to tie the name and the decor together. It's a little darker than I'd like, but it's cozy. Almost like a fancy farmhouse." Her gaze lands on the table centerpiece. "Putting the candle in a vintage Mason jar and setting it on a tray is exactly what the room needs. It's rustic *and* chic."

As I watch Lina effortlessly describe the restaurant's interior design, I finally figure out what's been bugging me about the wedding-godmother concept we chose for the pitch: It isn't the best vehicle for showcasing this incredible woman's talents.

I was so convinced that the personal element had to be front and center that I lost sight of the real person behind the service we're trying to sell. I fell into the trap of thinking the armor Lina had developed for herself was a bad thing. But, after our time at Surrey Lane Farm, I think Lina owes a large measure of her success to her skill in using that armor to her advantage if and when she needs it. Who she lets into her life, who she cries in front of, who she lets behind her walls, who she shares her emotions with, is ultimately her choice. And it doesn't diminish what she brings to the table; it just allows her to navigate different environments while remaining within her comfort zone.

Lina's strength is that she gets shit done. Like she's always acknowledged, she isn't going to be a client's best friend. Or cry at their wedding. Or jump around when the bride finds the perfect dress. That's not her style. But she'll organize the best wedding she can with the resources available to her. And *that's* what any client should want. Now I just need to explain why I'm advocating a change in tactics. "Can we talk about the pitch for a minute?"

She takes a sip of her water and folds her hands in her lap. "Sure. Is everything okay?"

"Yeah," I say. "It's just . . . I don't think we should use the wedding-godmother concept. It isn't you."

She sags against the chair, and her smile broadens in tiny degrees. "Can I tell you a secret?"

"Of course."

"I'm relieved. I've been thinking about it the past few days, and I was waiting for the right moment to talk to you about it. I started to worry that the concept would make us look like we're trying too hard. Or that we would be making me relatable at the expense of what I do best."

I nod. "Exactly. Fuck relatable. We don't need to change a single thing about you. We just need to play to your strengths, of which there are many. I'm thinking a theme focusing on your role as a wedding concierge could be effective. It ties in with the hotel's business, still evokes the idea that you'll give each wedding your personal touch, and would appeal to a broader cross-section of your client population. What do you think?"

She leans over and squeezes my hand. "I think I'm lucky to

be working with you, and now I'm really looking forward to making this pitch."

I'm probably beaming. Pleasing her pleases me, but it's extra special that I can impress her simply by doing my job. "Great. So I'll talk to—"

A hand lands on my shoulder, and a voice behind me bellows my name.

Startled, I twist around to see Nathan Yang, a childhood friend from the old neighborhood, grinning down at me. My heart resumes a normal rhythm. "Nathan, how the hell are you doing? It's been ages."

He nods. "It has, it has. Way too long." Nathan looks at Lina. "Sorry to interrupt, but I had to say hello to an old friend."

She gives him a friendly smile. "No worries."

"Are you dining by yourself?" I ask.

Nathan smooths his hands over the front of his black suit jacket. "No, no. I'm the manager here. This has been my gig for about a year now."

"Wow. That's fantastic," I say. "Congrats, man. Lina and I were just raving about the decor."

"Thanks a lot. I'm proud of this place." He glances at Lina again, his eyes narrowing as though he's trying to figure out where he's seen her before.

My mouth goes dry. *Oh, shit.* Nathan was Andrew's friend, too, and I'm pretty sure he was invited to Lina and Andrew's wedding. If there were a way to disable that part of the brain that controls facial recognition, I'd be performing surgery on Nathan this minute.

"Lina. Max. How good to see you," a voice behind Lina says. "Is Nathan treating you well?"

Rebecca? You're shitting me, right? Who the hell did I screw over in a former life? My gaze darts to Lina, who appears frozen in place. *It's okay. We can handle this, no problem. We're working. Not a big deal at all.* I stand and shake Rebecca's hand. "Hey, Rebecca. Good to see you. Nathan and I were just catching up. We grew up together." I wave my hand between Lina and me. "And Lina and I were just talking about the interior design. Trying to figure out the restaurant's main selling points. There's a lot to recommend. We're trying the food next."

Rebecca brushes her palms together. "Oh, I'm happy you're liking it so far." She leans in so only we can hear. "And the restaurant's at its most impressive during the weekend, so good choice coming during a peak time. Be sure to try out the special tasting menu if you get a chance. Nathan's done an amazing job drawing people in with that one."

Lina gives her a tight smile. "I bet."

Rebecca glances at her slim gold wristwatch. "I'm meeting my grandfather for dinner. He's checking up on our properties. And checking on me, too, probably."

Nathan places a finger over his lips as he studies Lina. "Sorry if I've been staring, but you look so familiar to me. Have we met before?"

Lina sinks lower in her chair and fans herself. "Is it hot in here? Someone must have turned up the heat."

Rebecca, meanwhile, is slipping curious glances at everyone, tennis-spectator style. "Lina, are you okay?"

"Oh, I'm fine," Lina says, her voice froggy. She clears her throat. "Just feeling a bit under the weather all of a sudden."

I want to wrap Lina in my arms and hide her from Nathan's scrutiny, but that would be unprofessional—and weird. *Play it*

*cool, Max. With any luck, Rebecca will leave before Nathan makes
the connection.*

"Hey," Nathan says, pointing a finger in Lina's direction.
"Now I remember. You're Carolina Santos. You were engaged
to Max's brother, Andrew. Sorry that didn't work out." His face
flushes. "Damn. This is me inserting a foot in my mouth. My
apologies for mentioning it."

Dammit. So much for luck.

Rebecca tilts her head and studies Lina.

Her expression devoid of emotion, Lina surveys the restaurant through narrowed eyes, as if she's searching for the most
effective escape route.

How she's holding it together is a wonder. Me? I'm ready
to crawl under the table, and my brain isn't operating quickly
enough to defuse the situation. Besides, what the hell would
I say?

Rebecca shakes her head. "Well, I must have missed a memo,
but we can sort it all out Monday morning." She looks between
Lina and me, her mouth set in a hard line, then she says, "First
thing Monday morning, perhaps?"

We both nod, neither of us meeting Rebecca's gaze.

"I need to use the restroom," Lina says, standing abruptly, her
face still blank. "It was great seeing you again, Rebecca." She
glances at Nathan. "And nice meeting you."

I watch her walk briskly in the direction of the restrooms.
Rebecca and Nathan watch her leave, too.

What a clusterfuck.

Chapter Thirty

LINA

Hope may spring eternal, prima, but deception will bite you in the ass.

Natalia's warning rings in my ears like a church bell. Bong. *Hello? Are you surprised?* Bong. *Of course you got caught.* Bong. *Now Rebecca not only pities you but also distrusts you.* Bong. *What are you going to do now?* Bong. *Guess you can forget about that position with the Cartwright.* Bong. *At least you didn't cry in front of everyone.*

With my fists clenched at my sides, I pace the length of the restroom, avoiding my reflection in the mirror. There's no need to see my tears. I can feel them sliding down my cheeks.

Someone knocks on the door.

I flinch, then quickly wipe my face dry—or try to. "It's occupied," I call out.

The door opens a crack. "Lina, it's me. Can I come in?"

"It's not a good idea, Max. I'll be fine. Just give me a"—I hiccup—"give me a second and I'll be out."

"Baby, you're crying. Let me help."

"How can you help, Max? I fucked this up all by myself."

He's quiet for a moment. Then he's talking to someone else. "We just need a minute, okay?" he tells the person. "She's having a menstrual crisis."

I probably misheard him. "Did you just say I'm having a mental crisis?"

"No, I'd never joke about that. I said *menstrual*. I only have a vague idea what that could entail, but she seemed to understand and backed away."

I snort. Even when I'm having a "menstrual crisis" he makes me laugh.

"Did you just laugh?" he asks. "See? I'm helping already."

Several seconds of silence pass, and my stomach churns when I consider the possibility that he's gone. "Max? Are you still there?"

"I'm here, Lina. Will you let me in? Please?"

The urgency in his tone suggests that he's asking for more than just my permission to enter this restroom. But if he sees me like this and doesn't judge or pity me, what then? I'll probably fall in love with him, that's what. Because he'll be the only man who's seen my truest self and doesn't think less of me for it. Andrew never saw the real me. And because of that, I was able to handle my breakup with him like a boss. Didn't cry, or yell, or make a fuss. I held on to my dignity in the face of Andrew's abandonment—because I never gave him my heart. Even when I asked him to reconsider his decision, I did it calmly and logically, pointing out the reasons we made sense. And when he declined to change his mind, I moved on.

So why should I ever give someone the power to make me feel

weak again? That would be the very definition of self-sabotage. Plus, I've already got that covered; considering what just happened out there, I think it would be wise to impose a moratorium on undermining myself.

"Hey, Lina," Max says.

"Yeah?"

"I'm just going to talk, okay? I figure it might help."

I hiccup again. "Okay."

"So here's the thing. I wish Andrew and I were closer. But we just aren't. From an early age, my parents encouraged competition between us. They think sibling rivalry can be a good thing. We push each other, they say. To a certain extent, that's true. But it also means we don't know how to engage with each other unless we're trying to outsmart, out-succeed, out-everything each other. And I'm just so fucking tired of it."

This is eye-opening. Andrew barely talked about Max when we dated. Now I understand why. When I think about what I knew about Max then—Andrew's younger brother in New York—and what I know now, the difference is laughable. The man at the door is vibrant and sweet and funny and sexy and so much more than Andrew's younger brother.

"I'm not exactly sure," he says. "The toilet overflowed, so they're cleaning it up."

I frown. "What?"

"I'm explaining why this person can't enter the restroom," he says to me.

"Oh."

"Anyway, this assignment with Rebecca," he continues. "I know I told you it's my chance to break away from Andrew at work. Distinguish myself so I don't have to be attached to him at every turn. But it's more than that. I just want to be my own person. Live my own life. Without reference to Andrew. Be Rebecca's first choice for no other reason than I'm good at what I do. Maybe then Andrew and I could learn to like each other." He's silent for a moment, then his voice fills the air again, though it's weaker than it was before. "I don't know why I'm saying all this. I just thought you should know that what went down tonight affects me, too. This client could help me stand on my own. And I think we can fix the situation together—if you let me in, that is."

Somehow Max knows that if he shares a piece of himself, I'll be inclined to do the same. I can't keep him out. It would be pointless to try. So I walk to the door, pull on the handle, and peek outside. Max is leaning against the wall to the right of the door, his hands behind his back and his head facing the ceiling.

"Hey," I say.

Max turns to face me, his body still propped against the wall. "Hi."

I take his hand and tug him inside the restroom.

Within seconds, he's sweeping his thumbs under my eyes and drying my tears.

"So brave," he says softly. After a pause, he adds, "Still a badass, tears and all."

I roll my eyes and wave a hand up and down my body. "Out there, yes. In here? This is not the look of a badass."

He stretches his arms out in front of him, and I fall into his body, releasing a shuddering breath as he envelops me in a tight embrace.

"Thing is," he says, his chin resting on my head, "there's no single way to be a badass. Your mother and aunts coming here and making new lives for themselves? Badass. My mother running her own firm even after she and my father divorced? Badass. You facing the obstacles in your path and reinventing yourself in the process? Badass. There's room for different kinds of greatness. Even if you cry doing it. Hell, *especially* if you cry doing it."

"It's not that simple and you know it," I say into his chest.

"You're right. I do know it. Or I know it now. Because you made me see that it's complicated. I just need you to understand that I think you're amazing and strong and yes, a fucking badass. I can't control what other people think, but I know what I know."

And to think I wasn't going to let him in this restroom. Or in my heart. I can no longer fathom not doing both. I don't share myself with many people. My family and Jaslene are my only exceptions. But I'm ready to make an exception for Max, too. He gets me. Like no other man ever has.

Someone knocks on the door, and seconds later, a server pokes her head in. "Folks, we've got a long line outside. Are you squared away with your menstrual crisis, ma'am?"

Max and I separate, my jaw dropping at her words. How did the night progress to the point that she's even posing this question with a straight face?

"I'm all set," I answer. "Thanks."

I drag Max out of the restroom, my face averted so I can avoid the annoyed gazes of the people waiting their turn for a restroom with only two stalls.

"I need to go home and drink myself to sleep," I tell Max. "We can talk about the Rebecca problem tomorrow."

He throws an arm around my shoulder. "We still need to eat, though. How 'bout we get the paella to go?"

I groan. "That sounds good, but it'll take forever to make."

"What if I told you I already ordered it?" he asks, his eyebrows waggling.

"I'd thank you from the bottom of my heart and tell you that we'll both be getting a workout tonight."

He grimaces. "Shit. That's a shame."

"Why?"

"Because I didn't order it yet," he says.

"But I thought . . ." I shake my head. "Never mind."

The man's ridiculous, but I wouldn't want him any other way. I drag him out the door. Paella or not, we're both still getting a workout tonight.

———

"Max, I need to get out of bed." I tap the octopus sprawled across my body. "Max."

He doesn't budge.

"Max, there's marble cake with buttercream frosting in the kitchen."

He stretches and lifts his head. "What? There is?"

I take advantage of his grogginess and slip out from under him. *So gullible.* As much as I'd love to cuddle with him in bed this morning, I promised Natalia and Paolo I'd meet them at Rio de Wheaton to go over their seating chart for the reception.

Max sits up, one hand stretched behind him and the other rubbing the back of his head, the sheet carelessly draped over his bottom half. "Did you lie to me about cake to wake me up?"

"I did. Sorry."

He scrubs a hand over his face. "Noted. But vengeance shall

be mine." After fluffing the pillow behind him, he leans his back against the headboard and watches me gather my hair into a high ponytail. "So, you ready to talk about a game plan for dealing with Rebecca Cartwright? Ignoring the issue won't make it go away, you know."

I brush a few strands of hair from my face—stalling. I don't know how to explain my actions to Rebecca without diminishing myself in her eyes even further. Plus, I suspect the chances that she'll give me a fair shot at the position are slim to none. If I think too much about the opportunity I wasted, I'll only get emotional about it, and that's not going to change anything. I guess at this point I should focus on owning my mistake and ensuring neither Andrew nor Max pays for it. Oh, and I should find an alternative office space. "Honestly, I'm not sure what I'll say to Rebecca yet, but I'd like to speak with her alone. This is my mess, and I'm the one who needs to clean it up." I clear my throat and rest my butt against the dresser. "Would that be okay with you? I mean, I know you'll probably want to touch base with her yourself, but I'd like to speak with her first."

He studies me a moment, then nods. "I trust you to handle the situation. Just let me know how she reacts and I'll follow up with her afterward."

"Deal. And now I *really* need to get ready."

"Don't let me hold you up," he says, shrugging.

Max pretends to have no interest in delaying my progress, but I know better. Out of my peripheral vision, I can see him slowly tracing his fingers over his lips in a circular motion. The bedsheet, which just a few seconds ago blanketed him below the waist, seems to have dipped to his lower thighs. As I dart around the room gathering discarded clothes and searching for fresh ones, I squint at Max whenever he's in my line of sight. This has the desired effect of turning my view of his body into an amorphous shape with zero appeal. It's either this or jump his bones and miss my appointment with Natalia and Paolo.

Max gets on his knees, his penis swaying as easy as it pleases, and then he hobbles over to the edge of the bed. "What's wrong with your eyes? Are you feeling okay?"

"I'm fine," I say, squinting harder. From this vantage, his junk almost resembles a parrot swinging in a cage. And . . . oh God, that's definitely my cue to go. "I think my eyes are just a bit tired from all that crying yesterday. My vision should improve soon."

"But why won't you look at me?" he asks, his voice forlorn.

I blow out my cheeks and face him. "Max, I'm trying to be good here. I need to make this appointment, but you're kneeling on my bed with your dick swinging." I chance a glance at it. "When is it going to stop doing that, by the way? Doesn't a pendulum settle down eventually?"

He laughs and shakes his hips, triggering the pendulum anew. "Stop doing what?"

Oh for goodness sake. I haven't even had coffee yet. Grumbling under my breath, I take my clean undies and robe and wave goodbye to him. "Tchau, Max. I'm going to take a shower."

"May I join you?" he asks, looking at me with puppy dog eyes.

I pause at my bedroom door and point a finger at him. "No. You stay there. If you care about me at all, you'll stay right where you are."

He puts up his hands as though he's surrendering and flops back onto the mattress. "I care about you way more than"—he makes air quotes—"'at all,' so consider me neutralized." He plumps the pillow and rests his head on it, closing his eyes. "Enjoy your shower."

Oh, he's wily. How am I supposed to resist him when he disarms me with his words alone? It's impossible. Accepting defeat (or maybe it's a victory), I saunter back into the room, press my knuckles into the mattress, and lean into him. "I'll enjoy my shower even more with you in it."

He steals a chaste kiss. "What about Natalia and Paolo?"

"I'll shave off some time getting ready." I tweak his nose. "Just for you."

As soon as I say the words, it occurs to me that I've been doing a lot of things just for Max lately—and that realization doesn't disturb me as much as it probably should.

Chapter Thirty-One

LINA

*A*n hour into drafting Natalia and Paolo's seating chart, we encounter a logjam, and her name is Estelle. She's that family friend who attends every gathering even though no one will admit to inviting her.

Natalia draws a red *X* over Estelle's name. "She can't sit anywhere near my mother. If Estelle complains about the cake, Mãe will smash it in her face."

Tia Viviane passes the table and adds her own commentary. "That's right. I'll smash it in her face and it will feel *so* good." Her feet never pause during this delivery, and by the time I look up from the chart, she's gone.

"Is that before or after Tia Viviane's had a few caipirinhas?"

"That's stone cold sober and at her happiest," Natalia says, jerking a thumb in the direction of our last Viviane sighting.

"Okay," I say. "What about putting Estelle at table twelve?"

Paolo shakes his head. "Estelle and Lisandro had a thing a

while back. A few drinks in, and they'd be all over each other. You have kids at that table."

"Okay, what about table seven?" I ask.

Natalia groans. "Estelle's mad at Lynn because Lynn didn't invite Estelle on a girls' weekend trip to New York a couple of months ago."

"I've got it," I say, snapping my fingers. "Give Estelle the wrong address for the reception. Problem solved."

"I wish," Natalia grumbles. "Wait. Let's put Estelle at your table. You'll be a positive influence on her. Jaslene won't need a seat because she'll be taking over the role of lead planner for the day."

That's a good point. Jaslene and I don't often switch roles during a pending client assignment, but I'm taking a back seat for this wedding because Natalia's my favorite cousin and I'd like to enjoy the time with her and my family. Plus, Jaslene recently asked for more responsibility, and this is the ideal opportunity to give it to her.

Paolo tries to nudge Natalia subtly, but nothing about Paolo is subtle.

She turns to him, eyes wide. "What?"

He nods his head in my direction.

"Oh shoot," Natalia says. "You aren't thinking about bringing anyone, are you? A plus-one or something?"

Interesting phrasing there, Nat. I gather she wants the answer to be no, but I *am* thinking about asking Max to join me—if I can work up the nerve. "Well, now that you mention it, I wanted to talk to you about that."

Viviane appears out of nowhere—as does my mother.

"Yes?" I ask them.

"Oh, nothing," my mother says as she wipes her hands on a towel and looks over my shoulder. "I just wanted to see the chart."

"We've been at this for an hour," I say, knowing a mother's lie when I hear one. "You need to see it now?"

"Yes," she says, nodding her head at me. "That's exactly what I said."

Tia Viviane's too impatient to absorb information on the sly. She's the type of person who extracts it—per her schedule. "What's this about a plus-one? Who would you bring?"

I suck in a deep breath and let it out slowly. "Max Hartley, okay?"

Viviane gives me a dismissive wave. "More of that job again? You think if you bring him to the wedding he's going to help you get it?"

Natalia and I exchange glances, amusement in our eyes.

Your mother's so clueless.

Girl, I know. Just let it go.

"Tia Viviane, I'm asking Max to come with me because I like spending time with him. Is that a good enough explanation?"

"Hmm" is all she says.

Natalia squeezes my hand. "Of course he can come, silly." She elbows Paolo. "Right?"

He shrugs. "Yeah, sure."

"This would just be a social thing, okay?" I slip in my latest news, hoping no one will make a big deal of it. "The job is no longer mine to try to get. My potential boss found out I lied about knowing Andrew and Max, so I doubt she'll even let me do the pitch."

Tia Viviane and my mother drag chairs over to the minus-

cule table and look at me expectantly. *Damn.* Of course they
want an explanation. Fortunately, my mother's called away to
the counter, her expression barely disguising her annoyance that
someone would want to *buy* something in a *store.*

Tia Izabel emerges from the back room. "What's going on?"

Tia Viviane fills her in. "That job Lina's trying to get? She lied
about knowing her ex-boyfriend and his brother. We're waiting
for the rest of the story."

My mother returns and stands over us, hands on her hips.
"Okay. Finish."

I give them the CliffsNotes version of the debacle. They supply the sound effects—a chorus of *oohs, ahhs,* and *ta brincando,
nés,* which loosely translates to "You're kidding, right?"

Tia Izabel fans herself with both hands. "You American kids
have too much time to get in trouble. Stay at home with the
family and things like this don't happen."

"Yeah, that's exactly why Solange went buck wild when she
left," Natalia says under her breath.

I kick Natalia under the table and mouth *shut up*; she rolls
her eyes in return.

Tia Izabel has no idea her only child, Solange, had a bit of
a rebellious period after she left home for college, and I'm sure
Solange would love to keep my aunt in the dark about her ex-
ploits. And anyway, it's old news. Now that Solange is in graduate school, she's calmed down considerably.

"Filha," my mother says. "So what happens now?"

"I'm not sure." I massage my temples. "And I'm sorry. I know
I'm squandering the opportunities you gave me, and I hate that
I let my silly emotions lead me down a destructive path once
again. Believe me, I know none of you would have made the

mistakes I made. But I'm going to figure a way out of this mess. One way or another, I'll make sure I'm not a disappointment to you."

My mother drops her arms and rests a hand on mine. "Why would you say something like that? You could never be a disappointment. All we want is for you to be happy."

"Happiness doesn't feel like enough, Mãe," I tell her. "Not when I think of the sacrifices you made." I look at my aunts. "Not when I think of the sacrifices you *all* made. I should be building on the foundation you gave me. Working harder. Achieving more. Isn't that what the next generation's supposed to do?"

My mother sighs. "I worked my butt off so you and your brother wouldn't have to. My reward is seeing that you're doing something you love and making a living at it. That's all I ever wanted—for you to be okay, and you're *more* than okay, Lina. Focus on that."

"I just wish I were as strong as you are," I tell my mother. "Look at what you've accomplished."

My mother shakes my arm. "And look at what *you've* accomplished. You own a business, filha. That takes skills and a lot of strength. Yes, you faced a few bumps along the way, but that's life. Don't ever think you need to be exactly like me. We're not the same person. I'm not perfect or superhuman. I just did what I had to do at the time. Now it's your turn. And you're much stronger than you realize."

She's echoing what Max told me when we were holed up in the bathroom at Blossom. Maybe they're right that I don't give myself enough credit for what I've managed to achieve thus far.

My mother walks behind me and throws her arms over my shoulders. "Live your life, not ours. You've been doing a great job of it so far. And if this job is what you want, fight for it. If it's your own business you want to pursue, do that instead. Build a future that makes sense for you, not anyone else."

God, she's right. Instead of worrying about living up to their standards, I need to focus on meeting my own. And while my mother's and aunts' lessons will always serve as a guide, what makes sense for them won't always make sense for me. That doesn't mean I'm failing; it just means I'm living my own life. I reach up and squeeze her hand. "Thanks for always being there, Mãe."

"Just remember one thing," my mother adds.

"What?"

She raises an index finger and narrows her eyes at me. "If you ever put me in a nursing home, I will haunt you from the grave."

Me: Just got home. Spent the evening with my mother.

Max: Next time you see her, tell her I miss the brigaderos.

Me: Brigadeiros.

Max: Right. Won't make that mistake again. How'd the seating chart go?

Me: All set. Except there's an empty space next to me. Want to claim it?

Max: What's the date? Never mind. Whatever date it is, assuming it's during a weekend, I'll be there. But I should know the date so I can put it on the calendar.

Me: May 18. 11 a.m.

Max: Damn. I'll be returning from a business trip that morning. I'd have to be a little late. Is that okay?

Me: That's fine. You can meet me at the reception. A little of
   Max is better than no Max at all.

Max: You're such a flatterer. It's a date, then.

Me: Nervous about talking to Rebecca tomorrow.

Max: She's more laid-back than most. I have no doubt you'll
   figure out exactly the right thing to say.

Me: Thanks. I'll give it my best shot. Going to get ready for bed.

Max: Good night, L.

Me: Good night, M.

I probably won't sleep at all, though. Not when so much is
riding on my meeting with Rebecca in the morning.

———————

The Cartwright's business offices are made for bustling. People
in small cubicles are shouting instructions into phones. Said
phones are ringing incessantly, as if no one knows how to answer a call. And a group of men are standing around an actual
watercooler, as though they're waiting for someone to capture
their likenesses in a stock photo.

Rebecca marches out of her office and removes her eyeglasses
in a very *Devil Wears Prada* way, complete with a hair flip that
tells me she means to set me straight during this meeting. Out
of the corner of my eye, I spy the men by the watercooler dis-
perse in various directions. It's as if Rebecca shouted *Ready or
not!* and now everyone's playing a game of hide-and-seek. This
isn't the Rebecca I'm used to, and the presence of this version of
her doesn't bode well for me.

"Lina," she says. "Where's Max?"

Whoa. It's apparently not even nice to see me.

I stand and smooth my hands down my slacks. "I asked him to give us an opportunity to talk alone first."

Rebecca crosses her arms over her chest, her brows snapping together as though the notion's absurd. "You weren't aiming to talk woman to woman, I hope."

"No," I say. "I was aiming to speak with you *person* to *person.*"

She sighs, drops her arms, and spins toward her office door. "Come with me, then."

On the way there, she doesn't engage with me at all. It's alarming to see how drastically her demeanor has changed since she discovered Andrew and I were once a couple.

I enter her office and sit in the chair she's gestured to. The decor in here is an extension of the hotel: nice but without any personal touches to mark it as Rebecca's domain.

She sits at her desk, her hands clasped in front of her, and peers at me. "I have nothing to contribute to the conversation at the moment, so you might as well say whatever you think you need to say."

I take a large enough breath that my chest rises, and then I do what I should have done from the beginning: tell the truth. "Andrew and I were engaged four years ago and due to be married three years ago. The wedding never happened. He decided he couldn't go through with it. Fast-forward to the day you ushered Andrew and Max into the conference room. I hadn't seen Max since the wedding, and I hadn't seen Andrew since a week after the wedding. In all honesty, I panicked. I wanted to continue to impress you. Wanted you to think I was this uber-professional wedding planner who had it together and was unflappable. Basically, be the person that attracted your attention in the first place. But I was worried about how you would react, and more than that, how I would react to the stress of facing an unexpected and unwelcome reunion with my former fiancé. Now that I think about it, what would have been really impressive is if I had acknowledged Andrew as my ex-fiancé without showing any feelings whatsoever. You probably would have hired me on the spot."

Rebecca's face softens from granite to sandpaper—still rough but now suggesting some flexibility.

I press ahead. "I didn't want you to see me get emotional, or worse, cry. And let me tell you"—I nod vigorously—"that was a real possibility. I hate the idea of appearing weak under any circumstances, and I cringe at the thought that someone would lose respect for me because of it. So I held out my hand and pretended not to know Andrew, and probably as a result of the shock or some sense of duty to me, Max and Andrew played along. It was not their idea, but once it was set in motion, I think they couldn't figure out how to come clean in a way that would satisfy you. I'm sorry I dragged them into this, and I hope you don't penalize them for my mistake."

Rebecca sits back in her chair. "You don't have to advocate for them. Your version of the events will suffice for now."

I blow out my cheeks and meet her lukewarm gaze. "Well, in the interest of full disclosure, I should tell you that Max and I are seeing each other. And Andrew doesn't know."

Rebecca's eyes widen and her jaw drops. "This is a fucking soap opera."

Oh. She's progressed to swear words. I'm in trouble now. "I don't expect you to understand why I did what I did—"

"Lina, I understand," she says calmly. "I don't like what you

did, but I do understand why you did it. You see, I'm the CEO
of a hotel group founded by my grandfather. My concern has always been that people will think they can pull a fast one on me
because I'm"—she rolls her eyes—"plainly in my position as a
result of favoritism. I'm not imagining this, either. It's happened
so many times that I expect it. With you, though, I didn't get
the sense it would be an issue. I try hard not to build the kind of
walls that would make it difficult to interact with my staff, but
I do have my days. And today's been that kind of day, in large
part because I discovered that you and Andrew and Max had
deceived me. People do what they need to do to protect themselves from the things they fear. I'm no different. Neither are
you, apparently. So, yes, I get it, but I don't like it. That's about
all I can tell you."

It's refreshing to speak with someone who not only relates
to my experience but also doesn't think the way I respond to it
is entirely flawed. Protecting yourself from hurt doesn't mean
you're broken. It means you're human. I'm thankful to Max for
helping me see that. Every person has to decide whether to lower
their shield and when. Lowering it won't happen with every
person. I didn't lower mine with Andrew. And sometimes the
privilege of getting behind that shield needs to be earned. In the
way Max earned a place behind mine. "It means a lot that you
understand, even if you're upset about it. I'll at least walk away
from this experience knowing my reaction wasn't completely
uncalled for. That's something." I rise from the seat and put out
my hand. "It was great meeting you, and I wish you the best of
luck with the search."

Rebecca stares at my hand, her brows drawn together. "Not
so fast, Lina. We're not done here. I view this as part of your

interview. I said I'd take everything into account when I make my decision, and that's still the case." She raises her chin and studies me. "Unless you want to withdraw your name from consideration?"

"Absolutely not," I say without hesitation. "I'd still like to be considered. Thank you."

She waves my thanks away. "Tell Max he's off the hook. For now. As far as anyone's concerned, I know nothing. I'll leave it up to you to work things out with him and Andrew."

I nod. "I appreciate the chance, Rebecca."

"Frankly, I hope you wow me during the presentation," she says. "Because this has been . . . a lot."

I couldn't agree more. But if Max and I focus on putting together a kick-ass presentation, we just might get what we want after all.

Chapter Thirty-Two

MAX

The intercom beeps and Sammy's voice fills my office. "Max, there's someone here who claims the two of you are best friends. He also says you've been doing a poor job of playing your part in the relationship."

I shake my head. *What a needy bastard.* "Tell him to come on back, Sammy."

Less than ten seconds later, Dean appears in my doorway wearing a cocky grin and a three-piece suit.

"It's spring, man," I tell him. "The vest is overkill."

He glides into my office and plops onto a guest chair. "I didn't come here for you to pick apart my wardrobe choices."

I get up and close the door—largely for insurance, because one never knows what's going to come out of Dean's mouth. "Why are you here, then?"

Steepling his fingers, he leans his elbows on his thighs and stares at me. "I've been trying to figure out why I haven't heard from you in a week and a half. It's cool if we don't see each other every day, of course, but we do have a weekly basketball engagement—which is my only form of exercise, by the way— and for the first time in forever you were a no-show. So I was trying to figure out what might be occupying your time." He sits up. "And a light bulb went off. He's spending a lot of time with Lina, working diligently on the Cartwright proposal, I thought. Then I asked myself, 'Self, if Max is spending a lot of time with Lina, what's a possible scenario that would lead Max to ignore his best friend?' And it came to me"—he pretends to crack a whip—"like a bolt of lightning, it came to me: Max and Lina are doing the horizontal samba."

I sigh. "It's the horizontal mambo, dipshit."

He puts up a finger. "First of all, she's Brazilian American, so we're going with the samba. I looked that shit up. Second of all, that's all you have to say?"

I scrub a hand over my face. When God was handing out best friends, I should have asked more questions about this one's qualifications. Dean consistently offers a baffling mix of sage advice and questionable commentary, the latter always making me question whether I should take the former. In any case, I can't trade him in. "All right. Here's the deal. We went on a little trip and things happened."

"Things happened?" he asks, raising both brows.

"And they're still happening. That's really all I can tell you."

"No, it's not," Dean says. "I don't need a blow-by-blow, but you can tell me what you're thinking. You know, drop a hint or two about your plans with this woman."

I can't help chuckling at the mock indignation in his voice. "Are you asking me if my intentions are honorable?"

He shrugs. "Something like that. And not just for her sake but for your sake, too."

There's no question Dean cares. I shouldn't be so hard on the guy. But this isn't the place to talk about Lina and me. And besides, I can't make plans with Lina if she and I don't make them together. "Man, I don't have any answers. I just know I like her. Way more than I probably should at this point."

He nods. "So how does your brother factor into this?"

I swipe up a pen from my desk and twirl it with my fingers. "He hasn't so far. We don't talk about him much. When we're together, it's just us, no one else. I'm not thinking about Andrew, and neither is she. I mean, depending on how things go, we'll need to tell Andrew what's going on. As a courtesy or something. But in the meantime, I'm focused on Lina."

"Well, what about all the stuff we discussed?" Dean asks. "The reasons you shouldn't be together. Getting out from your brother's shadow. Your family. The competition between you and Andrew. Is all that immaterial now?"

"All of it still matters," I tell him. "It just doesn't matter as much as I thought it would. For one, I'm not interested in competing with Andrew anymore. Lina says I need to be in competition with myself, with the best possible version of me out here. And she's right."

Dean nods. "I like this woman."

"Plus, as far as I'm concerned, Andrew's just a guy she dated a long time ago. Every person has a dating history. Lina's just happens to include my older brother in the mix."

"What about your parents?" Dean asks.

"My father won't care. My mother will adjust. And who knows? Maybe she'll get to be Lina's mother-in-law after all."

"Whoa, whoa, whoa. Is that where this is headed?"

I shake my head. "Not yet, no. Still, who's to say it can't happen someday? Look, I'm not going to lie and say none of it matters. But if I want to be in this relationship badly enough, and I do, I'll figure out how to deal with the issues that can't be easily set aside."

I replay my own words in my head: *If I want to be in this relationship badly enough, and I do . . .*

Why the hell am I sitting here talking to Dean about this? I need to speak with Lina and tell her that I want more than a fling, regardless of the obstacles. There's no reason we can't have a future together—if we both want it.

The way Dean's frowning at me dampens my excitement, though. "What's that face for? Say what's on your mind."

Dean sighs. "I don't know, Max. That stuff that went down with Emily made you question your own worth. I'm just worried you're glossing over that and not thinking about how it could mess you up here."

Emily did mess me up. I mean, it's not every day someone you've dated for a year tells you she wished she'd met your older brother first. But Lina's over Andrew. It's not the same situation at all. "Yeah, I hear you. And look, if I had any inkling that Lina's still interested in Andrew, I might think differently, but she doesn't seem even remotely interested in rekindling a relationship with him. That's good enough for me." I jump up from my chair. "Dean, I need to go."

I'm at the door, opening it wide, when he asks where the hell I'm going. "If I want to be in this relationship, I need to tell her, don't you think?"

"Tell whom what?" my mother asks outside my office. "Are you dating someone and didn't even tell me?"

Shit. I don't need this right now. I put my hands on her shoulders. "Mom, I love you. And I promise I'll explain. But I need to do something before I chicken out."

She cups my chin and grins. "Well, look at you. Someone's smitten."

My mother never engages in office displays of affection with Andrew or me. It figures that the prospect of my getting serious with someone would make her break her personal rule.

She raises her chin, pretending to be offended by my silence. "Well, fine. Do what you need to do. But let me ask you this: Have you seen your brother? There are papers for the presentation to the Cartwright strewn around the conference room."

"Saw him pacing in that same room on my way in," Dean says.

"No clue where he could be," I tell my mother. Then I glance at Dean, who's hunched over in the chair and massaging the back of his neck. "Dean, chill. It'll all work out. Let's meet for b-ball later this week."

He waves at me dismissively and puts a hand to his forehead. Which I'm going to ignore. Because right now, I'm focused on telling Lina how I feel, and I can't let Dean's worries drag me down.

As I'm climbing into the Lyft, it occurs to me that my plan to lay my heart on the line is flawed for at least two reasons: I'm still waiting to hear the outcome of Lina's meeting with Rebecca, and I don't know if Lina's at work. If the meeting didn't go well, I won't be making any grand declarations today. So I send her a carefully worded text to get the information I need while also concealing my intent to surprise her.

> **Me**: Hey, L. Back from your meeting with Rebecca yet?
>
> **Lina**: Was just going to text you. Great minds . . . Yes, back at the shop. Meeting went well. Want to talk about it over lunch?

Now that she's extended the invitation, there's no point in hiding the ball.

> **Me**: Perfect. I can drop by in 20 minutes.
>
> **Lina**: How? Aren't you at the office?
>
> **Me**: I'm in a Lyft. Already on my way.
>
> **Lina**: Ok. See you soon then.
>
> **Me**: 👍

As the car travels along the George Washington Parkway, I glimpse parts of the Potomac River through the clumps of trees lining the road. I can't look at anything related to nature without remembering when Lina and I made love on the hood of her car. Pretty flower blooming in a bush? *Hood.* Grass growing in the ground? *Hood.* Bird in the sky? *Hood.* And it's getting inconvenient—there's a whole lot of nature out here.

"What's got you smiling, buddy?" my Lyft driver, Benny, asks. He looks to be in about his fifties with a paunch that reminds me of my dad's.

I catch his eye in the rearview. "Thinking about a woman. Hoping to tell her I want us to be together."

He nods, his mouth curving into a wistful smile. "It's always best to tell the person you care about how you feel, good or bad. Honesty's the *only* policy, I always say."

"Yeah, let's just hope she likes what I have to say."

Fifteen minutes later, Benny drops me off in front of Something Fabulous. The window display features mannequins wearing wedding gowns with bouquets of flowers standing in for their heads. A pale blue awning adorned with bows serves as a canopy for the small storefront. When I enter, a bell above the door jingles.

A man with dark curly hair graying at the temples and a tape measure hanging from his neck greets me with a smile. "Hello. My name's Marcelo. How can I help you today?"

"I'm looking for Lina . . . Carolina Santos, I mean."

He tilts his head and narrows his eyes at me. "Is she expecting you?"

I take a deep breath and broaden my stance. "She is."

He smirks at me. "You can head to the back. She's finishing up with a fitting."

I walk down a narrow hallway until I reach four different dressing areas, each with gauzy curtains covering an arched entryway. There's activity in two of them.

"The girls—"

"Call them your 'women' if you must," Lina says. "Or your 'ladies,' although I'm not a fan of that one, either. But breasts aren't girls. *Tits* is okay. And please refrain from calling anything a 'girly part.'"

"Well, okay," the person says loudly. "When Paolo sees my *tits* his *dick* is going to burst."

Natalia. In a nutshell.

A gasp from another dressing area reminds me that I'm eavesdropping. I knock on the outside wall. "Lina, it's Max. I'm here. Want me to wait outside?"

She separates the curtains and sticks her head out, a sweet smile on her face. "Hey, there. We're almost finished and Natalia's already dressed. Hang on." A minute later, she pulls back the curtain. Shoes, open boxes, and tissue paper clutter the floor. Natalia's sitting in a chair lacing her sneakers, and Jaslene's carefully placing Natalia's outfit in a garment bag.

"Well, if it isn't the guy who's somehow managed to snake his way into my cousin's heart," Natalia says.

Lina looks at Natalia, mouth agape, then turns away.

"You mean *worm*?" I ask, grinning.

Natalia shakes her head, points her index and middle fingers at her eyes, then at mine. "No, I mean *snake*."

Jaslene zips up the garment bag and picks up a box. "Ignore her, Max. Natalia's like this with everyone." She rolls up a bunch of tissue and places it in a recycling bin. "Even her husband-to-be."

Natalia drops her head back. "I'm not an ogre." She looks me up and down. "But just so we're clear: You're still on probation."

"I welcome the opportunity to change your mind," I say.

Jaslene pulls Natalia away. "Come on, let's give them some space. I'll treat you to a smoothie down the block."

Bless that woman. I'm sending her something from the Sweet Shoppe today.

After placing the last of the boxes in a stack on a chair, Lina saunters over to me, her eyes dark and enticing. "Hey, there." She slips her arms around my neck, stands on her toes, and brushes her lips across my mouth. *This* is precisely what I want. For us to greet each other with kisses. For us to meet in the middle of the day and go to lunch. For us to wander off somewhere for a quickie when the mood strikes us. I settle my hands on her waist and draw her closer, deepening the kiss. We both moan when our tongues meet.

Somewhere in the distance a throat clears. Although I know enough to pull away from her, I'm still in a daze, which clears the moment Lina gasps.

"Andrew, what are you doing here?" she asks.

I turn to see my brother standing outside the dressing area. His face is blank, but one of his hands is clenched at his side.

"I came to ask you about your pitch," he says to Lina. "Wanted to make sure Max has been doing his job. Instead, I see this. My brother and the woman I was going to marry kissing in a bridal shop."

Lina, whose hand is covering the mouth that was just kissing me so sweetly, drops her arm and pivots to face him. "Oh, c'mon, Andrew. I realize this must be a bit of a shock, but let's not play the wronged brother here. You broke up with me, remember? On our wedding day, no less. *Three* years ago."

I never envisioned this scenario, so I'm having a hard time formulating the right words to respond to it. What comes out is clunky and ineffectual: "Andrew, we're not doing anything wrong. If you think about it for a minute, you'll see that I'm right."

Andrew stares at me and puffs out his cheeks. "I get it, Max. It's not like we've ever followed a bro code or anything."

"God, I hope not," Lina says, derision in her voice.

I raise my head to the ceiling and count to ten. *Do not let him rile you. He's going to lash out because he's been blindsided.* I regret that we didn't tell him sooner. I do. My brother and I may not be close, but if I put myself in his place, I can understand why he'd want to know what's going on.

"I guess I should have seen this coming," he continues. "Everything's a competition with you. Yes, it's possible you like Lina, but I know that in the deepest recesses of your brain you wanted to win what was once mine."

I step forward. "Don't be a prick, Andrew. She was never yours to begin with, and you know that's not—"

Lina steps forward, too. "I know all about your history of competition, Andrew. Max told me what I needed to know. It's pointless to even go there."

Andrew tilts his head and raises a brow. "Oh, is it? How can you be so sure, Lina? I've known my brother way longer than you have." He pins me to the spot with his smug expression. "Is this about Emily? Is this your way of trying to prove to yourself you can steal a woman's heart, too? Well, it won't work. Bear this in mind, little brother. *Lina* wanted to marry *me. I* decided not to marry *her.* And even after I didn't show for the wedding, *she* asked *me* to reconsider."

Lina sighs. My gut twists. I had no idea Lina tried to reconcile with him. Something about that fact unsettles me, and although I'd love to shove it aside, I can't. He's trying to get under my skin. I *know* this. But I can't deny he's succeeding. Lina wanted him first. She'd still be with him if Andrew hadn't walked away. Hell, she wanted him even *after* he jilted her.

"Think about it, Max. If I hadn't said no, we'd be married right now. You might have even been an uncle." He shakes his head. "I just don't get it. You've always been so worried about living in my shadow, yet you pursue the woman I was going to marry. Doesn't sound like a winning strategy to me."

My brother's on a fucking roll. I've never seen him like this. He keeps throwing verbal jabs and won't let up. Problem is, he's my brother. He knows exactly where I'm vulnerable. But Lina doesn't need to hear this shit. He's done enough to her already. "Andrew, this isn't accomplishing anything. Try to think about someone else for once." I gesture to Lina. "Whatever you want to say about me, fine. But she doesn't deserve this."

Lina places a hand on my back. That small show of solidarity keeps me grounded.

Andrew clucks his tongue. "Well, this is getting awkward, so I'll leave you two alone to sort this out." He turns to leave, then stops, lifting a finger in the air. "Oh, wait a minute. I forgot to tell you the funny part. You'll love this, Max."

"Oh good Lord," Lina mutters.

Jesus. Why won't he leave already? If I could be certain we wouldn't tear this place apart, I'd kick him out myself. "Andrew, just say what you need to say and get out."

"Consider this my little gift to you. An early wedding present, if you will. Max, you didn't encourage me to cancel the wedding. You spent most of the night talking about where you'd spend your honeymoon if you ever got married." He leans over and addresses Lina in a whisper: "Costa Rica's his fave, by the way."

I shake my head. "But in your text, you admitted I was right. That I'd made sense when I said you weren't ready to get married. I fucking saw it with my own eyes. Lina did, too."

"You saw it," Andrew says, "but do you remember it?"

My vision clouds, and a new rush of adrenaline courses

through me. He's got to be fucking kidding me. What diabolical bullshit is he up to? "Why the hell would you lie about something like that?"

Andrew sighs. "Honestly? I didn't want to face Mom and Dad alone. It was much easier to deal with their disappointment if my younger and mega-persuasive brother had a hand in the decision, too." He faces Lina, who's shaking her head and pacing behind me. "Anyway, they'll be happy to know you're returning to the family, Lina. I'm sure my mother won't care how your reappearance will affect the family dynamic. I'm also sure it's a relief to know there was no reason to hate him, especially now that you both have every reason to despise me. Thanks to yours truly, you can enjoy a sparkling fresh start, and we'll all be one big happy family."

Lina steps forward and stands by my side. We stare at him, both of us wearing stunned expressions.

Andrew sighs. "That last part was sarcasm, by the way." He waves goodbye to us, and as a final parting gift, treats us to the shit-eating grin he wears so well. "Take care."

When he's gone, I drop my head into my hands and take a deep breath. That text. That stupid-ass text that was passed around from family member to family member as evidence of my role in the whole fiasco was a lie. What bullshit. Still, as much as it makes me want to clip Andrew in the chin, that text is the least of my worries.

All relationships require work. But a relationship that starts out the way ours has isn't facing great odds. And would lead to what? Me ending up exactly where I don't want to be? Stuck in Andrew's shadow again? Living the life *he* walked away from? Loving the person who loved *him* first? Wondering if I'm good enough to replace the person *she* wanted to be with? I don't deserve that. Neither does she. I thought I could get past Lina's connection to my brother, but the truth is, I can't. I'll always worry that I'm second best. Or that she's settling. This is what Dean's been warning me about all along, isn't it?

It hits me then: I'm in a relationship that has no real possibility of flourishing. And that isn't fair to either of us. Honesty is the *only* policy, right?

Lina shakes her head. "Did that just happen? I feel like I'm in the twilight zone."

I blow out a long breath. "It happened."

And unfortunately, it's only going to get worse from here.

Chapter Thirty-Three

LINA

And to think I almost married the man. I certainly dodged a dickhead with that one.

Max is still holding his head in his hands. He must be heartbroken knowing Andrew pinned him as part of the reason he decided not to marry me. Shit, I regret all the things *I* said and did when I thought Max had been a partial culprit. But we got where we needed to be anyway, didn't we?

I squeeze his shoulder. "Hey. It's okay. The worst is over."

Max lifts his head and gives me a sad smile. "Yeah, I wasn't expecting to deal with that today. Had other plans, for sure."

I trail my hand down his chest and hang my finger on a belt loop in the waistband of his slacks. "Do you want to just head out? We can talk over lunch."

His gaze travels to a spot behind my shoulder. I know that move well, so I'm immediately on high alert.

"I think that whole confrontation wiped me out," he says,

massaging the back of his neck. He glances at me. "How about a rain check on lunch?"

That's understandable. It's not every day that your brother finds out you're dating his former fiancée. "Sure. But let me give you the short story on Rebecca. We had a great talk. Awkward but helpful. She understands why I felt compelled to lie. Doesn't appreciate it, but she understands. She called it a soap opera."

His shoulders tense. "She's not wrong. Honestly, this whole mess forces me to ask the million-dollar question: What the hell are we doing, Lina?"

I snap my brows together and step back, removing my finger from his belt loop. "What do you mean?"

He turns away and paces the dressing area. "I mean why are we"—he waves his hands around—"together. What do we think is going to happen here?" Still pacing, he rubs his temples as though answering his own question is hurting his head. "Here's what I think. We got caught up in a dream world. One where it didn't matter that you almost married my brother. One where I wouldn't care that he's always going to be somewhere in the background. You know my issues. The thought that Andrew will always be looking at us with that smug grin of his is"—he raises his hands and bends his fingers as if they're claws—"fucking infuriating. Hell, you even told me from the outset we wouldn't work in the long-term." He sighs. "Here's the thing: We both deserve a relationship that doesn't exist in my brother's shadow. And let's be honest, you know exactly what you want, and it's a lot closer to Andrew than I'll ever be."

Someone's got me all figured out, and he's so wrong. But

my gut tells me this is about his issues, not mine. "What do *you* want, then?"

He scrubs a hand down his face and blows out a long breath. "I want to come first. I want someone who thinks *I'm* the best thing that's ever happened to them. You were going to marry him, Lina. *He* chose to walk away, not you. Even after he was a no-show at your wedding, you tried to change his mind. That means something. I can't be your second choice, Lina. There's just too much history between Andrew and me to set that aside."

"Yes, I tried to change his mind. I thought he was what I wanted. What I needed. But I was wrong and—"

He throws up a hand. "And I want to know that I didn't pursue the woman I love because of some silly competition with my brother. I can't be one hundred percent certain of that, Lina. Ever. Could you? Is that fair to either of us?"

My stomach clenches. That part's total bullshit. An excuse to pull away from me. To pretend he's doing this partly for my benefit. If he'd pursued me to "win" me, he wouldn't care how I felt about him; he'd want to win at all costs. No, he's grasping at straws. After all the talk about *just being with him, letting go, letting him in,* a few conniving words from his jerk of a brother send him into a tailspin. *Unbelievable.* The pang in my chest prompts me to speak. "You think we're doomed from the outset."

We stare at each other. He breaks eye contact first.

"Yeah," he says. "What's the point of trying to fix something that may be unfixable? Wouldn't it be better to cut our losses now? Before anyone gets hurt?"

I want to scream that he's hurting me right the fuck now, but years of self-preservation clamp an invisible hand over my mouth. Why would he pursue me? Tell me all that stuff at the retreat? About our potential. About how he can't stop thinking about me. Why would he tell me he cares about me a lot more than "at all"? Why? Why? Why?

The space where my heart should be feels hollow, as though someone's torn the organ from my chest as easily as a person rips a page out of a notebook. If this is how I feel now—seconds away from wailing from the pain he's causing me—imagine what it would feel like a year from now. Or two. Or five. These big feelings aren't healthy. They draw emotions out of you best left under lock and key. Well, he's not getting them from me. Not today or any day.

Still, a small voice in my head tells me to fight for him. He's scared and I understand why. He thinks he's not enough. He can't wrap his head around the idea that I'd choose him over Andrew. He believes I'm settling for second best. But telling him none of that's true isn't going to change his mind, and I don't know that there's any way to convince him he's wrong.

He takes my hand and shakes it, pulling me out of my conflicting thoughts. "Hey."

"Hey," I say.

"This isn't easy for me," he says, "but you and I both know this relationship had an expiration date. Andrew showing up today just shortened our timeline. And maybe that's for the best."

Hearing him explain away our relationship so succinctly drains me of any energy to battle him on this front. I can't force him to be with me, and I shouldn't have to. The best approach is to say my piece and turn to the tasks ahead. Approachable-yet-badass bitch should work fine. "Look, I think you're selling us short, but I'm not going to beg you to be with me. If whatever we are ends here, then so be it. The great thing is, I'm confident we can handle this like adults. We have only two weeks before the pitch and all of that work can be done by email or phone." I shake my hand free of his. "So let's finish this pitch and get me a fucking job, okay?"

He smiles faintly. "Okay."

"You can let yourself out, right?"

He straightens. "Of course. We'll talk soon."

Just go already. Go, go, go.

When he walks out of the dressing area, I take a shaky breath and let the tears flow.

Good news: I didn't cry in front of him even though I desperately wanted to.

Bad news: Judging by how much it hurts to see him leave, I think I'm already in love.

———————

"Lina, what are you still doing back here? We left like an hour ago."

Jaslene stares at me from the dressing room entryway, a large paper cup in her hand.

What am I doing? Moping. Feeling sorry for myself. Retracing my steps to figure out what I should have done differently. "I just got tired and decided to sit down, that's all."

She walks over and puts a hand to my forehead. "Are you feeling sick? Need me to get you something?"

"I'm not sick, Jaslene. Not physically, anyway."

Because Jaslene takes on everyone else's problems, I'm not surprised when she sits in a chair on the other side of the table between us. "But you're heartsick. Is that it?"

The tears are flowing freely now. "Yeah. Is that what it's called when you wish you could remove your heart from your body and never use it again?"

Jaslene sets her cup on the table, making sure to place a napkin under the cup before she does, then she hands me a tissue. "What happened?"

"Andrew."

She twists in her chair, her eyes wide as saucers. "What? He stopped by?" Her eyes narrow. "Oh . . . *oh* . . . he saw Max, didn't he?"

"Yep."

"¡Chacho! What awful timing! Were you—"

Natalia bursts into the dressing area, a cup twice the size of Jaslene's in her hand. "I'm back, mulheres! Did you miss me?"

"Always," Jaslene says, her flat tone underscoring her sarcasm.

Natalia meows and hisses at her, adding a two-fingered claw scratch at the end. "Keep that up and I'll revoke your invitation to my bachelorette party." She plops down onto the floor in front of us, dramatically arranging herself in a cross-legged position. "Now, tell me what happened. Oh, shit, Lina, you're crying."

I nod, then tell them the abridged version of this afternoon's garbage fire, hiccupping on every fourth word. It takes forever.

Jaslene peppers me with enough questions to get the unabridged story out of me. Natalia, meanwhile, remains silent, occasionally slurping on her fruit smoothie. It's painful to go over it again, but I suppose this is part of the process. Catharsis.

"Nothing to say?" I ask Natalia.

She shakes her head. "Still absorbing. Also, feeling really guilty about the way I treated Max."

Jaslene sucks her teeth. "Max will be fine." She leans over and squeezes my hand. "I'm sorry you're hurting. If I could take just a little of your pain, you know I would. Want to go to capoeira class tonight? That might help get your mind off him."

I groan and slide down the chair. "I doubt that's possible, but I'll try anything."

Natalia takes another sip of her smoothie, then pops her lips. "Okay. So the way I see it is this. Max is scared. You're scared. Andrew's lost. And all of you need to get your shit together." She winks at me. "But know that I'm rooting for you."

I cackle at her concise summary. "Thanks, Natalia. I can always count on you to tell it like it is."

"Am I wrong?" she says, her hands raised in a question.

Of the three of us—Max, Andrew, and me—I'm probably the only one who recognizes that she's not.

MAX

*M*y mother tosses a pen at me. "Are you with us today?"

I fumble to catch it and sit up. "What? Yeah, I'm here. No need to resort to physical assault."

She leans back in her office chair and studies me for a good ten seconds before she says, "Well, if you were paying attention, you'd know that I posed a question."

"Which was?"

She looks over at Andrew. "Do *you* know the question?"

But Andrew's staring at the notepad in his lap, so she lobs a pen at him, too. "What the hell is going on with you two?"

It's been less than twenty-four hours since my relationship

with Lina imploded, so I know what's wrong with me. As for Andrew, who the hell cares.

Andrew's still not with us, though.

My mother bangs her fist against her desk to get his attention. "Andrew."

He jerks and scribbles on his notepad. "Got it."

"Got what?" my mother asks.

"Whatever you need me to do," he says uncertainly.

My mother rests her elbows on the desk and massages her temples. "Okay, let's start over. What's going on with the Pembley account?"

Andrew's the lead on that one. As usual, I'm his backup. He sifts through his notepad looking for the color-coded tabbed pages for that account. "Pembley. We're set to meet with them next week. That still work for you, Max?"

"Yes," I say.

"And the Cartwright Group?" my mother asks.

You mean the client I wanted to woo so I could show you that I'm worthy of managing my own accounts? Oh, I don't know. The client knows we lied to her. The planner I'm supposed to be helping would probably throw me in a wood chipper if given half the chance. And if I'm forced to sit with my brother for anything more than fifteen minutes, I'll lunge at him. "Everything's on track. I should be getting mock-ups from Karen later today. I'll share them with Lina soon after that."

My mother nods. "Good."

She peers at Andrew. "And you? How's it coming along?"

Andrew tugs on his tie. "Well, Henry's not on board with the current direction, so we're scrapping the plans and trying something new."

Interesting. Is that why he was pacing and throwing papers in the conference room yesterday? Can't wait to see what they come up with. Although now that I think about it, Rebecca hasn't suggested that we'd be watching each other's presentations. I should ask that Lina and I go first, just in case Andrew decides to steal our ideas. Wouldn't put it past him.

"That's not encouraging, Andrew," my mother says. "I need you to get a plan in place soon."

"Will do," he says. "I promise."

My mother clasps her hands on the desk, leans on her elbows, and looks at me. "I've been meaning to ask you. How's Lina? Is she well?"

I can't talk about her in a dispassionate way. It would kill me. And I've already taken enough hits where Lina's concerned. Fuck this. If I'm going down, he's going down, too. I jerk a thumb in Andrew's direction. "Ask him. He saw her as recently as yesterday."

My mother's head snaps back. "You did? Why?"

I twist my upper body in Andrew's direction and settle in for an explanation. "Yes, Andrew. Tell us why you visited Lina at her work even though I'm the one assigned to help her."

Andrew clears his throat. "It's like I said. I wanted to make sure you were doing your job."

"You were planning to fish for information about our pitch, weren't you?" I ask. "You didn't want me to know, so you went to her. Because you couldn't think up a single idea without my input."

Andrew sighs, feigning boredom. "Think what you want, but I had legitimate business reasons to be there. Unlike you."

My mother frowns at us. "What's that supposed to mean?"

This is ridiculous. Andrew and I are squabbling like children.

And for what? So we can one-up each other in my mother's eyes? I have zero interest in doing that. "What he means is, Lina and I became something other than friends or colleagues. Neither of us planned it, of course, and whatever it was is now over, so there's really no point in either discussing it"—I point at Andrew—"or, in your case, poking me about it. When we're in this office, I want to work. That's all." I slide to the edge of the chair, readying myself to leave. "But just so there are no more secrets between us, why don't you come clean, Andrew?"

My mother removes her eyeglasses. "Come clean about what?"

Andrew and I stare at each other for several seconds, then he drops his chin and loosens his tie.

"Max never discouraged me from marrying Lina," he says. "I made that up."

My mother gasps. "You what?"

I don't need to listen to this crap. "Are we done here? If so, I'll leave you two to talk."

My mother's gaze bounces between Andrew and me. "We're done."

I stand and walk to the door. My priority is helping Lina get the job of her dreams. Everything else is bullshit.

Before I slip out, my mother calls me back.

"Max, hang on."

I turn to face her. "Yeah?"

She meets my gaze, her mouth set in a determined line, then she says, "Whatever it is, we'll get through it. I promise."

I don't know what to say to that. There's nothing to get through. Not anything that matters, anyway. I give her a weak wave. "Yeah. See you later."

Chapter Thirty-Four

MAX

From: MHartley @AtlasCommunications.com
To: CSantos@DottingTheIDos.com
Date: May 1 - 10:23 am
Subject: Materials for Pitch to Cartwright
   Hotel Group

Hi Lina,

I'm attaching the mock website landing pages and social media graphics Karen prepared. Because the storyboards are more involved, we're holding off on preparing them until we know you're comfortable with the current approach. Let me know your thoughts.

Hope you're well.

—Max

From: CSantos@DottingTheIDos.com
To: MHartley@AtlasCommunications.com
Date: May 1 - 10:57 am
Subject: Re: Materials for Pitch to Cartwright
Hotel Group

Thank you.

I'm curious: What do you think?

Just seeing that she's responded to my email makes my heart thump hard in my chest. I'm squinting at the screen, willing it to make more words appear, but that's all I'm going to get. What else should I expect? She's doing just what she said she would: acting like an adult. I should do the same.

From: MHartley@AtlasCommunications.com
To: CSantos@DottingTheIDos.com
Date: May 1 - 11:02 am
Subject: Re: Materials for Pitch to Cartwright
Hotel Group

I think we were right to settle on the wedding-concierge concept. Your services fold in nicely with what the Cartwright's already doing. Makes me think the transition would be seamless. I'm hoping Rebecca Cartwright agrees.

p.s. How are you?

From: CSantos@DottingTheIDos.com
To: MHartley@AtlasCommunications.com
Date: May 2 - 9:43 am
Subject: Re: Materials for Pitch to Cartwright Hotel Group

Hello Max,

I've now had a chance to review the materials in full. Please extend my thanks to Karen for doing a superb job.

I agree that the wedding-concierge branding works seamlessly with the Cartwright's current services. I'm excited to make the pitch, and I can't wait to see the storyboards.

All my best,
Lina

I'm glad she's pleased with our work. And I wish she had answered my question. I struggle to come up with an excuse to keep the dialogue open. My response is, in a word, pathetic.

From: MHartley@AtlasCommunications.com
To: CSantos@DottingTheIDos.com
Date: May 2 - 10:13 am
Subject: Re: Materials for Pitch to Cartwright Hotel Group

Will send them soon.

Dean sends me a text a few minutes later.

Dean: You. Me. Drinks at Maroon next Friday.

Me: Why?

Dean: So you can spend some time with me. Damn. You're not
in mourning.

Me: Sorry. Sure, let's do it.

He's right. Breaking up may be hard to do, but I need to get
over her.

"Dean, why are we here?"

He cups his ear and leans into me. "What?"

"Why. Are. We. Here?"

He's bopping to the music, some techno shit I have no interest in listening to. "Just hanging out on a Friday. You do remember how to have fun, right?"

I wave off his question.

A server wearing silver wings leans over Dean and places two
drinks on the coffee table in front of us. If the other drinks we've
had are any guide, these won't be weak, either. The place isn't
crammed wall-to-wall with people, but I wish it were. That way,
I wouldn't have to see how sorry this place is.

We're sitting on a purple velvet couch. The people across from
us are draped over a green suede couch. Lina would love the
purple one. With that, my thoughts take a turn. I picture Lina
in her apartment. Then I picture *us* in her apartment. In her
bed. In her shower. At the kitchen island sipping coffee before
going our separate ways.

Dean taps me on the back of my head. "Stop that."

"Stop what?" I say in a tone that's more a growl than an attempt at conversation.

"Stop thinking about her," Dean says, his gaze following a woman across the room. "It's been over a week. Time to accept the choice you made and move forward."

That sounds final. And sad.

Dean hands me a glass. I have no clue what's in it, but I still throw it back in two gulps. Jack and Coke.

"Unless . . ." Dean says.

"Unless what?"

He points out at the people mingling in the club. "Unless this doesn't feel right to you. Is there some other way you want to meet someone? Dating app? Church? Blind date arranged by one of your friends? I could set you up if you want."

None of those options interest me. I'm fucking ruined and I'm not even mad about it. "I need to take a piss." I wobble off the couch, nearly face-planting in the process.

Dean jumps up. "Whoa, man. Maybe we should get you home."

"Okay, yeah. Let me just"—I motion like I'm holding a firehose—"take care of this and we'll head out."

I'm surprisingly steady on my feet in the restroom. When I return, the music's barely audible and a man's standing on a small stage in the back of the room. "Oh shit," I say to no one in particular. "Is it open mic night?"

The people around me cringe. Perhaps I should tone it down, but how else am I supposed to entertain myself?

A large hand slaps me on the back and squeezes my shoulder. "You ready, buddy?"

I shake Dean off, knowing I *must* take part in open mic

night. It is written. Somewhere. I point at the stage. "I'm going up there."

Dean frowns. "Up where?"

"There," I say, pointing. "I need to get some stuff off my chest." I raise my arms in the air and snap my fingers continuously. "Poetry or something. Yeah, a poem."

Dean scrubs a hand down his face. "You think this'll help, huh?"

I tap him on the chest. "I'm sure of it."

Dean nods. "Fine. I'll get you up there. Stay behind me." He weaves his way through the crowd as I hang on to the back of his damp shirt. Then he's talking to a woman, his thumb pointed at me. She gives me a once-over and nods at Dean.

He turns around and gives me the okay sign. "You're up next. Make it count."

The man at the mic and the woman Dean was just talking to chat briefly. Man at the mic says, "We're going to have a little spoken word by a gentleman who needs to get some things off his chest. Put your hands together and give a warm welcome to Climax."

I stumble onto the stage and whisper in the man's ear.

"Oh, sorry," he says into the mic. "It's just Max." He hands me the mic and jumps off the low platform.

I squint at the bright lights trained on the stage and step back to avoid the glare. After clearing my throat, I begin my one-man show, whisper-speaking in a slow cadence:

"Lina

Her name is Lina

Lina, Lina, Lina, Lina

Where's Lina now?

Why did I let her go?
Lina, Lina, Lina, Lina
She moves like a dance
Laughs like a bell
Would never . . .
Uh, drop my penny into a well
Sometimes so serious
Makes her mysterious."

The crowd's into it. I can tell. People are nodding their heads and smiling. But I can't stay up here too long because my stomach feels like crap.

"Anyway
Lina's my heart
Should have known it from the start
She's wonderful said my mother—"

"Aww," someone in the audience says.

"Only problem is
She was engaged to my brother."

"Oh damn," someone else says.

Then there's a collective *oooh* in the audience followed by excited chatter and murmurs. *Yeah. Exactly.* Everyone knows that type of situation is fraught with peril.

Dean collects me from the corner of the stage. "M, you were like Adam Sandler in *The Wedding Singer* up there. Classic." He puts a hand on my shoulder. "But I'm starting to think this thing with Lina isn't going to just disappear because you want it to."

It has to. I don't want to wonder whether Lina and I are together only because she couldn't be with Andrew. That would wreck me. I want to be the best thing that's ever happened to Lina in the same way she's the best thing that's ever happened to me. And Andrew isn't going anywhere. He'll be a constant reminder that I don't have her entire heart. Not completely. *No, I'll pass on that misery, thank you.* I may be hurting now, but the sharp pain of this loss will dull eventually. Someday.

LINA

*W*ho knew there were so many songs with a ride theme?

Natalia jostles me as she pulls dollar bills from her bra. She holds up the wad of money and waves it around. "Hey, cowboy. Save a horse and ride me."

Jaslene, who's tipsy, snatches the wad for herself. "Got my saddle, sweetheart. Where's my pony?"

I need to speak to the person who approved this outing. *Oh, wait.* That would be me.

We're just a week away from Natalia's wedding and I caved to her request that we take her to a male revue in DC. That's not the problematic part.

"Bring it here," Tia Izabel yells.

This is the problem: I'm wrangling Jaslene and four family members, not just one. Sure, I *want* them to have a blast, but I don't want anyone to overstep the boundaries of decency or the rules of the revue itself—touch where they're not supposed to, say something crass, or start removing their own clothes. Keeping track of everyone as they watch the show is like playing a game of whac-a-mole. *Stop that. No, you can't just throw the money. Put your hand down. No, you don't need another drink,*

Natalia. Yes, it's real. No, you can't touch it. Jaslene, that's not a vibrator! Hey, you can't go up there unless they invite you.

"Shake what your dada gave ya!" sings Tia Viviane.

How does she even know to change the lyrics?

"Shake what your dada gave ya!" Natalia chimes in.

Oh, that's how.

My mother's hand is vacuum-sealed to her face like a starfish. Interestingly, though, her fingers are spread in a way that allows her to peek at the show if she chooses to. I *should* be enjoying our night on the town. I appreciate an expertly choreographed dance performed by buff dudes just as much as the next person. But swinging boners make me think of Max in my bed, and my brain isn't interested in anyone else's erection at the moment.

My mother bumps me with her shoulder and tucks into my side. Everyone else is distracted by a new dancer strutting onto the stage. Assless chaps. Natalia must be pleased.

"What's wrong, filha?" my mother asks. "You look sad today."

"It's nothing, Mãe. Just tired."

We're essentially screaming at each other to be heard.

"Did you have a fight with Max?" she asks.

I pull back and furrow my brows, my lips pressed together in contemplation. "Where'd you get that from?"

She shakes her head. "It's just . . . I thought maybe there was something there. And now you're looking lost so I wondered."

I can't really hide anything from my mother. Not for long, anyway. "Yeah, there was something there . . . but now it's gone. His choice."

"It was a bad choice. I hope you know that."

"I thought so, too, at first, but now I'm not so sure."

I can't really blame Max for fearing that our relationship

would be doomed from the start. Maybe it was. It's one thing to fall in love with your ex-fiancé's brother; it's quite another to fall in love with your ex-fiancé's brother when those siblings have been locked in a competition since forever. Still, there were moments so bright and perfect between us that I can't help imagining we would have had tons more of them. And I miss being with the one man who adored the real me, who had my back, who made me feel safe to share my fears and my disappointments. I wish I could erase my memories of him—because you can't miss someone you don't remember.

Oh God, this hurts.

A flash of silver catches my eye, then the male emcee passes our table, looking for a volunteer from the crowd to sit in the place of honor onstage.

Tia Viviane waves her hands and points at herself as though she's an aircraft marshaller directing a plane on the tarmac.

The emcee keeps walking past her.

Tia Viviane cups her hands over her mouth and yells after him, "Don't just ignore the older woman with big hips and a big butt. I want to have fun, too."

He stills, then spins to face Tia Viviane. Wearing a wicked grin, he stalks back to her, stretches out his hand, and says, "Come with me, then."

Oh my word.

Tia Viviane takes his hand and skips up the steps. Not long after, a dancer—tall, broad-shouldered, and brown-skinned— circles Tia Viviane, eventually helping her to the chair. Viviane rubs her hands together and waits for the show. He teases as he dances, stretching out his tank top to give her glimpses of his hard pecs and washboard abs.

Tia Viviane makes a big show of yawning.

The dancer jerks his head back and places his hands on his hips; Tia Viviane's a puzzle he's trying to solve. Facing the audience and cupping his ear, he raises his free hand up and down in the air while the emcee says, "Make some noise if you want more."

The dancer slides his hands down his abs and gyrates his hips, then he pulls on the sides of his tear-away pants, revealing a black bikini thong, which disappears when he bends over.

His ass is in Tia Viviane's face.

His *ass* is in Tia Viviane's face.

Natalia falls over in laughter. Jaslene screeches, jumps up off her chair, and pumps her fist in approval.

Tia Viviane grins, but she doesn't look all that impressed. The emcee sidles up to her and places the mic near her mouth. "What's wrong? Too much for you?"

She snaps her brows together. "Too much? That's not enough." She crosses her arms over her chest. "I could see the same thing on the beach in Copacabana. A lot of them, too. Ass and butt floss everywhere."

The emcee and the dancer shrug at each other, and then the emcee's ushering Tia Viviane back to her seat.

You know what? I'll be fine, with or without Max. Would I prefer to be with Max? A thousand times, yes. But if it's not meant to be, I'm still blessed in countless ways—these wonderful women and my battery-operated vibrators chief among them.

Now I just need to snag the job of my dreams. That should be enough.

It *has* to be.

Chapter Thirty-Five

MAX

The day of the Cartwright pitch, Lina strides into the conference room, a tan satchel briefcase in one hand and a large travel mug in the other. A fancy clip holds her hair in a high ponytail—no strand out of place. Her navy pantsuit, which she's paired with a cream blouse, communicates authority and assurance, while the hot pink nail polish peeking out from her open-toed shoes hints at the playfulness I've witnessed firsthand.

As she approaches, I run my hands down my pant legs, trying to dry my sweaty palms. A pang of regret settles in the pit of my stomach when I realize I can't greet her with a hello kiss. My chest constricts the closer she comes, the need to touch her palpable but impossible to act on. My heart's gone rogue, skipping and tripping as it sees fit, probably based on her nearness alone. More than anything, I feel a sense of hope—hope that today she'll get the thing she wants most: the job of her dreams.

"Hello, there," she says with a polite smile.

"Hey," I say.

It's a struggle to put words together. My head's a jumbled mess of regrets and what-ifs. Thankfully, Lina's not relying on my speaking skills to land her this job. She'll make the pitch herself.

She waves her hand over the table. "Is this everything?"

I nod. "Yeah. I came a few minutes early and checked the stacks a fourth time. Feel free to do your own spot-check. If we're missing anything, I have the files on my laptop and we can print them out here."

"Let's hope that won't be necessary," she says, taking a seat at the table. She checks the stacks against her own notes on her phone. "So, any last-minute tips?"

I take a seat across from her. "Just be yourself. You're selling you. If you don't genuinely believe in what you're saying, Rebecca won't believe it, either."

"Good advice," she says, her hands still riffling through the papers. "Okay, I think we're all set. I'm glad we didn't go with a PowerPoint. Sometimes paper is best, especially when we're pitching brochures and the like. The run-through of the mock landing pages should be a breeze. I went over them myself a dozen times yesterday."

She takes a deep breath and rests her clasped hands on the conference table. I stare in her direction, willing her to look at me, but she's gazing out the window.

"Lina—"

She stands abruptly. "I'm going to use the restroom before we begin."

I stand as she leaves and plop down onto the chair when she's gone. *Focus on her. Focus on the presentation. Everything else is bullshit.*

Lina returns several minutes later. Rebecca follows within a minute after her.

"Good morning, Lina." My client nods at me as she takes her seat. "Max."

I reach over the table and shake her hand. "Good to see you again, Rebecca."

"You, too." She flips through the binder set before her. "Shall we start?"

Lina rises from her seat and takes her place at the front of the room. "Ready."

Rebecca looks at her expectantly. I give her an encouraging nod.

Lina squares her shoulders and begins. "Dotting the I Do's is a premier wedding planning company with a three-prong approach to serving its clients' needs. One, personal service is key. We pride ourselves on knowing the clients' individual needs and meeting them. Two, no detail is too small. We worry about every detail so the couple doesn't have to. Three, weddings are an opportunity to be creative. In other words, there's no one way to get married, just as there's no typical couple. This philosophy allows us to explore our imaginations and make them reality."

Her voice is strong, and her words are clear and direct. I'm mentally pumping my fist in celebration of how she's doing so far. If Lina impresses Rebecca, it stands to reason that Rebecca will be impressed with me, too.

"Now, the Cartwright brings its own legacy of excellence to the table . . ."

Rebecca tilts her head at Lina and smiles.

Lina highlights the reputation, amenities, and grandeur of

the Cartwright. Again, she handles the material easily and confidently.

"So how do we combine the skill set of Dotting the I Do's with the resources and service commitment of the Cartwright? We provide personal wedding-concierge services just as the hotel would provide its own concierge services to hotel guests . . ."

Lina makes the rest of her pitch flawlessly, even including the anecdote about Rebecca's cousin's shaved eyebrows, which earns Lina big laughs from us both.

"So that's it," Lina says. "Those are my ideas for filling the wedding coordinator position with the Cartwright."

Rebecca gives her effusive praise and rushes out for her next meeting.

Eyes brimming with happy tears, Lina throws her arms around my waist and rests her head against my shoulder. "We did it, Max. We did it. Even if I don't get the job, I'll know we put together a kick-ass presentation."

I know she wouldn't shed those tears around anyone, and I'm honored to still be in the small circle of people who get to see this unguarded version of her. "*You* put together a kick-ass presentation. I was just along for the ride as I always told you I would be."

Neither of us pulls out of the embrace even though we've been in it longer than anyone would consider professional. I'm tempted to tell her that I screwed up. That I want another chance. But I'm scared. Scared that she can't possibly feel the same way I feel about her. Scared that my feelings are too big to be reciprocated.

The embrace does end eventually, when Lina steps back and

shakes out her hands. "So I need to head back to the office. I have a few appointments to look at office space—in case this doesn't work out."

"Yeah, yeah. I understand," I say, straightening my tie and my cuff links. "Good job today."

She smiles and bounces in place. "Ahhh, I'm so excited. Fingers crossed, right?"

I cross my fingers on both hands and cross my eyes for good measure. "Everything's crossed."

She points at my feet. "What about those?"

I cross them as well.

"Good," she says.

"Leave any of the extra stuff here. I'll pack it up and bring it back to the office."

"You sure?" she asks.

"Positive."

"Okay, well, I'll let you know when I hear anything. Thanks again."

"You're very welcome, Lina."

She strides to the door, and I watch her take each step, until she spins around and gives me one of her smiles, the kind that used to be reluctant but now come freely; it both speaks to how much progress we've made in the short time we've known each other and underscores that our impasse is all on me. I wish I could reprogram my brain so that I didn't care whether I was Lina's second choice, but even thinking about that possibility makes my chest ache.

Still, I want to spend time with her, in whatever way she'll allow. "Lina, about Natalia's wedding reception . . ."

She faces me completely now. "Yeah?"

"I'd still like to go if that's okay with you. I said I'd join you, and I'd like to keep my promise."

Tilting her head, she regards me with a blank look. "You don't have to do that, Max."

"But I want to."

And as soon as I say it, I realize how unprepared I am for the possibility that I won't have a reason to see her again. What if she doesn't get the job? Or Rebecca decides she wants someone else to work on the account? Neither outcome sits well with me, both because it would mean we didn't meet our goals and because it would eliminate our remaining connection.

"I want to," I repeat.

She presses her lips together and nods. "Okay, I'll see you at the reception, then."

So I'll be spending time with Lina and pretending my heart's not shredded. Sounds like a blast. I'm a man of many talents, but coming up with brilliant ideas that won't torture me is not one of them.

Chapter Thirty-Six

LINA

"Breathe, sweetie. You're going to be phenomenal."

Jaslene takes my advice and draws in a calming breath. "Okay, okay. I can do this. I know. It's just . . . I want Natalia's day to be as perfect as it can be and I'm nervous about being responsible for making that happen."

I place my hands on her shoulders. "You're not alone in this. I'll be around all day if you need me. Now, let's go over your morning checklist and make sure we're on track."

She nods and pulls out her phone from the pocket of her light blue sheath dress. "Okay. Request ETA from off-site vendors. *Check.* Confirm connection to location app for all wedding transportation." She swipes at her phone. "Town car is on its way to the house now. *Check.* Change office voicemail message to include emergency mobile number." She gasps. "Shit. I haven't done that yet. I'll do it now."

She runs out of my office and scurries to her cubicle just as my cell phone rings.

I glance at the screen and immediately recognize the number as Rebecca's. A flutter zips across my belly. *Oh God. This is it.* "Hello, this is Lina Santos."

"Lina, this is Rebecca Cartwright."

"Hi, Rebecca."

"I'm not going to mince words here," she says. "You wouldn't expect me to."

That doesn't sound promising. I definitely flubbed a line or two during the presentation, but I thought I did well overall, and she seemed impressed. *Dammit.* Maybe Andrew's guy blew her away?

"I just met with the board and advised them that I would be extending you an offer to join the Cartwright Group as director of wedding services. I was impressed with your work on Ian and Bliss's wedding, and your presentation earlier this week was excellent. Despite a few hiccups, you've proven yourself to be the best person for this position. I'd be delighted to work with you."

I pump my free hand in the air as I clutch the phone against my cheek. "Rebecca, I'm thrilled by this news. Really, really thrilled."

"Well, that's a good start," she says. "Any objection to continuing to work with Max to develop our marketing materials?"

I don't hesitate. "None." I'm confident that Max and I can work together even if we're not linked romantically.

"Great," Rebecca says. "I'll be sending you an email with the details of your offer and information about benefits. If you have questions about anything, just give me a ring. I'll look forward to hearing from you when you've made a decision."

"Thanks so much, Rebecca."

I decide to tell the family tomorrow, because I want their

focus to be on Natalia and Paolo, but my instinct is to share the news with Max first.

> **Me:** I got the job!
> **Max:** Congrats, Lina. That's fantastic news. I couldn't be happier for you.
> **Me:** Now we'll have something else to celebrate.
> **Max:** Champagne's on me. ☺

There's so much I want to tell him. I want to thank him for encouraging me to be myself during the pitch and for not insisting on a theme that didn't fit my personality. I want him to know that I appreciate those moments when he was vulnerable with me—at the retreat and in Blossom's bathroom—because he gave me a safe space exactly when I needed it. I want to thank him for rescuing me during Brent and Terrence's wedding rehearsal, when I was overcome with emotion about my own romantic missteps. And I'd love to tell him that I want to return to that field of flowers and not hold anything back the second time around. Instead, I reply:

> **Me:** Thanks.

Because the truth is, nothing's changed, and I can't force him to take a chance on us.

Choosing instead to focus on my monumental accomplishment, I run out of my office to share the news with my best friend. "Jaslene, I got the job."

"Ahhhhh." Jaslene swivels in her chair, jumps to her feet, and tackle-hugs me. "I'm so excited for you."

I hold her hands as we do a happy dance. "You should be excited for you, too. If you want a position as assistant wedding coordinator, the job is yours."

"Yes, of course, *yes*." She tackle-hugs me again, until a throat clears and we spring apart.

Shit. The shop is closed today in honor of Natalia and Paolo's wedding, but I forgot to lock the door when I came in this morning. Now I'm forced to look at Andrew's face.

"Andrew, what are you doing here?"

I inwardly cringe. The last time I posed this question he had a tantrum and my relationship with Max crashed and burned.

"I'm sorry to just show up like this, Lina. If you could give me just a minute of your time?"

The apprehension in his tone makes me curious to hear what he has to say. I raise my index finger in the air. "You have one minute."

Andrew follows me into my office.

I fold my arms over my chest and hover near the threshold. "I'm listening."

He rubs his palms together in a circular motion before he speaks. "I'm sorry. It's as simple and as difficult as that. I'm sorry for canceling our wedding the way I did. You didn't deserve that. And I'm sorry for my behavior the last time I was here. There was no excuse for it, so I won't try to make one. I don't expect you to forgive me, but it needed to be said. I'm taking a good look at myself and not liking some of the things I see."

"Is your brother the next person on your redemption tour? Because he needs to be."

Andrew quirks his lips to the side, as though reasonable minds could differ on the issue and he hasn't decided one way or the other. "Dealing with Max is a little more complicated. But I'm working on getting there. In the meantime, I'm making some moves of my own, and I thought you should know, in case it affects your thinking about the position with Rebecca or your relationship with my brother."

I tip my head to the side. "You know about the job already?"

Andrew nods. "The coordinator I was helping let me know he didn't get the position, so I assumed you did." He sighs. "Anyway, working on the Cartwright account made me realize I'm falling back on bad patterns, like riding on Max's coattails and trying to get him to fix my mistakes. Truth is, I've been so caught up in my rivalry with him that I don't know who I am without it. That's terrifying to me. I'm in a rut, not really doing much of anything that speaks to me personally, and I think I need to push myself to do more on my own. So I'm leaving Atlas—well, my mother's giving me eight weeks to figure out where I'm going."

My mouth drops. "Your mother *fired* you?"

Heat stains his cheeks. "Well, I think it's fair to say it was a mutual decision. We both realized I wasn't thriving in my current situation. Max is much better at my job than I am. In any case, my old firm in Atlanta says they'll welcome me back with open arms, so that might be where I end up." He shrugs. "Who knows. But what happened here has been eating at me and I wanted to apologize."

I don't know if he's being sincere, and I'm not going to spend my time trying to figure it out. He's apologized, and I suppose if he's engaging in a bit of self-reflection there's not much harm in that. "I appreciate the effort, Andrew. Thank you."

Now that he's tried to make amends, I expect him to leave, but he's standing in my office staring at me.

So awkward. *Help me, Jaslene.*

I clap my hands. "Okay, well, I've got a wedding to get to so . . ."

His eyes widen. "Right." He shakes himself out of the daze. As he glides past me, he says, "Take care."

"Take care, Andrew."

Goodness. It's already shaping up to be a groundbreaking day. One brother down. But unfortunately, there are no more to go.

I can't stop smiling at the newly married couple as I watch them enter the reception site. And people can't stop commenting on the venue: an art gallery with outdoor patio space in the District's Penn Quarter neighborhood.

"Did you find this place for them, Lina?" the infamous Estelle asks.

She's sitting across from me, and she's been a perfectly lovely table companion. Her reputation for causing unnecessary drama seems undeserved.

"It was one of the options I showed them, yeah, but the idea of holding their wedding at a unique location was theirs."

Estelle smiles knowingly. "And probably cheaper, right? Everyone knows Viviane is"—she slaps her right forearm with her left hand—"with her money."

Never mind. Estelle's a wedding troll.

But she's not going to mess with Natalia's day. The weather's perfect—sunny but not uncomfortably warm—and Jaslene's averting catastrophes with her clipboard like Wonder Woman deflects bullets with her cuffs. My cousin Solange, who's here just for the weekend, is flitting from table to table, making the rounds and effortlessly charming the wedding guests as if she were a professional hostess. My mother, who's sitting with Tia Viviane, Marcelo, Tia Izabel, and Paolo's parents, waves at me. I give her a wink in reply, and then I clap enthusiastically when Paolo and Natalia glide onto the dance floor for their first dance.

I glance at my phone to check the time. Max landed two hours ago and has texted to say he's on his way. I'm hopeful he'll arrive in time to hear my toast to Natalia and Paolo. If I can focus on Max as I speak to everyone in this room, I might be able to hold my tears at bay.

Jaslene rushes over, her gaze ricocheting around the hall as though she's scanning it for potential problems.

"You're doing great," I tell her.

"Huh?" she says, turning back to me. "Oh, thanks. Listen, they're starting to serve the champagne, so I'm going to let the DJ know you'll be starting soon. Are you all set?"

I'm clutching a sheet of paper in one and holding an empty champagne glass in the other, so I raise both hands in the air. "As soon as I get my bubbly, I'll be ready to go."

"Excellent," Jaslene says. "Good luck." Then she's off, power walking in the direction of the DJ booth. My best friend is in the zone and has no time for chitchat. I'm so proud of her I want to cry. *Fly, baby bird. Fly.*

Not long after, a server arrives and pours champagne for everyone at our table.

The music fades, signaling that it's time for me to take my

place on the dance floor. The DJ meets me there and hands me a microphone.

I tap on the mic. "Hello, everyone. May I have your attention, please." The room goes quiet, and my gaze is drawn to a lone figure standing at the patio entrance. *Max.* He's wearing a cobalt-blue suit and a white and black polka-dot tie. My heart goes haywire simply knowing he's here.

He puts up his hand and mouths *Hello.* I watch him briefly speak with Jaslene, and then he finds our table, slipping into his seat as unobtrusively as he can while still acknowledging our tablemates.

Now that the excited celebration chatter is dying down as I requested, my failure to fill the silence leads to murmurs among the guests. *Oh right. The toast.* "I'm Natalia's favorite cousin, Carolina Santos. I—"

Natalia appears at my side and hands me a slip of paper.

I shake my head as I read it, then share the message with everyone. "Before I toast the couple, Natalia would like me to tell you that we should refrain from any public declarations of love, announcements of pregnancies, or wedding proposals at this event. Violators will be kicked out at their own expense."

That draws several hearty chuckles, after which Natalia hikes up the train of her jumpsuit and curtsies to the crowd.

Once Natalia's sitting next to Paolo again, I take a deep breath and begin again: "To be frank, I was surprised that Natalia and Paolo asked me to make a toast at their wedding. You see, although I'm a wedding planner by trade, I'm not exactly the most expressive person in public settings. But as I was preparing to make this toast, I realized that I have some definite opinions about love, some of which came to me only recently . . ."

MAX

*L*ina's poise and elegance suit the occasion. Her hair's swept to the side in a nod to Old Hollywood glamour, and her pale peach dress skims her body like a soft caress. Still, my mind wanders to the minutes when she was stuck in an inflatable ball at Surrey Lane Farm. The memory brings a smile to my face. That day's quickly forgotten, though, when I hear Lina say she has definite opinions on love, some of which came to her only recently.

I sit up and lean forward, ready to concentrate on every word she's about to say.

She licks her lips and gazes at me intently. "You see, for as long as I can remember, the idea of loving someone twisted my gut and made alarms ring in my head. I feared that loving someone would make me weak, and when the person inevitably left, I'd make a fool of myself trying to convince them to stay. Sure, love can be messy. It draws emotions out of you that can bring you your highest highs and your lowest lows. But here's what I've finally figured out. Love doesn't operate in the abstract, whether it's romantic or not. It's between *people*. So trying to avoid it in the abstract makes no sense. That would be as logical as trying to fight a ghost. And yes, opening yourself to love can reveal your weaknesses, but with the right person, it can reveal your strengths as well. The moment you let your guard down with someone and let them into your life—*truly* into your life— you are at your most vulnerable, *but* you're also utterly open to a beautiful experience *if* they reciprocate. I asked Natalia once how she knew that Paolo was the right person for her, and she said, 'I knew because I wasn't afraid to love him.' It was as easy as that. And now I get it. She found the person she was willing to drop her shield for, and he reciprocated. They didn't take advantage of each other's vulnerabilities. Instead, they nurtured each other, opened themselves up to love, and now they're here today sharing part of their beautiful experience with us."

My heart is drumming against my chest. So much of what Lina's saying echoes the conversations we had. Weeks ago, I described Lina's perfect match. That person would be full of life like Lina's family. That person would adore Lina, make her take down her bun from time to time, get her frustrated, but only make her cry for the sappiest reasons. Natalia told me that person was Lina's worst nightmare, and now I understand why. Lina wouldn't be able to hide behind her tough exterior with that person. That person would see the real Lina—like I have. And yeah, Lina would be vulnerable, but she'd also be open to love.

The implication of all this reveals itself like a spotlight suddenly brightening all the shadowy corners in a dimly lit room. Andrew wasn't that person. And that's precisely why she wanted to marry him. She didn't love him.

But even if Lina did love Andrew at some point, she certainly doesn't love him now. She just said so herself. Love means breaking down your walls for the person who's willing to scale them. Andrew never tried. But I did. Because I *am* that person for her.

In the end, it doesn't matter if I'm Lina's first, second, or fifteenth choice; what matters is that I'm the *right* choice. And the onus isn't on her to prove that I come first in her life. No, the onus is on *me* to prove that I'm the best man for her. Every day. For as long as she'll have me. *If* she'll still have me.

LINA

I lift my bubbly in the air. "So let's raise a glass to Paolo and Natalia. May your days be filled with love and your nights be filled with comfort."

"And sex," Natalia calls out before she takes a healthy swig and plants a loud kiss on Paolo's lips.

The guests laugh and the DJ spins a pagode song that gets people out of their seats. This style of Brazilian music is midtempo and tends to attract those people who aren't in the mood to shake their hips at superspeed in the way that samba requires.

I stroll over to my table as people rush past me to find space on the dance floor. When I reach Max, he stands and holds out his hand.

I take it without knowing what he wants or where we're going. "Hey."

"Can we talk?" he asks, not returning my greeting. His expression is tight and his voice is urgent. "Somewhere quiet?"

"Sure. There's a rooftop garden. Want to go up there?"

His features relax. "That would be great."

As we climb the two flights to the roof, I struggle to catch my breath. I poured a lot of emotion into that toast and now I'm drained.

Max pushes open the steel door leading to the garden and gestures for me to go out before him. Plenty of greenery fills the space and a few flower beds add a pop of color. The couches and chairs in the center of the garden are inviting, but I'm drawn to the ornate wrought-iron railing along the perimeter.

I drift over and Max follows.

"So what do you want to talk about?" I ask.

Max shakes his head, then peers at me. "I want to talk about the fact that I've been a pigheaded fool."

Oh, all righty, then. I raise a brow. "Go on. The floor is yours."

"I told you that I couldn't be your second choice. Said there was too much history between Andrew and me to get past it. But I was wrong. *Totally and completely wrong.* It doesn't matter if I'm your first or hundredth choice as long as I'm the *right* choice. And I am, Lina. I swear it. I'll scale your walls to show you how much I care. And I'll take every vulnerable part of you and handle it with care. I fucked up. I know this. But if you let me, I'll spend the rest of my days proving to you that I'm your person. Because I love you."

Oh God. I'm going to bawl, and I don't even care. The tears are there, waiting for my permission to drop. So I let them. Because Max loves me. This beautiful, smart, charming man who's been attuned to me from day one loves me. And that's worth a few tears.

He bridges the distance between us and caresses my cheek. "Let me in again, baby. Let me be the one who'll have your back. The one who'll never judge you. The one who'll adore you, and get you to let loose." He swipes his thumbs under my eyes. "The one who'll only make you cry for the sappiest reasons."

My heart is hammering against my chest as if it's trying to answer for me. But I'm happy to let my voice do the heavy lifting here. "I'll be honest: You've always scared me. By putting my trust in you and in our relationship, I'm exposing myself to the kind of hurt that I won't recover from easily. But I think you've earned that place, and I'm ready to take that leap. Because you've challenged me to think about the shield around my heart and who deserves to get past it. I'm certain that you're my safe space. That I can be exactly who I am with you, and you won't judge me for it. You'll actually love me for it. And I want to be that safe space for you, too. When you've had a terrible day or something's gone wrong, I want you to think of me and my arms as your place of comfort. Because I love you, Max, and I want to be with you, too."

He squeezes his eyes shut for several seconds. When he opens them again, they're bright and glowing with affection, as if he's envisioned what comes next and likes what he sees.

"And just so we're clear," I say. "You're neither my first choice nor my second choice. You're my *only* choice."

"Lina."

There's so much emotion packed into that one word. It's as though he's added a new entry in the dictionary for it: *Lina,* noun: *my love, my future.*

And with a smile that makes my heart gallop, Max pulls me into his arms and sweeps his lips across mine. His mouth is both enticingly soft and masterful as we seal our new status with a kiss. We're in love, and we're together, and I couldn't be happier to discover where we go from here.

Remembering where we are, I settle further into his embrace and say, "To be continued, right?"

He presses his lips against my forehead. "To be continued *forever.*"

The sound of someone sniffling pulls us apart. I turn to see my mother, Tia Viviane, and Tia Izabel by the steel door. Tia Izabel dabs her eyes with a handkerchief. My mother, who's wearing a triumphant smile, puts her hand out in front of Tia

Viviane. My aunt grumbles while she fishes inside her purse, then she slaps a twenty-dollar bill in my mother's hand.

My mouth falls open. "Mãe, you were betting on me?"

She shakes her head. "No, never, filha. I was betting on Max."

He leans over and whispers, "Your mother's a smart woman."

She certainly is—and as to this wager, I can easily follow her lead. The odds may not have been in his favor weeks ago, but from this moment forward, I'll bet on Max any day.

Acknowledgments

Writing rom-coms is never easy—what's considered good humor is entirely subjective and sometimes dick jokes fall flat—but writing rom-coms when the world is on fire is especially hard. It's an endeavor that requires discipline (because rationing your social media consumption is a must), an ability to focus for an extended time on spreading joy despite the sadness around you, and the enthusiastic assistance of a kick-ass support group that totally gets what you're trying to do. Oh, and you need yummy snacks—lots and lots of yummy snacks. Note also that the people in your kick-ass support group often prevent you from falling down the social media rabbit hole ("Mom, are you on Twitter *again*?"), bring you snacks ("What? You've never had a Krispy Kreme doughnut? We must fill that gap in your foodie journey, STAT!"), and are themselves experts in bringing joy to your life (keep the hilarious GIFs coming, Sarah). All this to say, the people in my support group deserve a mountain of thanks for their part in putting this book in readers' hands. So here's to the amazing individuals, named and unnamed, who are in my support group, and to the following people, who deserve an extra-special shout-out:

My husband: As I write this, you're driving the girls to school, two weeks after having foot surgery, because I need to get these acknowledgments to my editor this morning. That sums up the support you've given me over the years. You're one of the finest men (in both senses of the term) I've ever known, and I'm so blessed to have you in my life. Love you always and in all ways.

My older daughter, Mar-Mar, who kept me company when I was holed up in my office as I wrote and edited this book, held my hand as I wrestled the opening sentence into submission (yes, this was a thing), and contributed to the brilliant cover concept: Your check's *not* in the mail, but you *will* be compensated—in snacks and hugs. I adore you.

My younger daughter, Nay-Nay, who volunteered to bring me coffee as needed, left Post-its with random facts in my office for reasons that still escape me, and cheered me up whenever I was feeling down: You are one of the sweetest girls I know, and yes, I'm totally biased about this, but I make the rules here. End of.

My mother: Mãe, I didn't need to be reminded of all the reasons you're my inspiration, but it's nice to have them memorialized in a book. Eu te amo muito.

My superagent, Sarah Younger: I'm so lucky to benefit from your badassery. Thanks for being in my corner, knowing just how to handle every situation, and helping me grow as a writer and a person.

My fabulous editor, Nicole Fischer: Thanks to you, my word salad is now a book. See? I was right when I said you were a magician. Your guidance and patience are always appreciated, and your LOLs always make me smile.

My prima, Fernanda, who suffered through a million questions about Portuguese accent marks and spicy Brazilian foods:

It means so much to me that you were willing to jump in and help at a moment's notice. Love you, mulher!

My writing partner in crime and friend, Tracey Livesay: Our phone calls, DMs, and texts got me through some *rough* days. I hope I did the same for you. I'm so glad you're my "oh honey no" person.

My Romancelandia compatriots—My #4Chicas posse (Priscilla Oliveras, Sabrina Sol, and Alexis Daria), Olivia Dade, the #BatSignal Ladies, and the #STET Crew: Thanks for checking on me, challenging me, and cheerleading for me. Mwah!

My beta readers—Ana Coqui, Soni Wolf, and Susan Scott Shelley: This book is stronger than it would have been had I not relied on your invaluable feedback. I can't thank you enough.

Liz Lincoln: A million thanks to you for stepping in and being the extra set of eyes I desperately needed.

And finally, to all the wonderful people at Avon/Harper-Collins who have championed and continue to champion my books: You're the only A-Team I recognize.

Don't miss Mia's next sassy, sexy rom-com . . .

THE WEDDING CRASHER

Dean's story is coming early 2021!

About the Author

MIA SOSA writes funny, flirty, and moderately steamy contemporary romances that celebrate our multicultural world. A graduate of the University of Pennsylvania and Yale Law School, Mia practiced First Amendment and media law in the nation's capital for ten years before trading her suits for loungewear (read: sweatpants). Born and raised in East Harlem, New York, she now lives in Maryland with her college sweetheart, their two bookaholic daughters, and one dog that rules them all.

BOOKS BY MIA SOSA

THE WORST BEST MAN

> "A delightful read that is equal parts sexy, heartwarming, and seriously funny."
>
> — Elizabeth Acevedo, National Book Award Winner

CRASHING INTO HER

Mia Sosa concludes her fun, flirty romantic comedy series with a steamy story about a stuntwoman in training who can't help but clash with the instructor... her former one-night-stand and best friend's cousin.

PRETENDING HE'S MINE

> "With the second in her Love on Cue series, Sosa deftly combines her flair for nuanced characterization with snappy writing imbued with a deliciously acerbic sense of humor, thus making her the new go-to author for fans of sassy and sexy contemporary romances."
>
> —Booklist

ACTING ON IMPULSE

> "A fresh, sexy, laugh out loud funny rom com with characters you can't help but root for and a love story that will leave you smiling well after the book is finished."
>
> — Alyssa Cole

> "The first installment in the Love on Cue series is charming, witty, and consistently funny... Spicy sexual chemistry and a generous dash of authentic Puerto Rican flavor blend together in a sharp romance that begs to be savored."
>
> — Kirkus

Look for a New Book from Mia Sosa

☗HarperCollins*Publishers*

DISCOVER GREAT AUTHORS, EXCLUSIVE OFFERS, AND MORE AT HC.COM
Available wherever books are sold.